AN
INCONVENIENT
WIFE

Also by Megan Chance:

SUSANNAH MORROW

AN INCONVENIENT WIFE

MEGAN CHANCE

WARNER BOOKS

NEW YORK   BOSTON

Warner Books

Time Warner Book Group
1271 Avenue of the Americas, New York, NY 10020
Visit our Web site at www.twbookmark.com.

Printed in the United States of America

First Printing: April 2004
10 9 8 7 6 5 4 3 2 1

Library of Congress Cataloging-in-Publication Data
Chance, Megan.
    An inconvenient wife / Megan Chance.
      p. cm.
    ISBN 0-446-52956-7
    1. Upper class women—Fiction. 2. Marital conflict—Fiction. 3. New York (N.Y.)—Fiction.
  4. Married women—Fiction. 5. Rich people—Fiction. 6. Hynotism—Fiction. I. Title.
    PS3553.H2663I53 2004
    813'.54—dc22   2003015659

Book design by Giorgetta Bell McRee

For Maggie and Cleo

ACKNOWLEDGMENTS

As always, I must thank Kristin Hannah for her invaluable insight, Jamie Raab and Frances Jalet-Miller for their care and dedication in pointing the way, Marcy Posner for her unwavering support, Elizabeth DeMatteo, Melinda McRae, Jena McPherson, Liz Osborne, and Sharon Thomas for fifteen years of Thursday nights, and of course, my husband, Kany, for his belief, love, and insight.

"Love" is an elastic concept that stretches from heaven to hell and combines in itself good and evil, high and low.

—CARL GUSTAV JUNG
Two Essays on Analytical Psychology
"The Anxious Young Woman and the Retired Businessman"

Survival of the fittest does not always mean survival of the best . . . it means only the survival of that which is best suited to the circumstances, good or bad, in which it is placed—the survival of a savage in a savage social medium, of a rogue among rogues, of a parasite where a parasite alone can live.

—HENRY MAUDSLEY
Body and Will

PROLOGUE

New York City

Autumn 1884

An asylum!" William said. "Is there nothing else we can try? Nothing at all?"

My husband balanced on the edge of his chair. The electric light shone on his high forehead, glinting in the gray threading through his dark hair. He was only thirty-five. The aging was due to his profession, he said. Brokering was a hard business. But I knew it was not that at all. I knew it was because of me.

"You don't want surgery." Dr. Little adjusted his round spectacles. The myriad certificates that dotted the brown toile wallpaper framed him nicely, as if deliberately placed to give weight to his earnestness.

"But if you think it's best . . ." I said.

Dr. Little turned his mild, thoughtful gaze to me. "An ovariotomy is not always successful. Your husband feels the risk is too great."

"You could die, Lucy," William said.

"But there's the chance it would work."

Dr. Little nodded. "Yes, of course. We've made great gains with surgery of this type, but I would not be so anxious to try it—not when there is another option. Beechwood Grove is an excellent institution, Mrs. Carelton. We've had good results with hysterics and neurasthenics. A few months of enforced rest may be effective."

"A few months," William said in a low voice. "You've said six months, at least. It would encompass the entire season. What would we tell people?"

Dr. Little shrugged. "Perhaps you could suggest that Mrs. Carelton has taken an extended tour abroad."

"Lucy has always hated Europe," my husband said.

"Something else, then," Dr. Little said impatiently.

William exhaled. "I don't know. An asylum . . ."

"A *private* asylum," Dr. Little corrected. "You must believe me when I say this is nothing like the horror houses you've heard about, Mr. Carelton. At Beechwood Grove, all of our patients are from excellent families. We make it as homelike as possible. Mrs. Carelton would even be permitted to have many of her own things."

I looked down, unable to meet the doctor's gaze. "Perhaps it's best, William. . . ."

"No." He said it so violently that I looked up in surprise. "No. I refuse to believe this is the only way. An asylum, for God's sake. That's a place for the insane."

"Mr. Carelton, you came to me for advice; you said you had lost hope. I'm saying there is hope to be found, but it requires a great sacrifice on your part—"

"What you're saying is that Lucy belongs with madmen and criminals," William said coldly.

"There are no criminals in Beechwood Grove."

"Only madmen."

"Mad*women*. We do not accept men there."

"Madwomen, then. You would put my wife with them?"

Dr. Little looked at William, and I read the meaning in his glance. *Your wife is a madwoman. It's time to acknowledge it. It's time to send her away. . . .*

I could not bear to look. I felt the start of tears, and I dug my nails into my palm.

William got to his feet and pulled me to mine. "I appreciate your time and your advice, Doctor, but the season is just starting—"

"You may regret this," Dr. Little said. "Mrs. Carelton has been unable to meet the demands of society before."

"This year will be different. We still hope that there will be a child."

Dr. Little pressed his hands together. "A child. Mr. Carelton, I'm quite sure Mrs. Carelton could not care for a child. Not in her present state."

"Perhaps a child is just what she needs," William said hopefully.

"A good long rest is what she needs. An asylum, with round-the-clock care, is what she needs. I'm sorry, Mr. Carelton, but I see no other option for your wife."

William hesitated, and then he nodded. "Again, we thank you, Doctor. Now we must wish you good day." His fingers squeezed my arm; together we turned and left the doctor's office. When we were outside, into the growing chill that sharpened the air, standing amid the noise of carriages rattling down the street, the constant movement of the city, he turned to me. "Well." He sighed. "I'm sorry to have put you through that, darling."

I was cold; I could not feel my fingers at all. "He could be right, William."

"You would prefer to be locked away?"

"No, of course not, but—"

"There must be something else. Another way. Something we've overlooked."

"Dr. Little says there's nothing."

William ignored me. "Perhaps we should not have returned to

the city so quickly. Perhaps . . . a short trip to the country? What do you think, Lucy? Do you think they would miss us?"

I did not say what I thought—that our friends would be relieved. "No," I said, and though I tried to smile, I could not manage it. "A trip to the country would be fine."

PART I

New York City
Early January, 1885

Chapter 1

The supper had gone splendidly. The gaslight glittered on the gold-rimmed plates and the gold of the palm-adorned epergne that held oranges and tiny kumquats and blushing yellow tea roses and greenery spilling over in artful disarray. The conversation was sparkling; everyone kept saying so. I wondered if perhaps their words were only talismans against the dark—how could an evening be boring when all kept remarking that it was not? Or was it merely that I was the only one who noticed the way the gaslight wavered restlessly across the china, as if it could not wait to be gone, as if other voices beckoned it?

"It seems your visit to the country has done you both good," Millicent Wallace said. She and William traded a quick look, and I felt myself grow hot as she reached idly for a pear from the tray.

I spoke quickly. "Yes."

"The country is so restful," William said.

Thomas Sykes nodded. "For a time. I must admit that after a few days, I find rest anything but restful."

William smiled. "The market waits for no man."

"It was good of William to take time away," I said quietly. "Especially for such a long while."

"Thomas would have sent me on alone," Elizabeth Sykes said with a laugh.

Thomas said, "I'm surprised you could make such a sacrifice of time yourself, William, with things still so unstable after last year."

"William would not hear of me going alone," I said.

"How good is your concern, William," Millie said. "How lucky you are, Lucy."

William shoved back his chair suddenly. It was unlike him, graceless and loud. When I glanced up in surprise, I saw his pointed gaze, and I realized my hand had gone to my temple. With effort, I forced it to my lap.

There was an uncomfortable silence, a sense of waiting, and I struggled to find words to fill it.

William said gently, pointedly, "Ladies, I'm sure you'd prefer the parlor to our cigars."

They had been waiting for me to signal the end of supper. I was horrified at my lapse, and humiliated. I had forgotten, yet it was such a simple thing, something I'd done so many times before.

I stumbled to my feet, jarring the table, sending a kumquat rolling from the centerpiece. "Yes, of course. Shall we have tea?"

Millicent and Elizabeth followed me to the parlor, with its pale blue walls and heavy gold drapes, to the little gilded table and the elaborate crystal decanters upon it—wedding gifts from a faraway cousin. I pretended there was nothing wrong, nothing odd about pouring sherry into a glass—only a very small glass, only a small amount of sherry—but I was nervous, and I poured too much. It spilled onto the Aubusson carpet, and I blotted the stain into a woven rose with the toe of my shoe, pretending not to see it.

I turned and smiled and held up my glass. "Tea? Or something stronger?"

Millicent stood by the hearth, her skirts brushing the stiff brass feathers of the peacock fire screen, her expression impassive. "Tea, I think."

Elizabeth shook her blond head. Her plain pearl eardrops shivered against her jaw. "No thank you. I doubt I could manage another sip." Then, as I went to ring the bell for Moira, Elizabeth said, "William is doing so well. Thomas speaks of him often."

"William will be glad to hear that," I said.

They both looked at me as if I'd said something strange, and I took a sip of the sherry and wished the warmth of it would speed through my veins, though I could hardly taste it.

"Are you not well, Lucy?" Millie asked, narrowing her dark eyes as if studying some particularly intricate tapestry stitch. "You seem pale."

"I'm just a little . . . tired." The sherry was not helping, and the room seemed at once too small and overwhelming—so many things: the faint scents of gas and flowers and the lamb we'd had for supper, mirrors and gilt and those heavy, massive curtains closing out the light and the air. . . .

You must not. William will be so angry, I reminded myself.

I got up from the settee, meaning to go to the curtains and pull them aside, but I caught my toe on the delicate table, rocking the Chinese urn and the pretty jeweled birdcage and the coils of the gas line that fed the Tiffany lamp.

Millicent rushed to my side as if I'd slipped hard on ice, and she took my arm. Her hands were warm through the figured velvet of my sleeve, and I realized how cold I was—but then I was often too cold or too warm now. William said I was like a hothouse flower.

"It was nothing," I said, pushing her away again. "These new shoes . . ."

She glanced down at them but said nothing, only gave me a look that shamed me. I forgot about the window and went to the bell.

"Where is the tea?" I asked. I twisted the bell more viciously than I meant. "Where is Moira? She should have been here by now—" I twisted the bell again.

"Lucy, I think I won't have any tea after all," Millicent said.

"Where *is* she?" I twisted the knob once more. When Moira didn't appear, I went to the doorway and leaned into the hall. "Moira!" My voice disappeared into the heaviness of the dark flocked wallpaper, and the deep tapestried curtains that hid the servants' stairs at the end of the hall, and the patterned carpets unworn by the footsteps of children, because only one child had ever played in this house, only me. "Moira!" I raised my voice, and this time it seemed shrill. "Moira! Where are you? Can't you hear the bell! Moira!" I was angry, and I felt that anger slipping beyond me, and though a part of me urged caution and tried to stop, another part just kept screaming, "Moira! Moira!" even though Millicent and Elizabeth were calling to me from the parlor. I heard the men come from the dining room, and William— "Darling, what's the noise?"—in that calm and soothing voice I hated, as if he were approaching a dangerous animal.

"Moira!"

The maid rushed through the curtains, her face pale, her light eyes wide with fear. "Yes ma'am," she said, curtsying quickly before me. "I'm sorry, ma'am—"

"Where have you been?" I asked her. "How often must I ring a bell before you come? I won't tolerate this, I tell you. I cannot tolerate this—"

"Lucy, darling." William had my arm. He pulled me against him, whispering sternly in my ear, "Contain yourself," and then in the next moment, louder, "My dear, my dear. It's all right. Moira had gone to get a package from Charles's carriage."

I pulled loose from my husband. "I don't care where she was. She should have come. I rang three times. They are prostrate with thirst—how long must we wait for tea?" Such a shrill voice, but I couldn't call it back. I couldn't make it stop.

"Perhaps you should rest, darling," William said. He tried to pull me to one of the fringed horsehair chairs in the hall.

"I don't want to rest. I want obedience from my servants. Is that too much to ask?"

"No, no, of course not," William said. He glanced at our guests, who were standing at the edges of the hall, haunting the doorways, looking disturbed and embarrassed. "She's over-wrought," he said. "The journey home . . ."

Millie reached past William to touch my arm. "Lucy, why don't we go upstairs? I haven't yet seen your new gown."

"My gown?" Her words confused me, coming as they did through my anger.

"Yes. The green one." She moved behind me, and I felt her gentle push, and then I was going with her down the hall, past Moira and my husband to the stairs, and my indignation fled as abruptly as it had come. I felt weak; I did not think my legs could hold me. My temples were throbbing. The gaslight left heavy shadows on the stairs, so I could barely see what had been until that moment a familiar passage.

Millicent took my hand as if I were a child. She led me to the bedroom, with its familiar scents of lavender and rose sachets, and paused. I heard the strike of a match, then the gaslight went bright, bursting painfully before my eyes. I threw my hand up as a shield.

"Hush," Millicent said, and the hiss of gas weakened as she turned it down. "There now. You'll feel better soon."

She was right; already I felt better. There, in the sanctity of my bedroom, I was calm again, my nervousness gone—not for long, I knew. It was never gone for long.

The pain behind my eyes abated. I sagged onto the chair flanking the fireplace. My bustle jammed hard against my spine, but I was too tired even to relieve that irritation. I passed my hand over my eyes. "I cannot think," I whispered.

"Then don't think," Millie said. Her presence was soft and comforting. "William said you were doing so well."

"I was. I was."

"What did the doctor say?"

"Which one?"

"Did you see one in the country? No, I suppose you didn't. What about the last one you said William was taking you to?" Millicent hesitated delicately. "The one here in the city?"

I closed my eyes. I thought of Dr. Little's thinning hair, his probing fingers, his hopelessness. I thought of the one before him, who'd prescribed laudanum, and then still another, who'd thought chloral would be best, and the first: *There is a mass*, he'd told William. *An ovariotomy is the best course.*

Millicent rushed on, obviously embarrassed. "I don't mean to probe, Lucy, you know I don't. But I . . . have you considered going back to Elmira? The water cure seemed to do you good."

"No," I said. "It made no difference."

"William would send you again if you wanted it. He would do anything for you."

As if William's generosity was a benefit. I had begun to think of my husband's solicitude as the cold wrap at the water cure: tightly wrapped in cold sheets, water constantly running over my skin, wet and cold and warmth, constant touch, air and motion, always there, always hovering, never still. I wanted stillness. I wanted time to stop, motion to end. I wanted to sit for hours in this room, to watch the ceaseless waver of light trying to escape from the lily-shaped globe near my bed. *I understand*, I wanted to say to it. *I know you want to run. What I don't know is why you must go, or where you will escape.*

Millicent went to the rose brocade drapes and pulled them aside. "It's starting to snow again," she said, and then, as if that thought led logically to the next, "There are weeks left in the season, Lucy. How will you bear it?"

I could not help myself; I laughed. "It's not I who must bear it, Millie, but you and William and everyone else. You tell me, can you bear to be around me? Or will you withdraw too, as the others have?"

"They are all there for you, Lucy. All you have to do is call them back."

I laughed again. "Oh yes. No doubt that's true. Especially after that little scene with Caroline Astor last spring."

Millicent looked uncomfortable. She let the curtain fall. "William explained that you were not yourself."

"Not myself." Even the dim light was too bright, and the hiss of the gas made a ceaseless buzz in my head, the smell of roses nauseating. I wished for darkness and peace. "I am perpetually not myself."

"Perhaps . . ." Millicent paused. "Perhaps . . . another doctor could help. If there were a child—"

"Yes, yes, yes. If only there were. Millie, there's a bottle on my dressing table. A brown one. Will you bring it to me?"

I heard the swish of her skirts as she moved over the carpet, then the clink of glass as she lifted the bottle from the perfumes and powders and lotions there. I heard the little pop of the cork, her sniff.

"It calms my nerves," I explained. To my tired, aching eyes, Millicent was a blur of burgundy and gold fringe, ghostly skin and hair that disappeared in the shadows around her. She did not look quite real. "Please, Millie, bring it to me."

"There must be a spoon—"

I waved the words away and took the bottle. "I know how much," I said, and I brought it to my mouth, taking a whiff of the medicinal, faintly spicy scent before I sipped it. It rolled over my tongue, cinnamony-sweet, leaving bitterness behind as it went down my throat. I corked the bottle and handed it back to her, and then I rose and went to my bed. "I must leave you now, Millie," I told her. "I will be quite blurry soon."

She looked worried but said nothing, just sighed and set the laudanum back on my dressing table. By the time she reached the door, I was already languishing in anticipation of my shattered nerves dulling, my restlessness puddling into drowsiness.

"I'll tell William you're better," she said, and I could not keep from chuckling.

"Yes, tell him I'm better," I said. "Tell him to come kiss his princess good night."

I did not hear her answer.

When I came to myself again, I was not sure how long it had been, only that the lights were put out and I was undressed and in bed, though I had no memory of how this had come about, and no real concern—it was not unusual. The sound of my door opening had awakened me. William came inside. He carried a candle for a soft light, and it haloed and shadowed his face so that he looked like a demon. He was still dressed, and the smell of cigar smoke came with him, filling the room. I turned away.

"I'm tired," I said.

I heard him set the candleholder down, and then I felt the mattress giving way beneath his weight, his warmth as he sat beside me. "How much laudanum did you take?"

I spoke into my pillow. "Enough."

He was quiet for a moment. Then, "What did I tell you about making a scene tonight? Thomas Sykes could be very important to me—to us. It took me an hour to reassure him."

"I find it hard to believe he's never seen a woman scolding her servants before."

He took that overly patient tone again. "I doubt he's ever seen it done quite that way."

"Tell him who my father is. That's placated them well enough before."

"He knows who your father is."

Of course Thomas Sykes knew. That he was a newcomer to New York City meant he was probably more aware of it than the people who had watched me grow up in the shadow of my father's wealth and position. But they too were all old families with Dutch names, as secure in their place as I was in mine. Thomas Sykes and people like him needed us: our influence, our money, our social position. It was, I suspected, at least half the reason William had married me.

"I'm tired," I said again. "Please leave me, William."

But he did not go. Then I felt his hand, large and warm, on my back, through my nightgown, his fingers curving against my spine, a soft caress that nonetheless had me stiffening.

"No," I whispered.

He didn't stop. "Perhaps we should try again. To have some hope . . . I should think it would soothe you." He leaned toward me, whispering, so I felt his warm, moist breath against my hair. "Think of it, Lucy. A child of your own."

I felt his hand as a steady pressure, moving me, pulling me toward him, a familiar and irresistible force. I closed my eyes and listened to him unfasten his trousers, the soft snap of buttons, the *sssshhhh* of fabric as it fell to the floor, and then he was crawling into bed beside me, pushing up my nightgown, his hands rough and steady, unassailable.

I let him have his way. I had fought him only once, on our wedding night, when he came to me and I had not known what for. I had been afraid, and naive, and when it was over I lay there in terror, humiliated beyond bearing. But now I knew what to expect. Now I knew my duty. Now there was the hope of a child to sustain me. So I lay still, revolted and tense, passive as he forced apart my legs and entered me. I felt the rush of his breath against my throat, the grip of his fingers on my hips, and I turned my head to look at the wavering candle and waited impatiently for him to spend himself.

It did not take long. He collapsed on me, and I pushed him off and pulled my nightgown down again to cover myself.

"I'm sorry," he murmured, as he always did. He leaned over

and blew out the candle, then hurried from the bed to hastily dress. "I'm sorry, Lucy, to inflict such brutishness on you. You know I am. If it wasn't necessary . . ."

I made no reply.

"You're an angel," he whispered. "My sweet angel." He kissed me chastely on my forehead and was gone.

I grabbed the laudanum bottle in my shaking hands and took another sip, lying alone in the darkness until the blessed drowsiness overtook me.

Chapter 2

To say I remember when I first saw William would be not quite true. It is more true to say I remember the constant *presence* of him. One day he was not there, and the next he was, and always thereafter. I can't remember when I first thought him compelling, when it was that his laugh first arrested me, when I first took note of how beautiful his voice was as he accompanied me at the piano. That winter is like a blur around me, with him never far away, adjusting my wrap as it fell from my shoulders at the opera, murmuring in my ear, standing at the hearth with his elbow knocking the ruddy pears and yew set to decorate the mantel at Christmastime.

What I do remember is how ubiquitous he was, then how completely he disappeared that summer when we removed to Newport. How the days lingered on moist and heavy air that even the soft sea breeze could not completely dispel, and the hours dragged on and on without end, without diversion. I missed him terribly and was startled that I did—he was only my father's stockbroker, no one I should even take account of, much less miss. But miss him I did, so that my friends remarked at how dour I was, how dull. There was something lacking in the air, I told them; the vibrance was gone.

Then, one day in the late summer, only a few weeks before we were to return to the city, I sat alone on the beach. It was near twilight, with the sun setting pink and peach on the water and the thin waves breaking on the shore, barely nudging the mass of seaweed that seemed forever to mark the end of the surf at Bailey's Beach. Music from somewhere—a supper I had been invited to but could not remember where—had started, and it lingered on the air, underscoring a seagull's flight as the bird hovered and drifted, borne backward by the currents. I wondered whether he would rise or fall, land on the water or the shore, and then I heard the footsteps behind me, shoes scrunching in the loose sand.

I didn't bother to turn around. I was annoyed at the interruption—no one should be here this late, no one should have found me.

"How alluring. You look like a mermaid cast on the beach. Will you trade your fins for legs, my lady?"

I twisted to glance over my shoulder, startled at the sound of his voice, breathless with surprise and pleasure. "William! When . . . ? I didn't know you planned to come."

"Earlier than this, actually," he said. "But I couldn't get away." He leaned against the wall of the bathing pavilion, settling his shoulders against weathered wooden planks, crossing his arms over his chest. "What are you doing here so late? I had a devil of a time finding you. I probably wouldn't have done so at all if not for him." He nodded toward the watchman, who stood impatiently at the gate, his gold-laced uniform glinting in the sun.

"I'm surprised he let you in," I said.

William smiled. "I used my charm and told him I was with you. It wasn't too difficult. I think he wants to go home."

"Yes. I'm sure he does."

"Your father said you were going to supper at Bayside."

"I changed my mind."

"So I gather." William smiled again and came away from the pavilion to squat beside me. He looked as if he'd walked far in his flannel suit and boiled shirt. When he took off his hat, his dark hair was pressed to his head, damp with sweat. "What are you doing here, Lucy?"

"I was hiding," I admitted.

"Hiding? From what?"

"Everything."

"Ah. Everything." He made a broad, sweeping motion. "The water, the beach, the parties, the music, your friends, your teas . . . running away?"

"I was bored by their . . ." I bowed my head, embarrassed at what I was about to admit to him.

"Their company?" he teased. He tilted my chin so I had no choice but to look at him. His smile was gone, and I wanted to squirm at the expression on his face. "Now, I know that can't be true. Have you missed me this summer, Lucy?"

I pulled away from him and got to my feet quickly. The breeze blew the sand from my skirt into his face. I picked up my hat and shook it too. Sand floated from its pale satin flowers like pollen. "Why should I miss you?" I asked him, and though I meant my words to be careless and cruel, they sounded only fretful. "Have you written me a single letter? Sent me a single word? Did we make some promise to each other that you would do so? You're my father's stockbroker. Why should I care what you do?"

"Oh, Lucy, Lucy." He barely blinked at the sand I'd thrown so rudely in his face. That smile was there again, and a twinkle in his eyes. I turned so I would not have to see it and walked toward the water.

I heard him rustle in the sand, and then he was hurrying after me. "You did miss me, then."

"I've been far too busy."

"You've been sitting on the beach. Your father says you've been distracted."

"As distracted as I might be over a romantic novel. The days are long here. It's easy to get lost in . . . daydreaming. It's nothing to do with you."

"That's too bad," he said. "So if I were to—oh, say if I were to ask you to marry me . . . you'd certainly say no."

"Of course—" His words suddenly came to me, and I gasped and faced him, my boot sliding in the wet sand. "What did you say?"

He was expressionless. There was no smile, no teasing now. He said, "I've spoken with your father. I asked him for the right to—"

"How dare you," I said. "I've not heard from you for months. How dare you come here and surprise me this way."

"Lucy—"

"No." I backed away from him, holding up my hands as if I could keep him from me. Beyond him I saw the gatekeeper start from his post, heading toward us as if he thought I was in danger. I waved at him and shook my head, stopping him before he could come too close. "I thought you no longer cared for me. I was . . . To be truthful, I was not sure you ever had. You've never said a word to me. . . . I've had no idea of your feelings. . . ."

"Of course you had," William said gently, and he kept moving toward me, closer and closer, until I realized I'd been standing still, no longer backing away. He captured me neatly with his hands before I could rally myself to move. "You're no fool, Lucy. Don't act like one. You've known exactly how I felt. I thought you felt the same."

"You never asked me—"

"Should I have, when it was so clear to me? I've treasured your smiles, darling. I've thought of nothing but you all summer long."

"But you didn't write. You didn't visit—"

"I've had no chance. I wanted to make sure everything was right, that I was secure enough to come to your father, to be a viable suitor."

"There was no need. He anointed you from the first," I said bitterly.

"I've made him a fortune," William said, without pride or arrogance; it was simply truth.

"And I'm your reward."

He released me and stepped back. "Only if you want to be, Lucy."

I saw the hurt in his eyes and felt ashamed for having put it there when the truth was as he'd said it. I did love him, and I knew that I was merely punishing him for his inattention, for the hurt he'd caused me. But something in me would not let me stop—it was a flaw, one that I'd fought often over the years. Now I did not even try to calm myself.

"I don't know if I want to marry you," I told him, feeling a dim satisfaction when he flinched. "How can I believe you truly care for me? This summer I've seen no evidence of it."

"Because you haven't seen me—"

"Why is that, William?"

"I told you—"

"You said you'd been busy. Is this how it's to be when we're married? When you're busy, I just won't see you at home? You'll begin taking your dinners at the Knickerbocker or Union League—"

"Good God," he said. He lurched forward, grabbing my arms and pulling me hard so I fell against his chest. "Do you really think I could? Do you really think that I could keep from you a single moment longer than I must? Lucy, don't you know me at all?"

He held me away, and before I could answer, he kissed me.

I was twenty-five, and though I'd had suitors before, I'd never been kissed quite this way, so hard, with such need. I felt ravaged there on the shore, breathless as he pulled away and stared at me in a way that brought heat into my face. It was then that I first felt it: this sense that there was something hovering just beyond my knowledge, some vast landscape that I could not recognize, could not begin to know.

The tide had crept up higher so we were both standing in the weak surf. It lapped against the leather of our shoes. Above us, the gull keened and dipped; beyond us, the watchman turned discreetly away.

"We should . . . we should go," I managed, pushing away from William. I was shaky, the hem of my skirt wet and dragging against me as I tried to move. William took my elbow, steadying me until we had stepped onto firmer sand. I felt the press of his fingers on my skin. I was too tender; it felt like a bruise.

"Marry me," he whispered, and his voice called to some yearning deep within me, something untried, that had only just been summoned. When I looked at him, I knew that whatever this feeling was, it was not mine alone.

"Yes," I said.

That feeling did not go away. In the years since, it had grown stronger, until that odd yearning left me restless and weary. I had assumed children would silence it, and when there were none, I thought I should put my energies into filling the world with beauty. But William only laughed at my efforts: I was not a good pianist, and he was the much better singer. My father told him that as a girl, I had become unhealthily obsessed with art, so William brought me embroidery silks and gave me carte blanche to shop. *Make my world more beautiful, Lucy. I should like to come home to a palace of peace and contentment.*

Foolishly, I had agreed with him; I had thought being the queen of his castle might be enough. But that strange longing began to create its own place within me. Only the laudanum helped ease it.

William did not think the morphia was healthy, and I deferred to him; I did not take it as often as I wanted. Not in the morning, nor before a ball. Never—like tonight—before the opera, though my anxiety was such that I could barely fasten the diamond earrings William had given me. I glanced at the dark bottle on my dressing table, and Moira paused in brushing out my cape and said, "Should I bring it to you tonight, ma'am?" My throat constricted in want of it.

But William would know, and he would be angry, and I was tired of seeing that desperate concern in his eyes, so I shook my head and turned back to the mirror, finishing my toilette before I went downstairs to find William pacing the hall. He stopped when he heard me and grinned as if he could not contain himself.

"What?" I asked. "What is it?"

"Only that you're so beautiful," he said.

"That is certainly not why you're smirking like a fool."

"No. I've a surprise for you."

"A surprise?" I could not help my dismay.

"I know you dislike surprises. But not this one, I think."

"What is it?"

He clucked at me. "Not yet. Not yet."

I could not explain, but I felt anxious again, and afraid. From the corner of my eye, I caught sight of Moira coming down the stairs with my cape, and I grabbed hold of the newel post and said in a quiet voice, "Moira, will you bring me my cordial, please?"

"She'll do no such thing," William said. He held out his hand for my cape, and Moira, that stupid girl, hesitated between us, until she gave it to him and curtsied and slid past me. William draped my cape over my shoulders and handed me my bag. "Come along, Lucy. Don't spoil it."

He propelled me to the door, out into the cold evening. The air was clear and frozen, with small, dry flakes of frosted snow swirling in the streetlights, blown by the wind. The black iron frets and anthemion of the front fence glittered with ice, and beyond, Washington Square was silent, imprisoned by snow.

The carriage waited on the street; our driver, Jimson, was rubbing his hands together madly, trying to stay warm. Once we were inside the carriage, William sat heavily beside me, taking my gloved hand in his as if he wanted to anchor me there, as if he were afraid I would fly out the window and into the world. In truth, had I been able to do that, I would have been gone into that frigid air, breathing it so deep it stung my lungs.

Instead I looked out my window, watching the lights of Fifth Avenue flash by, until we jolted to a stop before the storied citrus-yellow facade of the Metropolitan Opera House, and I was both relieved and anxious again. It was William's way to deliver surprises before crowds, to shower largesse and distinction before those who still did not quite respect his background. He knew, too, that I would never challenge him before my friends, that I would feign the pleasure he wanted me to feel.

The door to the carriage opened, and William stepped down and waited as I came out. I took his elbow. His arm was like an iron bar beneath my fingers. The doormen ushered us inside, into globe-lit brilliance that played off marble and gold and elaborate chandeliers. The opera had already started as we went to our box, which was, as William was wont to say, one of the finest in the house, near the middle of the first tier of boxes— the Diamond Horseshoe. My father's name—or mine—would have brought us such positioning, but William had made sure of it by doing some business for the Vanderbilts and had procured this box well before the building was finished.

The talk and laughter were loud even above the music. William pushed aside the heavy plush curtains and stood back for me to go inside. We arrived well into the performance, but it was early yet, and many of the boxes were empty, as they would stay until near the second intermission.

William tapped my arm, and I reached into my bag for the opera glasses and handed them to him. I heard the little catch as he opened them up, then the quiet clicking of his tongue as he surveyed the boxes.

"Julia Breckenwood is here sans Steven," he leaned forward to whisper to me. "Ah, look at those diamonds at Daisy Hadden's throat. No doubt old Moreton is paying for last week's indiscretion." He handed me the glasses. "Look for yourself."

I took them, but not to look at Daisy Hadden's diamonds. I searched for Millicent, though I was not sure why. The intimacy of the other night was an embarrassment to me. When I did see her, sitting in her upper box with her husband, looking back at me with her own jeweled glasses, I glanced away, hoping she thought my attention had been elsewhere. Still, I sat until the first intermission in a gloom of anticipation; she would search me out, I knew.

But it was not Millicent who arrived first at our box. It was Charles McKim.

He was an architect who was developing a reputation for designing homes, and though I knew of him, I had never met him. Nor, I thought, had William. But when McKim entered our box, my husband nearly jumped in delight.

"Charles!" he said, shaking the man's hand and patting him on the back. "How good of you to come."

McKim nodded. "It was good of you to invite me. I confess I've been too busy this year to make many performances." He looked past William to where I sat and said, "This must be the lovely Mrs. Carelton."

"My wife, Lucy," William said. Then, to me, "My dear, this is Charles McKim. He's an architect with McKim, Mead and White."

"Yes, I'm familiar with your reputation, Mr. McKim." I held

out my hand, which he shook limply, his eyes lingering—as they were meant to—on my diamond bracelet.

"I'm delighted to be working for you, Mrs. Carelton. I cannot tell you how pleased I am to be of service."

"Working for me?"

"Your husband has graciously hired me to design your new home."

"Our new home?" I looked beyond him to where William stood beaming with pride, and I realized that this was his surprise.

"What do you think, Lucy?" William asked. He seemed hardly able to stay still. "I've been planning it for months."

"Planning . . . what?"

"That property on Fifth Avenue. I've decided to build. It's time, don't you think, that we leave the Row?"

I stared at him in shocked disbelief. Finally I said, "But . . . I grew up in that house."

"It was fine twenty years ago, Lucy, but things have changed. Why shouldn't we have a fine house? Everyone else has. Mansions are going up daily. Certainly we should be among them. There's electricity now. Electricity. Think of it—no more dim gaslight."

"No doubt Mrs. Carelton would be ecstatic about the chance to decorate such a home," McKim put in.

William came close to me and whispered, "What woman wouldn't love the chance? You can shop all day if you like. It will take your mind off—it will . . . ah, just think of it, Lucy." He turned to McKim and said silkily, "As you can see, my wife is quite overcome with excitement."

Just then, as if she'd planned the moment, the curtains swept aside and Millicent hurried in.

"William! Lucy!" She held out her arms as if we hadn't seen one another for a year. "Are you enjoying the performance?"

"I think LaBlache is in fine voice tonight," William said.

"Ah yes, but such a gloomy part! I own I can hardly wait until she dies at the end." Millicent smiled. "How lovely you look this evening, Lucy. I knew that green would be delicious against your pale skin. But where is your father? I haven't seen him for the longest time."

"He dislikes the German," William said. He looked at McKim. "DeLancey insists that he won't come here until they bring back the French or Italian opera. I'm afraid he misses the Academy—he kept a box there until the very end."

"Or perhaps it's only the Patti he misses," Millie said with a smile.

"I think we all miss Adelina Patti," William said. "But Millicent, you've come at the perfect time. I've just given Lucy the surprise of her life."

"A surprise?" Millicent's eyes went wide, but there was worry in them as she looked at me.

I tried to smile. "Yes. It was quite delightful. It seems all William's dreams are coming true. We're to build on that plat on Fifth Avenue."

Millicent clasped her gloved hands before her, smiling. "Oh, so he's told you, then."

"You knew?"

"Everyone knew. He's been keeping the secret for weeks. How glad you must be. I shall take you to the Art Association for the auctions. They have the most wonderful things. You'll need more Louis the Sixteenth, of course. Perhaps the Duveens will set aside an old master or two for you—"

My head began to ache. I put my fingers to my temples.

"Shall I bring you some punch, darling?" William asked me. I nodded, and he and McKim left.

Millie settled herself into the chair beside me. Her diamond tiara sparkled in the light, as did her earrings, so stars seemed to twinkle in her dark hair. She was wearing deep red velvet, and she looked young and pretty and alive, with her flashing dark eyes. I felt used up beside her.

"*Je m'étouffe*," I whispered, then regretted it; I had not meant to reveal how sick I felt.

Millicent grabbed my arm. "Come. Let's go outside, where the air is so much cooler."

I found myself rising, stumbling amid the chairs, pushing past the heavy curtains into the hallway, where the air was less close, less heavy. I could bring it into my lungs. I leaned against the wall, and my friend stood in front of me, shielding me from curious eyes, for which I was grateful.

"I thought you would be happy," Millie said. "We all thought you would be happy. The house he's planning—why, it's so beautiful. And it would be all your own. . . ."

"Papa has taken up residence at the Union," I said quietly. "He's there nearly every moment."

"But the Row house is so cramped and small. And really, Lucy, it's *Fifth Avenue*. I cannot understand you. Why aren't you happy?"

She sounded so plaintive and confused that it startled me. Then I saw Daisy Hadden just behind her, watching us, and I struggled to find solid ground, to soothe myself. "Why, of course I'm happy, Millicent," I said, wishing that simply saying the words could make it so. "Of course I am. It's just that I've a terrible headache."

Millicent looked relieved. "Oh, it's no wonder. I've nearly one myself. This terrible music."

"Yes," I said, relieved myself at our mutual deception. "I find I agree with Papa; I've a longing for the French or the Italian."

Millicent agreed: "The German is so hard on the ears."

We lapsed into silence. Once I would have said Millicent was my closest friend. She had been, and not so long ago, but these silences had begun to come more and more often, and I was not sure who to blame for them. She looked uncomfortable, and I felt nothing but a supreme weariness.

I had to force myself to turn around and go back to the box, to sit down. When Millicent left, saying, "Are you going to the Baldwins' after?" I could only nod numbly and stare at the stage before me, drowning in the dragging hours, wishing for my medicated darkness.

"I wish you had told me your plans before we went," I said to William as we made our way to the Baldwins' home on Madison Square Park. The bright arc lights streaked into the carriage windows, blinding for a moment before lapsing again into darkness, and I shielded my eyes with my hand.

"Really, Lucy," he said. "You had to know already what I planned. You knew when I bought that plat; I've held on to it for nearly a year. What else did you think I would do with it?"

"Sell it, perhaps," I snapped. "As ill-gotten gains."

He laughed at that. "How melodramatic. Don't tell me you've forgotten how your father made his money. You've lived for years on ill-gotten gains. I merely took advantage of an opportunity. Villiard wasn't the only one ruined by Marine Bank's collapse. We could have been there too, if I hadn't seen it coming—"

"Yes. Thank goodness you're so clever."

He leaned over me with a puzzled and slightly angry expression. "What makes you so particular of a sudden?"

I waved him away. "I like the Row."

He sat back against the seat with a heavy sigh. "It's your father's house."

"He's never there."

"But it's his nonetheless. It's been four years since we married. You're *my* wife. I can afford to keep you. I've been able to for some time. I haven't asked you to move before because I knew

it would upset you. But it's time. There's no need to be dependent on your father, and I think . . . I think it's not good for you."

"Not good for me?"

"Yes," William said thoughtfully. "It's time you stopped being
a daughter."

My head was pounding again. "Don't be absurd."

"I've thought it for some time, Lucy," he went on. "I think it's
time you were mistress of your own house. One where your father can't come in whenever he wants and reduce you to a blath-
ering girl. It's time we made our own life away from him."

I stared at him, bewildered. "I thought . . . you and Papa . . .
you're like his own son."

"I'm not speaking of me, Lucy, but of you," William said impatiently. "You even think of yourself as DeLancey Van Berckel's
daughter, not as my wife."

"Oh, good heavens, William. I do not. I'm Mrs. William
Carelton. I know that."

He studied me so searchingly that I had to turn away. "Do
you?" he asked. "I've wondered for some time if that house isn't
the reason we haven't had a child."

"The house," I said, meaning to be light, to joke. "Yes indeed,
it must be the house that holds such power."

William did not laugh. "We've seen so many doctors. None
has found a reason. What else am I to think?"

I gazed out the window, at the bright lights of the hotels, the
theaters. "That we aren't meant to have a child."

"I won't believe that."

"And you think a mansion on Fifth Avenue will change everything."

"I think it must," he told me.

"And if it doesn't?"

I refused to meet his gaze. "It must," he said, and I heard his
certainty and his will and the words he left unsaid, the threat of
Dr. Little's asylum.

Chapter 3

I used to dream of Rome. When I was a girl, I read everything I could about the city. I had dreams of wandering through the Piazza, of suppers eaten in warm, sultry air scented with olives and oregano. I formed an attachment to Italian poets, hiding their books from my father, sneaking them into bed to read by candlelight late into the night. I dreamed briefly of painting there—the landscapes here were too muted, too familiar. My brush longed to depict Italian hills and golden sunsets, Italian flowers and swarthy Italian peasants. *Rome.* The word was magical to me, as if just its conjuring could enable my soul to fly.

But I did not see Rome until William and I honeymooned there. It was only one stop on a European Grand Tour, before Paris—William had insisted that I be fitted by Worth for next season's gowns—but it was the place I longed to be every moment I was somewhere else. I wanted to see it through the eyes of the poets I revered, through the misty, earthy colors of the artists. *Rome.* Surely there could be nothing bad in a world that harbored such a place.

I did not see Rome through my poets' eyes. Nor did I see it through the brushstrokes of any artist. When I finally saw

Rome, it was through William's impatience, his longing to be farther on, in Paris and London, to finish business there, to have my hands modeled in clay, to see me dressed in Worth finery, to live up to my social obligations, which decreed that we should spend two months on our tour, and that it should include the places everyone went. There was no lingering at outdoor tables, breathing the scents of olives and oregano. There was no time to walk through the Piazza. The days were spent calling on friends of my father's, the nights dining at their tables. For me, Rome was just New York with different accents.

As William led me up the stairs to the Baldwins', I thought of Rome again, the Rome of my dreams, and how it had turned out nothing at all like I had imagined or wanted. It was impossible to believe that this life—the life of a wife, of a woman—had once been as intriguing to me as Rome.

The door was opened by a solemn-faced butler, and we went inside.

James Baldwin was a man who loved trees and forests, and the entrance hall was covered with pictures of landscapes, some by old masters and one by Millet that was greatly admired. Much was said of Ella Baldwin's decor, which was styled to match her naturalist husband's tastes, with pressed leaves imprisoned in glass, forever gold and red, and botanical studies kept immutable in tapestry and upholstery. I found it oppressive—nature forever inside, crushed by the massive weight of feathers and shells, stuffed birds preening on peeling branches beneath glass domes, wax flowers and paintings that echoed of what these things had forever left behind: the blessed course of life and death, nature at its cruelest and most sublime.

Dutifully, I admired a new painting, a landscape in the golds and browns of the Hudson River School, though to me it looked as if everything in the scene were dying.

"It is Father's new favorite," said Antoinette Baldwin—the pretty eighteen-year-old daughter—as she led us to the dining room, which was laid end to end with china and glassware that sparkled and twinkled in the light from a lily-globed gasolier. Candles had been lit as well, and the scents of wax and smoke and gas were heavy in the small room.

"There you are, Antoinette, darling!" Daisy Hadden was coming toward us, fluttering in deep rose lace, her new diamonds glittering blindingly in the candlelight. She touched Antoinette's arm and said in a low voice, "Your mama's asking for you, my dear."

Antoinette gave us a pretty smile and hurried off. When she was gone, Daisy said to William and me, "How nice to see you both. Lucy, how deliciously pale you look this evening. That gown is so bold against your skin."

William gripped my arm. "She has the headache. The opera was a trial."

"Well, yes. This season . . ." Daisy waved her hand languidly and lowered her voice. "This dinner should be just as wretched, of course. A pity Ella has such a lamentable cook. Although I suppose the good doctor might save us. Did you know he was here tonight? I thought Harry Everett might call him out last week. I quite imagined pistols at dawn."

"Doctor?" William asked. "What are you talking about? What doctor?"

Daisy looked surprised. "Why, Dr. Victor Seth. Don't tell me you haven't heard of him? I would have thought after all dear Lucy's trials . . ."

"I'm afraid not," William said.

"Oh." She seemed nonplussed. "But then I suppose the two of you have been in the country these last few months. Seth has become quite notorious recently. The guest du jour." She laughed. "They say he's a Jew, but you would hardly know it to look at him. He's very controversial, you know. He quite gives one the chills. Something about his eyes. But Ella swears by him. He's just over there."

I had barely heard her words, but there was something about Daisy's surreptitious curiosity that made me follow her gaze through the crowd to a man who stood near the back of the room, surrounded by Ella Baldwin and a group of our friends.

I had never seen him before. He was nearly as tall as William and of a similar age. His dark hair was thick and brushed into smooth submission. He wore a thin mustache and a Vandyke beard. Even from this distance, I felt how commanding he was. It surprised me not to have sensed his presence the moment we'd stepped into the room.

"He's a doctor, you say?" William asked thoughtfully.

"A nerve specialist," Daisy said.

"A nerve specialist?"

Daisy nodded. "Or something of the sort. I understand he wrote some brilliant paper, though there are some—Harry, for one—who say he's a charlatan. He has some new theory—Ella explained it all to me, but you know how I am, I can hardly grasp these things. Mesmerism or phrenology or something."

"Those are hardly new," William said.

"Well, then something like them." Daisy glanced back at the doctor. "He does seem to work miracles, though. And I suppose he's very charming. Why, look what he's done for Ella Baldwin—she was an invalid the entire summer, but you'd hardly know it now."

I hadn't known that Ella was ailing, but it was certain she was no longer. She was smiling brightly at the doctor, hanging on his every word, and with dismay I felt William's sharp interest in this man.

I touched his arm. "Darling," I said softly. "I'm quite parched."

"Yes, yes, of course," he said, forcing his eyes away from Dr. Seth, patting my hand. "Let's find you something to drink."

We left Daisy, and William's fascination with the doctor waned and disappeared as we made our way to the buffet. He was cornered by Richard Martin, who involved him in a conversation about bonds, and I was relieved.

We sat down to dinner so late that my head was spinning. It was the first time since we'd arrived that William and I were separated from each other, and even then there was only the width of the table between us. He had been seated next to Daisy Hadden, while I had to suffer the cruelly dull Hiram Grace, with his overgrown graying mustache and his ceaseless talk of Western Union, where he spent his days making so much money that his four daughters were perpetually dressed in Worth gowns. Dr. Victor Seth sat a good distance down the long table, involved in conversation. Far away from William, I was glad to see.

There was wine. I sipped until I no longer felt the pressure in my chest, despite William's warning glances.

"I hear you're about to join the others on Fifth Avenue," Hiram Grace said to me between the lobster bisque and the roasted partridge.

I reached again for my glass. "Ah yes. How quickly word spreads. William has decided to build. We've a plat on East Sixty-third."

"Hmmph. Going to tear down those shanties, is he?"

"I imagine so."

"You'll have a time of it, won't you? All that stuff females love: upholstery and paint and statuary and such."

"Oh yes." The damask tablecloth wavered before me as I set my glass down.

"So you'll leave Washington Square to your father?"

"It is his home," I said. "Though lately you would not know it, he spends so much time at the club."

"Got to give the newlyweds some room, don't you know." Grace lifted his glasses and wiped at his rheumy eyes. "Still and all, no doubt he'll sell that, too, before long. He's getting along in years, isn't he? Seventy or so?"

"Seventy-three," I said.

"Ah. I tell you, it makes me sad, all these good men passing on."

"Papa will outlive them all," I said.

"No doubt you hope so," Grace said. I did not attempt to enlighten him. "Even he can't stave off the march of progress."

"None of us can, Mr. Grace."

"That's so, that's so. They just keep coming in, don't they?"

"I'm not sure I take your meaning."

"Well, look at what happened to Lafayette Place and Tompkins Square. Nothing but immigrants. The Germans have settled only a few blocks from Washington Square—they'll take it next, you mark my words. We keep moving uptown to get away from 'em, and they keep following."

Gwen Sanders, sitting on Grace's left, chimed in. "It's bad enough to have to hire them. Why, Daisy was just saying that she already feels overrun with Irish! But what can one do? It's impossible to keep a maid longer than a few months, and to find a decent girl—"

"It's not in them to be reliable." Grace seemed unperturbed as he wiped at his mustache with a damask napkin. "No point in asking the impossible. They have smaller skulls, that's a proven fact. The Negroes and the Irish and all the rest haven't got the brainpower."

William spoke up from across the table. "All one must do is see how they live. Had they our intelligence, certainly they would better themselves."

My glass was nearly empty. I signaled for the serving girl.

On William's other side, Harrison Everett said thoughtfully, "Then you don't believe that all this talk of slum reform will make a difference?"

"How could it?" William asked. "These people haven't evolved enough to understand the consequences of vice. If you clean up the tenements, they will fall back into degeneracy. As Hiram said, it's in their nature."

Harrison persisted, "But if they were given jobs and decent places to live—"

"How can a change in environment possibly counteract generations of heredity?" William asked.

"Why, I'm not sure it can. But as the superior species, shouldn't we be expected to protect those less evolved?"

William laughed. "Good God, Harry, don't tell me you're one of those radical humanitarians."

Harrison smiled thinly. "I'm afraid so. You should be careful, Will, it might rub off on you if I stand too close at the next Glee Club practice."

"Gentlemen." Gwen put her long fingers to her forehead. "You're quite spoiling my appetite. Can't we discuss something better suited to such a delicious supper?"

William smiled at her, then at me—a smug, self-righteous smile cloaked in civility and refinement. "Forgive me," he said. "Perhaps we should change topics, gentlemen. We can't expect the ladies to participate in such indelicate conversation."

"I was finding it all quite interesting," Antoinette Baldwin said. She lifted her chin as if expecting a challenge and flushed the rosy pink that only the young can. She reminded me of myself at her age, forever wanting more, making myself heard, thinking I could change the world and my place in it. I was sorry for her and horribly sad for all the ways she would be shoved into silence, and the emotion overwhelmed me so that I dropped my newly filled wineglass, splashing wine all over the tablecloth, sending droplets scattering across the table to dot William's pristine white shirt like blood.

"Oh my, I'm so sorry." I got to my feet and wiped ineffectually at the spreading stain with my napkin.

The servant pushed in beside me. "Please, ma'am," she said, and I stepped back to let her clean it up. The wall was too close, and I crashed into it. I saw the doctor look up, his dark gaze sharpening; the others were staring at me oddly, the conversation fallen into disrepair. I shoved at a loosened hair and tried to smile.

"How clumsy I am." I tried to laugh, but the sound came out like a snort. I felt ridiculous tears start at my eyes, and I couldn't stop them. "And after such a lovely evening . . ."

Dr. Seth began to rise. "Madam, are you quite all right?"

William took his napkin from his lap quite deliberately and stood. "Thank you, sir, but I think it best if my wife and I excuse ourselves." Such a calm, even voice—I was quite sure no one but I heard his underlying disappointment. "Forgive us, James, for interrupting your supper. Lucy has had a headache all evening. No doubt we should have taken ourselves straight home from the opera."

James Baldwin nodded shortly. "Of course. I confess I've come home with more than one headache from this season's program." He glanced at me. "Do get some rest, dear Lucy."

I nodded, but I seemed unable to move from the wall. "I'm sorry," I whispered, and I could not find other words as William came around the table and unstuck me by putting his arm around my shoulders. I felt the doctor's gaze, unwavering, starkly curious, and then William was leading me away from the solicitous murmurs as he would a child. At the door, he took my cape from the butler and wrapped it around me. He shrugged into his own coat and hat, and we went out into falling snow.

I paused on the steps, feeling the snow melt on my skin, such a delicious cool, so that I lifted my face to it. "It's snowing," I said. "Oh, look, William."

"You've had too much wine," he said, pulling me down the steps and out to the waiting carriage, bundling me ungently into the dark, cold cocoon. He got in and sat silently, disapprovingly beside me.

The carriage jolted to a start, and I was flung against him. I could only burrow into his side, into the warmth of his sleeve. "I'm sorry," I whispered, too weary to move, wanting nothing but to fall into a deep, abiding sleep uninterrupted by midnight yearnings and vague dissatisfactions. What did that even feel like? Why could I not remember?

William sighed. "Ah, Lucy. What am I going to do with you?"

The next morning William went to the Exchange, and I laid in bed until noon. I'd instructed Harris that I wouldn't need the carriage; I was too ill to go calling today, as I usually did. Even when I did get out of bed, I lingered in my room, wrapped in my dressing gown, surreptitiously watching the snow fall on Washington Square from a crack in the rose brocade drapes. I remembered how, as a child, I had raced my nanny to the park despite her calls—"Slow down, Lucy! There's a good child! This is *not* ladylike behavior!"—and plopped myself down to make angels in the snow. She had laughed when she caught up with me, but that good humor was not enough to keep her from reporting my lapse to my father, who forced me to stay abed with a copy of Lydia Maria Child's *The Girl's Own Book* that afternoon instead of going with him to visit my cousin Hattie.

"Young ladies do not make snow angels in Washington Square," he said to me. "How glad I am that your mother is not here to see such a spectacle."

I could no longer recall the joy of that small defiance. I wondered: Had I felt the cold of the snow? Had I tasted it? Had the dull punishment of social catechism been worth that moment? There *must* have been joy. Or had I been then as I was now? Had the days always stretched so drearily before me that I could not rouse myself to step outside my bedroom doors?

But no; I remembered Antoinette Baldwin and the dull pain I'd felt at the anticipation of her impending womanhood, the knowledge that I had once been like her. To think of Antoinette, how trapped she was, how her wings beat so futilely against bars she could not see and did not even know were there, made me want to cry.

I turned from the window, too saddened to look at the snow, and my gaze went to the brown bottle on my dressing table. The rush of future days washed over me, the constant threat of Dr. Little's asylum.

I was hardly aware of going to it, only that it was in my hands, hard and smooth, the satisfying pop of the cork, and then the sweetness of it on my tongue, the bitterness after. I took more than I should have, but once I tasted it, I wanted more—a few hours of peace, surely that was not too much to ask? Only a few more hours.

William came to me through the haze of my dreams. I heard the door opening, more sharply than it should, and his exhalation of disbelief and anger. I felt him pushing at me: *Lucy, Lucy, damn it, what have you done?* I batted at him with my hands to leave me alone, and then he was gone.

When I woke up, it was the dead of night. There was only a candle, but its dim light hurt. I shielded my eyes and dragged myself from a lingering drowsiness to see a shadow in the chair next to the bed—William, still clothed, asleep.

I must have made a noise, because he roused, and I saw him looking at me with such tenderness and care that I could hardly bear it. He leaned over and took my hand, squeezing it between his soft fingers.

"I've talked to Victor Seth, darling," he whispered. "You're to see him tomorrow."

Chapter 4

The carriage wheels jolted and bumped on the settling paving stones as we made our way down Broadway, jerking to frequent stops for the traffic, which was horrible all the time, but particularly so that afternoon. I was nauseated from the night before, and the jouncing only made it worse. I did not think I could bear another doctor—not another suggestion of a cure that gave me hope for too short a time, or worse, another hopeless diagnosis.

"I'd never heard of him before Ella's dinner," I said again.

William sat rigidly beside me. Though he had brought the *New York Times* to read, it stayed folded neatly on his lap. "He's been given the highest recommendation."

"Daisy said he was controversial."

"That's not always a bad thing, Lucy. Apparently he has some new technique—"

"She said he was a Jew."

"No one knows that for certain. He did study in Germany."

"He's a foreigner, then?"

"He doesn't sound so."

"Well, I won't go," I said. I reached for the bell cord. "Turn the carriage around. I won't be examined by some poor immigrant."

William grabbed my hand before I could pull the cord. His grip was firm, his expression unyielding. "Last year you were willing to have them cut you open to end this. This man could be your salvation. *Our* salvation."

I sagged against the seat and closed my eyes. Images of other doctors ran through my mind. "I can't bear this again," I whispered. "I don't know how you can."

"Because I can't bear the alternative," William said. "Lucy, you've grown worse this last year. I have no choice but to hope that his new treatment may work. I'm surprised you don't feel the same."

"I do. I do. But to have hope dashed over and over . . ."

"We've never seen someone like this before. He's a neurologist."

"I don't know what that is."

"A doctor of the brain."

"Oh, William. The brain? All the others said it was . . ." I could not even say the word.

"He specializes in nervous disorders, Lucy. Especially in women. Ella Baldwin speaks very highly of him. We haven't tried this before. Perhaps . . ."

The hope in his voice nearly brought me to tears. I watched the respectable shops and hotels give way steadily to the red-brick buildings and warehouse trade of Lower Broadway, the advertising billboards pasted one over the other, layers of fluttering paper—TRY HOBENSACK'S LIVER PILLS, RHEUMATISM CURED IN THREE APPLICATIONS!—and I wished I were naive again, that it was three years ago, when I had faith that a doctor could easily cure whatever ailed me. How long had that hope lingered? When had it disappeared? After the second doctor? After the fifth? I could no longer remember.

William once more covered my hand with his own. "When we're done, we'll go to Delmonico's, and I'll buy you tea and a cake. Would that make you feel better?"

In spite of the fact that Dr. Seth was the current fashion, he could not afford the better offices in town. I grew more and more nervous, to think of myself walking into one of these side entrances, past iron gates and down narrow stairs to a darkened basement.

The carriage stopped, and this time it was not for traffic.

"We're here, sir," called our driver.

Jimson opened the door and helped me out, ushering me through the piles of stinking horse manure and garbage cluttering the street. I hung back until William put his arm around my shoulders and forced me forward. I was momentarily confused—this was no doctor's office before me but a shop. Its windows were full of handsome trinkets, stained-glass lamps, gilt boxes. A bell on the door tinkled when we went inside the incense-scented room, but no one was at the counter, and no one greeted us.

I hesitated, but William did not, and then I saw he was leading me toward a shadowed door in the back wall. Beyond it were stairs and a dusty, dingy hallway that was in desperate need of fresh paint. The faint light from a window slanted in from a landing above.

Our footsteps echoed up through the stairwell. We rounded the landing and went up another set of stairs that opened onto a long and narrow hallway with doors lining either side. The stairs continued on, but William took me down the hallway to a door at the very end. On it was painted in restrained black and gilt letters: DR. VICTOR SETH, DOCTOR OF NEUROLOGY.

I hung back and whispered, "Do let's go, William. We could be home in time for tea."

He grasped my hand and opened the door. We stepped into another dingy room with a small desk next to another door and an old rosewood settee against the opposite wall, its red-striped floral upholstery frayed at the corners. There was no one there.

William cleared his throat and had stepped forward to knock

on the other door when it opened. Out came a young woman with pale hair and eyes. She saw us and stopped midmotion. "Oh . . . hello."

"We have an appointment with Dr. Seth," William told her.

The girl went behind the desk and fumbled with a thin book that lay open on the blotter. "Of course. I see it right here." She gave us an expectant smile.

William reached inside his coat and pulled out his pocket watch. "I believe we're right on time."

She checked the book again. "Oh yes, you are. But . . . um, well, the doctor . . . he's not here yet."

"He's not here?"

"Well then," I said, backing toward the door, "perhaps another time."

William held me firm. "We have an appointment."

"He—he had an unexpected visitor," the girl said. "I expect him back shortly."

"This is unconscionable," William said. "I am a very busy man."

"Yes, of course you are."

The voice came from behind us. Startled, I jerked around to see a man wearing a heavy coat and a hat that shone wetly in the light. Dr. Seth. He had opened the door without making a sound, though it was impossible that we had not heard him.

He smiled smoothly as he pulled at his gloves. "Forgive me for making you wait. I was unavoidably detained." He glanced at the girl, who shrank visibly at the sight of him. "Irene, perhaps you could make yourself useful and find some tea for our visitors."

"Yes, Doctor," she murmured, leaving quickly.

He went to the other door and opened it, then stood back to usher us inside. I had expected William to continue to be angry, but he was uncharacteristically quiet, caught—no doubt as I was—by the presence of this man. I remembered my sense that

I should have felt him the moment I stepped into Ella's dining room; that feeling was more intense here, in this little office. It was unsettling, the way he took up space, as if something had entered the room with him, something large and intangible.

Wordlessly, William and I preceded him through the doorway.

The room was darkened. Opposite was a bank of windows, though all but one were covered by lowered blinds; the single open one looked out onto the brick wall of the building next door, at COXLEY'S CIGARS, PIPES, AND TOBACCO painted there in large black-and-white letters.

There was a click, and the room went bright, electric lamps blazing into brilliance. I blinked and gasped, used as I was to gaslight.

"You see, we have the most modern conveniences," said the doctor.

William murmured something, but I could not take my eyes from the room. The false light illuminated it to its worst advantage. It brought into relief the large table near the window, scattered with papers and open books. Behind it were shelves full of messily arranged books, shoved side by side, lying erratically one on top of the other. The only neat shelf was tightly packed with thin black leather-bound volumes bookended with a large white phrenology head.

There was a settee that matched the one in the waiting room, two chairs upholstered in a bright red brocade, and a ladder-back chair that sat next to a large wooden cabinet with several drawers. Near this was a long examination table. These—the cabinet and the table—made me most anxious: the cabinet because I had no idea what it was, and the table because I did. I glanced at William, who was frowning.

He turned to the doctor and said, "You *are* a phrenologist."

Dr. Seth was taking off his coat and hat. Though he spoke to William, his gaze went to me. "No more than any other self-respecting physician. The head is merely a personal reminder. Nothing to worry about." He smiled, and I found myself transfixed, uncertain whether to be charmed or afraid. "May I take your coats?" Dr. Seth asked.

William took his off, but I shook my head and grasped the front of mine, wanting the protection of it. Dr. Seth nodded mildly and gestured to the settee for us to sit down. I did not want to do that either, but these choices were not mine to make, so I went with William to the settee while Dr. Seth took one of the red brocade chairs.

Just then there was a knock on the door, and the girl—Irene—came in bearing a tea tray with service for three. She set it silently on the table beside the doctor's chair, then left.

When the door had closed, the doctor met my eyes. "You seem nervous, Mrs. Carelton. Perhaps some tea will reassure you."

William laughed shortly. "Lucy's nerves are the reason we're here to see you, Dr. Seth."

The doctor poured the tea with precision, added milk and sugar, and handed us each a gaily painted china cup. The rims were thick, the edges uneven, but the tea was hot and sweet and soothing; he had made it as I liked it, though I had not said a word.

"I have the feeling we've met before, Mrs. Carelton," he said.

"The other night, at the Baldwins' supper," William told him. "We had not been introduced then, but you must have seen Lucy's fit."

Seth straightened. His glance sharpened as it had that night. "Ah yes, of course," he said, and I was surprised to hear a brief impatience in his tone. "I assume that is why you're here, but why don't you tell me the whole of it?"

William said, "First, Dr. Seth, we need some reassurances. You've been highly recommended to us, but . . . well, you must see our situation."

"Of course." Dr. Seth nodded. "I can assure you of the strictest discretion, Mr. and Mrs. Carelton. As you saw, this office is deliberately situated to afford you the greatest privacy. I can promise that, should you decide to undergo treatment, my notes will be destroyed at the conclusion. Irene is highly motivated not to speak of your visit. I guarantee that no one will know you were ever here unless you tell them yourself."

The doctor wrapped his long fingers delicately around the thick cup as if afraid he might crush it. He looked directly at me. "Now, why have you come to me?"

William said, "We've been to ten doctors in the last three years. No one's been able to help. You're our last hope."

I felt the doctor's dark eyes on me. There was something improper, even dangerous, in the way he stared. My fingers shook as I brought my cup to my lips; I dared not look up.

William went on, "It's become unbearable living with her. We haven't been able to keep a maid longer than two months. Lucy's fits terrorize the household. She has temper tantrums, screaming hysteria—the smallest things turn her into a mad creature. When she's not having a fit, she's sad and inconsolable. She's barely able to rise from bed. I've despaired of her. Having anyone over for dinner is impossible, and in my business, it's necessary."

"I see," Dr. Seth said, finally turning to William. "What is your business?"

My husband looked surprised. "You don't know?"

"I confess not."

"Yes. Well." William looked discomfited. "Brokering. I'm a stockbroker."

Seth nodded. "Go on."

"Well, I . . . Last night Lucy took too much laudanum. It's really become—"

"Laudanum? Who prescribed laudanum?"

"Dr. Moore. About a year ago."

"How much do you take?" the doctor asked me.

"J-just a bit," I managed. "A few spoonfuls at bedtime. It . . . it helps me sleep."

"Tell him when else, Lucy," William said.

"There is no other time."

William gave the doctor a look as if to say: *Do you see what I must contend with?* I looked down at my tea, humiliated by my small lie.

Thankfully, Dr. Seth did not pursue it. "What have the other doctors said?"

William sighed. "Well, we've been"—he cleared his throat—"I'm sorry, this is indelicate."

"I'm a doctor, Mr. Carelton."

"Yes, of course. It's just that . . . well, Lucy has been . . . unable to conceive."

"And other doctors have attributed her moods to uterine monomania?"

"Why, yes, that's just what they've said—some of them, anyway. We've tried everything. She took the water cure a year ago, and then there was some kind of belt contraption that she had to wear. The one doctor thought an ovariotomy. Recently one suggested she was incurable. He said I should send her to an asylum. An asylum!"

"Has anyone suggested a clitoridectomy?"

I went hot. I could not look at either of them.

"One. But Lucy . . . she's not . . . not that way. It's just . . . except for this hysteria, she's the perfect wife," William finished lamely.

There was silence. I glanced up into the eyes of the doctor, which so agitated me that I looked down again into my tea, which was sloshing in my cup, so badly were my hands shaking.

Dr. Seth said, "I think I understand, Mr. Carelton. Now, if you will excuse us, I'd like to examine your wife. Irene will find you a newspaper to read, if you like."

"Of course." William rose from his seat abruptly. He set aside his cup and patted my shoulder and left. The door latched shut behind him.

Dr. Seth leaned forward. I pressed back into the cushioned settee when he reached out. "Your teacup, Mrs. Carelton," he said. When I gave it to him, careful not to touch him, he set the cup gently on the tea tray, much as a woman might. I had never seen a man move so gracefully.

"The examination is simple enough," he said reassuringly. "I trust you've experienced one before?"

I could only nod.

"I will try not to embarrass you unduly. But you understand, I do need to know these things to treat you effectively."

His gaze did not waver. I felt imprisoned by it.

"I understand," I managed.

"Good." He went to the door and called out for the girl, who came hurrying in. He said, "Irene will assist you. Please undress to your chemise. There's a screen just over there—" He pointed beyond the wooden cabinet and chairs, and I saw a red-and-black-lacquered Japanese screen.

He rose and went to the table that served as his desk, turning his back to me, and I slowly went behind the screen and let Irene help me. When I was ready, she gave me a small smile and left again. I crossed my arms protectively over my chest when I came out from behind the screen, clad only in my chemise. He was waiting by the table, his suit coat off, his shirtsleeves rolled up to reveal his bare forearms. The sight of that, along with the tangle of shining instruments gleaming beside him, made me hesitate, but he nodded reassuringly and gestured to the examination table. "Please," he said, and as I stepped onto a small stool and sat gingerly on the edge of the table, he took up the first of his instruments.

Notes from the Journal of
Victor Leonard Seth

Observation 38

Diagnosis: Hysteria (Neurasthenia?), possible Uterine Monomania

January 14, 1885

Mrs. C., thirty years old, consulted me for general hysteria. Married for four years, subject to hysterical bouts occasionally before then but with increasing attacks, especially in the last three years, probably related to an inability to conceive, though she has normal menstrual cycles. Has consulted ten doctors during this time, with diagnoses ranging from uterine monomania to displaced ovaries. Took water cure with mixed results. Laudanum at night (possibly more often) for the last year. According to her husband, she has developed an increased reliance on it, which resulted in an overdosage the night before, producing a deep, comalike sleep lasting fifteen hours.

Mrs. C. received an average education, comes from a wealthy and socially prominent family. Mother died from undisclosed causes when Mrs. C. was ten. Normal childhood. No siblings. Father is still alive. She is rather thin, of average height and normal intellect. Dark hair, face without color, white skin, with deep circles beneath her eyes belying her claim that she sleeps often and for long periods.

Mrs. C. is not completely forthcoming regarding her present medical condition, though she seems to desire help. She complains of a frequent inability to breathe, which no amount of relaxation or loosening of corset stays seems to relieve. Often has the sense of something blocking her throat—"suffocation," as she calls it. Complains of restlessness and the inability to experience joy or even contentment, along with frequent irritation and agitation that grows into "fits" during which she feels unable to control her emotions.

Present Condition: Temperature 99°F. Pulse 74, regular. Tongue slightly coated, whitish color. Thoracic and abdominal examinations revealed nothing abnormal. She complained of no tenderness or pain, yet I very easily created a painful spot beneath the xiphoid process and a corresponding one on the back by insisting she would feel such. Having thus established that the patient was suggestible, I did the customary vaginal examination.

There was no ovary pain. Vagina has normal sensitivity on both sides, with no evidence of abnormalities in coloration or tissue. Labia majora and minora are of normal sensitivity. Clitoris insensitive when not erect but becomes acutely sensitive during erection, which can be produced easily, with pleasant sensations, flushed cheeks and throat, and rapid breathing. Having determined that she had normal sensitivity, I then told her that cases of her type often came accompanied with numbness on the left side of the vagina and the corresponding side of the labia majora. I explored her sensitivity again and found a well-characterized hemianesthesia at both places.

Mrs. C. suffers from the usual malady of her class: spoiled, self-indulgent ennui, easily managed. Since she appears to be suggestible, I told her I thought she would benefit from hypnosis. She was not enthusiastic about the suggested treatment, and in fact seemed wary. When I called in her husband, he was highly opposed to the treatment, calling it "little better than phrenology." I assured him that the French were embracing the science, but he was not reassured. "We came here for real medicine, Doctor, not cumberlandism." I told him that I was highly trained, but he did not relax until I told him I would be combining the hypnosis with electrotherapy treatments, and that—as with most other patients of Mrs. C.'s type—I expected a radical improvement in his wife's temperament in a short period of time.

The electrotherapy will soothe them both; they believe in it. It's far better that I establish crédibilité in Mrs. C. especially, than tell her that I believe hypnosis can achieve results without the use of electrotherapy. Bernheim's maxim! <u>Suggestion is everything.</u>

I expect Mrs. C.'s results to be no different from those of my last several patients. A few visits, and she will be gone from my office completely, restored to her usual uncomplaining, parasitic existence. Though her husband desires discretion, they will both laud my accomplishments and recommend me to another bored invalid. These are the times I begin to despise the turn my practice has taken. Though I am adequately rewarded financially, these women only provide fodder for my critics and keep me from pursuing real knowledge.

I cannot turn my back on the money, but of late, it becomes wearying, and I must ask myself again: Is it possible for true science to exist and flourish in these conditions? I confess I despair of it.

Chapter 5

When we left Seth's office, I saw hope in William's eyes again, and I had to confess that I felt it myself. I determined not to—I knew already how this would end, the terrible disappointment, the paralyzing despair—but it was there nonetheless. Here was a treatment we had not tried, and Dr. Seth was a neurologist, a word I'd never heard before but which now sounded scientific and important. Despite my distrust of him, I wanted to be well. I wanted to believe that this time might work. I wanted it more than I could remember wanting anything. To see love in William's eyes again, instead of concern and despair, to ease my own sense of emptiness. . . . It was as William said to me: I had been willing to risk surgery to feel those things once before. I could do no less now.

So I didn't disagree with William when he said to me later, "I trust him, Lucy." His voice was full of yearning, as if he needed my reassurance. "Don't you? I believe this might just work."

"Neurology *is* a new science, as you said. There have been such advances—"

"Yes, there have been, haven't there?" he said eagerly. "It's impossible for one to keep up on all the different new theories."

"He's just come from Leipzig."

"Yes. Yes, he has. And this hypnotism, it's not the same as mesmerism at all."

"So he's said."

William looked satisfied. "I believe him, Lucy. I do. I think we're in good hands now."

"Of course we are," I said to him, wanting it to be true. "I'm quite sure we are."

It wasn't until the next morning that I realized how much I wanted to believe my own words.

I went downstairs to find my father breakfasting in the dining room. It was so odd to see him there that I stopped in surprise.

"Papa! What brings you here this morning?"

He was helping himself to eggs and toast from the sideboard while Moira hovered nervously behind. He glanced up when I entered, and his gaze swept me from head to toe. His thick mustache quivered; he frowned. My hand went reflexively to my hair; I forced myself to lower it.

"Lucy, my dear. How late you've slept this morning."

"Late? Why, it's only ten."

"The best of the day is long gone."

"Then you've missed it as well. You're only just now helping yourself to breakfast."

"This would be my lunch, since Cook cannot bring herself to roast a joint before noon."

I forced myself to smile. "You should have told me you would be here this morning. I could have instructed her to make something to your taste."

"I hardly need you to announce my presence in my own house," he said, turning from the sideboard. He went to the long mahogany table and seated himself at the end, William's usual place. "And I doubt you could have persuaded her to change her routine, in any case."

I hurried to the sideboard, where ham swam in juices already gelling into grease, and the white of the eggs was curling at the edges. I turned from both of those and took a piece of cold toast. Thankfully, the coffee was still hot.

My father was busily downing his breakfast, seemingly oblivious to cold eggs and greasy ham, but when I sat down, he gestured to his plate.

"Can't you do something about this, Lucy? God knows we pay that woman enough. You'd think she could make sure the food is hot, if nothing else."

"As you said, it's quite late," I told him. I tried to butter my toast; it crumbled beneath my knife, and because I was not the least bit hungry, I left it on my plate.

"It's no excuse. You should not let them be so lazy." He abandoned his breakfast to lean back in his chair. He was growing heavy, I noticed. His vest was pulling at the seams.

"You look well, Papa. Life at the club agrees with you."

"It suits me," he said. He poured another cup of coffee. "It's always clean there. Which reminds me—"

"The coffee's hot, at least." It was a futile attempt to distract him from what I knew must be coming.

"A man should have his comforts, Lucy. An oasis of peace from the world. When your mother was alive, I had that."

I looked down at the bits of toast on my plate, the nearly white lumps of butter.

"You should do more to help William, my dear. This house should be his castle, at least until he builds his real one." Papa chuckled. "Ah, I see that look on your face. I told William you'd like the idea. If you're anything like your mother, William will be looking at piles of bills. Grecian urns, stained glass . . . I hope to God you've inherited her taste."

I looked at the thick draperies, the heavy candlesticks on the mantel, turned and gilded, the endless display of gold and porcelain, and the suffocation started in my chest again. I could only murmur, "Yes."

"He deserves to be a king in his own house. The way I was until your mother died. That was one thing she was good at, anyway. If I wanted a roast at three in the morning, and a cook refused, she was gone by daylight. None of this tantrum-throwing nonsense. Your mother knew how to handle servants."

"I know, Papa. You've said so many times before."

"Pity you haven't retained her genius for running a household. You're too sensitive, Lucy. You must be more assertive."

"So you've said."

"If you hadn't spent so much time painting flowers and those silly little scenes—"

"Italian ruins."

"Ah yes." He nodded. "Thank God you've outgrown that. And the poetry—reams of wretched verse, I must say. I suppose I've that silly school to thank for all that, don't I? The Misses Graham, wasn't it? You'd think they could teach a girl her place in the world."

"Yes, Papa."

"Well, that's enough of that. You've taken my point, I assume?"

"Yes, Papa."

"Good. You make him happy, Lucy, or you'll regret it, that's all. Take my advice. Be a wife to your husband. If you make his world a comfortable one, that'll go a long way toward calming your nerves. William tells me he's been staying at the office late. I saw him at the lunch counter just yesterday, so I know he's not coming home then either. You will lose him, Lucy, mark my words, if you don't do something, and then where will you be? Back on my charity, that's where. And I can't live forever, you know."

"Yes, of course. Such a pity."

He frowned again and eyed me. "Yes, well . . . I'll tell you why I came over this morning. William tells me you've been ill. You do look peaked, but perhaps that's just your gown. You should not let yourself look so pale. You should not wear brown, I think. You're a pretty thing, Lucy, when you've a mind to be."

"I'll change after breakfast."

He nodded with satisfaction, and I looked away. His smug expression, his perfectly trimmed dark hair that was only now beginning to turn gray, his aged face that showed hardly a wrinkle—why should he be so young-looking, so arrogantly sure, so vibrant? It was as if he sucked the life from this room, from me.

"It's something more than your dress, I think, isn't it?" he asked. "What are you pining for now, Lucy? Music lessons? Travel?"

"No. There's nothing."

"I've seen that look in your eyes before. Go see another doctor, if you must. I've a friend in Philadelphia who tells me—"

"I am seeing another doctor," I blurted.

He looked surprised. "You are?"

I wasn't sure why I'd told him. To stop his diatribe, if nothing else, to end the ceaseless run of those words, their painful repetition. But now that I'd said it, I wished I hadn't. Reluctantly, I said, "William made the appointment. I've another one next week."

"Oh. Good. That's very good, in fact. Who is this man?"

There was no point in lying to him. He would find out, as he found out everything. "Just a doctor," I said. "On Broadway."

"On Broadway, eh? I hope he's discreet."

"I've no doubt of it."

"What's his name?"

I spoke as quietly as I could, hoping he would not really hear the name, would not really pursue it. "Dr. Seth."

My father had excellent hearing. "Seth? Seth? I've heard that name before, haven't I? Seth . . . Good God, Lucy, you don't mean Victor Seth?"

"Why—why, yes."

"What in God's name is William thinking?"

"He specializes in treatments for women, Papa."

"In cheating women, you mean."

My hand curled tightly around my cup. "I don't know what you mean."

"His own colleagues disparage him. Even that Dr. Moore of yours says he's a fraud. A dangerous one, no less, with all his talk of mesmerism and such."

"Hypnotism," I said softly.

"What? What did you say?"

"Hypnotism."

"Hypnotism?" Papa visibly struggled with his outrage. "Hypnotism?"

"And electrotherapy."

"Electrotherapy? With wires and such?"

"I suppose so."

"Electricity?"

"Ella Baldwin has nothing but praise for it. I understand it can be quite helpful."

"Helpful? I suppose so, if you've a mind to be a lamp. What's next? Spiritualism?"

I could not meet his gaze. "Now, really, Papa, how would talking to the dead possibly help me?"

He was quiet. When I looked at him, his lips were thin, his nostrils white. "Good God, Lucy, how can you not see the man's a fraud? Listen to your own doctor. Moore says he's irresponsible. That this is some kind of occult nonsense."

"Perhaps because it's a new science."

"A new science? How do you know this?"

"Dr. Seth has said—"

"Ha!" Papa jabbed his finger in the air. "This doctor told you. This fraud."

"He's not a fraud, Papa."

"And how would you know this, Lucy? Have you studied science and medicine?"

"No—"

He started to rise. "Where is this man? I'll go talk to him my-self. I can spot a charlatan in any guise."

I went still. The thought of it was horrifying. "No," I whis-pered.

Papa sat back down, thunderous, threatening. I knew why his business partners had always yielded to him. I had understood it for some time and never better than today. "I hardly need your permission," he said acidly. "I forbid you to see him."

"Please, Papa," I said. "Please. Don't do this."

"If William won't protect you, I shall."

"No, you mustn't. . . ." I struggled for the words. My faith in Dr. Seth grew in direct proportion to my father's outrage. "Please, Papa, I want to do this. He thinks it could help. William thinks it will help. And I want to be well. Please. I want it so very badly, and we've tried everything else. Everything."

I was trembling when I finished. Papa was stone-faced. My words had never silenced him before, and I had no idea what to do now that they had.

"Well now," he said slowly. "Perhaps I've been too hasty."

I wanted to cry with relief. "Oh, Papa, thank you. Thank you."

"Come now, girl, you know I dislike these maudlin displays."

I nodded, trying to gain control. "Yes, of course."

"You go to your doctor. But I warn you, I won't tolerate any strange goings-on."

"Yes. I understand."

"Good. Then for now I'll say no more about it." My father pushed back his chair and rose abruptly. When he came over to me and set his hand on my shoulder, I clasped it gratefully. He squeezed my fingers. "I don't hold with much of this nonsense, my dear, you know that," he said. "In the end it all comes down to accepting that you're a wife. Only then will you be truly sat-isfied. Find your duty. Happiness will follow."

*   *   *

I spent the next days in anxious anticipation. I had never experienced anything like hypnotism before. I had never even participated in the mesmerism parlor games that had been the preferred trick at parties only a few years before. To give oneself over so completely to someone else—I would have said it was not in my nature, though now I realized how often I had given myself over to my doctors over the years, how thoroughly I had thrown myself into their treatments and cures.

But that had been medicine; this suggested course of Dr. Seth's was unfamiliar to me. I hardly knew what to expect, so my apprehension grew even as did my eagerness.

The servants seemed to relish my tension. I was certain they deliberately worked to agitate me: Cook spoiled two sauces; Moira was unable to dust a single item adequately. Even Harris, whom I'd always trusted implicitly, lost an invitation to a late supper.

Truthfully, the last was a relief. I did not go out—to think of concentrating long enough to have a conversation put me in a desperate mood. I longed for my cordial, but William had taken to hiding it from me until bedtime, when he would magically produce it. I searched his bedchamber to no avail; I could not find it, and all I managed to achieve was his censure when he arrived home to find his drawers askew. He threatened then to throw it away, and though I could procure another prescription easily enough, I did not think I could face Dr. Moore again so soon. It had been only a week since I'd last asked him.

I behaved as well as I could. I embroidered. I tried to read. I attempted to write letters. When the twentieth came, I could hardly stand myself. By ten o'clock that morning, I was dressed and ready to go, and then I sat idly in my bedroom, alternately dreading the appointment and longing for the time to go more quickly. Finally it was time to call for the carriage, and I set off for Dr. Seth's alone.

When I pushed open the door to the little shop, the bell rang.

Again there was no one behind the counter, no one in any part of the shop, not even a woman searching for knickknacks—but then this was too far from the respectable shopping district for that. Those who came to this building no doubt came for only one purpose.

I hesitated, then went through the back door up those mean, dim, and narrow stairs. My footsteps echoed against the smoky ceiling, the unpatched, stained walls. Before I was ready, I was there, staring at his door. VICTOR SETH.

The door opened, and Irene stood there smiling. "I thought I heard you, ma'am. Please come in. The doctor's waiting for you."

I followed her inside, and the door clicked shut behind me with a sharp little sound that made me jump.

"May I take your cloak?" the girl asked. She was lifting it from me before I had a chance to respond. She hung it on an iron coat-rack and went to knock on the door leading to the doctor's office. "Doctor?" she called. "She's here."

There was a noise behind the door, a clatter, then papers shuffling, and I stepped back against the wall just as he opened the door.

I had forgotten how commanding he was. I was stunned for a moment, paralyzed until he stood back and ushered me inside his office.

"You did not change your mind," he said to me once the door was closed.

"No," I said. "Why should I?"

"More than one patient has been dissuaded by the gossip," he said. He regarded me carefully. "You are not?"

"No." My gaze fell to the floor. The wood was stained and worn. "I yearn for a cure, Doctor. I want to be well."

"Then we shall make you well. Won't you sit down? Or would you prefer the settee?"

I sat in the nearest chair. He went to the matching one and pulled it around soundlessly, facing mine but nearly beside it, so the arms were almost touching. It was as if we were lovers embarking on an intimate conversation. I flinched, and though I knew he saw it, he ignored it and sat with a slow, elegant motion, folding himself into the chair.

"You say you want to be well, Mrs. Carelton," he said. "I know what that means to your husband; now I would like to know what it means to you."

"What it means to me?" I said, nonplussed. "Why, I should think that's clear enough."

"Really?" He stroked his small beard. His gaze was so solid and penetrating, I felt as if he could see my very bones, and I squirmed, unable to sit still beneath such scrutiny. "Let's say it's not clear to me. What do *you* want from me, Mrs. Carelton?"

"My husband is building a grand house," I told him honestly. "He expects me to spend a fortune decorating it."

"Most women would delight in such a thing."

"Yes." I nodded. "And that is the problem, Doctor. The things that most women delight in leave me feeling exhausted. I cannot muster the strength to face a calling day or another party." The words came spilling from me then, things I had never been able to articulate, things I was surprised to find I even felt. "What I want . . . what I want most of all is to be like everyone else. I want to take pleasure in decorating the house. I want to enjoy a calling day. I want to be satisfied with what I have."

"I see," he said softly.

"My husband believes that having a child will cure me," I told him simply. "I don't know if that's true. It seems certain that I will never know. And so I want your help in finding the joy in life that everyone else seems to know how to find. I confess it is inconceivable to me that I will ever know it. I— I want you to save me, Doctor. I feel as if I am slowly drowning."

He said nothing when I was finished, merely continued that damning gaze. I fumbled with my bag, embarrassed to have revealed so much. "How foolish it must seem to you," I blurted.

"Hardly a medical concern, I know. My fits are what trouble William the most—"

"Lay your arm on the rest," Dr. Seth instructed.

Taken aback, I said, "What?"

"Lay your arm on the rest."

"Why?"

He smiled. "I promise I won't hurt you, Mrs. Carelton. Can you believe me?"

"I suppose. My husband would see you ruined if you did," I said.

"Yes."

I took a deep breath and laid out my arm, gripping the end of the armrest, feeling the purse of fabric beneath my fingers.

The doctor touched my wrist. I had not expected that he would touch me, and I jumped.

"Never fear, Mrs. Carelton," he said softly. "I only mean to turn your hand . . . like so." Gently, he lifted my arm and laid it down again so that my palm was up, so that the thin burgundy silk of my sleeve tightened around my forearm like the skin of a sausage.

His finger began to move on the underside of my forearm, soft and slow, back and forth. When I opened my mouth to protest, I could not make a sound.

"I'm going to put you into a little sleep," he said in a soothing, quiet voice, almost like a chant. "It will be as natural as if you were at home. Your eyes will grow heavy, your limbs have become limp. Sleep is coming. Let yourself go. Sleep."

I was tired. I had not slept well last night, even with the cordial, and it seemed my eyes had a will of their own. His finger kept moving, his voice droned on and on, and then I felt his hand on my shoulder. I opened my eyes, and he was sitting back in his chair, not touching me at all, rubbing his small beard, his dark eyes thoughtful and intense.

I felt as if I had come out of a deep and refreshing sleep, but I knew I had not. Only seconds had passed. Not long at all. Yet I felt disoriented and strange.

"You've just awakened from a rather deep sleep, Mrs. Carelton," he explained.

"But I— I have not slept at all."

"For nearly an hour," he told me. "Do you remember any of it?"

"No," I said, with rising panic. "No, no. I remember you touching me and saying I would sleep—"

"Nothing more?"

I shook my head.

"I've rarely encountered a patient who experiences such a profound trance," he said, rising. He went to the wooden cabinet at the end of the room and opened the top.

"But what happened?"

"I have established the beginnings of a cure. I believe you will feel much better quite soon."

I wanted to laugh. "A cure? But that's absurd."

He looked at me over his shoulder. "I assure you it's true. But there are one or two other things we can do to hurry things along, I think. I'm sure you'll find the results more tangible."

"What have you done to me?"

He sighed and turned completely to face me. "Mrs. Carelton, all I have done is to suggest to your unconscious mind that you will feel better. I've imposed no will upon you. I am not a magician; this is not an entertainment. If you cannot trust me, I fear there's no point in going further."

"No, no, I didn't mean to suggest—"

"Of course you did," he said. "But I believe that if you can bring yourself to overcome your objections and your fears, we can make great strides against your illness."

"Then it is an illness," I said eagerly. "It's not simply my imagination."

His gaze was arresting. "You are quite ill, Mrs. Carelton. Fortunately, you are treatable." He went and called Irene, then motioned toward the screen. "Now, please, Mrs. Carelton, if you will undress, we can continue."

I'd had no confidence when I walked into this office, but at once I was imbued with it. I could not explain it. Already I felt better.

When Irene and I came from behind the screen, Dr. Seth stood by that large wooden cabinet. It was opened from all sides, drawers slid out to reveal a mass of coils and wires and dials. He told Irene to go as I stared at it in repulsed fascination, my nervousness returning until he motioned to the chair he'd placed beside it.

"Sit down, please, Mrs. Carelton. I assure you, you won't find this unpleasant."

I did as he asked without question. I sat in the chair and put my bare feet on the metal floor plate and watched in absurd calm as he moved wires and adjusted dials. When he asked me to hold a hollow metal cylinder connected to a wire, I did not balk. Then I heard a hum. He held what resembled a wand, thicker where he held it, narrowing to a metal ball.

"This will feel strange," he told me. "But it won't hurt."

As he spoke, he went behind me, touching the base of my neck with the wand, and I felt an odd heat, a buzz, a motion that leaped through my skin and moved with him down my back, lingering at two spots near the bottom of my spine before he moved again in front of me, pulling a stool around between my knees, pushing up my chemise, parting my thighs with assured indifference. I said nothing—I felt paralyzed with shock and a faint horror—but when the wand touched me, I jerked. The doctor put his hand on my arm, and I was still again as the current pulsed through me, stronger and stronger. I felt a stranger take over my body, crying out, convulsing until finally he took the thing away, and I was left breathless and dimly aware that through it all, he had told me the truth: I'd felt no pain.

The hum stopped. He had turned off the machine; he set the

wand on the cabinet. "You may dress now, Mrs. Carelton," he said, and I realized that my chemise was still rumpled above my knees, that my body was still pulsing, that I was flushed and bewildered. Quickly, hiding my face from him, I raced to the dressing screen. I could not look at Irene as she came to help me dress, but when my bustle was buckled on, my petticoats fastened, I felt myself again. I heard a door open and close, and I prayed he was gone and I would not have to meet his eyes.

But when I came out again, he was standing by his desk, bent over a notebook.

"I've written you down for Thursday," he said. "We'll assess the treatment then. I think it best if you return soon and often to begin with. There will be less chance for interference."

Thursday was my calling day. It would be nearly impossible for me to avoid it. William would be furious if I did not see callers for a second week.

Dr. Seth put down the notebook. "Will two o'clock be satisfactory?" he asked as he came toward me, and before I could say *No, Thursday will never do,* he looked at me, and I immediately felt better: calm and reassured, as if some part of me—the tense, knotted part of me—had fled.

"Thursday," I said. "Two o'clock."

"You'll feel better immediately," he told me. "I'm sure of it."

The odd thing was, I did feel better. Much better. I could not keep from smiling as I left his office, and when I met Jimson waiting with cold hands and a pinched face at the curb, I suggested he drive me to a nearby restaurant, where I bought him a few small cakes and a cup of strong tea to warm himself. He was startled but obviously pleased, and the ride home was less bumpy than it had ever been before.

William was waiting anxiously when I arrived.

"I came home early," he told me when I stepped through the

door and handed Harris my gloves and cloak. "Come to the study, darling. I want to hear how things went."

"Why, I feel rested," I said as I followed him into the study. "Wonderfully rested. I bought Jimson a cake on the way home. He deserved it for waiting so long in the cold."

"You bought Jimson a cake?"

"Yes, he was out there nearly two hours."

"I . . . see. And the appointment?"

"I think you might be right about this doctor, William," I said. "Dr. Seth is . . . quite unusual."

William frowned. "Did he hypnotize you?"

"He says he did."

"He says he did. Weren't you aware of it?"

"Not really," I admitted. "But it hardly matters. Where was that invitation to the Harpers' late supper? I believe I feel like going after all."

Notes from the Journal of Victor Leonard Seth

Re: Mrs. C.

January 20, 1885

Today was my second appointment with Mrs. C. I had thought I would start with the electrotherapy to win her confidence, but then I noticed a pronounced languor in her eyes of a kind I have rarely seen, so I determined to try hypnosis first.

Mrs. C. responded immediately, with a deep level of unconsciousness that I have never encountered. I was able to produce rigid catalepsy by raising her arm and instructing her to keep it raised. Analgesia was produced as well—she was completely insensate to a pinprick on the tenderest spot of her forearm. When I told her to rise and walk, she continued until she nearly plunged out the window, and was riveted to a stop when I suggested it. I then told her that she was thirsty, and that I was handing her a glass of water, which she should drink. The water, the glass, all was imaginary, yet she took it from me and drank with gusto until I informed her that she was drinking urine, at which point she gagged and threw the glass from her, spitting and wiping at her mouth. I told her the sensation of having drunk urine was completely gone, and she then relaxed.

I then tried another simple illusion, telling her she was going for a walk through the woods on a lovely spring day, pointing out the things she saw along the way: a rock, a tree, a pretty bird. She responded to each item with obvious pleasure and interest.

I suggested to her that she would remain calm and happy over the next few days, that the memory of the walk would stay with her and relax her whenever she felt the urge to give in to hysterical fits. I also suggested that she would have more confidence in her doctor, and that when she returned home, she would feel refreshed and energized. I then proceeded to create hypnotic zones: A touch on the underside of her right wrist will send her into a deep hypnotic state, a touch on her shoulder will awaken her.

Mrs. C. woke with complete amnesia, which I have seen only twice. She did not even realize there had been any passage of time. I informed her that she had been "asleep" for nearly an hour. She was incredulous.

In an attempt to bolster my suggestion regarding her confidence in me, I then treated her with electrotherapy—

general faradization at the common areas of sexual neurasthenia: upper and lower spine, inner thighs, vagina, and clitoris, which seemed to have good effect.

She has agreed to return twice a week for treatment,
which I think necessary to fully effect a cure in as little time
as possible. Given the extent of her suggestibility, I think it
will not be long before Mrs. C. has no more need of me, for
which I am profoundly grateful—although I am uncertain why, given that there will simply be another to take her
place. Another invalid, another bored society matron, another reason for my peers to disparage me because they refuse
to understand or believe that there is room for hypnosis in
the treatment of illness and disease. How long must I bear
their criticism and their ignorant fear? What must I do to
gain their respect? Such a thing cannot be found in treating
upper-class neurasthenics, I am afraid. My peers can only
feel the same contempt for my patients that I do. To convince
them that the mind itself can cure, that the unconscious
can be trained to direct the will—they do not believe that
at Salpêtrière, Charcot himself is creating hysterics through
suggestion! They are afraid to believe such a thing is even
possible! And if they do not believe that such a thing is possible in those who suffer from true madness, how then will
they come to believe my own experiments, performed as they
are on those who suffer from self-indulgent invalidism?

They will not—that is the only answer. Yet I cannot
help but persist in believing that someday I will find a way
to convince them all.

Chapter 6

That night was as peaceful a one as I could remember. William and I went to a late supper at the Harpers', and though I knew William was watching me carefully, I felt none of my usual strain. It was as if I'd slept deeply for hours; my mind was clear, and I laughed and ate as I had not for . . . oh, as I never had. Even Elizabeth Sykes remarked on it, saying I seemed especially gay; had I had good news?

I thought I would not need my cordial that night, but when we arrived home well after midnight, I was more tired than I'd thought, and my good mood had inspired William in ways I had not counted on. He came to my room just as I was undressing, and when he left, I felt an overwhelming desire for my nightly dose.

I had the strangest dream. I was in Dr. Seth's office, and he was sitting in that bright red chair, watching as I walked across the room. The window beyond me was bright but hazy, and I was walking toward it. Walking and walking, as if I could some-how climb up into it and be lifted to the heavens, such a beautiful light. How much I wanted to be within it, I could not wait to be within it . . . when came the doctor's voice, a steady, sonorous "Stop, Lucy," though I had never given him leave to call me by my first name. Then the light faded to merely the thin, crisp sun of a January day, lapsing into late afternoon. I jerked to a stop at the sill, my hands against the glass, as sad as I had ever been.

When I woke, my cheeks were wet with tears.

I had grown used to odd dreams since I'd started taking the morphia, so I did not give this one any more thought. When Moira brought my morning coffee, she asked what I would wear to the Carrs' supper that evening, and the thought of that made me truly forget the dream and its sadness.

I had not remembered that William had accepted the invitation to Berry Carr's blue supper, though I should have. My friends had been talking about it for weeks, the plans, the orchestra she'd hired, the entertainment she'd planned—with several of the season's young debutantes playing out the drama of Tennyson's *The Charge of the Light Brigade*, all in the most elaborate costumes—and canvasback brought in at wretched prices for two hundred guests.

It was just the kind of event that usually sent my nerves jangling. I was surprised at my own calm when I said, "The black and blue Worth, Moira."

The Carrs lived on Fifth Avenue, near the site of our soon-to-be home, in their own plush château of pale limestone complete with all the worst accoutrements: elaborate dormers, balustrades, gaudy ornamentation. But for all Robert Carr's horrible architectural taste, Berry Carr had a genius for flamboyant interior decoration.

We arrived near nine, joining the long line of carriages that stretched from the Carr door down Fifth Avenue. A rich, thick blue carpet had been spread from the curb to the front door, with an awning—to protect it, no doubt, from the snow that had started to fall only an hour before.

William held tight to my arm as we handed our invitations to the doorman and made our way inside. He released me reluctantly, so we could pass into separate cloakrooms. There, a maid was waiting to take my cloak and hat. I went to join the other women who were preening in front of gilded mirrors.

"My, Lucy, how lovely you look this evening." Daisy Hadden turned from her primping as I approached. "I haven't seen that gown in— What has it been? A year, at least. How brave you are to wear it tonight. I never could have accomplished it."

"It's blue," I said, trying to think of a suitable lie, when the truth was I could hardly remember that I'd worn the gown before. Papa always said I should keep a record. William would have remembered, but I'd already had on my cloak when I came downstairs, and he hadn't seen it. "I had nothing else this color."

"Such a pity there wasn't time to order a new one. Who could have known Berry would decide on blue? I would have thought gold, perhaps, after the Goelings' silver supper. . . . Well, that one *is* lovely."

I smiled at her. "Thank you, Daisy. I've always liked it."

"Don't worry, I'm sure Berry won't notice. She's far too busy making sure the cooks don't spoil the ices."

I bent pointedly to another mirror, patting into place a loose hair, waiting until Daisy left before I fluffed the black lace demi-sleeves and adjusted my diamond and sapphire necklace so it fell just at the point of the heart-shaped neckline. I *had* always liked this gown, and I wished I could recall where I had last worn it—not to some huge entertainment, I hoped.

I went out of the cloakroom to find my husband waiting impatiently. He frowned when he saw me. "Lucy, that gown—"

"I'd forgotten," I interrupted, and together we went upstairs.

The entire ballroom, which had once been wallpapered in roses, was now papered in a deep blue brocade. The drapes were deep blue velvet with silver-embroidered hems. At the far end, an orchestra played a low, quiet tune meant not for dancing but for arrivals. There were orchids everywhere, a profusion bunching from blue urns and small silver and blue vases. Near the door, a table stood piled with rows and rows of white gloves and tiny blue velvet boxes holding some kind of favor.

"This is the kind of supper we shall hold," William whispered, "when our own house is built. Can you imagine it?"

I pulled away from him. "I see Millicent," I told him, and he let me go.

My friend stood not far away, talking to Major Grunnel. An orchid tickled her ear from the vase on the table behind her; she was wearing blue and fuchsia and sparkling diamond eardrops. I didn't know I had been anxious until she looked up with a smile and I felt something inside me loosen and ease.

"Lucy!" she said, and then her eyes widened when she saw my gown. "Oh, you look wonderful."

"Indeed you do, Mrs. Carelton," said the major with a slight bow. "In fine form, I should say."

"Thank you," I said.

We talked of the usual things, the beauty of Berry's room, the inspired choice of blue, the sweetness of the orchids. Then the gray old major walked away, limping slightly—a wound from some war—and Millicent and I were left alone.

"You must tell me," I said, "where did I wear this gown before? Do you think Berry will be furious?"

"A year ago, at least," Millicent said. "At some supper—I can hardly remember, Lucy, and Berry certainly will not. She was in London then. Don't you remember?"

"I don't think so."

"Yes, of course you do. There was a rumor of an affair with that old baron. They said she met him in his rooms at the Dartmouth House."

"No, I don't remember."

"Honestly, Lucy, it was the talk of the season. Robert himself went to bring her home. I can't believe you don't remember."

"Much of the last week is in a fog. Last year seems a century ago."

Millie looked at me oddly. "You seem well today."

"So everyone says."

"Did you see your new doctor?"

"Yesterday."

"And?"

"It was quite . . . interesting."

"What do you mean?"

"He is very odd. But the truth is, I do feel better today."

"And William, what does he think?"

I glanced through the crowd and found my husband easily. He stood talking to Robert Carr, who was smiling as William regaled him with some tale or another—it was one of William's talents, to engage people thoroughly. It was how he'd captured my father. How he'd captured me.

"He seems grateful," I said.

"How could he not be?" she said. "He has his wife back. No doubt he'll hold on as tightly as he can."

"Yes, no doubt," I said. I could not think of another thing to say, though Millicent began to talk of something else, and I didn't think she noticed.

By the time we went in to supper, I was exhausted from smiling and trying to concentrate on conversation. It was late—one-thirty—before we were called again to the ballroom. The young debutantes came out wrapped in gold tissue, with huge, elaborate winged breastplates made of gilded papier-mâché, their hair fashioned into elaborate helmets. They gathered, posing as they sang in unison:

> *Half a league, half a league,*
> *Half a league onward,*
> *All in the valley of Death*
> *Rode the six hundred.*
> *"Forward, the Light Brigade!*
> *"Charge for the guns!" he said:*

Into the valley of Death
Rode the six hundred.

"It's inspired," whispered someone to my right.
William touched my shoulder. "You look pale, Lucy."

Cannon to right of them
Cannon to left of them . . .

The gold of the breastplates was flickering. I recognized Antoinette Baldwin among the girls. She had a lovely voice, very
dramatic, and she struck a pose as if she'd been born for the stage.

It was such a pity, how that voice would go to waste. She
would have her debut this year or the next, then marry, and that
voice would be used for pointless gossip over tea, polite conversation, chastising children. The thought made me horribly
sad. I could not lose the sense of my own life unfolding before
me, so much the same, and my breath caught. I was suddenly
desperate for a place to sit down. William's arm was hard behind
me, holding me in place. *Not a fit. Not now.* I closed my eyes, forcing a breath, and a vision came into my head then, a pretty forest. I smelled the damp earth. I heard the song of a bird—a little
wren. I was walking.

But the forest was strange. There was a falseness about it, as
if it were a set staged for me alone, a memory told to me that I
had grasped hold of and made my own, though it was not mine.

While horse and hero fell,
They that had fought so well
Came thro' the jaws of Death
Back from the mouth of hell—

I didn't know where the vision had come from. There was an
insistency about it: The images commanded me to be comforted,

to be soothed. It was disconcerting; my head pounded. I had to find a place to sit down, to think—these were not my thoughts, not my memory.

I turned from William's arm and escaped the ballroom, past the table of gloves and gifts, down the stairs into the foyer, where a servant clad in black looked at me questioningly, saying, "Madam?" as I went to wrench open the door and rush into the cold night air.

But William was behind me. "What are you doing, Lucy?" He grabbed my arm, pulling me back again, slamming shut the door I had just begun to open. "What are you doing?" This time a hiss, an anxious look about, a reassuring smile for the servant. Then William grasped my wrist and backed me against the wall, leaning close enough that anyone watching might mistake it for a lovers' tryst. "Everyone noticed—what were you thinking?"

"No one noticed," I said. "No one at all. They were watching the six hundred—"

"Until you ran out of there."

"I cannot stay." I grabbed his arm with my free hand. "Please, William, take me home, or I swear I will go by myself."

"You'll do no such thing." His face was angry, intent. "You'll go back in there and dance with me."

"Oh, I can't. I can't." I could not bring my voice above a whisper; I felt the hot beginning of tears. "Please, William."

"I cannot go now. Robert Carr is unhappy with Stevenson. He wants a new broker."

"Please, William, if you love me, you'll send me home."

He paused. His grip eased.

"You can stay if you like," I plunged on. "Say I was taken ill."

"I don't understand," he said, and I saw the confusion in his face and was sorry for him in a way I could not communicate. "You seemed so much better. Last night . . ." He shook his head, and then he let go of me sadly and turned to the servant, who was trying hard not to watch. "Fetch my wife her wrap and summon our carriage," he said. He put his arm around my shoulders, drawing me back as the servant nodded and hurried out the door.

"When do you see Seth again?" William asked in a low voice.

"Tomorrow."

The servant returned with my cloak. Within moments, my husband was escorting me from the hall into the blessedly cold night air. He opened the carriage door for me and bundled me inside, saying, "I'll make your excuses," in a forlorn and familiar way. Then he closed the door, and I watched as he turned and hurried back up the stairs as if I was already forgotten.

Chapter 7

I'm not feeling well," I told Dr. Seth the moment I entered his office. "Last night we were at supper, and I began to feel ill. I had the strangest thoughts."

Seth rose from his chair, frowning. "Mrs. Carelton, you're trembling."

I was fumbling with my gloves, which I could not get off. "Yes, I . . . I've been like this since last night."

"Please, sit down."

"It's so odd, really. I was feeling better. Much better, and then I began to have these visions. It was like a nightmare, really."

"Please, sit down," he said again. He motioned toward the big red chair.

"A nightmare," I repeated. My bag was slipping out from beneath my arm. My right glove simply would not come off. I shook my hand in frustration. "Oh, this . . . this—"

He came to me and gently took my bag, setting it aside. Then he held out his hand. "Give me your cloak, and we'll discuss this."

"I just don't understand—"

"Forget your gloves, Mrs. Carelton. Your cloak. Please."

I hesitated only a moment, then I did as he asked, though I struggled with the cloak's clasp. He hung it on the coatrack and bade me once more to sit down. When I did, he pulled the other red chair to face me, sitting with a languid ease.

"Now, Mrs. Carelton, tell me exactly what frightens you."

"I'm not frightened," I said.

"You sound quite frightened."

"I'm not. It isn't fear, exactly. It's more . . . disturbing."

"Very well." He folded his hands together—long fingers, careful movements. "Then tell me what has disturbed you."

Faced with his calm, with his quiet, soothing voice, I found myself wordless. I struggled for something to say, a way to explain. "I—I had a dream."

It was not what I'd meant to tell him.

He waited.

"A dream about here," I rushed on. "This office. I was walking across the room to the window. I had my hands pressed to the glass. I was crying."

"Did anything else happen to you in this dream?"

"No, but it felt quite real. As if it had really happened. I could see the cigar sign and the light. . . ."

"It should feel real," he said. "You did walk, while you were in a deep hypnotic state."

"You mean . . . the last time I was here?"

"Yes."

"But you said I slept."

He shrugged. "It's easier to explain that way. The state of profound unconsciousness is most like sleep. Unlike sleep, however, you are quite aware of everything around you."

"But I remembered nothing of it."

"Your unconscious remembered it," he pointed out. "Which is why you had the dream. Now tell me: You said you were having disturbing visions. Did you mean the dream?"

"No, there was a forest."

"Ah," he said. "That was a suggestion I made to you. I thought such a scene would calm you. When you began to feel out of control, as if you were going into a fit, you were to think of a peaceful forest, a walk. There was a rock, a—"

"Bird," I finished.

He nodded. "A bird. A pretty song. Apparently it did not have the desired effect. You were disturbed by it."

"I didn't expect it," I said. "You said nothing about a forest. You said you made a suggestion that I would be calm."

"Which also apparently did not have the desired effect. The forest was only for oncoming hysteria. A secondary suggestion, if you will, in case the first did not work. Tell me, Mrs. Carelton, how you felt when you left my office."

"Rested," I said reluctantly. "Peaceful."

"Did that feeling last beyond the time it took you to reach your home?"

"Oh yes," I said. "It lasted until I had the dream, and it lingered beyond that, though not as strongly."

"Then we made a temporary improvement," he said with satisfaction. "A good sign."

"Is it?" I leaned forward. "Is it a good sign?"

"It shows your cerebral condition can be modified," he said.

"But it didn't last."

"It will," he assured me. "Your unconscious has been badly trained; we must retrain it to be well. What you must relinquish, Mrs. Carelton, is intellectual control. Reason is the enemy of unconscious suggestion. What occurred with the suggestion of the forest is an example: You realized the forest was not a real memory; your reason rejected it as impossible, and therefore you rejected the calm it was meant to convey. You no doubt began to feel hysterical."

"Yes. Yes, that was exactly what happened."

"It was my mistake. I should have told you about the image. I won't forget again. More importantly, you said you were calm until you had the dream that was not a dream, simply your unconscious memory. Were there any other details you remembered?"

I shook my head.

"How did you feel after remembering this?"

"Sad," I said. "I felt sad."

"Why is that?"

I tried to remember. "I don't know. My hands were on the window, and I wanted to cry."

"Did it remind you of anything else? Any other memory you have of a window?"

"No."

His gaze was solid, penetrating. I looked away, feeling uncomfortable again.

"What kind of a relationship do you have with your husband, Mrs. Carelton?"

I was startled. "What has that to do with anything?"

"It may have a great deal to do with everything," he answered. "Is it a loving relationship?"

"I don't understand."

"Did you marry for love?"

"Why, yes," I said. "Yes, I did."

"Did your father approve?"

"Approve? He did all he could to push me into William's arms."

"You don't sound happy about that."

"I was not at first," I said. "Then it didn't matter."

"And your conjugal relationship," he said. "Is it loving as well?"

I stiffened.

"Does he have a mistress?"

"Not that I know of. Really, Dr. Seth, I'm most uncomfortable with this conversation."

"Do you derive pleasure from sexual congress with your husband?"

"Dr. Seth!" I rose. My face was burning.

"Please sit down, Mrs. Carelton," the doctor said. "I don't wish to unduly distress you."

"I won't answer that question."

"You are unable to conceive," Dr. Seth went on matter-of-factly. "Your husband informed me that you have tried often but have never succeeded. He believes your illness is caused by the lack of children, and you have been diagnosed with uterine monomania at least once before. I believe that the state of your uterus—as well as your unconscious—is highly relevant to a cure."

I sat down, tight-lipped.

"If your desires are so concentrated on having a child, then we must—"

I rose and paced to the window, twisting my hands together. "I won't discuss this."

"How can I possibly help you, Mrs. Carelton, when you refuse to cooperate?"

"I don't know," I said desperately. I stared at the flaking paint on the brick wall outside, the blur of COXLEY'S CIGARS. "I don't know if you can help me at all."

His voice became cajoling. "Perhaps we should work on finding that calm again, hmmm? If you will just sit down . . ."

I felt a touch on my shoulder and twisted around to see him just behind me. How had he moved there so quickly, so silently? I had not even seen his reflection in the glass. I jerked away from him until the window was at my back.

"Don't!" I said, in a panic. "Don't touch me."

He held out his hand as if I were a wild animal ready to bite. "You are quite distressed, Mrs. Carelton. Forgive me. Please, if you will come back and sit down, we'll start with electrotherapy today. That should make you feel better."

I resisted his hand. I curled my fingers against the window. "Come," he said quietly. "I can help you."

Perhaps it was the way he looked at me, with that unwavering gaze, but I was afraid of him, of his questions, his interest. I was afraid of what I might tell him, of what that gaze would lure from me.

"I want only to be like everyone else," I said desperately, uncertain why I felt the need to say it. "I just want to be an ordinary woman. . . ."

He came closer, holding out his hand again. "I know exactly what you want," he said, and I found myself relenting. I put my hand in his; I let him lead me to the dressing screen and call Irene, and then, when I was naked but for my chemise, I sat in his wooden chair, and parted my legs when he touched my knee, and lost myself to the electric wand.

Notes from the Journal of Victor Leonard Seth

Re: Mrs. C.

January 22, 1885

Mrs. C. was extremely distressed over the suggestion I'd made at our last visit, that she visualize a walk through the woods rather than give in to a hysterical fit. I was surprised by how well her unconscious took to it, how intense the image seemed to her. I had expected to make the suggestion at least once more before her unconscious accepted it, but the problem seems to be not with her unconscious mind but with her conscious one. She recognized the image as a false one and found it frightening.

Unfortunately, my neglect in telling her of the suggestion has had serious consequences. Whatever trust she had been willing to give me has evaporated. She is wary and uncooperative, and my attempts to delve more deeply into her biography were met with violent resistance.

This turn is frustrating at best. She should not be so difficult. Mrs. C. is readily put into a deep hypnotic state, and her amnesia when waking from the trance is so nearly complete that she remembered what had happened to her under hypnosis during our last visit as only a vague, disturbing dream. This would all indicate a patient who is easily cured, and I have no doubt this is the case. Yet her reason has overcome a suggestion that offers her unconscious mind what she so clearly wants. Why did she fight it? Her dismay over it seems too extreme, as if she is afraid. I must admit I find this intriguing as well as annoying. It suggests she is hiding something—but that is absurd. I cannot imagine what a woman such as this would have to fear. She has everything she could want. No, I must assume that her rejection of such a suggestion of peace is simply an anomaly, and with a few more studied attempts, I can effect a lasting cure. I would like, at some point, to suggest another calming memory or image for her to rely on during the onset of hysteria, but given her distress over the last suggestion, I prefer to wait until I can discover an image from her own experience.

This may be more difficult now. I must reassure her that she can trust me. Fortunately, Mrs. C. is highly sensitive to touch. Faradization has brought her to climax quickly, and she achieved a trance through touch-induced stimulus—which leads me to believe that Mrs. C. has normal female passions that have been severely discouraged, *perhaps by her husband, perhaps by others in her life. Because she confessed that she married her husband for love—as much as that can be so—I suspect her nervousness and irritability may stem from interrupted coitus, an epidemic in the upper classes. If nothing else, faradization may ease these symptoms, bring her to my office in a more anticipatory state, and perhaps allow me to utilize her satisfied passions to regain her trust. If there is no trust, there can be no <u>crédivité.</u> And without that, I cannot be effective.*

Chapter 8

Over the next days, I felt remarkably rested. I had only a few arguments with the servants; I weathered my social schedule better than I had in some time and, according to William, was "delightful." I ran the household more efficiently than I ever had. My only complaint was at night, when my dreams were restless and strange, full of images I did not understand—most of which involved Dr. Seth's disturbing gaze. But these dreams did not seem to have any effect during the daytime. Then I scarcely remembered that I was having dreams at all.

"I'm glad to see Seth's methods are working so well," William said with satisfaction at dinner. "Am I imagining things, darling? Or *are* you feeling better?"

"I am," I said. "Much better."

"He said he believed you were making progress."

I stilled in the midst of taking a bite. "He said? You spoke to him?"

William nodded. "Yesterday. He was at the lunch counter at Bodes. We got to talking."

"The lunch counter?"

"His office is not far from there, I suppose." William

shrugged. "In any case, I'm very pleased with his efforts. I've asked him to come to the Athletic Club with me tomorrow."

I was dismayed, though I was hard-pressed to say why. "He hardly seems the sporting type."

"I would have thought the same myself. But he expressed an interest."

"I see."

"You seem surprised."

I played with the remains of my fish, my appetite gone. "Well, yes. After all, he's not like us. He's a Jew."

"He's no longer practicing, he says. I'm merely showing him my appreciation, nothing more. There are already plenty of doctors at the club. He'll fit in nicely. And perhaps he can use it to expand his practice."

"How thoughtful you are to suggest it," I said.

William's dark brows came together in a frown. "Are you telling me I shouldn't be grateful to him for restoring my wife to me?"

I could not answer. *Restore* seemed such a finished word, and despite my improvement these last days, I did not feel finished, hardly so. It did disturb me that William intended to form a friendship with my doctor, though I could not think of a reason why. After all, I had first met Seth at a supper, and it was clear he already moved in our circle of friends. It would be foolish not to expect to see him publicly.

"I've been hoping you might come with me to McKim's office tomorrow morning," William said. "He's finished the plans for the new house."

Our discussion about Seth was over. I forced myself to take a forkful of fish and put aside my dismay over the doctor. "Oh? So soon?"

"I'd like you to see them."

"I'm sure anything you've agreed to is fine."

"You're going to live there as well," William pointed out. "And

I'd like you to see the plans before you go to Goupil's. You should know what we need before you begin choosing things."

I gave him a weak smile. "Yes, of course."

"Then it's settled. We're to be there tomorrow at ten."

I did not argue. I feigned the excitement I wanted so badly to feel. I would do this for William, for myself. After all, I *did* feel better.

The next morning I met my husband in the foyer, dressed and ready. It did not take long to arrive at McKim's office, despite a cloud of snow that fell in a light and constant fog. We were met in the anteroom by an earnest young man who showed us into Charles McKim's office.

Charles was there already, seated at a huge maple desk, surrounded by rolls of paper. One wall was completely lined with bookshelves; the others held framed photographs of houses he'd apparently designed, though the electric lamp on his desk shone upon the glass at an angle, making the pictures hard to see.

He rose when we entered, extending a hand to William, giving me a warm smile. William and I sat in two silk-covered chairs.

"I've brought Lucy to give her final approval," William told him with a conspiratorial smile.

"I'm certain you'll be pleased, Mrs. Carelton," Charles said. He reached for a seemingly unmarked roll among a set of other rolls and spread it out over his desk, using paperweights to hold the corners. William rose and went to look over his shoulder, gesturing for me to join him. I did, but the drawing was impossible for me to decipher. It was only rows of lines, parallel and perpendicular, a semicircle here, words written in tiny letters.

"Look here," William said, pointing to a square on the paper. "This is the foyer. We'll have steps leading up to the front, all of cut limestone." His finger traced down a set of lines. "Do you see? They curve on either side down to the sidewalk. There are pillars here and here, and the porch roof is a terrace that leads out from the ballroom." His fingers moved over the plans so rapidly I could barely follow his motions; his voice was excited. "Do you see, Lucy? The entrance hall will be huge, with marble pillars reaching up three stories to a stained-glass dome. Mostly in rose, I think, so there will be a perpetual sunset over the floors below. Or sunrise, I suppose, depending on the light."

I began to see the plans as a house. It was simple to decipher now that I knew what I was examining.

"Yes," I said. "It's quite lovely."

"Do you think so?" William's face was more animated than I'd seen it for some time, and for a moment I felt a terrible jealousy that this house should command his affections when I could not.

"From the outside, it looks like a very large row house," I said.

Charles McKim nodded. "Yes. William planned it that way. He thought you would be more comfortable in familiar surroundings. But the inside is quite spectacular. Nothing like a row house at all."

"It will be beautiful," I said, stepping back from the plans.

William grasped my arm, bringing me gently back. "You must see this, Lucy," he said softly. "I've planned it all for you. Look, here is your suite. You'll have a sitting room that can be closed off from the bedroom by a set of doors. Do you see? There will be a window here—"

"A window?" I frowned. "Only one? It's quite small."

"Yes. Heating is more efficient that way," McKim said.

"We don't care about the cost of heating," I told him. "The window must be bigger. Where are the rest of them?"

I saw the way McKim glanced at William, but I did not retreat. I said insistently, "Show me where the windows are."

"In every room, of course," McKim said. "Here and here."

"There aren't enough. Really, William, there aren't enough. You know how I love windows."

"But Lucy—"

"There must be more," I said.

"But darling—"

"You said you wanted me to look at the plans," I said. I had wanted so badly to care about this house, and now I found myself caring too much. "You wanted my approval. It's a lovely house, William, truly it is, but the windows, there simply must be more."

"I can change the plans slightly without compromising the entire design," McKim said reluctantly.

"Then you must."

William looked at McKim. "Could you give us a moment, Charles?"

"Certainly." McKim stepped from his office, closing the door discreetly. When he was gone, William turned me to face him, holding my arms so I couldn't back away.

"Lucy, you must calm yourself."

"I'm quite calm."

He shook his head. "This thing about the windows—"

"You said I should have the house the way I liked it," I said. "You said I should approve of it."

"Yes, but not at the expense of everything Charles and I have worked for," he said. "I've done nothing but keep your interests in mind during this entire process. Charles and I have had several meetings."

"You never included me."

He gave me a chastising look. "Come, Lucy, you weren't the least bit interested until today."

"But now I *am* interested. And I want windows."

"Think of how cold such large rooms will be. The windows will only make it worse unless the drapes are quite heavy, and you don't like curtains."

"No," I said uncertainly. "I don't."

"You see?" He smiled a *how silly you're being* smile. "Really, darling, you can't want this at all. You only think you do. The windows we have are quite sufficient. If you like, I can ask Charles to make the one in your room larger."

His reasonableness was stifling; I felt myself surrendering, not caring any longer. "Yes," I said, breaking from his hold, turning away. "That would be nice."

"I knew you would understand," he said with satisfaction. He went to the door and sent the boy for Charles, who came back with a bounce in his step but a questioning expression.

"We'd like the window enlarged in Lucy's room, if you can, Charles," William said.

"And the rest?" Charles asked.

"The rest are perfect as they are."

"Excellent." Charles smiled, and the two of them leaned over the plans again, making little refinements here and there, while I tried to smile and listen to words that ran together in one long stream of nonsense.

"Excuse me," I said, making for the door. "If I could just go out for a moment."

William barely glanced up. "Of course, darling. I'll meet you outside. Charles and I are almost finished."

I slipped out and leaned against the wall. It seemed the plans of that house surrounded me, the lines and planes evolving into a skeleton of stone and wood, primitive and bleak, and in it I felt William's inflexibility of will. I was suddenly, unreasonably afraid that I could not live within those walls, that I should die if I had to beat my wings against them.

My next appointment with Dr. Seth was not for another two days, and the peace I'd found in his office began to erode, my pleasantness becoming edgy and brittle. The visit to McKim's had shaken me, as had William's adoption of Dr. Seth as a friend. I had not been able to regain my spirits.

That night was the opera. Merely the thought of the terrible, cacophonous music, the gloominess, the close air, the jewels and the perfume and the inquisitiveness—*How have you been, Lucy? You look tired, Lucy. Are you going to so-and-so's supper, Lucy?*— made me irritable. Worst of all would be William's cloying concern, his disappointment. *You were doing so well, Lucy. What happened?*

But I readied myself obediently. That evening, as I neared the bottom of the stairs, I heard my father's voice coming from the study. Then he came into the hall, followed by William.

"Ah, there you are, my dear," Papa said when he saw me. He was dressed for the opera, which I couldn't countenance. "Well, now, Lucy, you do look in fine fettle tonight."

"Thank you, Papa," I managed. "If I didn't know better, I would think you were planning to accompany us. But I know how you dislike the Metropolitan."

"As it happens, I am going," he said. "Much as I dislike it, I've promised to attend Dunsmuir's supper tonight after."

"I see," I said, though that hardly explained it. It would be easy enough for him to go to the supper with or without the opera.

William said, "I've managed to convince your father that he might enjoy the German style after all." Then he frowned. "Where are the emeralds, Lucy? The emeralds are for green."

I had chosen simple diamonds. "I didn't feel—"

"Moira!" He stepped to the bottom of the stairs. "Moira, bring Mrs. Carelton's jewel case here immediately, please."

"William, really," I said, putting my hand on his arm. "I thought the emeralds were too much for tonight."

"Don't be absurd. They'll wonder where the emeralds are."

I said nothing more. Moira brought the jewel case, and it was opened, and the diamonds were exchanged for a necklace of huge square-cut emeralds, the earbobs for elaborate emerald earrings that dangled to my jaw.

We arrived at our box just before the second intermission, fashionably late, to the murmur of voices and the turning of heads, the lifting of opera glasses. My emeralds reflected the stage lights, as they were intended to do. I removed my cloak and took my time sitting, as I knew William liked, giving them all a chance to see me, letting the glare of my jewels lure their gazes. I felt William's smile in the darkness. He put his hand possessively over my arm. Papa sat grumpily behind us.

I watched the last minutes of the performance before the break. I could not have said what the opera was tonight; my program lay unopened in my lap. I felt as if I were moving in a dream. Then the music stopped, and the lights rose, and I was revealed. William's hand tightened on my arm, and then he got to his feet and said, "I'll get us some refreshment," and left me there with my father.

He was gone only a moment before my father leaned forward and whispered, "Good God, Lucy, you're like a statue tonight."

"I haven't slept well," I answered.

"Of course not. No one has. It's the middle of the season." He harrumphed in my ear, a breath of sound that stirred my earrings. "That's no excuse. You're a Van Berckel. Be a credit to your family. And your husband. William said you've been better. I came tonight to see it for myself. I'm beginning to think William is being overly hopeful."

I took a deep breath. Just then there was a movement at the curtains, and I turned to see Clara Morris pushing through, her husband, Bartlett, in tow. Clara was a society matron of long standing, her pedigree nearly as exceptional as mine. She had enhanced it by marrying into a Knickerbocker family when she was barely eighteen. Tonight she wore a gown so bundled in lace that she looked more like an ancient schoolmarm than a youthful woman, an image she was obviously trying to recapture. That was accentuated by her keen gaze, which swept me from head to foot.

My father was on his feet in moments. "Clara. Bartlett. So good to see you."

"And how surprising to see *you*," Clara said archly. She rapped Papa with her fan, a flirtation that only looked silly. I saw Bartlett wince. "What brings you here after all this time, De-Lancey? I know I heard you swear you wouldn't set a foot in the opera house until they changed the program."

"I was persuaded otherwise," Papa said.

"How delightful." Clara's eagle eye swept past my father to me. "And how lovely to see you, Lucy. Mamie Fish and I stopped by on your calling day last week, to find you out."

At Dr. Seth's. I tried to smile. "I was called away unexpectedly."

"Well, I'm happy it was nothing more. We had thought— It's of no matter, of course, but there has been some talk that you haven't been home on your calling day for weeks. Have you been ill? Oh, I do hope it's not a reprise of last spring."

I heard the words she didn't say: *When you offended Caroline Astor and took to your bed for two months.*

Papa gave me a sharp glance, and I saw Clara catch it.

"No, of course not. Everything's quite lovely," I said, though I couldn't rid myself of the notion that she saw straight through me to the lie.

She gave me a little smile and looked smugly satisfied. "How good to hear that."

"Here we are." William came through the curtains holding two drinks. "Well, hello, Clara, Bartlett. Lucy, darling, you'll never guess who I found."

I reached for the glass. It was warm. The sweet, sticky scent of it was overwhelming. "No, I'm certain I won't," I said faintly. "Who did you find?"

Before he could answer, a man came through the curtains behind him. It was Victor Seth.

He was dressed as I had never seen him, in deep chocolate brown. His matching vest hung with two thick watch chains, each dangling a charm I couldn't identify from where I stood.

He looked like any of William's friends might, and his smile showed he was completely at ease in this society. His thick hair was swept back, his glasses were gone, and without them his eyes seemed even more piercing.

I stared at him, unable to speak, though I did gasp—I know I did that, because Clara looked at me with sudden avid curiosity.

"Have you met Victor Seth?" William asked the Morrises.

Clara Morris extended her hand. "No, I fear I haven't. Though I've heard so much about you, Dr. Seth. We both have, haven't we, Bartlett?"

Bartlett grunted.

William introduced them smoothly. Seth took Clara's hand with a smile and said, "Mrs. Morris, it's a pleasure to meet you and your husband."

"You're new in town, eh?" Bartlett said, the first words he'd uttered since entering our box. "You're a doctor?"

"Yes," Seth said, and to his credit, he didn't hazard so much as a glance in my direction. "I've only just opened my practice here a few months ago."

"A physician? Seems we hardly need another one of those."

"Perhaps not," Seth said graciously. "But one never knows."

William said, "Victor's interested in joining the Staten Island Athletic Club. I've been trying to talk him into polo, but he claims he has no talent for it."

"I'm afraid not," Seth said. He looked at me and said to my father, "Your daughter does you credit tonight, Mr. Van Berckel. Mrs. Carelton, you look lovely this evening."

"Thank you," I said. My heart was beating so hard I could barely hear my own voice. I did not know how to feel about meeting him here—it was so out of context. I had known I would see him in society again, and I thought I had braced for it, but not well enough, it seemed. To think of what he knew of me . . . I had the image of him seated before me, between my spread legs. My hand went involuntarily to my low décolletage. He did not miss even that small motion.

"Where is your office, Dr. Seth?" Clara asked.

"On Broadway, isn't it?" Papa said, then smiled at me triumphantly.

"Why, yes, it is," Seth said. "Not the best part of town, I realize, but I returned from France only last September. I had little time to find an office."

Papa nodded. "God knows we've enough ailments to fund a multitude of doctors. I've paid half of them myself."

I took a sip of my punch, pressing the glass hard against my lower lip.

"The fees today are so high." Clara shook her head in mock disgust. "I should think it would be economical to have a doctor as a friend."

"Which is precisely why I don't treat my friends," Seth said, and the others laughed.

I could not bear it, not another moment. The images from my dreams, from my times in his office, would not leave my head. I felt violated, invaded. I did not want him to have a life beyond the hours I spent with him. I wanted him caged there, cocooned in his office, contained so that I saw him only when I wanted to. This was impossible.

I put down my cup with a loud enough clank that Papa frowned, and then I touched William's arm and whispered to him, "I have a headache, William."

"One moment," he said to me.

I smiled weakly at the others. "You must excuse me for a moment," I managed. "But it's so warm in here—I really must get some air."

"Of course, my dear," Clara said, and then someone else said something, but I was already past them, through the curtains, into the hallway, where people milled, talking, laughing, looking at me curiously.

The lights went dim, the signal for the performance to start again. I made my way to the foyer, past the startled doormen, outside. It was cold; the snow had turned icy, drivers were huddled in a circle talking, rubbing their hands, burying their faces in scarves, and yet I hardly felt the chill upon my bared shoulders, or on the gold and gemstones that touched my skin. It was a relief to breathe air that burned my lungs, that smelled of ice and mud. I felt myself calming in only a few moments. Then one of the drivers caught sight of me and spoke to the others, and one of them—Jimson—hurried over, touching his hat, looking worried behind the bulk of his collar. "Ma'am?"

I meant to tell him to go back. I meant to say that I was going inside again, that I was escaping the headache. But before I could say any of that, I felt a hand on my arm, and I turned to see Dr. Seth standing behind me, with William coming quickly after.

"It's nothing to be concerned about," Seth said to Jimson. "Mrs. Carelton needs a moment to rest."

Jimson looked at me questioningly, and I found myself nodding my agreement, watching as he reluctantly went back to his friends.

William came beside me. He held my cloak, which he put gently around my shoulders. Surprisingly, there was no hint of irritation in his voice when he said, "Your father's quite worried about you, as am I. Do you wish to go home, darling?"

"Yes," I said, gathering my cloak close. "Yes, I would like that. I'm so sorry, William. It's simply that my head—" I caught Dr. Seth's gaze, how he watched us, how avid was his expression, and blurted, "I didn't know you cared for the opera."

He nodded. "I spent quite some time in Leipzig. I've developed a fondness for the German."

"I see."

"You seem distressed, Mrs. Carelton."

"It's just that I didn't expect to see you here."

"I don't know why not," William said. "You've seen him about before. And I told you I was putting his name forth for SIAC."

"I've distressed you," Seth said. He sounded chastened, apologetic, and that bothered me too, that he would know so well how I felt.

"It's only that I'm surprised."

"I'll go get DeLancey," William said. He was never so accommodating. I could only think it had something to do with Dr. Seth's presence. "We'll leave straightaway."

But William did not go, and Seth did not move. I did not move. Seth said, "Tell me, Mrs. Carelton, why seeing me here disturbs you so."

"Why shouldn't it?" I whispered. "You're my doctor."

"You seem afraid."

The word shook me. "Afraid? Of course not."

"Perhaps you're worried that your friends might reveal your secrets."

Something leaped in me, some twinge of feeling. I turned away.

William laughed. "Secrets? Lucy has no secrets."

"Is that true, Mrs. Carelton?"

I could not look at Seth. "Of course it's true. This is absurd, to be having this conversation here. It's freezing."

"Yes, it is absurd." Dr. Seth hesitated, then said, "William, might I have a few minutes with your wife?"

William frowned. "Whatever for?"

"I think I may be able to relieve her headache."

"It feels better already," I protested.

William glanced at me in worry and nodded. "Yes, of course. I'll go find Lucy's father."

"Don't be silly," I said. "Let's all go inside, where it's warmer. I am feeling much better."

It was as if I hadn't spoken. William hurried away, leaving me standing alone with Dr. Seth beneath the glare of streetlights and the icy brush of snow.

Dr. Seth turned to me. "Your husband insisted I come to your box. Otherwise I wouldn't have surprised you that way. Apparently your father had some desire to meet me."

"He thinks you're a charlatan." I had not meant to say the words, but he waved them off impatiently.

"He'll be impressed, then, when I cure you."

I forgot my discomfort in a rush of gratitude, and then was startled that he should so easily change my emotions. "When you cure me?"

"Yes, of course." He stepped closer. "But we've discussed this before, Mrs. Carelton. I can help you only if you trust me."

"I do trust you."

"Then why did you leave so hastily when I came to your box? What is it you're afraid of?"

He was too close. I took a step back. "Why, nothing."

Dr. Seth held out his hand. "Come," he whispered, and I felt helpless against him. I put my hand in his, and his fingers crept up, circling my wrist, pressing lightly, almost a caress. "Now, Mrs. Carelton, shall we find out what your secrets are?"

The next thing I knew, I was sitting in the carriage, dimly lit from the streetlamps shining outside. Dr. Seth was sitting across from me, his arms crossed over his chest. William and my father were nowhere to be seen.

Notes from the Journal of
Victor Leonard Seth

Re: Mrs. C.

January 26, 1885

During the last few days, I have happened upon Mrs. C.'s husband quite by accident. He has been most grateful about my treatment of his wife, and I have allowed him to

put forth my name for inclusion in the Staten Island Athletic Club. I had not seen the harm in this before tonight,
when our meeting ended in his taking me to his family's
box at the opera. Mrs. C. was there and was quite obviously
distressed by my presence. She left the box in a panic. I reassured her husband and the others that, as a doctor, I
could help with her admitted headache. I followed her
outside, where she stood shivering in the snow, and used
hypnosis in an attempt to soothe her.

Again she went into trance so easily. Again her unconscious seemed to find relief in relinquishing control. I have
always believed that hysteria lies in egoism and willfulness,
but tonight I had the opportunity to observe the etiology
that underlies Mrs. C.'s fits, and I begin to question my own
hypothesis.

Mrs. C. is depressive and highly strung. The events that
triggered the attack were my unexpected arrival at their
box, and her attempt to conceal her discomfort over the
true nature of our relationship. I begin to think that in her
case, hysteria is a form of self-blindness. Is it possible that I
am mistaken—that Mrs. C. does not understand herself
what her motives are or what she desires?

I was struck by the question and very much wished to
know the answer.

I am astounded at the result. Though I intended to
start with a simple questioning, Mrs. C. went far, far beyond
my expectations in revealing an obviously painful and
traumatic event. Under hypnosis, she is as open to me as
she was closed before. In the trance state, details of this incident seemed as clear to her as the day they occurred, and
it was evident from her reactions that she was experiencing
that day as if she were living it in the present moment.

After establishing that she was deeply in trance by use of catalepsy and analgesia, I embarked on my quest for answers.

S: Imagine a clear day, the sound of the ocean upon the shore.

She calmed immediately. It was clear the image had resonance for her.

C: Yes. The ocean.

S: Is this an ocean you recognize?

C: Bailey's Beach.

S: In Newport. Do you like this place?

C: I do. I love it there.

S: Why is that?

C: William proposed to me there.

I was surprised that she had expressed such a sentiment. In most of the female neurasthenics at Bernheim's school in Nancy—especially in the upper classes—a proposal of marriage may be satisfying: A woman has won the man whom her family supports, or who has the financial security she craves. The proposal may even be a relief. But it is rarely an occasion for joy or tenderness, as Mrs. C.'s tone implied hers was.

S: You wanted him to propose?

C: Yes. Oh, yes.

S: The last time we spoke of this, you said that your father had forced William into your arms. Isn't that true?

She spoke reluctantly.

C: He was my father's choice.

S: And you didn't resent that?

C: I did . . . and I didn't.

S: What do you mean by that?

C: It was another choice Papa made for me [there was bitterness in her voice], but I suppose in the end it didn't really matter. I loved William.

S: Loved. Do you still love him?

She paused here and then said, "I cannot make him happy."

S: That is not the question I asked. Do you still love him?

She bowed her head and said nothing. I assumed she was crying and had thought to calm her again when she looked up with dry eyes.

C: Sometimes I do.

S: Not all the time?

C: [obviously saddened] No.

S: When is it that you don't love William?

At this point she did begin to cry.

C: I don't know.

S: You said you cannot make him happy. How so?

C: Because I cannot . . . conceive.

S: Children would make William happy, then?

C: Yes.

S: And making William happy is what you want?

She was crying so that she could not speak. She only nodded.

S: Then we must try to find the reason that you can't have a child. Do you—

Here I stopped, because Mrs. C. was hiding her face from me with her hands. I gently forced them down, keeping them covered with my own while I gave her the command to remain calm and told her again to imagine the ocean. It had some effect, though she did not stop crying and in fact seemed disturbed by the image that had brought her peace only moments before.

C: I can't bear to think of it now. I have ruined things so badly.

S: Ruined what?

C: My marriage. My life.

S: Why do you say you have ruined it? What have you done?

C: If I could only be like everyone else. If I did not <u>want</u> so much.

S: It's no crime to want children. Women naturally—

C: I don't want children.

She spoke the words baldly, and with them, her tears stopped. She looked up at me in what could have been either shocked realization or a bold challenge.

S: You don't want children?

C: No.

It is not so unusual that women in unhappy circumstances do not wish to visit those circumstances upon their children and so choose not to become pregnant. But Mrs. C. does not live in poverty; her husband does not abuse her; she has a life envied by many.

S: I'm sure you believe that to be the case. The emotions you're experiencing—

C: I'm not deluding myself. I've never wanted children. I knew it when I was quite small.

S: Are you telling me that you feel no need to commit to what is considered to be woman's sole purpose?

C: To have a child is not my purpose.

S: I see. Then what is?

C: I want to paint.

I have seen this kind of displacement many, many times. Her disappointment in being unable to conceive has channeled itself into the urge for selfish expression for which there is no talent or real desire beyond the statement "I want to paint."

S: Hypnosis cannot give you talent. I can't create something from nothing.

C: I have talent. Or once I did. It's been so long, I don't know.

S: You have picked up a paintbrush, then? You've applied yourself to painting?

C: Yes.

S: But you no longer paint?

C: My father took my paints away when I was a girl.

S: Why?

Here she began to show distress once again. She could not keep still. I debated whether to calm her, but she continued before I could intervene.

C: He disapproved of it. He said it wasn't a ladylike profession, that I was embarrassing him by pursuing it.

S: Most women learn painting. How was your pursuit unladylike?

C: He said I was too ardent. He said I would make myself ill, as I'd been before.

S: You were ill before?

C: He took my paints and he threw them into the street. The horses . . . the carriages . . . they kept on going as if they didn't see, and I couldn't save them. He threw my canvas into the fire and said . . . he said, "You'll not get another one of those, my girl, not as long as I live. It's best you learn how to be a wife." He said I should have children and devote myself to them. Not painting. Not poetry. "You'll only be unhappy," he said. "Believe me. I know."

During this speech, Mrs. C. seemed most inconsolable. Her hands came up as if she were trying to stop someone, and her whole body was in a state of tremendous agitation.

S: Was this the end of it, then? Did you never paint again?

C: I tried. I bribed the maid to buy me some paints, but Papa caught her and dismissed her, and then no one would take the chance. Every time I came home from shopping, he checked my bags and boxes. He searched my room to make sure. After a while it seemed best . . . not to try .

S: Perhaps he was only trying to protect you.

C: Protect me from what? Being happy?

S: Is that what you think? That your father wants you to be unhappy?

C: I don't know.

S: Your father doesn't rule you now. Why don't you paint again?

C: William would never allow it. Papa told him early in our courtship that I was fragile. That I should be kept from paints and poetry. They were too overstimulating. He said I had a propensity for melodrama and illness.

S: Did William tell you this?

C: I was there when Papa said it. He wanted to make sure I heard.

S: So you would not try again?

C: Yes.

S: You said earlier that you had been ill. When was this?

C: I was thirteen, and I found poetry. I quite gave myself up to Byron.

S: To the point of illness?

C: I wanted to write like him, to _be_ him.

S: To be Byron would be to be a man.

C: Isn't it only men who live so passionately? Who experience every moment?

S: Is that what you wanted, then? To pursue moments?

C: To pursue life.

S: And you can't pursue life within your marriage?

Here Mrs. C. began to cry as passionately as she had spoken. The sobs seemed to come from deep within her chest. "Rest," I said, and she immediately quieted.

To see such emotion in this woman was fascinating. It explained much that has puzzled me. Her hysteria no doubt comes from her unconscious confusion—to long for something and be denied that longing with no hope of ever achieving it. I began to believe that despite the inclinations of her sex, perhaps she truly does *not* want children, that such a circumstance might drive her to deeper levels of despair. I also understood why her unconscious mind did not grasp my suggestions urging calm. To be at peace is not what she wants. To be like other women is also not her desire, as much as she protests that it is. It is clear that she does not want to be well in this world her father and husband have made for her, a world as a wife and mother, without the passion that exists within her, a passion that has no outlet but hysteria. Any suggestion I make that more firmly urges her adaptation to this world may not be successful.

Failure is not what her husband wants; it is not what

she claims to want. And yet I cannot deny the temptation such knowledge presents. In Mrs. C., I am reminded of the old questions: How much influence does the unconscious mind have over the will? How much control? If I discovered the wellspring of the inner life this woman claims not to want, and I planted the correct suggestions in her unconscious mind, would they overcome her reason? Her will?

Fascinating, but impossible that such an opportunity for research exists in this woman. This woman who is everything I've dismissed so contemptuously before now. I know I cannot pursue this. It is irresponsible. If my suspicions are correct, the passion she tries so hard to hide and control would ruin her were it brought to light. She would no longer be able to exist within her world, and I have no faith she could exist out of it.

Yet what could it harm to learn more?

Chapter 9

"Where is my husband?" I asked Dr. Seth.

He looked at me with grave eyes. "No doubt he'll be here soon. The opera is nearly over."

I remembered then. Seth's visit to our box, my escape. What I did not remember was anything after that.

"You hypnotized me," I accused.

He didn't deny it. He merely shrugged.

"What suggestion did you put in my mind this time?" I asked. I felt violated, as if he had somehow seen me unclothed and taken an image without my permission.

"I planted no suggestion," he said simply. "You will not yield to me, Lucy, and I cannot fight you. We are doomed to failure."

I was not sure which to be more stunned by, his admission of failure or his use of my given name.

"What do you mean, we're doomed to failure? Do you mean you can't cure me?"

"I mean you don't want to be cured."

"But I do. I do. I cannot go on this way." I was desperate, my anger forgotten in the realization of what I must tell William, at what would happen to me. Another failure. Dr. Seth was our last hope, and even he could not mend the break within me. "But you can't give up so soon. Why, we've barely tried!"

"I no longer believe that you want what your husband hired me to bring you."

"But I do. I want to be well."

"Ah." He uncrossed his arms and hesitated. I had the sense he was deciding something. He said, "There is a difference, Lucy, between being well and being alive."

I stared at him in confused silence. "I—I don't understand."

His eyes lit with a strange intensity that had me shrinking against the leather seat. He seemed driven by an excitement that animated him as he leaned toward me, so close I smelled the sage and citrus of his shaving soap. "Do you remember what we discussed while you were in a trance state?"

"N-no."

He put his hands on my forehead, fingers and thumb pressing into my skin. "You can remember," he said.

It was odd; suddenly I could. I remembered his questions, I remembered crying. I remembered the day my father took my paints from me, throwing them into the street, his words; and then later, William's compliance.

I recoiled from Seth's fingers, appalled, feeling violated again. "You stole my memory," I whispered.

"Not stole," he corrected. "You told me freely. I did not force you. I believe you wanted me to know."

"It was a long time ago. I was very young."

He hesitated. "Lucy—"

"I have not given you permission to call me that."

"Lucy, tell me something. These things you say you want: to be like other women, to be at peace—are you certain they would make you happy?"

I was filled with a terrible fear. "Yes. Yes, of course."

"You've led an entire life ruled by a will not your own," he said. "Your father's will, your husband's will. What if you could be the woman you were meant to be? What if you could escape from this"—he gestured futilely about the carriage—"this dull acquiescence?"

I stared at him. "Surely you're joking. My father would be appalled if I were such a woman. William would leave me. My friends would turn from me. It would destroy me. Surely you must understand that. I came to you for help. I want to be like everyone else."

He stared at me for a long moment, and then he said, "I'm not sure we can achieve that, Lucy."

"Stop calling me Lucy," I ordered. My voice was harsher than I intended. "My husband is paying you a goodly sum of money to make me well."

"Which I can do only if you're honest with me."

"Very well." I nodded. "I'll be honest."

At that he smiled, but it was a disturbing smile, one I didn't trust. I considered taking back my words, telling him it would be better not to see him again. But then I thought of William, of the asylum, and they filled me with such a terrible desperation that I said, "I don't want to fail, Dr. Seth. Please. I know you can help me. You must help me."

"Very well," he said, and though there was resignation in his voice, I had the strange feeling that he was not at all resigned. "Then we will try again. Be at my office tomorrow. At one o'clock."

"One o'clock," I agreed.

"What is it he does?" William asked for the dozenth time as we came into the house. He followed me as I handed my cloak to Harris. I headed for the stairs, pausing to adjust the gas, waiting for the little *pfftt* as it went out. "You were so calm when I came back with your father."

I sighed. "So you've said."

"I tell you, it was like magic. Like some parlor trick. What does he do to you?"

"It's hypnosis, William. He explained it to you."

"Yes, yes, I know. But I should like to see it."

"I'm tired," I said, reaching the first landing. "I should like to go to bed."

"But Lucy"—he reached for my hand before I could continue on, curling his fingers around mine to imprison my hand on the banister—"what does he say to effect it?"

"I don't know what he does or what he says," I said. I jerked my hand away and continued up. "He's a magician, I suppose."

"He is a genius." William's voice was hushed.

I turned on the stairs to look at him. "I wouldn't call him that. He hasn't cured me."

"Not yet. But I'm convinced he's the man who can. More convinced than ever. I forbid you to even think about not seeing him. In fact, I've asked him to attend to you more fully."

I stopped. "You've done what?"

"I think it's certain we'll begin to see him in social situations more and more often. I've asked him to watch—"

"You've asked him to spy on me?"

"No, no, no, not that. But if he can do what he did tonight . . ."

I felt ill. "I thought you wanted him to be discreet."

"I'm certain he will be. I've merely asked him to be aware."

I remembered how much I had disliked seeing Seth there, intruding upon my life, observing the things I didn't wish him to, and I began to move again, wanting the sanctity of my room so badly it was all I could do to keep from running there.

"How odd that you trust him so," I said, finally reaching my door. William was behind me. "It's almost as if he's hypnotized you as well."

William laughed. I pushed open my door and went inside, not even saying good night before I closed the door and leaned against it, keeping my hand on the knob, holding my breath, waiting for William to push inside. Instead I heard his laughter fade as he passed my door and went on to his own.

"Good night, my dear," he called, and there was a joy in the words that I had not heard for a long, long time.

Irene was not in the office the next afternoon. I paused, unsure of what to do. I knocked lightly on his door.

"Come in," he called.

When I went in, he was at the desk writing furiously, his round glasses nearly sliding off his nose, the hair that was normally swept off his forehead falling lankly into his face. A smoldering cigar perched on the saucer of a teacup next to his elbow, befouling the air.

"Am I interrupting?" I asked. "I'd thought you said one o'clock."

He looked up, and I realized he hadn't really seen or heard me before that moment. His gaze was blank at first, and then he broke into a smile. "Lucy," he said.

"Mrs. Carelton," I corrected.

He put down his pen and shoved back his chair, took off his glasses, and he was once again the doctor I'd grown accustomed to. He stood and motioned for me to hang my things on the coatrack. I glanced at the wooden cabinet, which was open to reveal the electrotherapy machine, and the sight of it sent a shudder through me—of revulsion or anticipation, I could not say.

"We won't do faradization today," he said, as if he'd read my mind. "Unless you'd prefer it."

"As you wish," I said.

"You seem nervous." The doctor took his customary seat in the wing chair and motioned for me to do the same.

"I am always nervous," I said.

"Shall we move beyond that, Lucy? You've promised to be honest with me. No edict of your husband's could force you to do that unless you harbored some hope of success yourself. Isn't that true?"

"I try to be an obedient wife," I said.

"But you aren't, are you? You've taken refuge in hysterical fits for years, and therefore achieved just what you wanted: some wretched imitation of autonomy. You've done everything you possibly could to fight the constraints of your life while still clinging to the semblance of it. In what way do you believe you're an obedient wife?"

I searched for the answer to his question, for some hint that I was no different from any other wife, that I inhabited my place with grace and humility. Only one thing came to me, and it was so intimate I could barely say it. "I continue to try to conceive a child."

Dr. Seth's gaze held me in place. It was as condemning as his words. "Unconsciously, you fight even that. Your body obeys your mind."

"What are you saying?" I asked. "That I don't want a child?"

"Isn't it true?"

"No! No, of course not."

"There's no need to lie to me," he said calmly. "I'm your doctor. I can't help you without some knowledge of your feelings, however unsavory they might be."

He knew, though he could not know; it was something I barely admitted to myself, something I tried to deny. But there was also relief in his knowing, and that was the worst of it—I couldn't acknowledge that relief, so I persisted with the fiction. "Why would you say such a thing to me, when I never told you I didn't want a child?"

"Under hypnosis you did."

"It was a lie."

"No," he said. "It was the truth. You know it was, Lucy. Stop trying to protect an ideology you don't believe in."

"I'm not. I'm not."

"The truth," he said gently, "is that you haven't conceived a child because you don't want one."

"But that's absurd! I could not possibly! There's something wrong with my womb."

"Who has told you that?"

"Why, other doctors."

"They've found abnormalities in your uterus?"

"Well, yes. Of course they have. They've suggested ovari- otomies—"

"To treat your hysteria."

"And rest—"

"To treat your hysteria."

"And the water cure—"

"To treat your hysteria."

Desperately, I shouted, "Shock treatments, nutrition, massage, blisters, leeches, camphor douches . . ." I ran out of breath and sputtered the last. "The only thing I haven't tried is an asylum."

"Which is where you'll end up if you continue to deny the truth."

I was clenching my fingers into fists so hard they hurt. "You're saying that it's only my thoughts that have kept us from con- ceiving."

Dr. Seth nodded slowly. "Yes. That's what I'm suggesting."

"Believe me, Doctor, I would like to think my mind is so strong. It's not, I can assure you. I feel I'm losing a little bit of it every day."

"Sit down, Lucy."

"I think I'd prefer to stand."

"Sit down."

I went to the chair across from his and sat, pulling my knees to the side so they would not brush his, pushing against the back of the chair to put distance between us. He would not let there be distance. As he had in the carriage, he leaned in so that his hands brushed my arms. *What if you could be the woman you were meant to be?*

I jerked at my memory of the words, which were so loud in my head it was as if he'd just said them to me.

"No," I said. "I don't want it. You told me you would not."

"Would not what, Lucy?" he asked calmly.

"I want to be like everyone else," I said. I could not stop the tremor in my voice. "I want to be what William wants."

"And what your father wants?"

"Yes."

"Don't worry, Lucy," he said. "You won't be sorry that you put your trust in me."

Then he took my hands.

Notes from the Journal of Victor Leonard Seth

Re: Mrs. C.

February 2, 1885

I find myself plagued by my questions re: Mrs. C. I have not slept for thinking of them. She resisted my attempts to convince her to give in to her inner life, and though that does not surprise me—in fact, it should quiet the ceaseless questioning in my mind—I cannot rest so easily.

Though I knew it would avail me nothing, I could not keep myself from suggesting my new theories to her husband. I met him at the Staten Island Athletic Club. It was a foul day, so I proposed we take ourselves to the boxing ring and spar. He is fairly proficient, though I beat him readily. Years of fighting the other boys on Hester Street have left their *mark upon me, I fear, and I don't wish to embarrass myself by admitting I have no idea how to row or play polo—rich men's games that I never learned.*

I found it the perfect opportunity to explain my new theories regarding his wife. I couched them carefully—he is quite ambitious and sensitive regarding his place in society and does not want to upset the balance he's managed to attain over the years. I understand that, but I begin to think that he could help his wife in some elemental ways. I told him that I believed Mrs. C. is a passionate woman caught in the confines of a society that reviles such passion.

At first he pretended not to know what I meant. Then he proceeded to tell me that his wife was everything he expected in a woman—she did her duty uncomplainingly, and he did not expect passion from one so well bred. He was even slightly repulsed by the notion. He confided to me that before their marriage, he kept a mistress, but he felt she was draining him of energy, so he left her. He has been "faithful, for the most part—more than any wife can expect," though he said there have been times when he has visited prostitutes in an effort to keep his filthy passions from sullying his wife.

These mindless notions weary me, but I pretended to understand his reasons and refrained from telling him that his wife would no doubt benefit from his filthy passions. Only a few days ago, I had a letter from my old mentor, William James, who has recently been made professor of philosophy at Harvard. I had felt confident in revealing my problems with Mrs. C. to him—my peers in Boston are more open to ideas of the brain as a psychic organ and are not so insistent on the centrality of the somatic as the cause of nervous disorders. Though James strongly disapproves of my reliance on hypnosis, he has spoken of Mrs. C.'s case with G. Stanley Hall

at Johns Hopkins. They both wonder if the root of her problems is sexual in nature: i.e., that the repression and subli-
mation of sexual instincts, particularly in women, may lead
to intense hysteria and/or neurasthenia.

This indeed may be the case. I strongly suspect that the
only orgasm Mrs. C. has ever experienced has been through
faradization. She, like many women of her class, has
learned to subvert her sexual passions. Most women chan-
nel such passions into their children, of which Mrs. C. has
none, so she may have channeled this sexual passion into religion, poetry, and painting. When even these were taken
from her, she had no outlet for her passion but hysteria.

But when I suggested to Mrs. C.'s husband that she be
satisfied sexually, he was profoundly opposed to the idea. He
muttered of corruption and indecency and reminded
me forcibly (by boxing me into a corner and nearly spitting
in my face) that they had come to me for help in making
Mrs. C. more normal, not less. "My wife has fits, Victor. They
already talk of her as if she doesn't quite belong, and her lineage beats any of theirs. Make her well. What I certainly
don't need—and what no one in our circle will accept—
is one of those New Women."

His refusal will cost me. Treatment would move much
more quickly if Mrs. C. experienced sexual release other
than through faradization. For now I did not gainsay him.
But I could not stop myself from the smallest of tests, from
planting a simple suggestion in Mrs. C.'s unconscious, only to
satisfy my curiosity. Perhaps I will be wrong, and her reason
will once again overcome her unconscious, in which case I
will return to my earlier attempts to treat her. In any case,
it can do no harm, and I shall be satisfied once I know for
certain if I am correct.

Chapter 10

The Morris ball was the following night. Clara Morris was not the most effusive of hostesses. I knew no one who actually looked forward to attending one of her entertainments, but there wasn't a soul who would send his regrets. Clara rarely gave a supper or a ball—she was too parsimonious for that—but to be invited was a mark of distinction outdone only by Caroline Astor's suppers. Like the Astor events, the Morris invitations determined once and for all who was acceptable and who was not.

Even the worst headache would not have kept me from the Morris house, but thankfully, Dr. Seth's calming instruction had relieved that worry. As William and I made our way up the stairs to the third floor of the Morris brownstone, the ballroom, I felt calm and happy, hopeful that I could have the peace I craved.

There was to be no late supper, but canapés were set on silver trays throughout the room, and champagne was poured liberally—on that Clara Morris would not have dared to skimp.

The room was crowded and hot, and the musicians in the corner looked as if they'd been squeezed into place. Clara had lit candles throughout, and their light glittered on gold tassels and fringe. A profusion of gilded mirrors and frames encompassed the large, dark paintings that had been in Clara's family for years. The whole effect was like being in Midas's cave, both blinding and ancient.

"I wish Seth could have been here tonight," William said in a low voice.

"I've been to hundreds of balls," I said, unable to completely disguise my resentment. "I hardly need him here. And he could not have hoped to win an invitation to this."

William sighed. "That's true enough."

"I feel quite well, William." I put my hand on his arm and smiled. "You worry too much, my dear."

"It's become a habit."

"One I hope to break you of soon."

He smiled. "I hope so, darling."

Just then the musicians began tuning up in preparation for the dance, and there was a flash of white as the men began to take their gloves from the table near the door. William went to get a pair himself, and then he was back again, leading me onto the floor for the first dance. To say we danced would be an absurd overstatement; the room was much too small, but we moved in time to the music.

"How little I'll miss this when we move into our new home," William murmured. "To have a full-size ballroom . . ."

"Yes," I said. The room was growing hotter; the smell of perfume was a heavy cloud that competed with candle wax and smoke and the increasing odor of chilled salmon.

"I've had McKim install ventilation shafts to warm it in the winter. In the summer we can open the attic dormers to bring in the cool air."

"How wonderful," I said.

"We'll need simple furniture for the ballroom. Nothing too elaborate. It should be easy to move but elegant. Have you visited Goupil's yet?"

I felt an urge to take off my gloves, such a foreign thought that it surprised me. I pushed it away, but it was back then, fiercer than before. My fingers clenched against William's hands.

"Is something wrong?"

"No," I said. "No." But my fingers were sweating inside my gloves, and the fine seams irritated my skin. I wanted nothing more than to take them off. I could think only of how fine it would feel to have the air on my skin. I fought the urge. How odd it was—I had not felt this way since I was a girl, when I was growing accustomed to wearing them. I could not take them off while we were dancing. It would be improper, against tradition and etiquette. I would not take them off. But the urge was so great within me that it was like a physical pain, and I could fight it no longer. Before I knew it, I had taken my hands from William's, muttering "Excuse me" while I pulled them off furiously, as if they were burning my skin. I let them drop to the floor, and then I could breathe.

William's face was baffled. "What are you doing?" he hissed, glancing around to see if anyone had noticed. "Good God, Lucy, what has come over you?"

I prepared to explain, then paused, suddenly horrified at what I'd done. I wasn't certain why I'd gone against convention. I had never dared to do such a thing, and gloves had not bothered me for years and years. Why they should do so today—

"I could not wear them another moment," I explained weakly.

William bent and picked them up, holding them out to me. "Put them on."

I stared at that pile of crumpled white kid. I did not want to touch them again, and to put them on . . . but that was ridiculous. It wasn't me. I didn't understand.

"Come, Lucy. You're causing a scene."

People were indeed beginning to look our way. I took the gloves from William and forced them on, stretching my fingers into the kid, pulling them over my arms, and it felt as if my skin were shrinking, smothering. *Take them off*, I thought, and that voice was so insistent, it took all my strength of will to deny it, to take William's hands again.

He swept me onto the floor, though his face was set in a tight mask, and I felt his disapproval. I danced with him, but all I could think of was how I wanted to feel his hands bare against mine. How much I wished to touch him the way I had at Bailey's Beach that long-ago day when he pulled me close.

The next afternoon I was alone in Victor Seth's office. Irene had shown me in, telling me he would be late, and now I wandered around the room, running my fingers along the leather spines of the books littering his shelves, many of them with fading foreign titles. *Du Sommeil et des États Analogues, Sur la Baquette, Divinatoire, Illustrations of the Influence of the Mind upon the Body in Health and Disease, Essays on Phrenology, The Principles of Medical Psychology,* and *The Temples of Aesculapius.* The last one intrigued me. I had just taken it down when the door opened and Dr. Seth came in.

He looked flushed, as if he had come some distance, and quickly. He still wore his coat and his hat, which he took off with an apology when he saw me.

"You're late, Doctor," I said.

"Forgive me. I was unavoidably delayed." While he unbuttoned his coat, I opened the book in my hand, letting the pages turn without intervention, watching the words go by. Then he was behind me. He took the book from my hand and snapped it shut. Startled, I stepped away.

"You move too quietly," I said.

"*The Temples of Aesculapius,*" he read. "Are you interested in the ancient Romans?"

"I hardly know."

"Asklepios was the son of Apollo. The cult named after him flourished for many years, well into the Christian era. They built temples for healing. Particularly for hysteria."

"Did they use hypnosis as well?"

"A form of it. They worked often through dreams." He put the book back on the shelf. "Now, Lucy, suppose you tell me how the Morris ball went last night."

"William was worried that I might do something foolish."

"Did you?"

"I don't know," I said. I moved away from him, running my gloved fingers along the edge of his desk, picking up a fine film of dust. "I had the strangest thought while we were dancing."

"Yes?"

"I took off my gloves," I said. "I couldn't bear the feel of them another moment. It was so odd."

"How did taking them off make you feel?"

"As if I could breathe again," I said. "It was such a relief—at first. And then I was appalled. I haven't done anything like that since I was a girl."

"Before your father threw your paints away."

"Yes." I glanced at him, and then I remembered. "But I was always too rebellious then. Thankfully, I've learned my place."

"You were rebellious," Dr. Seth repeated. He leaned against the bookcase lazily, but his eyes were alert, intense. "How so?"

"With my painting, of course." I moved to the window. "But even before that. There was the poetry, and before that, the church."

"The church? I fail to see how those things are rebellious. It sounds like the usual course of events for a young girl."

I laughed a little nervously. "Yes, perhaps. But not the way I went about it. I was in the grip of religious fervor. I went nearly every day until Papa put an end to it, and then I fought him. I cried and cried. I told him I would run away and join a convent."

"What happened?"

"It passed. That was when I found Byron." I touched the window; the cold of the day seeped through the glass and my gloves into my fingertips. "He thought I would run off to the

Continent and learn terrible French ways and be irredeemable. It would not do. I am his only child."

"Would you have done that, given the chance?"

"I don't know," I said, and the knowledge made me sad, though I was not sure why. "I don't know what I would have done."

In the glass, I saw the vague image of him behind me, but only as the fading color of his reflection, only the slight movement of his fingers as they moved upon his face. Then he said, "The window. Once again, Lucy, you seem drawn to the window."

I jerked back my hand.

"How old were you when your mother died?"

I turned, confused by his question. "Ten."

"When did you turn to religion?"

"I suppose it was not long after that. I was eleven, perhaps, or twelve."

"How did she die?"

I did not like to talk of it. "She drowned."

"Were you with her when it happened?"

"No, I wasn't. That is, I was at the summer house, but I wasn't at the beach with her."

"Was this in Newport?"

"No, no, it was long before we took a cottage there. It was up-river—on the Hudson." I remembered it well, though I had been there so long ago. "It was a beautiful place. It had been my great-grandfather's summer house."

"Do you go there still?"

"My father sold it after Mama died. I heard it was torn down."

Seth stroked his small beard. "What was your mother like?"

"Papa says I look like her, but I don't remember her well any longer."

"Did you love her?"

"She was my mother."

He smiled a little. "Did you love her?"

I was growing used to these questions. "She was . . . very quiet. Her voice was hardly more than a whisper. Papa was a much bigger presence."

"Did you love her, Lucy?"

"I don't remember," I admitted. "I don't really think of her at all. I'm not sure I ever did, even when she was alive."

"Do you remember the day she died?"

"Only as a great fog."

Again the thoughtful expression that made me nervous. Dr. Seth went slowly to the red chair, then motioned me to the other one, and I went as though under his spell, unquestioning.

When I was seated, he leaned forward and took my hand, turning it in his so my palm was up, and then he said, "We're going to remember that day, Lucy."

When I woke, it was to find my arms around his neck and my face pressed into his shirt, which was wet with my tears. He was holding me tightly, but as I came to myself, he let me go.

"You'll be at peace tonight, Lucy," he said, but I only nodded, embarrassed at such intimacy, feeling awkward and nervous as I pulled away and went for my coat.

I did not ask him what had happened. I did not want to know.

From the Journal of
Victor Leonard Seth

Re: Mrs. C., whom I will now refer to as Eve C.

February 3, 1885

*Things have transpired in this case that I could not
have dared to imagine. I find myself unable to proceed as I*

have been directed. I cannot, after all, resist the temptation that has presented itself.

But to start at the beginning: At our last meeting, I made a suggestion during hypnosis that Eve C. remove her gloves when she was dancing with her husband. I had hoped to gain some insight into whether Eve's unconscious would respond to a suggestion that fed in to her innermost wishes, or whether her will would overpower it and the habit of reason would hold. Eve would have been brought up with the severe etiquette of dancing with gloves on. The upper class do not touch; bare skin is anathema to them. The suggestion went against everything Eve has known, learned, or understood about her life. I had to know: Would she do it? And if she did, what would she feel about it?

She told me during our appointment that ultimately she had taken off the gloves and, in doing so, was struck by an intense sense of pleasure and freedom.

My theory had proved correct. When presented with the opportunity, her <u>unconscious mind can overpower her will.</u> This is a stunning discovery, and it made me wonder what power her unconscious could have if it were given free rein. Could I lead it, through hypnosis, to completely overtake her reason? Could I change her will?

To be given what I so ardently wish for—to have in my hands a subject who can help me win the respect of my colleagues, one who can help me prove the power of the unconscious mind, and yet to be told to ignore this knowledge, to proceed as she and her husband wish, to rid her of her unconscious passion—

To remake her in the way I wish is to destroy the life she claims to want so desperately; I know this, and yet what shall I do? Make her into another useless parasite? Shall I let scientific knowledge pass because of the wishes of one woman who cannot hope to understand the secrets she possesses? I would be less a scientist—truly worthy of the contempt of my colleagues—if I conceded to her wishes. She is only a woman.

I do not walk blindly into this experimentation. In an attempt to gain more insight into the genesis of her behavior, I took her, in a trance state, to the time of her mother's death. As she did when describing the trauma of having her father throw her paints away, Eve went easily back through time and described the incident to me as if it were currently happening. This is most important, because consciously she claims to remember nothing about that day.

Apparently her mother committed suicide while the family summered at their country home. Eve had been playing in her bedroom, which overlooked the Hudson River. She went to the window and watched as her mother walked purposefully into the water and kept walking until she foundered and was gone. "I called and called, but it seemed like hours until anyone came, and then it was too late. When they found her, she looked only as if she were sleeping."

Though Eve speaks of sorrow and disbelief and grief, I detected envy in her tone as well. Before I could question her further, she broke into such copious, heart-wrenching sobs that I was obliged to comfort her.

I had no opportunity to make another suggestion; my main goal was to determine the effect of a mother's suicide on such a young, passionate girl. It is clear that Eve suffers from both a desire to have a full life and the fear that such a longing can only ruin her, as it did her mother. I must work to overcome that fear—it is a strong barrier to the desires of her unconscious mind. I must work to erode her reason, to make her inner life seem the more attractive one. The strictures of society are not easily overcome, and it is true that Eve could correct my suggestions according to her own flawed judgment if she were left alone long enough. I cannot allow that to happen. The more time I spend with Eve, the more I can bolster the suggestions I make in her trance state.

To that end, I suggested Eve meet me at Delmonico's for luncheon. I explained that I wanted to observe her in a social situation, and though this seemed to trouble her, she agreed. The truth is that not only do I want every hour possible to work with her, I must also strengthen any bond she feels between us. I must make my influence stronger than any of the other influences in her life, including those of her husband and social ostracism. Only then can I achieve what I mean to.

February 4, 1885

Today I met Eve at Delmonico's, as we had agreed. It was a very cold day, with a chill wind that seemed to cut through my coat, and I was a few moments late. Though I did not expect to find her waiting outside on such a freezing day, she was by the front stoop, half sitting on flower boxes covered with snow. When I asked her why she did not wait inside, she replied that she would not be welcome as a woman alone, and gave me such a glance that I was reminded of the class difference between us.

To cover my embarrassment, I ushered her inside. They knew her—it seems everyone does, and she took charge of the situation as if she had been born to it, which of course she had. I was left feeling a bit useless. She asked for a quiet table, and we were led there right away.

I had not been inside Delmonico's before. We were placed close to a window in the main dining room, which I appreciated for the view it afforded of Fifth Avenue and the frostbitten greenery of Madison Square. I could tell from her anxiety that although we were in the corner, she would have much preferred the safety of darkness. I told her she should like the chance to stare out a window, and she smiled in a jittery fashion and confessed that she was unused to being alone with a man who was not her husband—something that I am ashamed to admit I had not thought of. She made furtive glances throughout the room, and her movements were nervous: the folding and unfolding of the napkin in her lap; the clasping and unclasping of her gloved hands; and when the soup was brought and she took off her gloves, she often fiddled with her wedding band.

The noise of the dining room left us ample opportunity to talk without being heard, so great was the clatter of dishes and silverware, the shouts of orders, waiters yelling back and forth to one another. The dining room was quite full.

I asked her if she knew anyone here. She gave me a quick nod and then confessed there was no one she knew well, which seemed to relieve her somewhat. She ordered a glass of wine. I did not drink but watched her as she did. She is a fount of nervous habits, as if it is only by sheer dint of will that she keeps hysteria at bay. I found that curious and oddly sad (a surprising reaction, I must admit).

She seemed possessed by some tension, and with every gulp of wine it seemed to grow within her until she spilled out with it. She spoke carefully, as if she did not wish me to know of her discomfort or her need for an answer.

E: What did I say at our last appointment?

S: You told me of your mother's death.

E: I was ... crying when I woke up.

S: Yes. You were quite distressed.

E: I remember nothing of it.

S: Not even in dreams?

Here she closed her eyes, and her face twisted in distress.

E: Oh. Yes. A few things. Nothing I understand.

S: It's no wonder your conscious mind has refused to remember it. It was a terrible thing to witness.

E: You mean ... I saw her drown?

S: From the window of your bedroom.

She gave the window a quick glance and swallowed.

S: What you saw would be traumatic for anyone. Since your visit, I've gone back to my case studies. You should take comfort from the fact that it's not unusual for hysterics to forget the incident that brought on the hysteria to begin with.

E: I wasn't hysterical when she died.

S: But soon after, perhaps. Isn't that when you turned to religion?

She was quiet for a long moment. There is intelligence in her eyes that is sometimes quite astounding. I waited to see if she would admit the connection between her mother's death and her search for fulfillment.

E: Why . . . yes.

S: As a substitute for your mother?

E: I've told you I barely remember her.

S: Your unconscious remembers her quite well. She was very kind to you, and quiet, as you've said before. She guarded you from your father's outbursts, though you were always aware of them, and it was impossible not to feel the tension of his disapproval in the house. She came from old money, and she smelled of it in a way your father did not: She wore the same perfume her mother— your grandmother—had worn. Something imported from Holland. It smelled of tuberoses and ivy. When you smell it today, you feel faintly nauseated. She had soft hands, and she preferred colors in plums and roses, though your father did not, and she ultimately gave in to him.

When I finished speaking, Eve reached for her wine so convulsively that her wrist caught the fork and sent it clanking hard on her plate. I could barely hear her when she spoke.

E: I . . . I told you all that?

S: How else would I know it? I did not know your mother.

E: I don't understand. How could I have forgotten so much?

S: You haven't forgotten. Your unconscious remembers it all.

The waiter came, looking embarrassed as he brought the next course, partridge in some winey sauce. I put my hand over Eve's to calm her. She gripped my fingers hard, as if she took strength from them.

When the waiter left again, she gave me a thin smile.

E: I'm sorry. I had not meant to—

S: It's quite all right.

E: We're in public, after all.

S: It is nothing to be ashamed of, missing your mother.

She looked thoughtful, and I asked her what she was thinking about.

E: How much I have longed for her. Or perhaps not her but <u>something.</u>

I explained that what she felt was <u>sehnsucht,</u> as the Germans call it. The longing for something that can't be named. She agreed that her bouts with religion and poetry and painting all may have related to the loss of her mother, and with the sense she had that there was something more for her, something she couldn't see and did not understand.

This was my opportunity. How easily she presented it. I admit I did not feel a moment of guilt as I suggested she make an attempt to somehow regain the satisfaction she had felt from her religious frenzy and her poetry and painting, before her father took those things away.

E: I could not. William would never allow it. Papa would—

S: Don't tell them.

The notion shocked her.

I did not want to frighten her into retreat, so I suggested that she start slowly, perhaps by sketching in pencil in her garden at times when neither William nor her father are at home.

She seemed to come alive at my words. Though she was still wary, I detected a certain glow in her eyes: The idea appealed. I told her I thought it would help to ease her feeling of emptiness, that elusive <u>sehnsucht,</u> and when she agreed to try, her fingers linked through mine. I was aware that I had not released my hold on her hand, nor had she on mine, and I felt the sheer exuberance that power can bring.

Chapter 11

He had given me permission to be free. When I left him, I asked Jimson to stop at some little shop on Lower Broadway. Careful that no one saw me, I ran inside and purchased a small sketch pad and pencils, along with a little cloisonné box that was quaintly pretty. I hid the sketch pad and pencils beneath my cloak and gave a vapid smile to Jimson as I came out into the freezing air, muttering some nonsense of how I'd seen the box earlier and it was the prettiest little thing. All of which puzzled him, I'm sure, because I'd never made a habit of talking with him before, and it was none of his concern where I might have him stop or why.

But I felt safer for the lie. I could not take the risk that William or Papa should find out. I felt a little guilty about it as well, but that feeling fled nearly the moment I got back into the carriage and went home.

My fingers itched to do as Dr. Seth had bade me, but it was too late in the afternoon. William would be home soon, and though I was tempted to draw only something small, I was glad I had not when he came home earlier than expected, bringin Papa with him for supper.

"I heard you were at Delmonico's with some gentleman today," Papa said as he applied himself to a saddle of mutton.

Papa's tone was insinuating, and William looked up with a frown on his face, his fork poised in the air. "A gentleman?" he asked.

I felt a twinge of guilt that made me angry. I had done nothing wrong. I met my husband's gaze steadily. "It was Dr. Seth, William. He said he wanted to observe me again in public, and it was time for luncheon."

"I see." William looked uncertain.

Papa frowned. "I've never heard of a doctor taking a patient out for luncheon."

"I admit it's unusual," I said. "But William felt I should spend as much time with him as possible. You *did* think it would be beneficial, William."

William seemed about to protest, but then he glanced at my father and said with false ease, "Yes, I did. Well. I certainly hope you introduced him to anyone who might not know who he is."

"Thomas Crowe was there," Papa said.

"Was he? I didn't see him."

"He said you looked right at him and looked away again as if you didn't want to be seen."

"Of course I didn't do that," I said, though I had, of course I had. To him and to several others. It had been the wrong thing to do, I saw that now. William was right. I should have introduced Dr. Seth. I should have made sure everyone saw how innocent it was. Why hadn't I done that? "I don't remember even seeing Thomas Crowe."

"He said he was at the table next to yours. That you and Seth seemed to be quite involved in your conversation."

I didn't turn to William, but I felt the question in his gaze, and flushed again, as though I were lying or trying to keep something secret. The store flashed through my mind, my surreptitious visit, the sketch pad and pencils that were hidden in a box beneath my bed, the doctor's words, *Don't tell them*, the way his hand had covered mine.

"It was merely lunch with my doctor."

"No doubt it was. It was simply the way it looked."

"And how was that?"

"You should have introduced him," William said quietly. "It looks bad, darling, not to do so."

I glared at him, and William had the grace to lower his gaze.

After dinner, when Papa had excused himself and retired to his room, I said to William, "You were the one who wished for Seth to be seen more in our circle."

"I know that."

"How am I to deflect gossip, then, if I'm to see him constantly and not let anyone know why I do so?"

"Introduce him as a friend," William said calmly. "Let Victor find ways to deflect their suspicions. He's promised to do so. Don't act as if you're ashamed to be seen with him."

"You're angry that I went there with him," I said.

"Not angry," he corrected. "Surprised. It was hardly a clever thing to do. And you said nothing of it to me."

"There was no reason to," I said. I fingered the gold-embroidered edge of the tablecloth. "It was only another appointment."

"In a restaurant."

"It was his suggestion."

William was silent. I looked up at him again.

"What else has he suggested to you?" he asked.

I had to work to meet his gaze. "Nothing."

"Nothing?"

"Well, the usual things. To control my fits. To be at peace."

He nodded and picked up his glass of port, taking a deep sip before he said, "As long as it helps you, we'll continue on as we've been. But try to remember your place, Lucy, when you're in public."

"Of course, William," I said, so relieved I had to turn away to conceal my smile.

After William left for the 'Change the next morning, I break-fasted and dressed and gave instructions to Moira and the menu to the cook. Then I pulled the box from beneath my bed and took out the sketchbook and the pencils. As I held them, it seemed as if a spell had been cast upon me, for the feel of them in my hands was luxurious—almost sinful. It had been so long since such paper had touched my fingertips, since the point of a charcoal pencil had marked my skin. It was true that I felt guilty; if William or Papa knew of this, they would see it as a manifes-tation of my illness. They would take it away. And yet I felt as if I held myself, as if this empty sketchbook held my soul in a way my own mind and heart did not; as if I were nothing without this emptiness to hold on to, to fill.

I wrapped myself in warmth: a cloak, a hat, warm boots. I put on gloves, though I meant to take them off the moment I was outside.

I paused at the parlor door and told Moira, "I'll be in the gar-den." I'd startled her as she cursorily passed the feather duster over a table laden with tiny boxes—including the little cloisonné I'd bought yesterday—and she flushed as if I'd caught her in a lie, as she certainly should have, for the lackluster way she was cleaning. But just then I didn't care.

"In the garden?" she sputtered. "But ma'am, it's quite cold."

I didn't bother to answer her; I could hardly keep myself from running as I passed through the house and out the door into the back garden.

The garden was narrow but deep and beautiful in the summer. I loved to sit there, surrounded by leaves and flowers. I did not visit it often at other times, and never in the winter. The grape as a dead-looking brown, vines tangled about the rounded te trellises bordering the garden. The small cherry tree was little more than graying branches rising from a thin, icy layer of snow that was mostly melted but for in the hollows and the lee. The seat of the stone bench was covered with ice, and the border beds were filled with brown vines and crumpled leaves that had once been flowers. I remembered them as a profusion of color without knowing their names or even the shapes of their petals, despite the fact that as a girl, I had spent two months one summer pressing flowers and naming them in painstaking copperplate on waxed pages.

Just outside the door, I gripped the sketchbook, finding the bleakness of the garden more lovely than I could have imagined. I had not done this in so very long that I was uncertain how to start. Once it had seemed that my mind nearly swelled with ideas of what to draw—to look at a landscape was to pick out the one thing I wanted to show. But today it seemed there were too many choices, and I'd lost the habit of critical faculty. Should I draw the tree, or the grapevine on the trellis, or the way the clouded sun cast shadows on the weakening snow, or the dead flowers, or the shape of the border, the bench, the crushed stone beneath it? I could not decide; I sat on the bench and felt the cold of it seep through my cloak and my gown and my petticoats, and finally it was the cherry tree that caught me: the way its limbs set out from all directions, the way it struggled from the snow. I took off my gloves and opened the sketchbook to its first pristine white page, and I took the pencil between my fingers and began to draw.

To say I lost myself would be an understatement. I was drawn in by the first line, and though my fingers were stiff with disuse, and I retraced my steps a hundred times, trying to regain the ease with which I'd once done this, I was captivated by the pursuit. More than captivated: giddy, unfettered. There was a cold wind, but where I sat, I was protected, and though the cherry tree bowed this way and that, I was unmoved. I did not feel the cold, not in my bare fingers nor from the ice on the bench, now melting into my clothing. I lost track of time until I heard a faint call, and then a louder, more insistent "Mrs. Carelton?"—a name that suddenly wasn't mine. I was a girl again, I was Lucy Van Berckel, I had no idea who Mrs. Carelton was—perhaps a friend of my mother's—and then I came to myself with a start to see Moira standing in the back doorway, hugging herself against the cold and saying, "Pardon me, ma'am, but Cook asks if you wanted tea?"

The one thing I did not do was think of the house slowly emerging on Fifth Avenue. William was immersed in every detail. He went almost daily to the work site to see how things were progressing, and one morning he told me in exasperation that he was worried—where was the enthusiasm I had shown that day he'd taken me to McKim's office? Why had I not yet visited Goupil's?

It was clear that he expected me to relish this new occupation—what woman wouldn't love the opportunity to completely furnish and decorate a new home?—and I knew he was right. I hated that I could not manage excitement over the task. Millicent asked me at nearly every supper when I planned to start. So, in the hope that her enthusiasm would bolster mine, I asked her to accompany me to Goupil's one afternoon. I convinced myself I would enjoy it.

She arrived promptly at one o'clock. "I knew you were feeling better when you told me how anxious you were to begin," she said, smiling a bit too brightly when I met her in the entry.

"Yes," I said, putting on my gloves and cloak. "I'm quite looking forward to it."

She was visibly relieved. I realized with a start what a toll my friendship must take on her. I had never thought of it in those terms before. Impulsively, I squeezed her arm. "I appreciate all you've done for me, Millie, truly."

She looked surprised and a little embarrassed. "Why, Lucy, please don't speak of it. I *am* your friend."

"Yes, you are," I said.

We went to her waiting carriage. The sky was overcast and heavy, but it had warmed since yesterday so that the snow was melting and slushy on the edges of the walk, and the talk was of rain. There was a gray, foggy look about the streets, veiling the carriage windows so it was hard to see anything beyond muted colors and hazy shapes. The city felt closed in.

Jean-Baptiste Goupil was no longer the most fashionable importer in New York City, but my father had used him, as had many of the old Knickerbocker families I had grown up with, so I knew him well. His studios were small compared to some of the others, quite crowded with paintings and sculpture. The heavy curtains were closed against the sunlight, the room lit dimly by sputtering gas, and the ceilings were high and hung with paintings to the rafters. The smells of dust and canvas and oils were heavy as we came inside, the air close.

"Mrs. Carelton!" Jean-Claude, one of Goupil's assistants, came hurrying over to greet us. He wore a brown suit that almost exactly matched the brown of his hair—like a wren, I thought, with the same kind of fluttering, nervous movements. He took my cloak and Millicent's, handing them off to some faceless clerk while he ushered us deeper into the darkness. "Oh, Jean-Baptiste will be distraught to have missed you, but he is gone to see to a shipment today."

He called for some tea and led us to a table surrounded by three chairs and a settee. While Millicent and I settled ourselves, he hurried off for his notebook.

"Such an impressive display," Millicent murmured.

"Yes. Papa has always admired his taste."

A woman came with tea. Jean-Claude was back in moments, smiling beneath his thin mustache as he took a seat beside us, pulling at his absurd little tie. "You must tell your father, Mrs. Carelton, that we have just received the most glorious bronzes.

Jean-Baptiste has set one aside just for him. He believes it will be perfect for your father's parlor."

I could not think of a single spot in the parlor for another thing. I sighed, knowing already that Papa would buy whatever it was Goupil had set aside for him, as he always did.

"Now," Jean-Claude said, settling back, "I understand you are building a new home, Mrs. Carelton. I do hope we can be of service to you."

"I would not trust such a job to anyone else," I said. "My husband wants old masters. He particularly likes landscapes."

Jean-Claude scribbled in his notebook. "We shall look for some French portraits as well. I think Mr. Carelton will be suitably impressed, and they are increasing in value every day."

"Yes, of course."

"You must have some Chinese porcelains, Lucy," Millicent put in. She leaned forward eagerly. "And a few sculptures in the entrance hall. I've always loved alabaster."

"Yes, but just now it is the Pompeiian bronzes that are de rigueur." Jean-Claude scribbled again.

"Then the bronze," Millicent said. "But perhaps one or two marble pieces would not be out of place?"

"I think that would be delightful," Jean-Claude said.

"And tapestries. They must be Gobelins. Last year Julia Breckenwood bought counterfeits."

"I can assure you that would *never* happen here," Jean-Claude said.

"Nevertheless, it's worth mentioning," Millicent said. "One never knows. What do you think, Lucy?"

"Do you mind if I walk around a bit?" I asked Jean-Claude. "To look at some things myself?"

"Indeed not," he said. "Please do. There are some exquisite paintings just over there"—he waved to a far wall—"that I know you would find perfect."

"Thank you." I rose.

I ignored Millicent's surprise and left them there. I walked farther into glowing semidarkness, past brown landscapes and mythical scenes, a Venus rising from the sea, a Cupid sending his arrow into a rounded, dimpled Venetian exquisite. Although these were all paintings my friends would buy to hang in their already crowded dining rooms, I was impatient with them. I wanted something else, though I could not imagine what.

Beyond me was a curtain that obviously concealed a small room. I was curious. I could not remember ever being in there before. I pulled aside the heavy velvet and plunged into an alcove lighted by a single sconce. It was a tiny room, every inch covered with paintings hanging on golden cords. The gaslight cast everything in a murky glow; the images were like a kaleidoscope—too many of them, all jangling together, and I turned again to leave, overwhelmed.

Then I saw the painting.

It hung beside the curtains, and the velvet of the drapes half covered it, but what I saw was arresting. A woman's nude back, glowing white in the darkness like a ghost. She was not a woman, or at least not yet one. She was stone from the thighs down, but above that her flesh was pale and slightly tinted, obviously alive, and she was bending toward something. A strong, dark arm gripped her waist, and fingers cupped a breast. Despite myself, I was drawn to it. I pushed aside the draperies to see more, and I realized the arm belonged to a man: the sculptor, who was holding on to the woman with a desperate and hungry passion. She was bending to kiss him, an alabaster statue brought alive by the arrow of Cupid's bow. Pygmalion and Galatea.

I touched the canvas, tracing down her calf to her foot, still encased in marble, and it seemed I felt the chill cold of the stone. I longed to pull her foot free, to finish the job Cupid had started. I felt how she strained; I felt her restlessness.

"Mrs. Carelton? Mrs. Carelton?"

I snatched back my hand. The curtains parted, and Jean-Claude was there, an anxious Millicent close behind him.

"Oh," he said, smiling. "I see you have found Jean-Baptiste's special room."

"His special room?"

"I am surprised you haven't seen it before," Jean-Claude said. "This is where Jean-Baptiste keeps the things he has brought over for certain clients. Items he has chosen specially. Your father has been in this room many times." He glanced at the picture. "Ah, *Pygmalion and Galatea*. A fine work. It's a Gérôme. He's a student of David, I believe. This is reserved for Robert Carr. He asked specifically for a mythical scene for his guest room."

"I see." The news brought a keen disappointment.

"If you like it, perhaps we can find something similar for you," Jean-Claude went on. "This is the original. We could have it copied or perhaps find—"

"No," I said forcefully. "I don't want it copied. I want this one. I'll pay double what Robert Carr commissioned for it."

Jean-Claude looked dismayed. "Mrs. Carelton, I'm afraid I—"

"Has Mr. Carr even seen it?" I asked.

Reluctantly, Jean-Claude said, "I don't believe so, but—"

"Find him another mythical scene," I said.

Millicent broke in. "But Lucy, I thought you said William wanted landscapes."

I hesitated. William had indeed wanted landscapes, but surely he would not mind this one choice. I would put it in the sitting room he planned for me if he truly hated it.

"Yes, he does," I said slowly. "But I simply must have this Gérôme."

I saw the faint worry puckering Millie's brow, but I could not help myself. As I talked Jean-Claude into selling it to me, I felt the oddest sense of power, of strength—the same sense I'd had yesterday in the garden. As if there were some force directing my actions, something that was wholly myself, a freedom. . . .

What if you could be the woman you were meant to be?

It was only a painting, a single choice, but I felt a secret pleasure in it, and that pleasure frightened me—it was like the feverish days of poetry and religion. Perhaps my father was right after all, and I should not indulge my passions.

But I made arrangements for the Gérôme and told Jean-Claude that I would be back in a few days to see what else they had found for me. Afterward Millie and I enjoyed a pleasant luncheon, during which we spoke of ordinary things. Yet all the while I felt a guilty kind of joy.

When I arrived home, Dr. Seth's words haunted me. *What if you could be the woman you were meant to be?*

I went for my pencils and sketch pad and tried to forget Dr. Seth, and the Gérôme, and that persistent, guilty pleasure. I wished I had not gone to Goupil's at all.

The fear—and the secret pleasure—only increased over the next days. It was as if spring had lit within me. I drew feverishly and long and at every spare moment sketches of everything in the garden, and of Washington Square, where I now walked almost daily. Though I went to suppers and balls, I could not have told you when or where I'd been, what I'd done. I thought of nothing but my hidden sketchbook; my fingers ached constantly for a pencil.

I saw Dr. Seth twice a week. His treatment was working as he'd promised: I was calmer, less given to fits. But my dreams had grown strange. I could not stop thinking about Dr. Seth, and the images from my dreams intruded at the strangest times—when I was among my friends or choosing fabrics for the new house—leaving me distracted and troubled.

I found myself doing odd things, as I had at the Morris ball, when I'd removed my gloves. At the opera one night, as I stood in the lobby with Hiram Grace, listening idly to his latest harangue about the growing invasion of immigrants, I heard him as

I never had before. His complaints and opinions had never had any impact; I usually barely listened to him, but I *was* hearing him when he told me that he felt the surest way to eliminate crime and immorality was to keep degenerates from procreating and allow that right to moral men only.

"How could that succeed?" I asked, professing an opinion of something I'd never bothered to think of. "I've heard you say yourself that women possess smaller skulls, that they're less developed. How, then, can moral men pass on their superior intellect when the vessel for doing so is clearly inferior?"

Where the words came from, I had no idea. Someone who stood near us laughed, and Grace reddened in embarrassment before he moved quickly away.

I had never done such a thing before, and I was humiliated at my unkindness. Yet in my heart lurked that secret joy, the happiness of rebellion I'd felt as a girl. I was afraid of it, and horrified that it had gained sway. I didn't understand; it was not me who said those things, and yet I'd heard my own voice. Who could it be?

There were other things. I went to Goupil's, as William still expected me to do, and I found myself again ignoring his wish for landscapes. I was taken by bright colors and interesting scenes, by rustics and exotics. Jean-Baptiste urged caution; he had heard from my husband what he wanted, but I insisted. The only landscape I bought was a fuzzy Turner that was chaotic and interesting, and which I hoped William would like but sensed he would not. I purchased a sculpture of two people caught in an embrace, tangled about each other, nude, licentious, and was arrested by the feelings the sculpture raised in me. It made me frankly hungry, made me want to be touched. Such obscene thoughts, thoughts that were growing bolder and franker day by day and especially at night, when they tangled with my dreams.

I was myself and not myself. But it was not until the last night of the season, and the Fitzgeralds' masquerade ball, that I realized how strange I had become.

Chapter 12

The Fitzgeralds' masque was an annual event. Preparations had been made months in advance. This year the theme was Ancient Egypt, and William and I had long ago been fitted for our opulent disguises as Julius Caesar and Cleopatra.

But as the night of the ball approached, I began to view my costume with dread. It had too much gold appliqué, too much fringe, too many jewels about the golden girdle. I had once loved it, but now it offended me. Late one night I began cutting away all the ornamentation.

When I was finished, my urge to wear the costume was overwhelming. It was of gold and white tissue, with one shoulder completely bare. I wore my hair down, so it fell to the middle of my back, and adorned it with only a thick gold ruby-studded circlet to match William's fire: my one nod to my husband's ostentation, to his full red and golden Roman armor.

When I came down the stairs, William said, "Good God, what happened? That isn't what we asked for at all! Didn't you look at it before now, Lucy? Do you think there's time to rescue it? Moira! Moira!" When the maid came running, he said, "Fetch the seamstress who sewed this debacle. We'll have her fix it immediately. We'll be late, but there's no help for it."

"I did it," I admitted.

He stared at me, dumbfounded. "What?"

"I changed it," I said.

"Why?"

"It just seemed too much."

"Are you mad, Lucy? You'll be the poorest-looking woman there. What will they all think?"

"Let them think what they will."

"This is ridiculous." William began to pace the hall. I had to stifle an urge to laugh as his Roman skirt bounced against his knees; his feet looked so strange and bare in his open sandals. "You cannot go this way."

"I will not go any other way," I said. I wanted to wear this simple costume more than I could say. The thought of jewels and ostentation were anathema to me as they had never been before.

"I cannot afford to let them believe we're in financial trouble. Not after last year. I have clients, Lucy, who expect me— This doesn't befit our status."

"For heaven's sake, William, it's gold tissue. It cost a fortune." I came fully down the stairs. "Do you think I look ugly?"

He stopped and looked up at me. "No. No, of course not. You look beautiful."

"Then this is how I shall go."

He hesitated. "At least wear the ruby necklace I gave you last fall."

"No, William," I said gently.

He did not know what to make of me, I could tell by his sudden uncertainty, as if I had become as much a stranger to him as I was to myself. I could not explain my insistence, and I did not try as we went to the Fitzgeralds', where we were to meet Dr. Seth. He had met Stewart Fitzgerald at the Staten Island Athletic Club and secured his own invitation, much to my surprise and William's, though my husband took a possessive pride in having been the man who embraced Dr. Seth and introduced him to SIAC. It was still hard for me to assimilate Seth into my circle of friends, so personal was my relationship with him, and it was difficult to treat him as an acquaintance when it seemed I spent every moment with him, even in my dreams.

Dr. Seth was already inside, and I was surprised to see him equally simply dressed, in leather and linen, as Mark Antony, though we had never discussed it. He looked nothing like the doctor I knew; his glasses were gone, his legs bare beneath the Roman costume.

"What is this?" William asked as we approached him. "Mark Antony?"

"At your service." Dr. Seth made a little bow. He looked at me. "Mrs. Carelton, you look captivating."

"She does, doesn't she?" William said. "I would have preferred jewels, but she wished this. The two of you look quite matched."

I glanced at him, thinking I'd heard some little anger in his voice, but his expression was open and guileless. I felt vaguely uncomfortable. "It's quite a coincidence," I said. I looked at Dr. Seth, unsure. "We never discussed it, did we?"

He smiled and shook his head. "A coincidence, as you said. Nothing more. Shall we go inside? It all looks quite fantastic."

It was true; the Fitzgeralds had never skimped when it came to their decorations, and this year was no exception. There was golden satin draped to look like the pyramids of Giza, and there were bright sarcophagi, golden urns filled with palm fronds, burial masks, and stiffened muslin painted with desert scenes covering the walls. Dark blue bunting painted with sparkling stars billowed from the ceiling.

"Do I hear water?" William asked. "Is there a fountain?"

"The Nile," Seth said, nodding to the side of the ballroom, where there was indeed a sinuous trough of water about five feet wide. It trailed from the back of the ballroom, where a small or-chestra gathered, to the opposite wall. It appeared to sink into the floor, but if one looked closely, it was plain that the floor sloped upward to greet it. They had built a platform to house it, and sand covered its banks; rushes and palm trees bent toward it.

"Stewart has outdone himself this time," William said admiringly.

I knew what he was thinking: *When our house is built . . . What we will do then . . .* I turned from the pretend river and thought of how tonight was the end of the season. Lent began tomorrow. Until the summer, when we all retired to Newport, there would be no more of these balls where we each tried to outdo the other. Until August I would not have to endure parties or late suppers. I would not have to pretend.

I drank champagne and mingled with my friends. I felt William's eyes on me, but he let me go, and after a short time I lost him in the crowd. I tried not to think of Dr. Seth, though I knew where he was at every moment, and I knew he watched me as well.

Waiters dressed as Egyptian slaves began to circulate with trays of champagne. I had turned to take a glass when my hand met Millicent's as she reached for the same one.

"Lucy!" she said in surprise. She was dressed as an Egyptian priestess. "My, Lucy, you look lovely. Who would have thought such plainness would suit you?"

"William doesn't like it."

"You're not wearing his rubies."

"He was not happy about that either." There was a thoughtful set to her face that made me curious. I said, "What are you thinking, Millie?"

"You seem . . . changed," she said.

"Do I?"

"Less . . ."

"Caged?" The word came from my mouth before I could stop it.
She frowned. "Perhaps it's only the gown."

But it was not, and I knew it. "No," I whispered. I pulled Millie closer, half behind the open door of a sarcophagus, and said urgently, "It's more than that, Millie. I do feel different, and I don't know why. It's . . . I've been saying things and doing thing

I don't even understand. This gown . . . it wasn't like this at all. It was jeweled and beaded, and there was a girdle, and I couldn't stand it. I spent all night cutting it off."

She looked uncomfortable but not surprised. "Don't be silly, Lucy. It's quite striking. You're the center of attention."

"Yes," I told her miserably. "Because the gown is so plain. But it was not what I wanted. And Millie, I'm having the strangest dreams. I don't understand myself at all."

The silence was loud between us before she looked at me knowingly and said, "Hiram Grace."

"Yes." I gripped her arm, grateful that she understood. "Yes, exactly. I have no idea why I would mock him so. I care nothing for those things. Why, I never knew I had an opinion on them. And then that—to say that—it's not like me. I've never done such a thing before."

"You could not have picked a worse man, Lucy," she said. "You humiliated him. He's been saying that he thinks you were drunk."

"Drunk?"

"That's not all," Millie said in a low voice.

"What do you mean?"

"Your behavior's been noticed, Lucy. Hiram Grace is only part of it. Others are talking. They've seized on his idea that you're drinking. Some are even saying you're verging on mad."

"Oh, for goodness' sake."

Millicent turned, dislodging my hand, and gave me a look that was like a shake. It sent me shrinking into the corner. "Lucy, listen to me. I've meant to talk to you about this before now, but . . . It doesn't matter why I haven't. Are you still taking laudanum?"

I frowned at her. "Hardly. A small bit sometimes. I don't seem to need it so much."

"And you're still seeing this new doctor?"

Inadvertently, I searched for him. He stood at the punch bowl beside Hiram Grace, who was dressed as an Egyptian prince and looking absurd in the costume, with his white fleshy, hairy legs peeking from layers upon layers of what looked like gold foil. A headdress was slipping from his thinning gray hair. Beside him, the doctor looked young and vibrant. I felt his presence from across the room.

Millie had followed my gaze. "Him?" she asked. "Victor Seth is your doctor?"

I shook my head. "He's simply a friend."

I knew Millicent heard the lie in my voice. "Lucy, you have a husband who adores you. William would do anything for you; you've the funds and the position to have anything you desire. To turn elsewhere for happiness is foolish."

I stared at her, puzzled. "What do you mean?"

"You must be careful," she said. "Your behavior was acceptable as long as it was simply a fit now and then, or headaches. There isn't a one of us who hasn't felt the same. But no one will tolerate what you've been doing. You haven't had your calling day for weeks. Daisy Hadden said she saw you drawing in Washington Square, and when she spoke to you, you looked right through her."

"Daisy Hadden? I don't remember that at all."

Millie leaned close. "Tell me you didn't leave Julia Breckenwood's entertainment to sketch a picture of her garden, even when there was nothing there but vines and dirt."

"Well, yes, I did that, but—"

"Good Lord, Lucy, you must see how unacceptable that is. What is wrong with you? Ask Seth—or whoever your doctor is—to prescribe something else. Take the laudanum again if you must. After tonight the season is over. You have weeks before Newport. As your friend, I feel I must warn you: Take some rest, or whatever you must do to be yourself again. You know this. Clara Morris and Mamie Fish and the others will have nothing better to do in Newport than make you the summer's sport. They'll ruin you without compunction. The Van Berckel name will be no help to you then." She squeezed my arm. "Please, Lucy. Be careful. You must be careful."

She gave me a final pleading look, and then she left me standing there alone. I was afraid. I felt as if my friends stared at me when I passed. I imagined them turning to one another, I imagined their words.

The room wavered around me. I clutched my skirt in my hand and went searching for air, but the crush was such that I could not get through.

"Lucy."

It was as if I imagined his voice, coming as it did so strongly into my head. I stopped and turned to search for him, and he was there. He held two glasses of champagne, and he smiled and pressed one into my hand, tapping the bottom of the stem with his finger, urging me to drink it. I did, caught—as I always was—by his eyes.

The champagne eased the tightness in my throat. I curled my fingers around the stem and held it close to my lips.

"Breathe," he whispered, and I did. "Now," he said, "do you feel better?"

He seemed to read my mind, and the thought made me nervous. I laughed a little giddily and said, "How did you know?"

He nodded toward the doors that were closed against the night. "You were making a beeline for the window."

"You were watching me."

"That is my job."

"Yes," I said, taking refuge in the champagne. "Yes, of course."

"Come, let's get some air." He put his hand on my bare arm, urging me forward, but I did not move. He looked down at me with a little smile and said, "What is it, Lucy?"

Suddenly I understood. I wondered why I hadn't thought of it before this moment. The memory of that image he'd suggested to me so long ago—the walk in the woods, the bird—came back to me. "You knew," I whispered. "You've done this to me."

"Done what?"

"Changed me."

"Changed you?" He gave me a distracted smile and said, "Of course I have. It's what you wanted. You're having fewer fits. Aren't you happier?"

"Yes," I said. "No. I— There are so many strange things."

"What do you mean?"

"Why, tonight. This costume. You knew what I would wear tonight. That William and I were coming as Julius Caesar and Cleopatra."

"How would I know that?"

"I don't know," I said. "Perhaps I told you when I was asleep."

"You were never asleep."

"Whatever it was. That's what happened, isn't it? I told you I was coming as Cleopatra."

"If you did, I wouldn't have expected this kind of costume," he said. "I would have expected something a bit more . . . elaborate. How could I possibly know that you would choose this?"

That stopped me, but there was something wrong with his logic. His eyes were dark; was that truth I read in them? "I suppose that's true," I said reluctantly.

"Come," he said. "Let's talk about this outside." He urged me forward again. His hand had been on my arm all this time. I felt a flutter of fear, and of pleasure too. I could not deny the pleasure, and that frightened me more than anything else.

I told myself that I went with him only to be away from watching eyes. We went out onto the pavilion that at the beginning of the season would be lit by lanterns and candles, with the doors open to extend the ballroom into cool autumn nights. Dr. Seth closed the doors behind us, and the music turned faint and whispering, the steady hum of talk disappeared. Now there was only the night, and the two of us alone together.

As we often were, I reminded myself. It was all quite innocent. I pulled away from his hold and walked to the edge of the pavilion, where the marbled floor ended at the narrow lawn overlooking the Astor mansion next door. All the lights in that house were dim; I had seen Caroline Astor earlier that evening, holding court in Malva Fitzgerald's ballroom as if she owned it.

Seth's voice came to me across the darkness, nearly disembodied. "What is it that bothers you tonight, Lucy?"

"I don't understand myself," I said. "I've been doing things, saying things. People are beginning to talk."

"What are they saying?"

"That I'm drinking. Or worse."

"You aren't drinking."

"But they don't know that. Or they wouldn't believe it."

"Why do you care what they think?"

I turned to look at him. He stood near the door, haloed in the light coming through the windows. He could have been a god. "It matters to me what they think."

"You don't need friends like that."

I said disbelievingly, "How can you say such a thing? I want them to be my friends. To have them talk like this, they could ruin me. They will ruin William."

"What did he think of your costume tonight?"

The abrupt change of subject flustered me. "He was unhappy with me."

"Because of what you chose to wear? Or because of what your choice shows you to be?"

I crossed my arms; the air was freezing on my bare skin. I felt the rise of gooseflesh. "I don't understand."

"It's simple enough," he said. "You look unfettered tonight. Free. Like a woman of passion. Don't you feel so?"

I shivered. Did I feel pleasure or fear at his words? "I am not a woman of passion. I don't want to be one."

"Why is that?"

I laughed bitterly. "Look around you, Doctor. This is the world I live in. Would you have me live outside of it?"

"That's not up to me, Lucy," he said. He stepped closer. "My goal is only to help you find happiness."

"Yes. So you've said."

"Aren't you happier?" He was in front of me, only a few steps away. I felt his warmth. "In this costume, don't you feel more free? Since you've been drawing again? The truth, now."

"Yes," I said. "Yes, of course. But—"

"But there's so much more," he said. He stroked my cheek, and the touch made me uncomfortable, but I did not pull away. "Can you live within these constraints, Lucy? Think about the way you used to feel. When you read poetry. When you painted. Can you live without feeling that passion again?"

"I don't want to feel it." I heard my own voice as the merest of whispers.

"Yes, you do," he said quietly. "I understand you, Lucy. Look at me: You know it's true. I know what you want." His eyes were burning in the near-darkness. His hand was a comfort, and in that moment, I felt it was the only comfort available, the one I should take. His eyes urged it; I yearned for it.

I heard the pull of the latch, the scrape of the door. Seth's hand dropped. I jerked from him and saw William stepping from the shadows of the door.

"There you are," he said. "What are you doing out here? I've been searching for you."

"Lucy needed some air," Seth said mildly. "I was just bringing her in."

William nodded. "Thank you for seeing to her. It's time to come to dinner, Lucy. The first course has nearly started."

"Yes," I said, stepping around Seth to my husband, acquiescing when he took my arm possessively.

Notes from the Journal of
Victor Leonard Seth

Re: Eve C.

March 17, 1885

I have ceased making suggestions that Eve be calm; I no longer try to safeguard her unconscious with suggestions that she refrain from fits. My hope has been that with every suggestion I make that leads her closer to her passionate inner life, her hysteria will naturally cease, and I have found that to be the case. I have encouraged her drawing and made several suggestions during trance that she put aside the ostentation and social obligations that so obviously frustrate and constrain her. I have encouraged her to test the limits of the cage she finds herself in.

I have written to William James regarding my discovery and my experimentation, and have had a letter back from him and G. Stanley Hall urging caution. Hall in particular accuses me of attempting to play God. Yet what else is God but a manifestation of our will? What is a soul but the melding of our conscious and unconscious minds? I intend to prove that our will can be molded, that a "soul" can be created. I am creating a new woman—and succeeding beyond my greatest expectations. To have such astounding results through the use of hypnosis is something I could not have imagined. This is the kind of experimentation and research I had only dreamed of, those days in Nancy. I have come an even greater distance from my colleagues who still hold dear their insistence on the centrality of the somatic. In Eve there is a compelling argument for Beard's theory of mental therapeutics—that the will rules the body. Eve desires no children; therefore she becomes physically unable to have them.

She denies her sexuality and therefore becomes passionless. But I must go even further. I believe that the will itself is controlled by the unconscious mind. Eve's hysteria is proof of that. When her unconscious mind could no longer accept its subjugation to her will, it rebelled and caused her great illness. Now that I have allowed it power, her hysteria is gone.

The only question that remains is whether or not these changes will be permanent. If I can take her even further—if I can create in her the _need_ to be free, rather than a vague and simple longing—she may sustain them. She is still constrained by society's measure, and by her husband. These artificial chains must somehow be thrown off. How to do so?

It has not escaped my notice that Eve has recently become quite attached to me. This is quite common in patients of all types. At Nancy there were several women in the laboratory who desired a sexual relationship with their doctors. There forms a great attachment between patient and doctor, as is inevitable when one divulges one's greatest secrets. Hypnosis—especially for those who achieve trance through touch—can be quite seductive: putting oneself into the hands of another person, surrendering completely. This is the root of the fear my colleagues hold against hypnosis, and there _is_ a compelling aspect to such power. It can also be difficult to detach from such a relationship, though in my experience, it has seldom lasted long and is rarely completely satisfactory.

Yet I wonder. If I were to utilize this attachment, to show Eve what true satisfaction can be, to lead her ever further into the sublimity of the experience that her upbringing has kept from her—

The idea is tempting. Perhaps even intoxicating. To be able to mold her passion, to watch her come alive—I must admit to feeling a certain headiness over the possibilities.

Chapter 13

Once the season ended, I wanted to leave the city, to go somewhere—away from Seth, away from expectation. Away.

My friends were leaving; Millicent and her husband had gone to the Breckenwoods' country home for a month; the Villiards had departed for the continent, the Goelings to the South, to visit relatives. I had thought William would insist on attending one of these country affairs. In spite of the fact that he could not leave his work for long, we often spent the months after Easter visiting. But this year he refused to do so.

"There's the house," he told me, "and I cannot afford to leave just now."

So I spent my days drawing and longing for paints. I wanted to show William my sketches, but I remembered too well Papa's admonitions and my husband's solid acceptance of them. So I brought my sketches to Dr. Seth.

I had a case full of my work—studies I had made of the garden or the park. I drew these out and handed them to him one by one, sitting on the edge of my chair to hear his opinion, wanting his approval so much it was like a fever.

He said nothing. He leafed through them one after another,

with little expression in his face. When he was done, he handed them back to me, and my heart sank.

"You don't like them," I said, stuffing them blindly back into the case.

"On the contrary," he said. "I like them very much."

"You do?"

"Yes."

"Oh." I couldn't help my smile. "Do you think them good, then?"

He steepled his fingers before him. "What do you suppose William would think of them?"

"William? Why, he would hate them."

"Why do you think so?"

"Because he would. I know it. He'd rather I was spending my days shopping for trinkets and carpets and curtains. I tell you, I hate curtains. If I could, I'd have every window bare."

Seth looked thoughtful. "Why?"

"So I could see the outside. The sky, the trees . . ."

"If you cannot be among them, then you can at least see them."

"Yes, that's it exactly!"

"It's more than a longing to be outside, isn't it?"

I frowned.

"You can see it in your sketches," he went on, motioning to my case. "Every stroke of your pencil is in motion, every scene is open. There are no houses or windows. No dark places. I think you're right. I think William wouldn't like them. I think he would find them threatening."

"Threatening?"

Dr. Seth leaned forward, and his face filled my vision. "Every page shows your longing, Lucy. For freedom. For passion. Just think of what you could be if William encouraged you, if he wanted your passion." His hand dropped to cover mine, settling on my knee. "Just think of it."

I barely heard his words. He had curled his fingers around my hand. As if he realized my discomfort, he drew back again so quickly it was as if he hadn't touched me at all.

"Was there ever a time when William wanted your passion, Lucy?"

I did not need to search my memory; the scene was there. Seagulls and salt wind. Sand in my boots, the rising tide. The smell of seaweed in the sun and William's warmly astringent bay rum. *Do you really think that I could keep from you a single moment longer than I must? . . . Marry me.*

"I see there is," Seth murmured.

I shook away the memory. "It was a long time ago."

"Before you were married?"

"The day he proposed to me."

"Show me," Seth said.

Obediently, I began. "It was during the summer. My father and I were at Newport, and I hadn't seen William—"

"No." Seth rose from the chair and stood before me. "You must show me."

"I don't know what you mean."

"I will be William, and you must be yourself."

I was confused and a little appalled. "You mean I must act it out?"

"Yes."

"I fail to see what good could come of that."

"Because I believe that you have refused to feel such emotions since that day. I would like to know why. What did William do or say to show you that such feelings were anathema to him?"

"There's nothing—"

"We will try to see if we can reach some conclusion," he went on. "But you must try to describe your feelings to me as we progress. Now, where are we?"

Reluctantly, I said, "At Newport. Bailey's Beach."

"You went there together?"

"I was there alone. He came after me. It was the first time I'd seen him all summer."

"And you were angry."

"Of course I was angry!" I rose. "I had thought he no longer cared for me."

"Very good," he said. "Then let's proceed. You are on the beach, and I am William. I've just come upon you."

"I can't do this."

"You must try, Lucy," he said, and his voice lulled me into submission. "I've come upon you at the beach, and I say, 'There you are, my dear, I've been looking for you.'"

I shook my head. "No, no, it wasn't like that."

"How was it, then?"

"I was watching the surf, and he stole up behind me."

"And said?"

I turned my back to him, trying to remember. "Something about mermaids trading their fins for legs. How I reminded him of that."

"Very poetic," he said. "Very well. Lucy, my dear, you look very like a mermaid who's traded her fins for legs."

Not right, but this entire exercise felt so odd to me, I only wanted it to be over. I turned to face him. "William," I said, then nearly laughed at the ridiculousness of it. "I didn't expect you."

Dr. Seth gave me a chiding look. "I had trouble getting away."

"The entire summer?"

The doctor shrugged. "It's been a busy season. I came as soon as I could."

"You could have written. Or sent someone to explain."

"But I thought you would know," he said, stepping closer. "You must have known I would come if I could. You must know how much I love you."

I winced. "William was not so . . . passionate."

Dr. Seth raised a brow. "No? But I think that's how you wanted him, wasn't it? Passionate."

"Perhaps a little," I admitted.

Seth came closer still, only inches away, and he took my arms, lightly holding me in place. "It was a romantic evening, wasn't it? Near sunset?"

"Yes," I said. I began to feel a little breathless.

"The sky was pink. There were seagulls—"

"A single gull."

"A single gull. Dipping with a wind that was barely there. The waves were soft on the shore."

"Yes."

"You were longing for something. For me."

"Oh, yes. . . ."

"I love you, Lucy," he said. "I want to marry you. Say you'll have me."

"Why should I . . . have you?" I managed. My throat was dry. The doctor's face was wavering before me, so I could not see it clearly. "You're nothing to me. My father's stockbroker—I shouldn't care for you at all."

"But you do."

"Yes. I do."

"Then perhaps I can convince you how much *I* care," he said, and he kissed me, and for a moment I forgot it was not William; I closed my eyes, lost in the experience, in the hard softness of his lips. I opened my mouth to him and stepped closer and felt that dip deep in my stomach, that turning over, that yearning that made me moan against him and grip him.

"Is this what you want?" he whispered in my mouth, and I said, "Yes. Yes. . . ."

I was still saying *yes* as he drew back slightly, saying, "What do you want to say, Lucy?"

"Don't leave me," I whimpered. "Oh, why won't you take me there? Why must you leave me?"

"Because I'm afraid of you," he whispered back. "A woman like you, Lucy, would suck me dry. You're a vampire."

I felt as if I'd just awakened from a deep sleep, from too vivid dreams. I opened my eyes and broke away, seeing not William but the doctor, his expression contorted and angry, speaking the words William had never spoken but which I knew were true.

"Oh dear God," I said, putting my hand to my mouth, trembling.

Impatiently, Seth said, "Isn't that what he would say?"

"Yes. Yes. But how do you know this?"

"You forget, I know William. I've talked to him. Do you think he's so different from anyone else? Half the men on Fifth Avenue think the same way." Seth turned on his heel and strode to his desk. "No doubt he's even afraid of self-gratification," he said contemptuously. "Such absurd ideas run rampant among supposedly learned men. To think that a woman's passion can steal the energy from a man . . ."

"It's not true?"

"There are no scientific grounds for such a belief, only moral claptrap."

"And morality cannot be truth?" I asked.

He was at his desk riffling impatiently through papers, but when I asked the question, he stopped and looked at me. "Do you think you're a vampire, Lucy?"

"Sometimes," I said carefully, "I believe that marriage has taken the best from William."

"Really? I rather think the opposite."

"The opposite?"

"That marriage to William has taken the best from you."

I could say nothing to that.

"I believe," he said, leaving his desk and coming toward me, "that William felt your passion that day at the beach—it would have been impossible not to—and it frightened him. I believe this is one of the reasons he's never encouraged it. The only question is why he went ahead and married you, if passion was not what he wanted."

"Perhaps he wanted love," I said.

"Or social advancement?"

"He does love me."

"Conditionally," Dr. Seth said. "If you were to give in to your passion, do you think he would accept it?"

I knew the answer, but I would not tell the doctor. "We both had expectations when we married," I said stubbornly. "I know of no one who doesn't."

"I'm not speaking of expectations," he said. "I'm speaking of conditions. What were yours, Lucy?"

I could not answer.

"You said: 'Why won't you take me there?' What there did you mean?"

"I don't know," I said. I felt undone. I could not think. "It was just something I said. I don't know."

"Perhaps you should think on it," he told me. "What was it you wanted from your marriage? Did you perhaps think that at least one aspect of your longing could be fulfilled? Did you think your husband would satisfy your desires? Or did someone tell you that only coarse women experience sexual fulfillment?"

"My father," I whispered. "My husband."

"Ah," he said with a sharp smile. "The two men who have kept you in chains. Tell me, Lucy, what does your husband call you when he makes love to you? 'My angel'? 'My savior'?"

Startled, I said, "A-angel."

"A man worships angels, he does not screw one."

His crudeness brought tears to my eyes. I backed away from him. "How can you say such things to me?"

"I'm trying to help you, Lucy," he said, and his voice softened. His eyes became gentle. He came over to where I was, nearly at the door. "Do you remember how you feel when you're drawing?"

"Yes," I said.

"And when your mother drowned, wasn't there a moment when you envied her?"

"For dying?" My voice was shaking.

"For escaping," he whispered. "For finally being free."

I could not deny it. He reached for my cloak and put it around my shoulders, fastening the clasp. I fancied that his hands lingered there overlong, that his fingers stroked my shoulder.

"Come, now, Lucy," he said tenderly. "I want to help you to be free."

When I returned home, Harris informed me that William was at the building site and would be home late, so I had the hours to myself. I went to my bedroom and stood at the window looking out, thinking over what Seth had said, and my body yearned. I allowed myself to think of how I'd felt in his office, and I could not deny that I wanted it again—but this time with William. It had been the overriding sense in my dreams, what I'd searched for in every painting I'd bought, every sculpture. I wanted to feel passion with my husband that was real and welcomed.

I changed into my dressing gown and stood again at the window, watching the sun go down and gild the sky above Washington Square. I watched the carriages and the fading light and knew exactly how the air felt; the days were reluctant to give up their growing warmth to the night.

I asked Moira to send William to me when he arrived home. I told her that I would take supper in my room, but when she brought the plate, I let it lie there. I took the glass of wine and drank that—for courage as much as any other reason, though the truth was that I did not feel nervous or afraid about what I was to do. It seemed I'd been waiting on such an occasion for some time; it was my doctor who had brought it to the fore.

I saw him come home. He stepped out of the cab and came

up the stoop with rushing steps, as if he could not wait to be here. I wondered if he did that every day, or if there was simply some good news to tell—good enough to make him want my inconvenient company.

The door opened and closed; there were voices in the hall, Harris's soft whisper, William's boom. He did not come up right away. He would go to his study, of course, and pour himself a drink. I knew his habits better than my own. When, moments later, I heard his step on the stair and the soft knock on my door, I turned with the words already on my lips.

"Come in."

He stepped inside, closing my door behind him. He held a glass of bourbon in his hand. On his face was a look I had seen many times before. It was wary.

I smiled at him. "Which Lucy will you find today?" I teased. "Isn't that what you're thinking? Will I be hysterical or sad or disobedient?"

"I would prefer," he said slowly, "that you be the wife welcoming her husband home."

"I am that," I told him. "Welcome home."

He frowned at me. "What ails you, Lucy?"

"Nothing at all. I feel fine, in fact."

"Did you see Victor today?"

"Yes. I've missed you," I said.

"Well, I've been quite busy. You know that. I've taken on two more clients at the 'Change, and what with the house and the clubs—"

"I don't mean today," I said. I put down my wineglass and moved toward him. "I mean that I miss the man you were; the man I married."

He looked confused. "What's this about?"

"Do you remember that day at the beach, William? The day you proposed to me?"

"Of course I remember it," he said, though he squirmed a little, and I was not sure he told the truth.

"Do you remember kissing me?"

He went still. His hand gripped his glass. "Yes."

"You never kiss me. I don't think you've kissed me since the night we wed."

"I've kissed you," he said.

"On the cheek. Chaste pecks to wish me good morning and good night. I miss the way you kissed me then."

He looked a bit displeased. "You do?"

"Why wouldn't I?"

Carefully, he said, "I would think, with your delicate sensibilities—"

"I wish you'd offend them," I told him. I came closer, though we were still so far apart. We had long since grown accustomed to space between us. To be close . . . it felt awkward to me, and there was no doubt he felt the same.

"I don't understand."

"Maybe once or twice I'd like you to . . . kiss me."

He set down his glass so hard bourbon spilled on my dressing table. "What's this about, Lucy?" he demanded. "What's got into you?"

"Nothing," I said. I took a deep breath and went right up to him, inches away. I touched his arm, letting my hand linger there. "I love you, William. I should think we could . . . celebrate . . . our feelings for each other."

I let my hand slip to his chest, to the buttons of his vest. I slipped one loose and pushed inside to feel the warmth of his chest through his shirt.

"What are you doing?" he whispered.

"Touching you," I said.

"Good God, Lucy."

"Ssshhh." I stretched on tiptoes to brush my lips against his. He backed away so quickly his head banged on the wall, and I smiled. "Come, William," I said. "I'm your own wife. How can this be wrong?"

He grabbed my wrist, keeping me from the fastenings on his shirt. "You are a lady," he said.

"I don't want to be a lady tonight." I twisted loose of his hold and kept on undoing buttons, pressing my hand past fabric to touch his skin. I kissed him again, whispering against his mouth, "Take me to bed, William. Please."

"Damn it, Lucy," he murmured. He held my hands again, stilling them. "Have you been drinking?"

"Not a drop," I lied.

He took my arm and pulled me to the bed. "You should lie down. It's clear you're not yourself."

I sat upon the mattress and grabbed him before he could back away. I looped my arms around his neck, pulling him down to me. "Please, William, don't leave me. I—I want you to stay. Please, stay."

He hesitated, and I took the opportunity to kiss him, opening my mouth against his lips, touching them with my tongue. He stiffened in obvious surprise, and I pushed my way into his mouth until I felt him relax, until I felt him surrender. When his hands slipped past the ties of my gown, I moved to allow him greater access. He pushed impatiently at the chemise I wore, jerking it up over my hips, unfastening his trousers. I had wanted to feel his skin on mine, something I had never truly felt. I wanted his hands on my breasts. I wanted the things I had only imagined. But though I had pushed William past endurance, nothing else would change. He did not touch me except to thrust inside me, but I was desperate enough to take even that. I raked my hands through his hair and held him tight to me so he could not put distance between us, so he could not run when I twisted my hips against his. But William spent himself quickly, and after that he did not linger. He rose as if the touch of my skin was unbearable. He fastened his trousers and looked at me as I lay with my legs spread, yearning, my chemise rucked above my hips.

"For God's sake, cover yourself, Lucy," he said. "You look like a common whore."

Then he left me.

I pushed down my chemise and tied my dressing gown about me, and I sat on the edge of my bed, burning and unsatisfied. I tried to think of that day on Bailey's Beach, to remember a long-ago kiss that had promised something more than this, but it was hazy, like a dream I couldn't quite remember. What was clear was the memory of this afternoon, of a mouth that opened to mine as William's never had.

Notes from the Journal of Victor Leonard Seth

Re: Eve C.

April 14, 1885

We have acted out the first time Eve C. apparently felt and recognized sexual desire, with mixed results. Though Eve was obviously aroused and enlightened, her husband was concerned about his later encounter with his wife, which he explained to me in deepest confidence when we met today at SIAC. He expects Eve to be a well-bred lady, and thereby passionless, and he is concerned that I mean to turn his wife into a whore. I restrained myself enough to explain that this is all part of Eve's treatment, and that it is only with the full exploration of all aspects of her unconscious that we can help her.

I reminded him of the masquerade ball, when she

showed no evidence of depression or hysteria (at least to his knowledge; I didn't inform him that I had staved off a possible fit). This was a mistake—he mentioned his worry that people are gossiping about her behavior—but it did remind me of the greatest threat to my treatment of Eve: that her husband will realize what I am attempting to do and remove Eve from my care. I reassured him this time, but I must be more careful in the future. I cannot risk him discovering my intentions toward his wife—at least not until it is too late for his actions to affect them.

My colleagues will be astounded when I present my findings at the Neurology Association meeting this year. When I think of how the scientific community will respond to my discovery, I am reassured that what I'm doing is the right thing, the best thing. Such an achievement is the pinnacle of all I have reached for, studied for, worked for. To have it hinge on one woman seems remarkable. It is not surprising that I think of her constantly, that my mind persists in working out the puzzle of her, that deep into the night, I debate the best way to proceed. I am consumed by her.

Chapter 14

The next morning William left early for the 'Change. When he returned that evening, we sat at dinner—ever the civilized couple—and did not refer to the night before. If we did not talk about it, it would be as if it never happened. The night was put away, folded into a drawer that was already full of things we never talked about.

I felt guilty and ashamed. I had become someone I didn't know. The urges that came more often, more intensely, the desire that plagued my sleep—these things did not belong to me, yet they seemed increasingly to be mine. I began to understand, as I had not before, the things I wanted: to spread my wings, to fly. But these were not what I'd been taught to want, and they seemed infinitely dangerous. Who would I be without the life I'd been trained to live?

The next days I lived in this hinterland, feeling the memory of desire curling like a wretched traitor inside me. I spent more time than ever in the garden, which was bursting to life in the spring days. The cherry had bloomed and was lush with glossy green leaves. Crocuses and snowdrops had given way to tulips and then to lilacs. Birds began to frolic in the marble bath I filled for their pleasure. I sketched the changes every day, as if by measuring the garden's growth, I could decide my own.

I fought my longing for Dr. Seth; instead I tried to engage a husband who looked upon my efforts with tolerant wariness. We had grown used to our progression away from each other, and I sensed that William was happier ensconced in the parlor, smoking a cigar and reading, than he was talking with me. I wanted to cry out to him, to warn him that I felt myself sliding away, that he would lose me, and that I did not want to be lost.

Then came the day that Goupil's delivered the crates. I had Harris pry open the wooden boxes, and as the pieces I'd bought emerged, I realized with a shock that each thing I'd chosen— every one—was an example of how tortured my thoughts were. It was no wonder Jean-Claude and Jean-Baptiste had been distressed; I must have seemed nearly unbalanced.

I knew I should send everything back before William came home. But I could not. I kept opening the boxes, each painting, every sculpture, the Turner and the bronze of the couple entangled in a kiss, until I reached what I'd been searching for: the Gérôme.

Gingerly, I took the canvas from its crate. I set it on a chair in the hall and stood back to stare at it. There was a part of me that hoped it would no longer arouse the same emotions.

But it did. Its effect was even greater than I'd remembered. The picture made me think of Dr. Seth, and that was so pleasurable and shameful that I grew flustered. I left the painting and went into the garden, forgetting about William.

He called me almost the moment he arrived home. When I came to him, he motioned to the art littering the hallway. He pointed to the painting—set as it was on a chair, separate from the others. He looked not angry but disturbed. "What is this, Lucy?"

"That's a Gérôme. *Pygmalion and Galatea.*"

"Well, yes, I see that," he said. "What's it doing here? What is all this doing here?"

"They're the things I've chosen for the new house," I said, clasping my hands tightly before me. "They've just arrived from Goupil's. The Gérôme was quite difficult to procure. It was meant for Robert Carr."

"No doubt it would look better on his walls than on ours. I thought we agreed on landscapes."

I felt something twist and give inside of me, some last remnant of desire, the frustration of longing. "I liked it," I whispered.

He shook his head with a smile and came to the stairs where I stood. He put his hand over mine on the banister. He smiled indulgently. "My dear, you know Jean-Baptiste won't hesitate to foist a rejected import onto someone else. You really shouldn't let him push you into something you don't want. I'll have to go with you to make sure this doesn't happen again."

I wanted to fight him. But that was wrong, that wasn't me. I was the woman who surrendered to her husband, who wanted to be his queen, who wanted his house to be his castle.

"Yes," I said weakly.

He patted my hand. "Send it back to Carr, Lucy. If Jean-Baptiste bought it for him, then he must be the one to take it. Send it all back."

"Very well," I whispered.

"What has Cook prepared for supper this evening? I hope it isn't mutton again."

He left me, laughing to himself, shaking his head at my folly as he went into his study. When he was gone, I stared at the painting of the woman emerging from stone, and I understood how it all must look to him, how insane I must seem. The whisper came to me: *like your mother,* and abruptly I remembered how she had stepped into the Hudson that summer, how purposeful she'd been.

*   *   *

"He's sending it all back, of course," I said dully. "I am not to be allowed to choose anything more for the house." I laughed a little. "Except angels for the bathrooms."

"Angels?"

"William has a taste for them," I told him. "He has been quite specific. They must be Romantic. Fat little cherubs with wings too small to carry them."

"Like Cupids, then."

"Yes."

I stood near the window, leaning against the bookcases. The sunlight was streaming in, heating the little room unbearably, raising the musty scent of dust.

Dr. Seth was sitting indolently but he watched me with careful attentiveness. I felt a shiver at it—a shiver of anticipation—and in distress, I shook it away.

"Will there be anything of you in the house?" he asked.

"Why, Doctor, it will all be me," I said lightly. "Don't you realize that my husband's taste is mine? Ella Baldwin did her entire home in leaves and stuffed birds simply because her husband has naturalist leanings."

"While William leans toward angels."

"Cupids."

"Cupids, yes, as you said."

A man worships angels, he does not screw one. I could not look at him any longer. I sighed. "Papa only encourages it. I think William's tastes might really be more subdued, given where he comes from."

"Where is that?"

"His father was a lawyer. His mother a seamstress, I believe."

"The working class?" Seth sounded surprised.

"Oh, a bit above that. They were highly respected, I gather."

"You gather. Don't you know?"

I shook my head. "I've never met them."

"Are they dead, then?"

"William's never said."

"And you don't find that strange?"

"William is quite ambitious. It bothers him enough that people know he's not quite of our class. He would hate for them to know the details."

"Yes, but you're not 'people.' You're his wife."

"Yes. That doesn't necessarily mean we're confidants."

"No?"

"No. It's hardly unusual. Most of my friends—"

"You said your friends know William is not of your class. Does this offend them?"

I shrugged. "If it did, they'd never say. At least not to my face."

"Why is that?"

"Because he was my choice. And as you said once—because of who I am." He sat with his elbows balanced on the armrest, his hands clasped before him, listening. "In the end they'd accept anyone my father and I brought before them. They knew almost nothing about William. But I loved him, and my father approved. That was all they needed."

"And what about you?" he asked. "Did you need more? Did it distress you to know so little of William?"

"I know nothing of you either, and you hold my deepest secrets."

"I'm your doctor," he pointed out, "not your husband. There's no need for you to know anything of me."

"What if I want to know?" I asked him, though I had not meant to; I had not even wondered about him before this moment. I had taken what I knew about him—his castaway Jewishness, the degrees on the walls of his office, his books—and those things had formed my opinions of him. He had sprung to me fully formed: Where he came from, who he was, had not mattered. But now I wished to know more. "What if I insist you tell me something of yourself?"

He was quiet for a moment. Then he said, "It's unnecessary. It could even be harmful."

"How could it be harmful?"

"Should a child know its parents' secrets?"

"I'm not a child."

"I should be a mystery to you, Lucy."

I felt oddly as if I wanted to cry. "I don't want you to be a mystery."

"This is not unusual, what you're feeling."

"Isn't it?" I asked bitterly. I could not help myself; I went to stand before him. "Is this what all your patients insist on, then?"

He looked at me calmly. "Most of them," he said. "At one time or another."

I felt an irrational surge of jealousy. "Have you made such strides with all of them? Do you understand all of them the way you understand me?"

He hesitated. Then he rose and took my arms, holding me loosely, rubbing his thumbs against my silk sleeves. "None of them are like you, Lucy," he said, and there came into his eyes a look that made me both afraid and glad. I pulled away from him and stepped back, though there was a part of me that wanted to stay.

"So in the end, you're just like William," I said. "You're just like my father."

"I am nothing like them," he said angrily. I'd never seen him be anything but in control, and though it made him more human, more of a man, I was distressed by it. I think he saw that. The anger left his face after a visible struggle for control, and then he was mine again, the doctor I knew, and I was reassured.

"You said I was like your father," he said. "How is that? Was he a mystery to you?"

"It's as you said," I told him. "There are things a child should not know about a parent."

He took a deep breath and sat down again. "Which do you

mean? Do you mean that you're relieved he's a mystery, or that there are things you wish you didn't know about him?"

"My father is a tyrant," I said simply. "There was a time, when I was a small child, when he was a god to me. But then I saw his flaws, and if a god has flaws, how can he remain a god?"

"Most gods have flaws," Dr. Seth said. "Even your God. He punishes beyond rationality. He changes His mind. He demands sacrifices to His ego. Like any common man. Science has no ego. It's rational and logical."

"Science has all the answers?"

"Yes."

"So there can be no mystery?"

Seth shook his head. "In the end, all things can be explained."

"Can they?" I smiled bitterly. "Can love be explained?"

"A change in the brain," he began, "purely physical reactions. Love is entirely somatic."

I thought of the way my body had yearned for my husband. Of the way I'd once felt about him, the racing of my pulse, the shortening of my breath, the excitement I'd felt when he came into a room. "Yes," I murmured. "Perhaps so. And hate?"

"Hate is learned," he said with certainty.

That I knew was true. "Yes," I said. "I learned to hate my father. How easily love turns."

"In the face of unbearable flaws," he said gently.

"Is that how you lost God?" I asked.

Dr. Seth smiled. "You're searching for answers to me again, Lucy."

I nearly held my breath. "Yes. But it's such a little thing, isn't it?"

When I thought he would refuse me, I felt desperate. I could not explain why I wanted to know this so badly, or why it should matter, only that it did.

Then he said, "Unbearable flaws. Things I could not reconcile. Little injustices."

I felt a rush so dizzying it was as if he had filled my lungs with his words. "But we all experience that. We don't all turn away from God."

"No," he said, and then he pierced me with those too knowing eyes. "But we don't all turn away from life either, do we?"

I was struck by his words. I thought of myself, yielding to my father, to a husband I barely knew. Packing up the Gérôme, hiding my sketching, buttoning up my passion. Little injustices.

I had allowed William to do this to me. Suddenly it was unbearable, to be so worshiped and untouched, to be denied as if I were nothing more important than a pretty doll. I wanted a husband who knew me and accepted me. I no longer wanted to hide. I wanted life.

I said, "You think that I should show William who I really am. You think I should insist against . . . angels."

"Cupids, I believe you said it was."

"Angels," I told him. "I meant angels."

I went home. Once there, I went to my room and took from beneath the bed my case of sketches. They were crumpled, the charcoal broken into little bits from how rapidly I'd put them away. Now I laid them upon my bed, smoothing them as best I could, then I took the pile of them downstairs into the parlor that had once served as my mother's ballroom. I drew open the curtains to let the sunlight in, and then I laid out the sketches—some on the upholstered window seat, some on the table, over the settee. There were so many of them. But of the best there were twenty in all, and when I looked at them, I felt a sense of accomplishment, of pride, of pleasure.

I stood in the middle of the room, so nervous I could not be still. I touched the sketches, smudging a little here, wishing I'd thought to bring the charcoal with me so I could fix a line, a shading. I wanted them to be perfect. Dr. Seth had seen me in them, who I was, what I wanted to be. I prayed William would see the same things. I did not allow myself to think of this as a desperate attempt to stave off the sense that I was leaving him behind, or the truth of my increasing awareness that I would never be happy with William.

By the time the sun began to dip low in the sky, I was so nervous I could barely contain it. When I heard William arrive home, my heart beat irregularly. I went to the doorway so I could hear him ask Harris where I was. I heard the butler answer that I was in the upstairs parlor.

He did not come up right away. First he went to pour a drink, and then I heard the heaviness of his step on the stairs. Then he was at the door of the parlor, looking in with a puzzled expression and saying, "Lucy? What's going on?"

I should have realized then. I should have hurried him from the room and swept up the sketches and kept them secret. I should have known by looking at him that the day had been hard, that he'd suffered disappointment, that he was weary. But I rushed to him, pulling him into the room, saying breathlessly, "William, I've something to show you."

I pulled him so impatiently to the drawings on the table that his drink splashed over the side of his glass, smearing the charcoal. It was a sketch of Washington Square, and in dismay, I grabbed my handkerchief and dabbed at it, trying to make it right again, and when it was not, I cried out, "Oh, but now it's ruined!"

William pulled it away from my ineffectual patting and said, "What's this?"

"It was Washington Square," I said.

"I can see that," he said. Then it was as if he was just noticing the others. His gaze swept the room, alighting first on one, then another. I stood there while he took a slow turn about the room, looking and looking, so silently. I felt an overwhelming sense of pride that was so elating I could only stand there, waiting for him to see, to know.

"Who did these?" He was bent over the ones at the window seat, staring at them intently.

"I did."

"You did?" He straightened and stared at me so incredulously that I had to smile. I rushed over to him and grabbed his arm in my excitement.

"Yes, yes. I did them. I've been working on them since the start of February—months now—you can't imagine how much I've loved it. It's starting to be quite colorful—I was hoping to get some paints, and then you would see—"

He was still staring at me, but his incredulousness had faded. In its place was a distress that completely stole my words.

"You drew these?" he asked slowly.

"Y-yes."

"You?"

"Well, yes, William." I reached around him to pick up the nearest one, but he grabbed my wrist, keeping me from reaching it.

His words were too careful. "I thought you were forbidden to paint again."

"I haven't painted. It . . . it's charcoal."

He shook my arm impatiently. "You were forbidden!"

"By my father," I said, "not by my husband."

He sighed and went to the window seat. He stood looking at the pictures, and I saw a deep sorrow in him before he swept up the drawings and crumpled them in his hands.

I cried out and ran to him, reaching past him, trying to save them, but he wrenched away from me. Before my eyes, he tore the drawings into bits and scattered them over the carpet. I raced before him to save the others, but I tripped over my skirts, falling against the settee, and could only watch helplessly while he destroyed those as well. He took each drawing and tore it until the floor was littered with bits of paper, and when he was done, he came to stand before me, his chest heaving as if he'd just come from the athletic club.

"Where are the rest?"

I buried my face in my arms. "There are no others."

He jerked my arms away. "Where are they?"

"I tell you, there aren't any."

He was gone before I could finish. I heard him on the stairs, and in horror I knew he was going to my bedroom, where he would see how many there were.

I ran after him, barely seeing Moira, who stood trembling in the hallway. I lifted my skirts and rushed up to my bedroom. William was already inside. On my bed was my case, the box of charcoal, the pile of sketches. William took them up, and I launched myself at him, grabbing his arm.

"Please, William. Please don't . . . let me explain."

"Explain what?" he asked impatiently. "Explain how obsessed you've become again?"

"No, no. You can't take this away from me. Not now . . . Oh, please, William." I pushed against him, trying to take his face between my hands, to keep him still, but he would have none of me. He pushed me away so roughly I fell, and then he threw the case into the fireplace. The fire caught and leaped, consuming the case, the papers; they curled into ash, the smoke filled the room.

Then he turned to me and said, "It was Seth who told you to do this, wasn't it? Wasn't it?"

Teary and stunned, I shook my head. "You don't understand."

"I understand enough. I told him how ill this made you before. You won't be seeing him again."

"No," I said, crawling to my feet. "No, William, please. You can't do this."

"You are my wife, and I know what's best for you. And this"— he motioned to the fire, to me—"this is clearly not it. Painting, again, for God's sake. He must know what will happen."

"William, please."

He twisted away, and I slumped against the wall, blinded by tears.

"I'll send a messenger to him tonight telling him that I'm ending your treatment." Then he gave me a terrible, pitying look and said, "This is for the best, Lucy. It's all for the best."

He closed the door, leaving me in the smoky room with the ravenous, crackling fire, and for a moment I could not move. I could see nothing but that my life was over, that I was a prisoner forever.

Without thinking, I grabbed my cloak and my hat and ran from the house.

Chapter 15

There was only one person I wanted to see.

As I reached Broadway, I saw an oncoming stage. I hailed it and felt an overwhelming relief as it stopped and the driver said, "Climb aboard, ma'am."

It was awkward to make the step, and the stage started even before I was inside, so that I nearly fell into the lap of a businessman who was engrossed in his newspaper. I mumbled an apology and slipped into the seat beside him, clasping my naked hands together. I had forgotten my gloves.

There were three other men aboard, all dressed like businessmen, and they spared me only a glance before politely sliding their attention elsewhere. We tried not to bounce into one another as the stage made its uncomfortable way down Broadway.

A small gong sounded, startling me. The men were all moved to action, each reaching into his coat pocket and pulling out a coin, then tossing it into a small basket lowered through a hole in the roof. The fare. I'd forgotten the fare.

"How much is it?" I asked.

"Ten cents," said the man with the paper.

I made a show of reaching into the pocket of my cloak, of

pulling it aside to search for a purse, though I knew already there would be no money. Shopkeepers sent the bills directly to my husband.

My movements became more frantic. I tried to stem my mounting embarrassment and horror—I could not pay, and it was too far to walk, and I must get there, I could not go back home.

The man beside me touched my arm, and I froze.

"Let me get this for you," he said, reaching into his vest pocket, tossing up the coin. His face was kind. "My wife forgets her bag from time to time."

"Yes, that's just what I did," I said, my words stumbling over themselves. "It was so silly. Thank you. Thank you so much."

"Some days are like that, eh?" He brought up his paper again, burying himself within it, and I had to bite my lip to keep from crying in sheer gratitude.

The ride seemed so long. I stared out the window, but I could see nothing but the fire licking at the paper of my sketches, Washington Square curling into ash. The sorrow and pity on William's face fueled my anxiety, until I nearly jerked loose the string signaling my stop on White Street. I gave a smile to the man who'd paid for my trip, and he tipped his hat to me, and then I jumped from the stage into a puddle of mud that splashed into my boots and wet the hem of my gown. I hardly cared; I was too busy looking at the building before me. It was dim, the store beneath was dark. For a moment I thought I would have to break the glass to get in, but the door was unlocked.

When I reached his office door, it was locked. I tried the handle again, sure I was mistaken. Of course he was there; where else would he be? I rattled it until I was sure it would come loose. Then I knocked on the glass window that bore his name in black and gilt letters. Harder and harder until finally a light came on. I nearly cried in relief. I saw a shadow behind the patterned glass, and I laid my hands flat upon it and burst into a smile. When it opened, I nearly fell into his arms.

"Oh, thank God you're here. You'll never—"

I stopped short of pitching myself into him, because it wasn't Victor at all. It was Irene, looking annoyed.

"Mrs. Carelton," she said. "Whatever are you doing here at this hour?"

"I want to see him," I said firmly, pushing my way past her to the office door. "Where is he? I demand to see him."

"He's not here," she said, rounding me, blocking my access. "Really, Mrs. Carelton, he's not here. You should go home. I'll be sure and tell him in the morning—"

I pushed past her. The door was open, and I burst through.

"Mrs. Carelton, please. He went home hours ago."

"Home?"

"Yes, of course. Where else would he go now that his appointments are done?"

"And where might home be?"

She hesitated only a moment. Then she went to the desk and scrawled out the address on a scrap of paper. She handed it to me, and I turned on my heel without even a thank-you. The paper was precious; I wrapped my fist around it and headed to the door.

"You might want to have your driver take a weapon, ma'am," she said. "It can be dangerous in that part of town."

I went out the door and closed it behind me. When I was standing on Broadway, I opened my fist and looked at the paper. The address was unfamiliar; I did not even begin to know where to go, and the stage was already gone.

A street sweeper was raising the scents of manure and garbage down the way. I hurried over to him and said, "Excuse me, but could you tell me where Essex Street is?"

He gave me a queer look, one almost too familiar, that took

in my lack of a bustle or gloves. "Essex Street? You sure you want to go there, lady?" he asked.

I assured him I did.

"Go up a block," he said, "and then take Canal Street to the East River."

Canal Street. The East River. I felt faint. "Are you sure?" I asked. "I fear you must be wrong. It couldn't be—"

"Well, it is," he said. "You want to know the direction or not?"

"Yes, yes. Please."

"When you get to Allen Street, turn left. Essex crosses it. You'll have to ask around there for who you're lookin' for."

"Allen Street," I said.

"You'd best take care, lady," he said, and then he went back to his sweeping.

I could not seem to move. The twilight was coming on strongly, the sky darkening. Soon the arc lights would come on, the rest of the world would be cast in darkness, and I was alone here on Lower Broadway.

I should go home. I didn't belong here. Not here, and certainly not on Canal Street, or Allen Street, or any of those little streets that gathered beneath Houston and stretched to the East River. I should not be here. I should be at home. With William. I should be living the life I was meant to lead.

Before I knew it, I had started to walk up Broadway, past the street sweeper, ignoring the stares and curious glances of those who wondered what a lady alone was doing on Lower Broadway at twilight. I walked quickly, afraid I would change my mind, grow weak somehow in my own steps. I knew if I went home, if I went back to William now, I would never see Victor Seth again.

The night began to come down around me, and still I walked. Canal Street began as retail shops and warehouses, and as it went on, the streets on either side became narrower and dingier, the smells grew stronger, less familiar—fish and sausage and garlic and garbage and manure—and the buildings changed from warehouses to small frame houses nearly falling apart.

The streets were muddy and strewn with garbage. Pushcarts were being led slowly home, moved by men and women with weathered faces and gray clothes, holding what fish or rags or tin had not been sold. I pushed past a woman with cages of chickens that squawked loudly as I went by, and she screamed after me in some foreign guttural language.

It was as though I had entered another world. I was afraid and more certain with every passing moment that I had made a mistake, that he could not possibly be here. Not here, not my Victor. He was a doctor, a brilliant neurologist. How could such a man live in a hell like this, its tiny little stores emblazoned with signs I could not read, and the terrible smells: urine and death and rot and blood from carcasses hanging in windows and bad fish and spoiled milk and sweat and greasy smoke. . . .

I hugged myself close and walked faster, through a warren of old row houses that had been altered beyond recognition, windows boarded up and possessions piled in what had once been tiny yards and stoops. There were no signs now, at least none that I could read. I had to stop finally to catch my breath, to get my bearings, and when I did, some filthy little man came from the shadows and spoke to me in a language I couldn't understand, though I knew what he wanted.

"No," I said in horror, backing away from him. "Oh, no, no, no—"

He muttered at me and walked on, but I was shaken. I had no idea where to go. What had the street sweeper said? Walk up Allen to Essex, but where was Essex? How far had I gone?

I drew into the shadows, huddling there, afraid. Irene's words came back to me—*You might want to have your driver take a weapon*—and I was certain I would not get from this place alive.

The noises around me grew louder. Men laughing, shouting.

Faint music. Coughing. The squeak of pushcart wheels. Weary footsteps. The high voices of women calling out in singsong.

I heard them before I saw them. The swish of a gown, of two, the step of heels. When they came nearer, I saw what they were, but I was afraid enough that I didn't care. I stepped from the shadows as they neared me. They laughed nervously and gave me a critical eye and began to walk by.

"Please," I whispered, and one of them stopped. She had the hardest face I'd ever seen. She looked at the woman with her— a younger version of herself, with a tattered kerchief hiding her hair—and rattled off a long string of words. I held up my hand to stop her and said desperately, "I'm looking for Victor Seth. On Essex Street. Essex Street."

"Essex," the younger one said, and I nodded in grateful relief. "Yes. Essex."

"Seth?" She pronounced it oddly—a long *e*—but again I nodded. She looked to the older woman and said something to her, and the older woman laughed and pointed to the corner beyond, saying over and over a word I couldn't come close to making out. Then she crooked her finger and held up her fingers—one, two, three—and then the two of them laughed again as I stared uncomprehendingly.

The older one grabbed my arm. She was quite strong, and I was tired and afraid, so I didn't protest; I stumbled along behind her. They led me down the street, and I had the dim thought that they were taking me to some terrible little house where I would be held prisoner. They could have thrown me into the East River, and I would have been helpless to stop them.

But they did not. They took me to the corner and turned right, and we were on a street lined with row houses and tenements indistinct from the first, and then we were before a ramshackle row house that looked to be sinking beneath the weight of its misery. They pushed me up the cracked and weathered stoop and left me sagging against the door before the younger one said, "Seth," in her odd way. They walked away again, chattering between themselves, abandoning me.

I was cold and sweating at the same time. My feet would no longer hold me, and I was so afraid I was nearly paralyzed. But I held one last hope that the women had brought me where I wanted to go—in any case, I had no choice—so I lifted my hand to the door and knocked.

There was no sound beyond. I knocked again, louder this time, and when that brought no answer, I began to pound. Someone must be there. There was a dim light coming from the second floor—someone had to be there. My pounding became rhythmic, almost soothing. I think I might have pounded forever, too mindless to stop, too terrified to leave, but then I heard footsteps beyond, and a muttered curse in something that sounded like German, and then the door was pulled open so abruptly I nearly fell into the man who stood on the other side.

He was short and wizened, with rheumy eyes that squinted at me before he straightened in surprise and said, "Fräulein, you must be lost."

It took me a moment to realize that I understood him. All I could say was "Victor. I—I'm looking for Victor Seth."

"Ah," he said, nodding. "Victor. *Ja, ja,* Victor. Come. Come." He stood back, motioning me inside. I almost collapsed in gratitude and relief.

He closed the door behind me. The house had been converted into flats, and we were in a dimly lit hallway littered with old mattresses and straw and rags; with bodies that huddled, stinking, in the shadows beyond. There were boxes and cans, heaps of clothes, piles of fabric tied with twine. From somewhere came the monotonous hum of some kind of machinery. The smell of kerosene was strong, along with the smells of cooking—onions and cabbage and grease—and the stench of urine. The doorjambs were grimy with fingerprints, the stairs before us sagged in the middle, and the finish had been worn to bare, filthy wood. The banister shook as the man put his hand upon it and gestured for me to follow him upstairs.

We climbed the creaking stairs to the next floor, where wash lines were strung with clothing from room to room. One of four doors had been eased open to cast its faint light across the hall. From inside that room came the guttural sounds of talk punctuated by the clatter of dishes, and again that whirring sound.

The man pushed open the door. "Victor!" he called, and then he said something in German. I heard an answer, low and deep, in Victor's voice, and then there was the sound of a chair pushing back, and footsteps, and he was there, stepping around the old man, pausing in the doorway, staring at me.

"Lucy," he said.

I fell sobbing into his arms.

Chapter 16

"My God, Lucy, what are you doing here?" He tried to hold me away from him, but I could only cling more tightly, so relieved to have found him, so certain he would make everything all right.

He gave me a little shake. "How did you find me? What happened?"

I could not answer. Finally he pulled me close while I sobbed against his chest, and I heard him say something to the old man in German—the gutturals made his chest rise and fall in jerky movements—and then he was leading me into the room beyond, where the *whirrr* became louder, the smells of food overpowering. I buried my face in his shirt; the scents of soap and sweat were oddly familiar and comforting.

"Come," he whispered to me. He spoke again to the man and to someone else—there was someone in the room whom I saw indistinctly—and then he led me across the room, which I had no sense of through my tears, into some small dark space. He shut a door behind us. "Here. Sit down."

My knee bumped into something—a bed, I realized, and I sank down upon it. It sagged beneath me, and when he sat beside me, it sagged even more. His arm was still around me; I leaned into his side, my sobs easing. I felt him fumble, and then he was shoving a handkerchief into my hand.

"Would you like something?" he asked. "Something to drink?"

"No." I shook my head, dabbing at my face. "No, nothing. Just you. I . . . I had to see you."

"Yes," he said. Then, "I'm going to light the lamp." He took his arm from my shoulders, and I heard the strike of a match. There was the flicker of flame and the small, dim light of what I realized was a kerosene lamp, and the darkness of the room eased. It was not a room, even, but a closet, like the closet between my room and William's, but smaller still than that. It held only the bed we sat on, no more than a cot covered with a stained, frayed quilt. The lamp was set on a shelf built into the corner, and piled around it were books, and above them a top hat. A brown suit hung on a hook in another corner, along with a coat. There was a lock on the door. The room held the strong, familiar scent of cigars.

"What is this place?" I asked. "You can't possibly live here."

I realized how undone he looked. His shirt was collarless. His braces were loose, looping at his hips, and his hair was tousled and curling at the nape. He looked younger than I'd ever imagined. "Why are you here, Lucy? Why have you come?"

I had thought of nothing but getting to him. He was to be my salvation. He understood me as no one had. But his questions were cold and faintly hostile, and I felt uncertain and embarrassed.

"I'm sorry," I said, crumpling the handkerchief. "I should not have come."

"No, you should not have," he agreed. "How did you find me?"

"I . . . I went to your office. Irene gave me your address."

His gaze was assessing, dark. He was like another man altogether. "How did you get here?"

"I walked."

"You walked?"

"I didn't realize how far it was . . . or what it would be like—"

"You could have been killed out there. Didn't you know—"

"How could I have? Why should I assume a doctor—a neurologist—*my* neurologist—would live in a . . . in a . . ."

"Tenement."

"Yes," I whispered. I looked at him. "Yes. Why? Certainly you could live better than this, with the money William pays you alone."

"The old man you met out there is my father," he said grimly. "He and my mother have lived here since they came from Germany thirty years ago. He owns it now."

"Then he could sell it. There are other places, better ones."

"For Jews, Lucy? Jews who aren't of your class? Where else would they go?"

I had no answer.

"They have a decent life here," he said, "though you wouldn't know it just to look. He does piecework. That noise you hear—those are sewing machines. They go nearly all night. He contracts with the mills and hires women to sew. Twenty, thirty women and their families live and work on this floor alone. The money he makes paid for my schooling. That and a donation from a generous mentor sent me to Leipzig."

I did not know what to say.

"You wanted to know more about me," he said bitterly. "Does this satisfy your curiosity?"

"I understand about your parents," I said. "But you—"

"They're getting old," he said. "They struggled to give me a better life, and they deserve a son to look after them now."

"I'm sorry," I said. "I'm sorry."

"Sorry for what? Sorry that you know where I come from? That I'm not what you wanted me to be? Or is it only that you're sorry you've trusted someone like me?"

"Don't."

His hand was on mine, holding me in place. "Why did you come, Lucy?" he said roughly against my ear. "Why are you here?"

"It doesn't matter. Truly. I'll go back home." I was crying again, and I dashed my hand across my eyes, muttering fiercely, "God, how stupid I am. What a silly, stupid woman."

I rose. It was a single step to the door. He was there suddenly too, grabbing my shoulder, forcing me to face him. I put my hands on his chest to push him from me. My vision was blurred, and I felt desperate in a way I could not explain, as if just his presence was too much; as if I could not find ground steady enough to hold me. "I'll be fine. If you'll just let me go."

He took hold of my wrists and moved my arms as if they were made of clay, pliable, elastic, down to my sides, trapping them there so I could not move, and then he kissed me.

I felt his lips on mine with a little shock, and then he was pressing against me, his body holding me to the door. I had both wanted and feared this, perhaps it was even what I had come to him to find, and I opened beneath him. He loosed my arms and put his hands on either side of my face, and I leaned in to him and followed when he pulled me with him to the bed and we fell onto the ragged quilt together. I did not hesitate but only reached for him when he backed away to slide up my cloak and skirt and petticoats, when he pushed between my legs. Though we were both clothed when he came inside me, it seemed I felt him with every part, that he freed me so I was thrusting against him, impatient, yearning, pleading, and then stunned as the pleasure coursed through me, leaving me mindless and crying out into his mouth, gripping him until he collapsed upon me with a final groan. We lay there for some time, it seemed, until the pleasure died, and I could not move for the intensity of my release.

When he stirred, I did not want him to go. But he slid from

me and sat up, tucking and buttoning while I lay there with my clothing pressed up to my hips, my boots and stockings still on, my hat falling from my head, clinging to a loosened hat pin.

He sighed, and I became self-conscious. I pushed down my skirt and sat up. The hat pin fell out. My fingers trembled as I reached for my hat and held it in my lap, afraid to look at him, to look at anything but a burgundy rose and a jaunty dark green feather. I could not say anything, and I wanted him to stay silent as well; I did not think I could bear whatever it was he would say.

But then he turned to me, and his gaze caressed me, and I found myself saying, "I . . . I've never felt like that. Not even the electrotherapy . . ."

"Yes," he said quietly. "It's not the same." His eyes darkened and he said, "Someday I would like to see all of you."

I reached for the fastening of my cloak, embarrassingly quick, to please him. "Yes," I said. My breath came fast again; I looked at his mouth. "Yes, of course. Just let me—"

His hand came over mine, stopping it. "Not now," he said. "Not here."

I was disappointed. "Oh. I thought—"

"It's late."

"Surely it's not—"

"Where does William think you are?"

William. I had so completely forgotten him that when Victor spoke his name, it was like that of a stranger. I was horrified at what I'd done, at what we'd done, and I scrambled off the bed, shamed by the wetness between my legs, by the scrapes of mud my boots had left on the quilt. "Oh, I didn't think . . ." I twisted my hat in my hand.

"Ssshhh," he said, coming to me, taking the hat from my hands. "It's all right, Lucy."

"No," I said desperately. "No, it's not all right."

"He keeps you caged."

"Yes," I said breathlessly. How much I craved the touch of him, already—so quickly—yielding to him again.

"You mustn't feel guilty for this. You needed this."

"Oh yes."

"Does he know where you went?"

I shook my head. "I just left. I came by myself. I didn't tell anyone."

"Good," he murmured against my ear. "That's very good."

I lifted my mouth to his. "I suppose that he should know. . . ."

"We'll talk about that later," he said.

"But he'll have to know. If I don't go back—"

"You have to go back," he said. It was a breath against my lips, but it startled me.

I jerked away from him. "What?"

"You have to go back," he said. "Come, Lucy, you know this. You can't stay here."

"Why not?"

"Look around you." He motioned impatiently at the room. "You don't belong here."

"But . . ." I stared at him, uncomprehending. "But you can't want me to go back to my husband. Not after this."

"Where else should you go?"

The question had no meaning, no relevance. I could not bend my mind to it. "But we've—"

"You would be ruined, Lucy," he said softly. "If you were to leave him now, I would be ruined."

"I don't care," I said. "It doesn't matter to me."

"Yes, it does."

I was humiliated beyond bearing, but I could not escape him. The room was too close, he was too close. I looked at him in confusion. "I'm falling in love with you," I said miserably.

"Listen to me, Lucy," he said. "You must listen closely. We must be careful. It's not unusual for a patient to form such an attachment to her doctor. Or to mistake feelings of gratitude for love."

"Gratitude? That's absurd. I know the difference."

"Oh, Lucy," he said. "We still have so much work to do." He reached over to the bed, where my hat pins lay scattered, and gathered them up. Then he set my hat on my head, gently—far too gently for any man—fastening it to my hair. He grabbed his coat from the hook by his suit, and then his hat, which he tucked beneath his arm. "It's late. You must go home. Come. I'll take you there."

Chapter 17

He opened the door and took my hand, and I let him lead me out without a murmur. The old man—his father—and an old woman who must have been his mother sat at a table with another woman who was bent over a sewing machine that she operated in fits and starts.

His mother was sewing by hand, by the light of a kerosene lantern. She was so hunched her eyes were nearly on the fabric. As we came out of the room, her expressionless gaze raked over me, taking in everything, and I felt she knew exactly what had gone on behind that door, what I had done with her son, what I had come for.

He said something to them in German, and they both nodded.

"You should lie down, *Mutter*," he went on in English. "Your eyes are too tired for that."

"*Pssshhh*," she said, waving at him in disdain before she bent back to her sewing. The father did not take his gaze from me as we went to the door.

"You be careful, Victor," he said, and then, "Take care, Fräulein."

We went out into the hall, where the darkness was more pronounced, and the huddled sleeping bodies were harder to see. Victor held my elbow, directing me down the stairs. At the foot he paused to lift a bundle of bound pieces and move it out of the way, and then we were back into the night, which was cold now, and foggy, and very, very dark.

"Stay close to me," he ordered, though I was pressed into his side, with no desire to leave it. There were only a few people on the street, mostly women. As we passed them at a fast clip, one or two of them murmured to Victor, and he called back a greeting.

"You know them?" I asked.

"I grew up here," he told me curtly.

"So you know everyone."

"No." He shook his head. "When I was a boy, these were all German houses—German Jews. Now most of them are from Russia. They aren't like us at all."

"Us? I thought you didn't believe in religion."

"I don't practice Judaism, Lucy, but I can't escape my heritage, no matter how I try. It's changing here, faster than anyone likes. These signs you see all over, they're Yiddish. My parents don't speak it. I don't speak it. My father considers them fanatics. They're clannish and backward. But there are so many of them that any ground we've managed to gain has been stripped away. When your people think *Jewish*, they no longer think of men like my father, who have come to terms with Western culture, who have even embraced it. They think of the unemployed masses in the *Khazzer-Mark*."

"My people?" I asked, hurt. "You sound so contemptuous of us. Of me."

"Come, now, Lucy," he said. "When you first heard of me, what did you think?"

I remembered Daisy Hadden's words—*They say he's a Jew*— and my own repulsion that a Jew might touch me.

"You see?" he asked, taking my silence for assent.

We walked on without speaking. Gaslights were here and there on the streets—dim gas here, while elsewhere in the city, arc lights shone brilliantly. We passed men huddled in the corners; on Hester Street the market stalls were empty and the streets were muddy and strewn with whatever garbage was too useless for even the rag-and-bone men. There was sound everywhere: talking and coughing, girls calling out, music.

But we went quickly and soon left it all behind. We were again on Lower Broadway, where the warehouses were shut tight and shops were dark and nothing but the ghosts of the day were left to haunt the streets.

"I'm sorry I don't have a carriage," he said. "How are you doing?"

"I'm fine," I said, but that wasn't the truth. My feet still hurt within my now torn boots, and I was tired and sweating, but these were the least of my discomforts. When we had been near his home, I had not felt like myself. There was no one there to recognize me; I was so profoundly out of place that it seemed I had lost Lucy Carelton. But now we were in places I knew, and I felt myself coming back slowly, bit by bit. I began to watch for bright windows, people staring out, those who would know me. I began to think of the row house where William would no doubt be waiting. I began to wonder what excuse I would make, what I would say to him, where I would tell him I'd been. The lies came easily to me now, when only a short while ago I had thought to end my unhappiness, to tell him the truth.

The truth was so far away already. I'd left it in that little closet of a room, on a cot that shrieked beneath our weight, and the memory was already fading—I could not quite believe it had happened. The man walking beside me now was so distant; had we been intimate? Had I truly felt the pleasure I'd thought I had? Had that been Lucy Carelton or someone else entirely? It seemed impossible to know.

When we were a block from the house, I stopped. "You should leave me here," I said.

He looked down at me and then at the long row of houses that stretched before us, all the same, all guarded by the black iron fences, the fancy stoops, the restrained elegance. This was where I lived. This was who I was.

I had hoped he would argue with me. _No, Lucy, I'll walk you to your door. To hell with William. To hell with all of them._ But I was also relieved he did not.

"I'll watch from here until you're safely inside," he said. "What will you tell William?"

"That I went to Millicent's house," I said. "She'll lie for me if he asks her."

"Very well," he said. He released my arm. "I want you to come to my office tomorrow. Around two o'clock."

"I can't do that," I said.

"You can cancel whatever social obligations you have," he said impatiently. "This is important, Lucy."

"No, I— That's not what I mean," I said. "William has . . . Before I left, he burned my sketches, and he accused you. He said it was all your fault. My drawing again. My behavior."

"You didn't tell me any of this."

"No," I said miserably. "He's forbidden me to see you. No doubt he'll come see you himself tomorrow."

"I see," he whispered.

I stood there uncomfortably until I thought he would say nothing else, and then I turned to go. "Well, then. Good-bye."

"Wait." He grabbed my arm, hard enough that I stumbled into him, and he held me tight against his body and put his hand to my cheek and kissed me, and it all rushed back as if it had just happened. The little room, the feel of him, my pleasure, and my desire for him rose up to overwhelm me, so that I cried out in desperation against his lips, "Don't make me go back. Don't make me go."

"Let me talk to him," he said, tangling his fingers in my hair. "I can change his mind."

"There's no need. I can stay with you. There's no need to talk to him at all."

"Ssshhh, Lucy, we've discussed this already. You must go back for now. But you can't stop coming to me, do you understand? Whatever happens, we must find a way to meet."

"Yes," I said, my joy rising at his words. "Yes. Whenever you say. You have only to send word."

"Let me talk to William tomorrow," he said. "I'll send word to you then. Watch for my note, Lucy. If I can't make him see reason, you'll need to make sure he doesn't see it. Can you do that? Can you lie to him?"

"I will," I told him. "Yes. I'll keep it from him."

His hand fell from my face. He gave me a final kiss. "Go on, then," he whispered. "Until tomorrow."

"Until tomorrow," I answered him, and then I hurried away, warm and reassured until he was only a shadow blurred by fog and darkness. I was ready to face my husband.

But once I reached the gate, I began to tremble, and I stumbled going up the stoop. I had no key. I hadn't thought of this, of knocking, of waking someone, of facing them all so soon. Before I could ready myself, the door opened, and I tripped over the threshold into light and warmth. Harris caught my arm, steadying me, but before I could say thanks, I saw a shadow looming beyond him. William stood in the hallway, wearing his dressing gown over a pair of trousers, his arms crossed over his chest.

"Lucy," he said. "Thank God you're home."

He was furious. He stood stiffly, his expression hard, his gaze focused on Harris, who closed the door behind me and held out his hand to receive my cloak and hat. I gave them to him, saying softly, "Make sure Moira cleans them."

William's gaze moved over me with such suppressed anger it seemed to burn. "What happened to your boots?" he asked.

I glanced down. The seams were torn; they were spattered with mud. "I—I stepped in a puddle."

"Take them off," he ordered, and then, to Harris, "Throw them out."

"I need a buttonhook," I said. "I'll send them down later."

"They're filthy."

"Yes. It's a long walk to Millie's. I didn't take the carriage."

"Millie's?" William's tone sharpened. "Is that where you were?"

I felt a surge of relief, but I could not look at him as I spoke the lie. "Yes. Yes. I had supper there."

"I see," he said. I saw his skepticism, and my relief fled. "Come upstairs with me, Lucy," he said. "We have some things to discuss."

"Of course. Yes, of course. Perhaps I could change—"

"Later," he said. He took my elbow, and his fingers were hard and unyielding, where only moments before Victor had held me gently.

"Will you be wanting anything, sir?" Harris called up. "Some tea?"

"No," William said curtly. We went up the stairs to the door of my bedroom. He released me, allowing me to go in before him. I had no sooner gone inside than he shut the door firmly behind us. The sound made me wince.

I went across the room to the window, as far from him as I could. Numbly, I pushed aside the curtains, searching the street for a shadow—his shadow—but the street was empty except for a passing carriage.

"You weren't at Millie's," William said. "When you disappeared, I sent Jimson there first. She hadn't seen you or heard from you."

I should have thought of that, I should have known. clutched the curtain. I could not think of what to say.

"Why the lie, Lucy? Where did you really go? Did you go to meet Seth despite what I told you?"

I had rarely heard him so angry. Despite myself, I glanced toward the fireplace, where there was nothing but a pile of ash. My drawings. The sight gave me strength. Slowly I turned from the window to face him.

"He's my doctor, William," I said. How calmly I said it, how strong I sounded. "I have been seeing him nearly every day for four months. Of course I went to him. I was distressed."

"You mean he *was* your doctor," William said.

"I went to his office," I went on. "But it was late. He wasn't there. And I didn't know what to do. I was so upset. So I stayed there."

"You stayed there?" William was incredulous. "In his office?"

"His office was locked," I said. "I stayed in the hall. At first I had some thought that he might come back, but then I fell asleep."

"You fell asleep. In the hall."

"Yes."

"You expect me to believe this?"

"What else was I to do?" I asked him. "Where was I to go? To Millie? To Papa? What should I have said? That I was afraid of my husband? That he had hurt me unbearably?"

William had the grace to look shamed. "No. No, of course not."

"You see? I had nowhere else."

"You did not meet Seth."

"He wasn't there."

"You saw no one else?"

"No one who knew me, William, if that concerns you."

"Lucy, what was I to think? You just left without a word. And you haven't been yourself. You can't know what I've been going through, how worried I've been."

"You needn't have worried."

"But those sketches—"

"The ones you burned."

"Your father said—"

"I was a child then. Now I'm a grown woman." I met his gaze. "A wife. The sketches were harmless, William."

"You've always been so fragile. You can imagine what I thought." He came to me, putting his hands on my arms, stroking me hesitantly. "I'm sorry, Lucy," he said. "I lost my head. It was a terrible day—an argument with a client, and then when I saw those drawings, when I thought . . . I love you, darling, and I was afraid. I hope you can forgive me."

I was not sure I could. My own anger was a tight knot, a terrible bruise, but I thought of what Victor had said, of how William could ruin us, and I contained it as best I could.

"Certainly," I whispered, looking at the terrible condition of my boots, remembering. "Of course."

He let out a breath. "Thank God."

I felt his kiss on the top of my head, and I pulled gently away.

"There's just one other thing," he said.

I went still. "Yes?"

"I think . . . Well, I do think it would be better if you didn't draw again. It seems to agitate you so."

I closed my eyes, breathing deeply, clasping my suddenly trembling hands together. I made myself remember Victor's words. "But I love it."

William was behind me, his hands on my shoulders, squeezing. "Yes, but you must admit you've grown too attached to it. It's unhealthy, Lucy. Surely you must see that. After what happened to your mother."

I turned, startled. He had never mentioned my mother before, never even alluded to her. "My mother?"

He looked uncomfortable. "You are very like her, I understand. Your father's been worried on that score for years. Please,

I don't want to lose you that way. Remember what Dr. Little said."

I struggled to control my emotions. "And Dr. Seth?"

"There are other doctors. Better doctors."

"You said he was our last hope."

He kissed my shoulder. The heat of his breath made me shiver and grow cold. "I don't believe that any longer. We can try again for a child. All that electrotherapy—perhaps it made a difference, hmmm? Come, should we try again?"

I could not bear his touch a second longer. I pressed from his arms, trying to smile—a weak attempt, I knew, when I saw how his eyes darkened, how his own smile faltered. "I . . . not tonight, William. I'm so tired. The walk was long, and I'm still not recovered."

He was not soothed. I ran my fingers over his arm and kissed his jaw. "Surely you understand. I was so upset, and now, I must admit, I'm still undone. I really must get something to eat, and some rest."

He relaxed, and nodded, and backed away from me, saying, "Yes, you should rest. I'll have Cook send something up. A bowl of soup, perhaps."

"That would be lovely."

He went to the door. I tried not to look as relieved as I felt, but only smiled at him when he turned again to me with an uncertain expression.

"You do forgive me, Lucy?" he asked. "You will do as I ask? Do we understand each other?"

"We're in complete harmony," I reassured him, and I stood there smiling until he left.

Notes from the Journal of
Victor Leonard Seth

Re: Eve C.

April 23, 1885

I fear I have made a grave mistake in treatment. Yesterday Eve came to me at my home, obviously distraught, and I was so concerned to see her there that I rushed into a crucial step in her treatment. I had meant to take things more slowly, to bring Eve into the world of physical passion more carefully, and now I am afraid I have undone all my painstaking work. She responded eagerly, of course—her reaction was exactly what I would have wished it to be in its right time and place. But now is too soon. Now she wants to reveal all to her husband, to leave him, and this would only cause a scandal, which would hopelessly cloud the acceptance of any scientific strides I have made. I should have planted the ground more carefully, more judiciously. I do not understand myself. I was never so careless before; in the past I have approached this level of treatment with the utmost care, as have all of the physicians I've known. Such treatment requires the most exacting dispassion. All I can think is that I have spent so much time thinking about her, agonizing over the correct path, caught up in the excitement of creating such a vibrant being—to mold her with my own hands!—that my judgment was momentarily impaired. Thus far I have been meticulous and deliberate. I cannot afford to be so careless now.

I can only hope this does not have the consequences I fear it will, though I am not confident. She told me that her husband has forbidden her to see me again. If she were to tell him of this episode, I have no doubt she would be removed from my care—from my reach—completely. I cannot allow that to happen. Not when I have come so far. I must meet with him, take pains to reassure him, and then I must retread this ground carefully and not allow my success to lead me into false confidence. I must not allow her presence to muddy my own thinking. Once the experiment is done, she will be free to pursue her own path, whatever it may be, wherever she can climb from the rubble of her past life, and I will ascend to greater heights, to the accolades of my peers. This is my purpose. Scientific inquiry. Knowledge to change the world. I must remember this and not allow my own passions to gain sway.

Slowly. I must go more slowly.

Chapter 18

Two days later, Moira came into the parlor bearing an envelope. "This just came for you, ma'am."

My fingers trembled as I tore it open.

You must come today at two o'clock. —S.

Relief made me giddy. I nearly broke into a smile before I remembered Moira, who stood waiting in the doorway, naked curiosity on her face.

"I must go out," I told her. "Ready my burgundy walking suit."

"Will you be needing the carriage, ma'am? Should I tell Jimson?"

"Yes. Tell him to bring the brougham around."

I turned to the window and stared across at the park, allowing myself the smile I'd hidden from Moira.

I knew that William had gone to see Victor yesterday, and that Victor had persuaded him that I still needed care. William had reluctantly allowed me to continue seeing the doctor "for now," as he put it, but I had heard nothing from Victor and had worried. I'd thought so much about him that I assumed it must be obvious to everyone, and now my anticipation threatened to burst through my skin. He had sent word, as I'd wanted, but I had expected more. Words of love, perhaps, some sign that he felt as I did, anything. The note was so brief and so plain. What would he tell me when I went to his office? What did he mean to do? Would it be as it had been two nights ago, or had that simply been an aberration, something he would apologize for, a terrible mistake? I did not know whether I could bear it if he did that. I tried not to question myself or think about what my desire really meant or how I had betrayed my husband.

When the outfit was laid out, I dressed as quickly as possible, cursing Moira inwardly for her fumbling slowness as she fastened the tapes of the bustle about my waist. My mouth was dry, and I felt I was shaking, though I saw in the mirror that I looked perfectly composed. When I left the house, not a hair was out of place; I looked like a woman going about her business, not what I felt I was: a woman rushing to an assignation with a lover.

Jimson was waiting. When we reached Lower Broadway and he helped me down, I stood looking at the building before me. How things had changed since I'd last seen it. But now it was not evening, and the lights in the little shop were on, the sidewalks were full of men bustling about and street sweepers brushing madly away and men unloading crates and barrels onto the walk. I hurried through them, not wanting to waste a single moment. I could barely contain myself when I reached his door, when I pulled it open.

The outer office was empty. Irene was nowhere to be seen. I did not wait to see if she would appear; I went to his door and rapped sharply upon it. I did not think I could bear those few seconds before he called, "Come in."

I turned the knob and stepped inside, unsure of what I would see, afraid that it would not be what I wanted.

The electric lights were off; the room was dimly lit by the bright daylight surging around the cracks of the lowered blinds. He was at his desk. There were dark shadows beneath his eyes, and his hair was tousled, much as it had been the other night. I carefully closed the door behind me and stood there composed and erect, searching his face for something, some sign.

He'd been writing. He put down his pen and said, "I wasn't certain you would come."

"Of course I would come." How breathless I sounded.

"William told you, then, that he came to see me?"

"Yes."

"And the result?"

"He said he had agreed to continue my treatment. 'For now,' he said."

"Is that how he worded it? Did he tell you that he told me it was you who wished to end it?"

"No," I said. I pressed my hands together. I felt a little faint. "No, of course not. Of course that's not what I wish."

"Are you sure, Lucy?"

"Yes. Yes, I am."

He looked satisfied, even smug, but not relieved, as I had hoped. He had said nothing to reassure me; he had not referred to the other night at all. I felt miserable again and could not take my eyes from him, yearning for him so that I could not quite think.

He had not moved from his desk. He jotted a note in his notebook, and I began to perspire.

Then he rose, and I began to resent him for his obvious calm, for not mentioning the other night, for not touching me or kissing me, for not seeing how I wanted him.

"Take off your cloak," he said. "Come and sit down."

"Only my cloak?" I asked him, and his gaze shot to mine with an intensity that took my breath.

"Sit down," he said.

I did as he asked. He had turned to the window, and when I sat, he turned back again. I saw how restless he was now that he was standing, how he could not quite be still. He came toward me.

"Are you going to hypnotize me?"

He paused behind the other red chair.

I reached for the buttons on my collar. "You said you wanted to see all of me. Shall I start now?"

He swallowed. His voice sounded strangled when he said, "There are other things we must work on."

"Such as?"

"I'd planned to make a suggestion regarding your drawing."

"It's unnecessary. William has forbidden it."

He didn't look at me. "If you truly want to be the woman I think you can be—"

"I want only you, Victor. Please, I've thought of nothing but you. Haven't you thought of me? Didn't the other night matter to you at all?" I rose and stepped toward him, moving around the chair that shielded him. "The woman you talk about, the woman you want me to be, shouldn't this be a part of it? Shouldn't I know about passion?"

"Yes, of course," he said.

"Then I want you to show me," I said. "Teach me how to be that woman. I want to learn."

"Your . . . expectations must be . . . tempered," he said. "Only then can . . ." He looked at me. "Only then . . ."

I hardly heard his words. I knew only that he was wavering, that I had him, and I reached for him, putting my hand on his chest, curling my fingers against his suit coat.

"Lucy," he whispered, and I was triumphant.

He pulled me close and kissed me with his open mouth, as desperate and hungry as I was.

"I've given Irene the afternoon off," he murmured, kissing my cheek, my jaw, my throat, fumbling with the buttons at the front of my bodice until we were both working together. My fingers jerked against his as we unfastened them.

"The things women wear," he said as I shrugged from my bodice and stepped from my skirt. He was struggling with the tapes of my bustle and the crinolette. When they were loose, he flung them away from me; I heard the springy scrape of the bustle as it bounced against the wall and slid to the floor. I stood before him in only my corset and stockings, and he fell to his knees before me and unfastened my garters, pushing the stockings down my legs, rolling them off. I took off the corset cover and undid the front fastenings of the corset, and then he was standing again, pressing against me, roughly shoving the straps of my chemise from my shoulders so it pooled at my waist, and I was naked in a way I had never been before. I could not remember even William having seen me thus, and when Victor backed away to look at me, his gaze was so assessing that I crossed my arms over my breasts in sudden shyness.

He shrugged from his suit coat, pulling his braces down and unbuttoning his shirt, and then his underwear, so that when he came to me and pushed my hands away, I felt his skin against my breasts, and I lost myself completely. I had no more sense of who I was or what I was doing, only that I wanted him, and before I knew it, we were on the floor, completely naked, and I could hear nothing but my own cries and the rush of his breath.

"Is this what you want, Lucy?" he asked. "Is this why you came to me?"

I could only say, "Yes, yes," and move against him and clutch him, gasping and trembling as I climaxed in his arms. How had I lived without this before now? How could I live without it after?

"I've changed my mind," I whispered. "I'm no longer falling in love with you. I am in love with you."

He looked up, his weight still on me, his hair falling into his face. "This is all simply—"

"Don't say it," I warned, putting my finger against his lips. "Don't ruin it."

He pushed my hand away. "Love only complicates things. It can only imprison you. You said you loved William when you married him, didn't you?"

"I don't want to talk about him," I said. "Don't say his name."

"You can't deny it. You did love him."

"I thought I did," I protested. "But I didn't know. There was never anything like this. There won't ever be. My life with him is over."

"It can't be over, Lucy."

"It is. I'll tell him the truth. I'll tell him I'm in love with you."

"No." His gaze was burning. His weight pressed me into the floor. "It would ruin everything." His insistence surprised me. "You're weak now," he went on before I could speak. "If you tell him the truth, he'll destroy you. You're not strong enough to withstand social destruction alone."

"But I won't be alone. I'll have you."

"A Jew who lives in a tenement?"

"A doctor. A neurologist."

"A hypnotist, Lucy. Think about it. You yourself called me a charlatan when we first met. Your father still believes that's what I am. This city hasn't even begun to understand science. They don't hear the word *hypnotism* without thinking of Mesmer. To them it's some ridiculous parlor trick without study and experimentation, without results. We would be pariahs, both of us. Is that what you want?"

"We would be together."

"Your romantic notions are misplaced," he said dryly. "Poverty is its own kind of prison. Social banishment is only another set of chains."

"You want me to stay with William."

"For now."

"For how long?"

He rolled onto his side, tracing my breast and stroking to my rib. I began to melt again, to want him.

"Just tell me what to do," I murmured as his hand stroked down the soft underside of my arm, a steady caress. "I'll do whatever you say."

Notes from the Journal of
Victor Leonard Seth

Re: Eve C.

April 25, 1885

I have convinced Eve's husband to allow treatment to continue, and Eve has not only agreed, she has given me carte blanche.

Today I planted the suggestion that she would want above all things to see me, in spite of any persuasion by her husband or anyone else against me. I have also reinforced my insistence on secrecy and instructed that she continue her life <u>as it is</u> until I determine she is ready to make decisions about her future.

PART II

Newport Beach, Rhode Island

June 1885

Chapter 19

This year I packed for Newport with an excitement that far surpassed any other season's.

Though I'd always loved Newport, and the chance to summer at the cottage my father had owned since he sold the summer house on the Hudson, I had been growing to love it less and less. When I was a child, it had been a wonderful place, full of sea breezes that rushed through the open windows and swept papers and knickknacks to the floor, and the sound of the waves rushing upon the beach, and an expanse of lawn that rolled right to the edge of the sea. But now the rest of New York had discovered it as well, and the summers that I'd spent alone and free had become full of social strictures and rigid schedules and notions of etiquette that were as confining as New York City's, with the addition of hot summer weather and sand.

This year, however, I was restless with my haste to go. The months could not pass quickly enough for me. Though I had held tight to Victor's conviction that I must stay with William, I wanted to spend some time without my husband. He would be able to leave his work only on the weekends, and I was giddy with the freedom that promised.

The strain of this last month had worn on me. In the beginning I could not look at my husband without remembering what
Victor and I had done together—what we continued to do—but
it became easier, my guilt and shame fading to acceptance; no,
more than that. It was as if my relationship with Victor were
somehow a reward for all that marriage to William had taken
from me, all that my father's dominance had taken from me. It
had become my birthright, and in light of that, my guilt faded.
But what took its place was harder and less elastic. What took
its place was resentment and impatience. I could not see William
without wishing him away, and the time we spent together became harder to bear.

Victor and I still met twice a week, but we gradually saw each
other even more often. First an extra hour seized in his office,
and then, as he continued his ascent into my social circle, minutes grasped on an outdoor terrace, in an abandoned room
down a darkened hallway, stolen kisses. Oh, how I loved him. It
seemed that the stronger my love grew for him, the more I
chafed at the social schedule that had kept me so bound for so
long.

It began with my unwillingness to go to Daisy Hadden's
country house for two weeks.

"But you've always gone," William protested. "She expects it
of you."

"Well, I don't wish to go," I told him. "I haven't time."

"You haven't time? Good God, Lucy, you do nothing."

"Daisy hasn't a brain in her head," I said. "She's the most boring company I know, and I won't spend another moment admiring those diamonds Moreton gave her because he feels guilty
over meeting Madeline Hoover at the Metropolitan Hotel."

"Lucy!"

"Well, it's true, William. You know it as well as I."

"But—"

"Daisy knows it too. As long as she gets a weekly box from Tiffany's, she doesn't care."

He was quiet, and I looked up to see him staring at me, a speculative expression on his face.

"What?" I asked. "What is it?"

"What's happened to you?" he asked. "What's happened to my kind little wife?"

"Perhaps she's grown tired of kindness."

He took a deep breath. "Perhaps we should stay home for a while."

I waved him away. "Soon it will be summer and you can send me off to Newport, where I won't embarrass you."

He looked thoughtful, and I felt a twinge of guilt that I banished quickly.

"Perhaps we should stay home this year," he said. "The house . . ."

"William, it won't be finished for months. There's no reason to stay in the city."

"McKim expects it will be done by the start of the season," he said.

Already the house was rising into the air, brownstone and wood. I could not drive by it without thinking of it as prison walls. "There will be something else to change," I said. "There always is."

"It will all come together more quickly than you think. And we've barely begun to furnish it."

"Jean-Baptiste has it well under control," I said. "Oh, William, you can't mean not to go to Newport. I simply must."

"I wouldn't miss it," he said.

"But I would."

"Yes. You'd shrivel up without your sea breezes and that wretched seaweed."

"You can mock me all you like," I said, feeling defiant. "I will go alone, then."

He took a deep breath. His eyes grew sad. "You've changed, Lucy," he said.

I turned away. "Yes, thank God. You should be grateful. I haven't had a fit in ages."

"That's true," he agreed, but I sensed that he was less happy about that than he had expected to be. When he said, "Don't make me regret being generous, Lucy," I stared after him, perplexed and anxious as he left me.

I wanted no more of his silent thoughtfulness, or my sense that he saw more than I wanted him to see. Newport lingered like a beacon before me.

My trunks were packed days before we were to take the steamer over, and I was not relieved until Narragansett Bay was before me and I saw the huge yellow pagoda of the Ocean House Hotel and the waves splashing lazily against the boulders of Purgatory Rocks. Then I felt my spirit leap to meet it.

A local woman, Sadie Longstreet, cared for the house during the rest of the year. As in other years, she had sent her son David with a wagon for our trunks. The breeze was slight and full of salt, the elms bordering the street lending graceful shade. Budding hydrangeas were bright green against weathered clapboards.

"Right on schedule," David said as he tipped his hat to William and me. His shaggy dark hair fell forward, and he shoved it back again beneath the brim. His teeth were stained from tobacco, but other than that, he was a handsome young man and much stronger than his lanky frame suggested. He lifted our trunks easily and settled them in the wagon, then he helped me up beside him while William perched in the bed.

"What's changed, David?" I asked him, and he gave me a sideways glance.

"Now, ma'am," he said. "You know nothing ever changes here."

"Isn't that the truth," William muttered from behind me.

I ignored him, and we moved off, leaving the weathered and picturesque little town behind, making our way down Bellevue Avenue, where the rocky, shallow cliffs and hills gave way to rolling lawns and summer cottages that had grown steadily larger in the years since we'd first come here.

Seaward, our cottage, was one of the smaller ones. It was wood, instead of stone or marble, and no château. It was a charming house, with mansard roofs over the dormers and striped awnings covering the porch that wrapped all the way around, with graceful steps down to the lawn and bushy hydrangeas and climbing roses bordering the sides. The windows were wide and blinking in the sun, the drapes already opened by the efficient Sadie, the wicker furniture set out on porch floors swept clean of sand or debris tossed by winter storms.

When we arrived, I was so eager I leaped from the wagon nearly before it was stopped. I hurried from the drive to the front porch, where Sadie waited at the door.

"Welcome, Mrs. Carelton," she said. "It's all ready for you. I had David repaint the porch in the spring, and I made sure to scrub it this time, like you asked last year. I've removed all the dustcovers and aired out the mattresses. I think you'll find it quite satisfactory."

"Oh, it's lovely," I said.

She frowned. My arrival last year came to me: how tired I'd been, how nervous. How the porch was in such a state, and the rooms felt damp, and I needed to lie down immediately to quiet my pounding head.

The thought embarrassed me, and when she stepped back from the door, I went inside quickly. The entryway was big and square, the hardwood floors gleaming. In the middle rose the staircase with its simple balustrades, smelling of beeswax. The doorways were large and arched, so it seemed all the downstairs rooms connected to the hall and to one another. The breezes whirled through on hot summer days, crossing in little eddies of current, so it was impossible to stand in the entry and not be cooled.

It looked as if I had just left yesterday. I went from room to room as David brought the trunks inside and lumbered upstairs with them. The door of the first parlor, whose windows fronted the ocean, led onto the wide porch that shaded it. The back parlor was all in green, with a calm, even light that shone on the piano and shelves filled with books—they would not fade here, where the sun was not so harsh. The dining room opened onto the porch as well, and the kitchen held on its shelves green and cranberry glass, dishes sturdier than what I kept in the city; there were so many alfresco dinners here.

Then there was the upstairs—five bedrooms, all with large windows and shining wooden floors covered by rugs in stripes or florals. The room I'd had as a girl, done in roses, opened onto a small terrace; the room that had been Papa's and now was mine and William's fronted the beach and led onto a huge balcony covered with an awning. In the past, we'd often taken our morning coffee there.

I went up to the third floor, where the rooms, tucked under the eaves, were hot even in the early summer and would be sweltering later. Those in the back of the house were the servants' quarters; the front rooms were used for storage and sometimes as extra guest rooms. There were fishing rods and nets and baskets for gathering shells, and wardrobes filled with bathing costumes and boots and old summer hats and gloves for gardening.

I stood in the most forward of these and shoved open the window—a hard pound at each corner, because it had shrunk into the frame during the winter—and leaned out and breathed in the fresh air and watched David unload the trunks, and William as he walked out onto the lawn, examining it for flaws, pausing halfway across, putting his hands on his hips to stare out at the ocean and the rocks that jutted from a promontory.

He seemed a stranger to me, a man wearing a dark coat and hat where they were so unsuited. I thought of Victor, of when he would come, and I felt both elated and nervous, because I had not yet told William that Victor was coming to stay as a guest for a time—we had not yet determined how long. In my mind I had outlined already the entire summer with him at my side, and though I did not think my husband would protest—many guests had stayed for so long—I did not think he had quite put aside his reservations about Victor's treatment. I was unsure what his reaction would be.

Better not to give him notice at all, I had determined. Better to bring Victor out to play the available bachelor during the summer, the way Lester Hines had done last year with Minnie Stevens, and that writer fellow with Alva Brooks. The ladies loved it. Men to play escort during the week, when husbands were away. Yes, that was what I would pretend.

William glanced up at the window where I stood, and I felt caught by my thoughts. When he waved at me, I could barely lift my fingers in answer. Instead I shut the window and hurried downstairs to the bedroom and began to fumble with the trunks David had brought up, unpacking feverishly. I could not wait to be ensconced, to be permanent.

That night the two of us had supper on the veranda. It was a beautiful night, with the sunset gold and pink and purple and the water deepest blue, with dark, foamy crests, and a breeze that pushed away the heat of the day. Sadie had set an intimate table, with candles that called moths to flitter about the flames. William seemed preoccupied, and I wanted nothing more than for the next day to fly by, to reach Monday again, so we ate in silence. When Sadie took our plates away and brought a final course of pretty strawberry ices, my appetite was gone. I slipped my spoon into the molded pinkness and stirred it into a melted puddle.

"Is something wrong?" William asked.

I glanced up, startled by the sound of his voice. "No, of course not."

"You seem especially quiet tonight," he said. He pointed with his spoon to the mess on my plate. "And you haven't eaten any of your ice cream."

"I'm quite full."

"I see," he said. He took another spoonful of his own. When he'd swallowed, he said, "You could have stayed in town, you know, Lucy."

"Why would I do that?"

"You could keep your appointments."

"My appointments?"

"With Victor."

I was conscious suddenly of making a great mistake. I tried to smooth over it; I laughed lightly and said, "Oh, that. Yes, well, you see, William, we've talked quite a bit about that, and we decided it would be much better if I didn't stop seeing him over the summer. He believes I'm not quite ready to be on my own for so long."

"Does he?" William spoke wryly. "Yes, that doesn't surprise me. He's said as much to me before. How long does he expect this to go on?"

I began to feel nervous. "I don't know. He's never said."

"A year? Longer than that?"

"I . . . I don't know."

"Perhaps it would be best if you *did* take the summer off. We could see then how well you do without him."

"But you see, he thinks it's too soon to try."

"Really, Lucy, you can't expect to take the steamer into the city twice a week. You might as well stay at home."

I fingered the lace edging of the napkin in my lap. "Of course you're right."

He was quiet. When I glanced up again, it was to find him

staring at me. "Why do I have the idea that you're not telling me something?"

"It's just that I hadn't the opportunity," I said, rushing on. "I meant to tell you, but there was so much to do to get ready, and I thought you'd disagree—"

"Disagree about what?"

I tried to smile. "Why, that Victor should come here. It's truly the best plan all around. He doesn't think it's a good idea to end my treatment for the summer, and I had no wish to stay in town, and many of his patients will be summering elsewhere, and so it seemed best for him to come to Newport."

"He's closing his practice for the summer so he can attend to you?"

"No, that's not it at all."

"I don't pay him enough to do that."

"That's not what he's doing. He won't be dancing attendance on me constantly. He'll go into the city occasionally, I'm sure."

"Occasionally?"

I squirmed. "Or perhaps more often than that."

"This is beyond absurd. Who ever heard of a doctor doing such a thing?"

"I've told you, he believes there's still so much work to do."

"I see. And where will Victor be staying while he attends to you? At the Ocean House?"

"The hotel is falling apart, William, you know it is. Hardly anyone who's anyone goes there anymore, and we've so much room here."

"You've invited him to Seaward."

His voice was flat. I said as brightly as I could, "Why shouldn't I? We have guests here all the time. Last summer you brought James Willard to stay the entire month of July, and left it to me to entertain him."

William looked thoughtfully at me. "I suppose you're right," he said at last, reaching for his glass. "I suppose there can be no harm, especially now that Seth is linked to Julia."

I blinked. "What?"

"I said: You're right. There's no harm in it, certainly."

"No, what did you say about Julia? Julia . . . Breckenwood?"

"Didn't you know?" he asked rather smugly. "I would have thought you'd heard the gossip."

"No, of course not," I snapped. "I'm not about all day, listening to stock messengers and standing at lunch counters."

"I'm too busy to come home at noon, Lucy, you know that. And I thought you preferred it this way."

"What gossip have you heard?"

He shrugged. "John Bradley said he saw them together at Daisy Hadden's country house. I believe Victor was there for the weekend, and Julia had come down the day before."

It took all my will to adopt a nonchalant tone, to say, "Perhaps she's become his patient."

"If she has, she'd never say, though I've heard nothing of her health failing. No, Steven was out of town last month. No doubt Julia was just lonely."

"No doubt."

"Steven says she'll be coming to By-the-Bay next week."

"How nice," I managed.

"So Victor will have someplace else to go, should he grow tired of playing doctor."

He was watching me, measuring. I smiled, though it felt a tremendous effort, and said, "Yes. I would hate for him to be bored."

William reached into his pocket for a cigar and bit off the end, spitting it into the hydrangeas. Then he lit it in the candle flame, puffing so the flame grew high and bright. A nearby moth nearly singed its wings.

He sat back in his chair, puffing contentedly. The smell settled in a cloud around my nose, so I thought of Victor and his cigars, and the sickness rose in my stomach. I could barely sit there companionably with my husband.

"Victor should like Seaward," he said. "But don't feel the need to show him around too much, Lucy. You leave that to Julia, and to . . . whoever else might take a fancy to him."

"I'll be sure to do that," I said quietly.

William's gaze went hard. "Just remember, my dear," he said, "I expect you to remember who you are."

Chapter 20

When William at last kissed me good-bye and had David drive him to the steamer, I was so relieved I sagged into one of the wicker chairs on the veranda and watched him drive away.

When he was gone, I could not be still. Victor planned to arrive in the afternoon, after wrapping up his morning appointments. I paced the gardens and wondered jealously if Julia was one of them; if he dismissed Irene to run errands when she came, as he did with me; if the blinds were lowered and dark, so the phrenology head gleamed bone white and ghostly in sunlight filtering past the edges.

The thought of it made me so irritable I snapped at Sadie and watched her mouth go tight and drawn and realized that that was the expression that was familiar to me, that her pleasant smile these last days had been odd. I felt a niggling guilt and walked down to the edge of the lawn to stare out over the sea.

It seemed to call to me, the way it always did, and in other years I'd ignored the call until eleven, the fashionable hour to go to Bailey's Beach, when I would swim among all the others. Not since I was a child had I clambered down these rocks, and then only when Papa was not there to see and my nanny had turned her back.

I had not forgotten how. Huge rocks bolstered the six feet or so to the beach. I lifted my skirts and climbed down them, my inadequate boots slipping on the smooth edges, my petticoats catching. I tore my stocking and scraped my shin, but at last I stumbled to the sand. The tide was coming in, so I had only a short distance to go, and little time, but I decided to walk, as difficult as it was on sand that slipped and gave beneath my heels. I went down the beach, past the cottages like Seaward and the marble châteaus beyond that were growing more prevalent every year, with their staffs of gardeners and butlers and servants, their fountains and pagodas and ballrooms.

I did not look to them but out at the sea, at the change of the light upon the water, the shifting colors, the tangles of seaweed that swayed with the waves yet amazingly did not move at all. I lifted my face to the salty breeze. Before I knew it, the water was to my feet, wetting my hem, and the sand I walked upon was only a narrow strip that would soon disappear. I had no choice but to turn around.

When I reached the rocks of Seaward again, the tide was in so far I had to walk through inlets of water that came to my ankles. My boots were ruined. It was more of an effort to climb the rocks back to the lawn, and my stockings squished in my boots. I sat down on the lawn, silk gown and all, and grappled with my boots, but even had the water not swollen the leather tight, I could not have begun to loosen them without a buttonhook. I got up again and trudged the expanse of lawn, holding my hat in my hand, bedraggled and dirty, sweating. I felt alive; the walk had soothed me; the wet flap of my gown about my ankles was a sound I had not heard since I was a girl.

I was halfway across the lawn when I heard a call. Victor was coming down the steps of the porch, striding toward me.

I felt ensnared again, jerked to him without will or sense, suddenly so dizzy and desirous that I was both material—a body only, simply visceral sensation—and without substance at the same time.

All I could think was that I loved him, and that he might be lying to me.

"Lucy," he said. He started to reach for me, and I jerked away. He frowned. "Isn't William gone?"

"He left this morning. He'll be back again on Friday."

"So we've a week to ourselves."

I could not contain myself. The words came bursting from my lips. "William told me you were at Daisy Hadden's that weekend—that weekend I did not go—with Julia Brecken-wood."

He looked surprised, and then angry, and then his expression settled into a careful mask. "Ah," he said.

"Is she your patient? Does she require your assistance day and night? Do you 'take care' of her the way you take care of me?"

"Julia Breckenwood is a lonely woman who's donated money for my research."

"Is she a patient?"

"Come, Lucy, you know I can't tell you that. My career depends on my discretion."

"Her husband would ruin you if he found out, you know this, don't you? He would ruin you. All you've worked for—"

"It's not what you think, Lucy."

"Has she formed an 'attachment' to you too? Does she tell you she loves you?"

"Lucy, hush." He took hold of my arm, pulling me closer. His thumb stroked the silk of my sleeve. He bent to whisper in my ear, "I haven't laid a hand on her."

"Why should I believe you?"

"Because Julia Breckenwood is not you," he said, tracing down my arm, winding his fingers about my wrist. "I would not risk losing you, Lucy. You must believe me. I would not risk it."

His breath sent a shudder along my skin, and I could not bear it. To be so close and not to touch. I looked up at him. "Perhaps I could show you to your room."

"Yes," he breathed.

With effort, I stepped away from him and turned to the porch, where I saw Sadie, standing near the table, darting quick glances at us.

That first week, there were still so few people that it was as if we had Newport to ourselves. Outwardly Victor was the perfect guest. He was entertaining over supper, kind to the servants, and he kept me in high spirits. We spent every day in idle pursuits: long, leisurely breakfasts on the porch, walks along the beach from which we returned damp and sandy and laughing, and early afternoons when I sat on the lawn and Victor wrote furiously beside me. The servants had been told that Victor was my doctor; it explained too well why he must attend to me constantly.

There were no stolen hours here, they were full of him already, and there were too many risks to be taken in the daylight, so we would wait until nightfall for our trysts. The day would be one long aching stretch of need and anticipation, so when he came to my room, my need of him was so intense I did not waste a moment. It was luxurious and fine, to make love on a bed instead of an office floor or a settee, and it always seemed that exhaustion came far too quickly, that the night should stretch on longer, that I should take every minute until the early hour before the servants woke, when he would disentangle himself from me and return to the rose room, the room that had once been mine.

I spent those hours in a daze of happiness and contentment. When he touched me, I forgot everything: who I was, William, the world. I was under a spell, with Victor the magician keeping me bound and I a willing victim.

When Friday came and William drove up in the late after-noon, looking tired and anxious, I felt his presence like a gash in the landscape. I was angry at his interruption of these rainbow-hued days.

"Hello, darling," William said as he came walking around the side of the house. I was lounging on a blanket laid upon the grass, staring up at the sky. Victor sat beside me, the sleeves of his boiled shirt rolled up over his arms as he scribbled away in a ledger.

William squatted down beside me and kissed me lightly on the head, while I suppressed a shudder, and then he looked at Victor. "Why, hello, Victor. I see you managed to tear yourself away from the city."

Victor smiled at him. "A pity you can't do the same."

"Yes, well, most of us must work during the week. How lucky you are that your work is here." William threw a glance at me.

"You've a charming home," Victor said.

"Enjoying yourself, are you?"

"Immensely."

"The weather to your taste?"

"It's been clear every day."

"I assume Lucy has been seeing to your needs adequately."

I could not look at him. Or at Victor. I squinted at the clouds in the sky, trying to find a shape, but they were frayed and loose and would not coalesce into anything I recognized.

Victor laughed. "To be honest, William, it's the other way around. I'm at her beck and call, as is so often the case with pa-tients. But she's doing better these days. I assume you've seen the difference."

"Oh yes," William said. I could not decide if there was sar-casm in his tone. "No more fits, no more moods. Cook has fi-nally decided to stay—she was threatening to quit twice a week. You've worked wonders with her, Victor."

"I am sitting right here," I said. "There's no need to talk about me as if I were some piece of horseflesh."

"You see? Delightful." William looked to me. "What have you been doing this week, my dear? Busy planning parties and such?"

"So few people are here yet," I said. "And I've spent quite a bit of time with Victor, of course."

"Still the hypnosis?" William asked.

Victor said, "It's best to continue the suggestion until it's firmly planted in the unconscious."

"Is that so? How long must this 'planting' continue? Do we expect a harvest anytime soon?"

"Not before the summer is over, I would think," Victor said.

"That long, then? Nine months? A child takes as much time." William squeezed my shoulder. I stiffened.

"Victor tells me there are some patients who must be treated for years," I put in.

"Oh, I should hope not," William said. "Surely not that long."

"Lucy is making great strides, but the mind is an impossible thing to predict. We don't understand it fully even now."

"Yes, yes, so you've said." William was impatient. "But we're not talking of just any mind, we're talking of a woman's. Lucy's. How complex can it be?"

I began to rise. "I think I'll see about tea."

"Thus far, I've seen little real evidence that a female brain is simple," Victor said.

"But certainly more primitive, isn't it?"

Victor shrugged. "Perhaps. Certainly they don't seem capable of specialization in the same way as a man."

"You see?"

"Yes," I said wryly. "I'll just see about the primitive necessity of food."

"Call Sadie," William said. "Where's the bell?"

"The bell? I haven't used it since we've been here."

"How are you calling the servants, then?"

"I've been walking into the house to find them," I said. "Really, William. The bell seems so insensitive, don't you think?"

He looked at me as if I had fallen into a fit before him. "You're the lady of the house," he said. "Their job is to serve you."

"Yes, but it seems so ludicrous when it's just as easy for me to—"

"Sadie!" he called. "Sadie!"

Victor was watching us with interest, and I was embarrassed. "Please, William."

"Sadie!"

She came hurrying onto the porch, flustered. "Yes sir, Mr. Carelton? Is there something you're needing?"

"The service bell, for one thing," William snapped. "Mrs. Carelton is not to rouse herself. She is your mistress."

"Please, William, there's no need for this."

He ignored me. "Where is the bell?"

"On the piano, sir, where it's been since last fall."

"Bring it to me."

Sadie began to turn back into the house.

"No," I said. I spoke more sternly than I had intended.

Sadie stopped. William looked at me in surprise. "What?"

"I don't want the bell. Sadie, please leave it where it belongs." I turned to my husband. "I'm not an invalid, and I won't be treated like one. If my mind is so primitive, William, my body is not. I can walk. I can skip and jump too, if I care to. I won't be catered to like some delicate flower."

Under William's eyes, I felt as if I were some oddity in Barnum's museum—a two-headed calf, a dried mermaid. "As you wish," he said finally. Then he said to Victor, "What the hell are you smiling about?" before he turned on his heel and strode angrily away.

Sadie lingered on the porch, confused.

"We'll have tea on the porch, Sadie," I said gently, and she nodded and hurried into the house as if she were relieved.

Only then did I look at Victor.

He was sitting up, and slowly, quietly, he clapped his hands. "That was magnificent," he whispered. Then he dipped his head and smiled, turning back to his ledger, to his endless writing.

That night I lay in bed, waiting in dread for William to come to our room. He and Victor had gone to the porch after supper, to smoke their cigars and drink port. I could not bear the tension of it any longer and left them to themselves. I tried to read, but I could not concentrate, and when at last I heard the closing of the door and footsteps on the stairs, I blew out the candle and closed my eyes and pretended to sleep while I listened to Victor's low "Good night," and his footsteps passing my door on the way to his room, his infinitesimal hesitation.

It was some minutes before I heard William's heavy step on the stairs. I turned on my side and evened my breathing, but I could not relax. When he opened the door and paused, letting his eyes grow used to the light, I knew he wasn't fooled.

"Asleep already, darling?" he whispered. "Such a pity. Not even a welcome for your husband after all these days without me?"

I did not answer. I heard him fumble on the tabletop beside the door, the strike of a match, the lighting of another candle. He closed the door and came to my side of the bed, where he stood, shining the candlelight on me so I could no longer pretend. I opened my eyes.

"What are you doing?" I asked.

"Looking at you," he said. "Wondering whose spirit has taken over my sweet wife."

"Don't be silly, William."

"Does he tell you what to say?"

"No, of course not."

"What does he tell you then?"

"Nothing. He's helped me, William—even you must see that."

"Yes." He sounded confused. "You do seem better, but—"

"But what?"

He paused. "Nothing," he said, and then, "I went to the house before I came here today. It's progressing rapidly, Lucy."

"Is it?"

"McKim is certain we'll be able to move in by mid-September. I've told him I want to hold a ball to open it at the start of October. The sixth, to be precise."

I rolled onto my back, shielding my eyes from the light. "I can't possibly have everything ready by then."

"You will," he said easily. "I've ordered the invitations. Three hundred of them. They should be done in a few weeks. I'll have them sent here, and you will address them and have them delivered."

"But William—"

"I don't ask much of you, Lucy, but on this I must insist. This is the start of our new life. I want nothing to go wrong."

I could not imagine it. That life seemed so far away.

William stood there holding the light, wavering. I closed my eyes. "I'm tired, William. Put out the light."

He sighed. "You know, Lucy, I do love you."

"Yes, I know," I whispered.

"We'll be so happy there." He remained a moment longer, and then he went to his side of the bed and set the candle down. I heard him undress, and then the sputter as he blew out the candle and crawled in beside me. The bed sank beneath his weight, and I stiffened to keep from rolling into the valley between us. My breath came shallow as he turned toward me and put his arm around me, pulling me to him.

"I'm tired, William," I said.

He released me.

"Yes, of course," he said, rolling onto his back again, and his voice was so resigned it ached within me. "Forgive me."

In the morning he was out of bed before I woke, but I heard him talking downstairs, and I smelled the heavy, greasy scents of bacon and potatoes and eggs. Sadie had remembered William's favorites. I rose and went to the window, pulling aside the drapes. I heard the front door open and close, and then I saw William stepping onto the lawn, walking toward the rocky seawall. He was alone.

I quickly put on my dressing gown, opened the bedroom door as quietly as I could, and hurried down the hall to Victor's room. The door was closed; he wasn't up yet. I tapped on it lightly, and before he could answer, I cracked it and peeked in.

He was still abed but awake, staring out the windows. He wore only his union suit, and he looked sleepless and weary, but his face lit when he saw me.

"William's gone down to the beach," I whispered. "But I've only a minute. He hates the sand."

I stepped inside and closed the door behind me, and he lifted his hand. "Come here," he said. I went to him, sitting on the edge of the bed, letting him wrap me in his arms, breathing deep his scent. He kissed my jaw, my ear. "How are you this morning, my darling? Do you still belong to me?"

I was so enraptured by the endearment that I barely heard the rest. I was breathless with his affection, with the words he'd never used before. "Yes," I said. "Oh yes. Always. Tell me to leave him, Victor. Tell me and I will. I swear I will."

But he did not say the words, and soon I forgot I had asked him to.

Notes from the Journal of
Victor Leonard Seth

Re: Eve C.

June 22, 1885

I have retired to Newport Beach with Eve, as her personal doctor. At this critical stage of her treatment, it is preferable that I be with her as often as possible. Here, where she is at her most naturalistic, where she feels an affinity for the endless ocean, her mind is at its most accepting. In the city her newfound self might crumble beneath the onslaught of social habit and the control of her husband. Removed from all of that, under my constant influence, she is becoming a truly marvelous creature.

While her husband is away in the city during the week, Eve is mine to manage without interference. We have spent nearly every moment together, and although one's environment is uncontrollable and I cannot completely protect her from those who would come between us, I am confident that I have strengthened our bond. She is a strong and vibrant woman, one I have fashioned from whole cloth; one I have improved from a submissive, tentative, neurasthenic woman groping for some way to drug herself into passivity. I continue to be amazed at my success and preoccupied with her every nuance. She belongs to me in a way that no human being has ever belonged to another.

I have had another letter from Hall. He cautions me to temper my enthusiasm. He says I am spending far too much time with a married woman, and that such far-reaching exploration of her sexual being is too dangerous—

he believes it can have only disastrous consequences—such hypocrisy from the man who counseled that interrupted coitus and suppressed passion may be a leading factor in her unhappiness, which I have proved to be true. I had quoted Aristotle, "All men by nature desire to know," and his answer was to accuse me of sophistry: "With your emphasis on the development of the self at the cost of everything else, what then is individualism truly but selfishness? In this poor woman, who has a life beyond yours, who must return to it with a soul that has since known a freedom she cannot hope to grasp again, have you not simply destined someone to be unhappy? To be a pariah? She is a woman, meant to serve others, to live within a certain prescribed world. You have not thought of her life but only of your own scientific inquiries. Is it your right to ask those sacrifices? Is it your right to play God with this poor woman's mind? Your goal, my friend, should have been to teach her to find happiness in her role, to teach her to be happy within her femininity, and not to urge her to seek pleasure and fulfillment in a world she is not allowed access to. She is not, after all, a man."

He misses the point: that I have <u>created</u> someone; that hypnosis and other aspects of treatment have forged a new soul. The idea that it can even be done is remarkable, and yet he dares to question me on the grounds of morality. What is morality but another way humans hold one another in bondage? Should science and truth be held in thrall to such a manufactured thing?

Hall is wrong; I find no agreement with the Sophists and their beliefs that absolute truths are unknowable. Socrates said that through rational thinking and logic one can find universal truth, and that is what I believe, <u>that</u>

is what I have found in Eve. I have proved that the will is not only knowable but pliable. She is on her way to becoming the kind of woman I have never before seen. I must continue on, I cannot rest, I am full of her. When Hall and the others see what I have done, they will understand. Until then she belongs to me.

Chapter 21

When William left again, the rest of the world came knocking.

As Victor and I sat on the porch or in the side yard, I saw the wagons come. There was a regularity to them, at least one a day, loaded down with trunks and boxes, with women who waved at me and men who tipped their hats. The cards began to make their appearance, sent by servants to announce arrivals; they rested in a pile on the silver salver in the foyer. The early time, the alone time, was over so soon. I cursed myself for not coming earlier, for not finding weeks alone with Victor instead of only days. But William never would have allowed that, so I resigned myself to the ending of idyllic hours.

The first supper was at Millicent's. She had been coming to Newport only the last two years, and her husband had bought a house farther down Bellevue Avenue—a ten-room cottage they were busily adding onto and redecorating.

The regular crowd was still small and intimate, so Millie had invited a faster set as well. They were a welcome diversion now, before August brought Caroline Astor and her social watchdogs. Twenty or so of us gathered that night in Millie's seamotifed dining room, and I was aware every moment of where Victor was in the room; it took all my will to keep from monopolizing him, touching him, showing them all that he belonged to me. I was distracted enough that I found it hard to listen to Alma Fister as she leaned close to me at the table.

"I could hardly bring her with me," she was saying in a loud whisper. "She insisted that she be allowed to go back to the city once a week to take her wages to her mother. How could I possibly allow such a thing? I mean, really, how important can a few cents be? I've half a mind to let her go as it is—the way she looks at me is so impudent. I can hardly give her an order that she isn't mocking me with her eyes. But you know how difficult it is to get a good servant, and she does my hair so wonderfully."

"Perhaps she only wants a few hours to herself," I said.

Alma looked at me as if I'd just committed heresy. Her dark brows rose high, accenting the odd contrast between them and her rapidly graying hair. "Why, she's a servant, Lucy. She'll take what hours I choose to give her. And I simply can't afford to lend her the time. What with all the promenades and parties, I need someone constantly to attend to my hair."

"You could forgo one or two hours. I expect it would hardly make a difference. You might even find you like it. I've taken several hours for myself. Just to sit idly on the beach is invigorating."

"Have you?" Alma's blue gaze darted down the table. "How do you manage to do that with a guest about?"

She had looked to where Victor sat, not far away, engaged in conversation with Millicent. I smiled patiently. "Victor spends much of his time engrossed in his work, I'm afraid. I've tried to convince him to go out himself, but he claims he came here for peace and quiet."

"A pity William doesn't find his way here more often. He could take Victor out to the Reading Room or the Casino."

"Yes, but William's quite busy. It's a wonder he's managed to be here every weekend."

"It's so hard for them to get away," Alma commiserated. "Gerald complains of it often." Alma's husband usually spent his weekends not at his summer estate with his wife and her friends, who searched constantly for the next amusement, but anchored in the bay, watching the goings-on from his yacht, the *Mary Dare*.

Alma whispered, "You would think Steven Breckenwood would at least attempt to do the same." She glanced at Julia Breckenwood, who sat a short distance away, and whose presence made me anxious—I had not forgotten William's words regarding her and Victor—and wrinkled her nose. "Poor Julia. Everyone knows he's been seeing that little actress. It's quite scandalous. We must do what we can to keep Julia occupied this summer."

There was laughter at the end of the table. Victor was smiling in that diffident way he had. I heard him say, "Mesmer was interested primarily in magnetic energy."

"Oh yes, I've read all about it," Leonard Ames—one of the few men at the table and well known as Alma's Newport monkey—spoke eagerly. He took a sip of his wine. "Something about some energy fluid that runs through the body, isn't it? Didn't he use magnets to direct it? Quite fascinating, really. Is that what you do, Victor? Have you your magnets? Perhaps we can try it out."

"It's not the same thing at all," Victor said impatiently. "There was nothing scientific about it. Human magnetism has nothing to do with hypnosis—nor, for that matter, does celestial magnetism."

Alma frowned. "Celestial magnetism?"

"A kind of spiritualism, I gather," Leonard put in. "Can you summon the dead, Victor? Let's have a séance."

"And wake them from their graves?" Victor asked wryly. "Leave that to the charlatans. I've nothing to do with it."

"Then what do you do?" Alma asked. "I'm afraid I don't understand."

"Hypnotism is simply a form of sleep," Victor explained sharply, "where a suggestion is made to the unconscious mind to modify behavior."

Leonard leaned forward eagerly, sloshing droplets of wine on the tablecloth. "You mean that if I were having trouble sleeping, you could make a suggestion that I sleep and I would?"

"It depends on the strength of your will," Victor said. "But yes, essentially."

"You mean you take over someone's will?"

"It's not possible with everyone, but in some cases, yes."

"You could make me do anything you wanted me to do?" Leonard poured more wine. "Could you make me do something like, well . . ."

"He's terribly shy, really," Millie said, and everyone laughed. "Could you make him do something truly outrageous?"

"Probably." Victor eyed Leonard speculatively.

"Oh, please, try," Leonard said. "Show me how this hypnosis works."

"Will you, Victor?" Alma asked.

"It's not a parlor game," Victor said.

"Well, of course," Millie put in. "But perhaps seeing it would explain it to us a little better. And it's been such a dull week. I'm sure we could all use some amusement."

It surprised me when he considered it. They were all sitting forward, as if by the very pressure of their movement they could get him to agree. I found myself urging him as well. He was a brilliant man, and I wanted them to understand him. I wanted them to think of him as I did. When he looked at me, I nodded and said, "Perhaps you can make them understand."

He set down his goblet. "Very well," he said, "but I must remind you that this isn't a game."

"Take me first." Leonard stood, spreading his arms as if sacrificing himself. "I've a longing to see how it feels to have no will."

"I would have thought you'd already know what that feels like," Julia said.

The rest of the table laughed, as did Leonard. "Well, then, to see what it feels like to have someone else's." He widened his eyes. "I shall be a new creature. Like Frankenstein's monster."

Victor stood. "Perhaps someone less dramatic," he said. "Perhaps Julia?"

All eyes went to her. Julia set down her napkin, licking her lips with a little nervousness. Her expression was reproachful, even petulant, but she smiled and said, "Of course," and rose against Leonard's loud protests.

"Do you have a comfortable chair, Millie?" Victor asked.

"In the parlor." Millie got to her feet, ushering us all from the dining room. They followed Victor like rats after the Pied Piper, seduced by his charisma, as I had been. We went from the dining room into the first parlor, which also was decorated in a sea theme, with settees and chairs of aqua silk, glass jars of shells, wallpaper flocked in shades of sand. Victor motioned Julia to the settee and pulled a chair opposite her in a formation that reminded me of his office. I knew what Julia was feeling as he sat across from her, and I saw with a small shock that it was familiar to her as well. She seemed comfortable and calm, as if she knew what was going to happen. I felt a keen stab of jealousy. I wondered why he had not chosen me.

"Everyone must be quiet," he said, keeping his gaze on Julia, who blushed beneath it. "It cannot work if you aren't."

"Silent as the tomb," Leonard said, putting a finger to his lips, and there were nervous giggles and a few hushes. When the room was quiet, Victor began.

I had only ever been the victim of that gaze, and I watched

with a kind of repulsed fascination as Victor took Julia's thumbs
in his fingers and began to speak in a quiet, singsong voice.
"Look at me, Julia, and think only of going to sleep. How you
long for it. How good it will feel to close your eyes. Your eyelids are growing heavy. Heavier. Your eyes are very tired."

Julia's eyes began to redden.

"Yes, that's it. Your eyelids are flickering, your eyes are water-
ing. Your vision is blurring. You want to close your eyes. Sleep
is all you long for. Yes, close your eyes."

Her eyes were tearing now. When he said the final words, she
closed her eyes in obvious relief. I had known that relief once,
the first time he'd put me into a trance. Since then, I had never
needed such a ceremony. My fingers curled about my wrist.
There was a murmur from someone, quickly hushed. Victor did
not take his gaze from Julia.

"You will no longer feel anything. Your hands are motionless,
you see nothing more. You are sleeping. Sleeping." His voice
trailed off in a whisper.

"That was remarkable," Leonard said.

"Quiet, Len," Alma ordered.

Victor released Julia's thumbs. They fell lax into her lap.
"Now," he said, "I am going to raise your arm. It will stay frozen
in the air. No amount of strength will move it."

He raised Julia's arm until it was outstretched, so the candlelight shimmered off the purple silk of her sleeve. The sinews in
her arm were pronounced; her hand was rigid. Gently Victor
tried to move it. It did not budge. He turned to Leonard.
"Would you care to try?"

Leonard swallowed and nodded. He came forward and
pushed on Julia's arm. "It's solid as a bar," he said in amazement.

"You may use all your strength," Victor told him.

Leonard put both hands on Julia's arm and tried to lower it. It
did not waver. "My God," he said.

"Does one of you ladies have a pin?" Victor asked.

"Yes. Yes, of course." Alma reached into her chignon and pulled out a bejeweled hairpin that glittered citron and amethyst. She put it in Victor's hand.

"You may lower your arm now, Julia," he said, and she did so. He took her hand and turned it palm up. "You will feel nothing," he said, pressing the pointed end of the pin into the soft center of her palm, hard enough that it made an impression. She didn't move.

"What else can you make her do?" Leonard asked.

Victor handed the pin to Alma, who stood staring as if it held some magic power. He sat back in his chair and said to Julia, "Rise and open your eyes."

Julia stood obediently.

"Walk."

She walked, neatly avoiding the chair, crossing the room as if she could see everything within it. I began to feel strange, as if it were me Victor was putting through the paces.

"You can't go any farther," he said, the tone of his voice never wavering. Low and smooth, with a rhythm that held us as spellbound as Julia. "On the table beside you is a glass of wine. You will drink it."

There was no table beside her, but Julia reached out. Her hand curled around an invisible glass. She raised it to her lips. Swallowed.

"You've had your fill of it," Victor said, and Julia put the glass down. "Now you will return to your chair and sit down. When I count to three, you will awaken. When you do, you will hear the sound of a violin coming from the beach."

Julia moved back to him. She sat down, calm and still, and Victor counted slowly. "One. Two. Three."

She blinked. She saw us watching her and flushed deeply.

Leonard clapped his hands. "Bravo, Victor. That was truly remarkable."

But no one paid attention to him. We were all watching Julia as she tilted her head. "Do you hear that?" she asked, rising, going to the window. "Why, it sounds like someone is playing a violin on the beach."

Victor sat back in his chair, crossing his arms over his chest. He smiled smugly while the others oohed and aahed and crowded around him, and it was clear he enjoyed their adulation. I looked at Julia, who had turned from the window with a frown. Our gazes met, and I felt hollow and alone. I remembered a walk in the woods, a singing bird.

"There's no violin," I said softly to her, and her expression cleared. She nodded and went again into the dining room, to where her glass of wine—a real one this time—waited. She took a long swallow.

I heard Leonard ask, "Can you do that to anyone?" and Victor's assured assent, and then a chorus of "Oh, I'd like to try" and "Put me to sleep, Victor" and "No, no, it's my turn now." I turned away from it all, bedeviled in a way I couldn't explain. I went out the screened door and onto the porch that looked over the darkness that was the sea. The moon was slight. I could see the crests of waves, dimly white and ghostly, floating, disconnected. From somewhere came the scent of roses.

That night, as we walked from the carriage house around to the porch, Victor caught my arm, stopping me before I climbed the stairs. "You seem quiet tonight," he said.

"I'm a bit tired."

"You've said nothing about dinner."

Sadie had lit a lamp that beckoned from the window. It cast Victor's face in shadow, but I could see the avidity of his stare, how hungry he was for praise. I said, "You were quite a success. I think they all love you."

"Yes," he said with satisfaction. "Did you hear how they all begged for it? Two minutes before they had called it mesmerism."

"They couldn't know the difference," I said dully.

"I had to show them it was a true science. They didn't believe."

"Now they do."

"Yes, now they do," he said. I felt his excitement. We went up the stairs, and he pressed me against the wall near the door and kissed me. "They'll know now," he murmured into my mouth, and my sense of disconnectedness fled. I felt again the passion I always felt for him, the longing so intense it took away doubt as he lifted my skirts and plunged his hands beneath them, holding me in place, taking me there on the porch while the sea rushed onto the beach beyond.

Chapter 22

Victor became a luminary in Newport. He was invited to the Reading Room, the exclusive men's club that William had spent most of three years trying to join before they accepted him last summer. Women could not get past the first step onto the large piazza without encountering a clubman, so I only heard about how Victor entertained them, how he made Gerald Fister attempt to light his cigar with a stem of mint from a julep, and how even Cornelius Vanderbilt had clapped him on the back and asked him to attend one of their parties. When we went to the Casino to listen to the orchestra, he was surrounded by those who wanted to be turned into trained monkeys, and every supper we went to ended with a display of hypnotism. Even Millicent had taken her turn on the chair, exclaiming when she woke over how loud the military band on the porch was—where had it come from?

Victor had told me in the past how hypnosis was not successful on everyone, and to others only to a certain degree. I noticed how carefully he chose—Julia, whom he had hypnotized before; Leonard, who wanted it so badly he would no doubt pretend even if Victor could not take him into a trance; Gerald, who accepted with alacrity anything that made Alma happy. But never me. Victor never put me into a trance before a crowd.

It was mid-July already. The sky was clear blue and cloudless, and the mornings came humid and hot, so we woke often before dawn, bathed in sweat, to open the windows, and we kept them open far into the night. Even the water felt warm when we swam.

We began to live for the night, for the suppers we went to and the ones that we increasingly hosted together. William had not visited Seaward for the last two weeks. He would come on the fourteenth to spend a week, but he was busier than ever. He sent his love, along with the invitations to our ball for me to address, and hoped that Victor was not monopolizing my time.

Victor threw himself into the entertainments, and these scenes played anxiously about my mind. I did not like the game hypnotism had become; it made too little of my own experience. I did not like seeing how easy it was for Victor to make a fool of someone. I began to wonder about the control he had over my mind. Though I was uneasy and fretful, my passion for him had not abated. If anything, it had grown, so my fingers itched for him constantly; I grew less discreet. Occasions like the one on the porch grew more frequent—once on the beach, along the seawall; once in the carriage house, while David was outside washing down the landau; once midday in the little rose bedroom that had been mine, with his papers crumpling beneath me and Sadie moving around downstairs. I searched for ways to bind him to me, because my own doubts plagued me. I did not like my feeling that the Victor I knew was changing into one of the tricksters he claimed to despise. I wanted his hypnotism play to stop, and I told myself it was because I feared for him: I knew how soon people's affections could turn, how the newest entertainment passed so rapidly into the next. How much longer before hypnotism bored them the way phrenology had? But the truth was that I didn't like the intrusion of my own reason; every time he put someone in a trance, I was reminded of the control he must have over me.

I thought Victor must sense my uncertainty, but he said nothing, though I often found him staring at me as if he could see into my thoughts.

Early one afternoon, two days before William was due to arrive, Millie came to call bearing rolls of wallpaper and swatches of fabric and chunks of marble. I welcomed her with a smile, but those things only reminded me of the pile of invitations on my desk, ready to be sent out, and of the huge mausoleum that I would be returning to, of William's expectations.

She knew this, of course. Perhaps it was part of the reason she'd come. As she laid a chunk of pink Italian marble next to one of sparkling marbleized granite, she gave me a sideways glance and said, "I wouldn't have brought them all this way, but I do need help choosing, and I thought since you've so recently been through this yourself . . . Oh, and Lucy, wouldn't this pink look lovely in your new foyer?"

"William has already decided on something," I said.

"Oh? What is that?"

"I don't remember."

She gave me an odd look, and then her glance went beyond me to where Victor was idly glancing through rolls of wallpaper. "You didn't help him choose?" she asked me.

"William has his own ideas for the house," I said. "My opinion hardly matters."

"Really?" Millie stepped away from the marble samples. "But you went to Goupil's so often this spring."

I had to turn away as a burst of bitterness came upon me. "He didn't like my choices. He particularly disliked the Gérôme."

"Oh? Well, you knew he would. He did say landscapes, Lucy."

I saw Victor's shoulders tense. I wondered what he thought Millie was saying, why it mattered to him. When I looked back to Millicent, I saw she had followed my glance, and her own expression was assessing, faintly worried.

"In any case, Charles says he drove by your new house the other day, and it looks nearly complete."

I thought of the walls looming against the sunset, the dark stone, William's enthusiasm, and I nodded, fingering a swatch of multicolored tapestry. "I've invitations to send out for the opening. William wants a grand ball."

"How wonderful. Alma Fister was saying the other day that jewels would make such an elegant supper theme. Can you imagine? A pearl supper or an emerald one. Which would you choose?"

I felt the dull start of a headache. "William's planned something already. I have no idea what it will be."

"William?"

"He's much more dedicated to the house than Lucy is," Victor said. His interjection was so out of turn that both Millie and I went silent.

"It's true, you know, Millie," I said. "Victor is only saying what we already know. I prefer the Row."

"I know that was so once. But I'd thought—"

"I'd rather be here at Newport."

"Perhaps you won't feel that way once the house is finished."

"I cannot imagine."

"Lucy," she said. She bent close, as if she did not want Victor to hear. "You should at least feign interest. No one will understand why you care nothing for it. And William has been so good to build it for you."

I stepped away from her. "He's built it for himself, Millie."

She frowned. "But I thought—" She glanced again at Victor. "You said your doctor had worked miracles."

I worked to keep from looking at Victor. "He's quite brilliant."

"Yes." She said the word slowly, as if by lingering she could make herself believe it.

Victor straightened from the rolls of wallpaper and came over to us. "You seem skeptical, Millie," he said.

Millicent fingered the small gold dragonfly at her collar. "You must forgive me if I speak bluntly. It's just that I've known Lucy for so very long, and these last years have been so difficult for her. There have been so many doctors, and none has effected a cure. I'm happy that she feels so much better, but it seems so closely tied to you, Victor, that it gives one pause."

He smiled his charming smile. "I'm simply Lucy's guest for the summer. It also happens that I'm a doctor, so I'm available to help her should she require it."

"Victor specializes in nervous disorders," I said. "He won't say it, but I know you're already aware that Victor is more than my guest. He's the doctor I've been seeing—the one I told you about—and he's been most kind to stay here with me this summer." As I spoke, I touched Victor's arm.

Millie's gaze went to my hand. "Your doctor," she said softly. The doubt did not leave her expression as she looked at Victor. "You must truly be a genius, then. No other doctor has been able to help her."

"No other doctor has bothered to understand her," Victor said. "None of the others have been trained in neurology."

"Neurology?"

"The study of the mind."

"Ah. You're an alienist, then?"

"I'm a scientist," Victor said. "Unlike most alienists, I'm not concerned with asylum problems but with the true understanding of the brain and nervous system."

Millicent did not look enlightened. She seemed impatient, even angry. She said, "Would you mind, Victor, if I had a word with Lucy alone?"

"Certainly not," he said, but he was slow to leave.

Millicent waited until he was gone, then drew me to a corner of the room, next to a potted fern, as far from the doorway as we could be.

"I know what you say, Lucy, but there's something more here," she whispered urgently. "It's only a matter of time until everyone else sees it too."

I frowned. "What are you talking about? He's my guest for the summer. It's not at all unusual. Look at Leonard Ames—he spent all of last summer with Alma. No one questioned it."

She shook her head. "This is not the same as Leonard Ames with Alma Fister. Victor is no charming, harmless bachelor, Lucy, and you are too attached to him. You've hosted dinners together; he hovers around you as if he can't bear to leave you alone, and you're no better. You watch him constantly. People have noticed."

"You're being ridiculous, Millie." I backed away from her, loosing her hand.

"I'm not, and you know it," she said. "I remember when you were a child, Lucy. You've always been so passionate about everything. Too much so. Once you found something to engage you, you grew too involved. Nothing else mattered. I see it happening with him. You must send him away before everyone else sees it. They'll destroy you, Lucy. You've already caught their attention. You've changed, and they'll blame him when they see— don't you understand?"

"He's my doctor, Millie. Nothing more," I insisted—a little too desperately, I thought, and she noticed that too.

"Perhaps not yet," she said thoughtfully. "But I know you, Lucy, and I see what's happening, if it hasn't happened already. Send him away. Please. Don't ruin yourself or William."

"But I'm so much better."

"There are other doctors. It's unhealthy the way he controls you. It's as if he has you under his spell."

Her words shook me: They mirrored my own thoughts. "That's absurd," I said, though I heard my lack of conviction.

"I've seen what kind of power he holds," she said. "I've seen what he does."

"That's simply medicine."

"No it's not." Millicent grabbed my arm again, pushing me into the fern so its fronds brushed my shoulder. "Give him up."

The very thought made me ill. "I won't. I've found my life again. He's shown it to me. I'm happy for the first time in years."

"Happiness is not the most important thing. If we all did as we pleased, where would the world be?"

"I'm done caring about the world. It's time I started caring for myself."

"And it's you who will pay the price when this turns into what I suspect it will," Millicent said. "Or perhaps I'm too late. Perhaps he's already your—"

"My what?"

Her face hardened. "Don't be a fool, Lucy. You're my friend, I don't want to see you hurt."

"I won't be hurt," I said.

She stepped back and sighed. "Lucy, I have heard you say such things a hundred times before. What has it ever brought you but grief?"

I felt cold. "This is not the same thing as painting or poetry."

"No," she said. "But I remember William's courtship, if you don't. You expected him to create happiness for you, and as a result you've been miserable for the last four years. Look at yourself, Lucy—you've never been able to find satisfaction in the things that were possible. You're always reaching for something that isn't there. Don't doom yourself to unhappiness again."

"I appreciate your concern, Millie," I said coldly. "But you've misspoken."

Her lips pursed. She adjusted her hat, reached for her shawl. "Very well. I've done what I can."

Her resignation caught at me, and my annoyance over her

words dissipated. I touched her arm as she went to gather up her things. "Please don't worry. I know what I'm doing."

She looked up at me and sighed. "For your sake, Lucy, I hope you do."

I tried not to think of Millie's words past the time she left. When Victor came back, he gave me a searching look, but I only shook my head and said, "Millie's worried about me," and laughed it off as gaily as I could manage.

The late afternoon grew hot; I could barely feel the slight breeze coming off the sea. Victor and I had accepted an invitation to a party tonight at By-the-Bay; Julia Breckenwood's husband, Steven, had at last come to spend the weekend with his wife. But there were hours until I had to start preparing. I stared out at the water and thought of how good it would feel to bathe in it. I had not done so since Victor had arrived. When I said as much to him, he motioned to the waves lapping against the beach below the rocks and said, "Get your bathing costume. We'll go now."

"Oh, not here," I told him. "The currents are too unreliable."

"Then where?"

"Bailey's Beach. But it's long past eleven."

"What does time have to do with it?"

I thought of the crush of the fashionable eleven o'clock hour, the crowds of people, the women delicately dipping a toe and then stepping back. I turned to Victor with a smile. "Nothing at all."

It was not far to the beach. The guard was too well trained to show surprise at the lateness of the hour. He opened the gate for us, and I hurried off to the pavilion and changed into my bathing costume of heavy dark flannel.

When I came out, Victor was nowhere to be found. He was no doubt changing still. The beach was empty; of course it would be now. The waves beat steadily but limply against the shore. I spread the blanket I'd brought. I went to the edge of the water, which was deliciously cool as it wet my slippers, as it wicked up my stockings. I moved farther and farther out, until the water was at my waist and the flannel grew heavy and wet, and then I set into an easy lap along the shoreline, never so deep that I could not put a foot down.

The water was cool and luxurious. I felt strong and good, buoyed by salt. I didn't know how long I swam, only that I tired and stopped and walked back to the beach while the water surged and pulled against me. I broke from its grasp to the shore. The sand drew away beneath my feet with the tide. The flannel weighed on me now that it was no longer borne by water.

Along the shore walked a man wearing trousers with no shoes, and no hat, and no coat over his boiled shirt, the sleeves of which were rolled to his elbows. I watched him idly before I realized it was Victor.

"Where's your bathing costume?" I asked as he drew near, and I saw the fine veil of sweat on his forehead.

"I haven't one," he said.

"You haven't?"

"They weren't necessary where I come from," he said with a wry smile. "We wore our union suits when we jumped into the East River. Or nothing at all. I didn't think that would be approved of here."

"Oh." The image momentarily distracted me. Together we walked to the blanket and sank down onto it. "You should have said something. There's one of William's in the attic. I'm sure it would fit."

"No," he said, and there was a harshness to his voice that made me pause.

"It's only a bit of flannel," I said.

"And you're only his wife."

I was surprised by the quiet force of his words, by the jealousy

I heard behind them, and pleased too. "Because you want me to be. If you said the word, I would leave him."

He stared out at the water. His toes dug into the sand.

I couldn't help thinking of William. This was where he'd proposed to me. Until this summer I had never spent a moment on this beach when I didn't remember that day and yearn for his touch, just that way—again. Now it seemed so ridiculously civilized, so unreal, such a little passion. I'd experienced so much since then that it was hard for me to recall how much I'd wanted him, how frustrated I'd been.

Victor looked out toward the tangle of seaweed at the mouth of the bay. I laid my hand on his arm, which was hot from the sun, darkening, it seemed, even as I watched it.

"I don't want you to leave him," he said without looking at me. "Not yet."

"Not ever?" I asked.

He closed his eyes. "Not . . . yet," he repeated. "I must think. This has gone so much further than I intended."

"Than you intended?" I asked, afraid. "Don't you love me, Victor? Tell me you do. Tell me you don't want me to stay William's wife forever."

"No," he said violently. He twisted, reaching for me. His hand tangled in my hair, which I'd plaited for the swim, and which was rough and stiff with drying salt. "You are not William's but mine. I created you."

He held me close, so tightly I could barely breathe. He ravaged me with his mouth, and I let him. I went weak for him. I would have let him take me there on the beach, for anyone to see. And when he released me, his gaze went beyond me, freezing to some point over my shoulder. I turned to follow it.

There was William standing just beyond, booted and jacketed, as he'd been the day he proposed to me on this very beach. William, arrived two days early and come to look for me here, where he knew I could always be found.

Chapter 23

I pulled away from Victor, and he let me go; his hand dropped from my hair as if he had lost sensation. We sat there like statues as William came toward us. His face was expressionless. It was only when he came near that I felt the shuddering chill of his fury.

"I came early," he said quietly. "I thought you would be glad."

I didn't know what to say; I could only stare at him.

Victor said, "William—"

William cut him dead with a look. "This is a public beach. Anyone might see."

It was a reminder, a warning: We might have been heedless enough to display our affair at Bailey's Beach, but William was civilized. He would not brawl there; he would not give us the chance to appease him, or even the satisfaction of his anger.

"I saw David outside with the landau," he said tonelessly. He held out his hand to me. "He's waiting to go home."

I got to my feet, and Victor unfolded himself. I took up the blanket, bundling it, sand and all, my fingers trembling. I looked to Victor for support, but his features were etched in taut relief;

his tension was unbearable. I turned back to William, who said to Victor, "You'll come with us."

Victor said, "Of course."

"I'll let no one accuse me of leaving a houseguest to walk the distance home. After all, I'm a generous man. Generous to a fault, some have said." He laughed shortly. "Generous enough to offer up even my wife, it seems."

"William," I said.

He turned, his nostrils white, his hands fisted. "I don't want to hear a word from you."

It was not until I'd endured the horrible, silent ride home that I realized I'd left my gown behind in the bathing pavilion, that I was still wearing my bathing costume, that my skin was dry and sticky with salt. Once we were at Seaward, William dismissed David with a curt word. Sadie was in the kitchen, in the midst of putting together tea. He told her to go home for the evening, that we had no more need of her today.

It was only when they were gone that William turned to me and Victor.

"Who else knows?" he asked me. His voice was slow and quiet and deadly.

"No one," I rushed to tell him. "No one. It's not what—" I stopped, unable to say the words *It's not what you think*. Because it was exactly what he thought, and I could not make myself lie.

He nodded shortly. "I understand we've accepted an invitation to By-the-Bay for supper tonight."

I could not bear his civility. I felt like crying. "Oh, for God's sake, William. Please don't do this."

"Have we accepted the invitation?"

"Yes. Yes. But I'll send our regrets right away." I turned to go to my desk.

"No," William said. He was looking at Victor, who stood expressionless. William's face was terrible in its humiliation and rage. "We'll go tonight."

I was stunned. "Are you mad?"

"We'll go tonight," he continued. "And we will enjoy ourselves as if nothing has happened. Victor will enjoy himself. I
want him to remember how much. I want him to revel in it. Because it's the last time he'll ever attend such a thing."

I stared at him, aghast. "What do you mean?"

William ignored me. He smiled at Victor. "Victor, my friend,
after tonight, your career as a 'brilliant' neurologist in this city
will be over. You won't be welcomed in any home. If I were you,
I'd return to Leipzig. When I'm finished with you, it will be the
only place that will have you."

"William," I said. "You can't—"

He leveled a look that both silenced and stilled me. "You're
wrong, Lucy. I can. And I will. Tomorrow. Tonight you will do
what I want for once. I won't be humiliated. We will go to By-
the-Bay. We will be the happy couple, and Victor will be our
grateful houseguest. You will be my obedient wife. No one will
know about this. I won't drag your name into the mud, *darling*,
nor mine with it."

For a moment I thought insanely of Robert Carr, of how he'd
gone to London to bring his wife home from an affair with an
English baron. Of how she'd come. Of how they played the
happy couple at her blue supper.

I looked wildly at William, and then at Victor, who continued to stand silently. Why had he said nothing? "I won't do this,"
I said. "I won't go tonight. I can't."

Victor said, "Lucy, do as he asks."

William said sarcastically, "Yes, Lucy, listen to Victor. Do as
he tells you. How well he controls you. Better than your own
husband. Tell me, Victor, did you summon her to your bed, or
did she come of her own accord?"

Victor looked away.

"I trusted you, you bastard." William's control looked as if it might snap. Then he struggled, his teeth clenched; he calmed himself.

I felt sick. "William, please, don't do this. Scream at me if you must. Be angry. Just don't be this way."

"I've had enough of passion," he said. His pale gaze made me shiver; I knew he spoke of me, of what I was, of who I was. "Get dressed for Julia's supper, Lucy. You look a sight."

I turned away, unable to face him or to bear Victor's stolid acceptance of his fate. I did as he asked; I went to dress for supper.

By-the-Bay was alight and glorious. The middle of the dining table had been made into a pond that held pink water lilies; everyone said the soft-shell crabs and roasted partridge were sublime, though it was impossible for me to try even a bite. There was plenty of champagne, and William drank more than he usually did so that his cheeks were faintly reddened, and his eyes were glassy with a good humor that held cynicism and pain beneath it.

He kept me hard by his side most of the night, forcing me to smile, to pretend that all was well, to fight the tension that made me feel ill, that made my head pound. He caught every glance I threw to Victor, who showed no ill effects of this afternoon; he was circulating, smiling, his usual charming self. Desperate for instruction, I wanted to ask him what he wanted of me, what my role should be, but William made sure that such a meeting was impossible. I had no hope of rescue. I was paralyzed by the weight of my future.

"Victor seems to have enraptured them all," William whispered to me. He took a great swallow of wine. "You didn't tell me he's become the darling of Newport."

"Yes," I said absently. "He's quite requested."

"Why?"

I nodded toward Victor, who was talking animatedly to Gerald Fister. "He's worked magic among them. They adore him."

William's mouth tightened. I said to him, "I'm asking you not to destroy him. I'm begging you."

"I've given you everything you've ever wanted, Lucy, but I'm done with that now." He frowned, his gaze passing across the room. "What's going on?"

I saw that Victor's magic was happening already, as it always did after supper, when it was quite late, and everyone was too drunk to dance and too awake to go home. Victor would be talking, and someone would find him, touch his arm, whisper into his ear. Across the room two chairs would already be facing each other, ready for the night's entertainment.

I saw the touch, the whisper. I saw the chairs set up where the orchestra was packing up their instruments and readying to leave. It was almost two o'clock in the morning. I looked back at Victor to see that he was staring at me, so intently that I looked down, trying to warn him with my inattention. I felt William put his arm around my waist. He staggered a little with the movement; he was quite drunk.

"What is it?" William asked. "Where are they going?"

"It's Victor," I said, wanting to leave.

"Victor?"

"You once asked how he hypnotized me. Now is your opportunity to find out."

William frowned but went with all the others, and because he did not release his hold on me, I went too. There was muttering and the growing sound of laughter, of suspense. There were those in this crowd who had just come to Newport and not yet seen Victor's performance. And it was to be a good one. I saw Victor's charisma in full force. I wondered how he could be so calm, knowing that everything would be gone tomorrow. That I would be gone.

He began with Millie, who smiled and giggled nervously, like a girl, as he called her name. She went to the chair and sat, pulling her saffron skirts around her demurely, looking at him expectantly as Victor took the seat before her and held her thumbs in his.

"I must ask for silence," he said. I knew these words so well, this performance so intimately. "Complete silence."

The crowd went dead. Beside me William went taut. His fingers stiffened against my waist.

It went as it always had, every move perfect. Millie's trance, the stiff arm, the pinprick. Victor varied the hallucination, as he sometimes did. This time Millie went to the table, which was being cleared, and moved aside the glasses and silverware as if preparing for bed. Then she crawled onto it and lay down, pulling up imaginary blankets, fluffing nonexistent pillows. When he woke her, she heard a flute on the porch.

William was astounded. "Is this what he does to you?"

"I don't know," I said.

Leonard Ames, dancing attendance on Alma, was next. William watched with unease. Finally I felt him snap. His hand tightened on my arm as he pulled me from the crowd. His voice was clipped when he said, "We're going home."

I could not stop him. He was an immovable force, and he took me from that room as if I were a child. The others were too enraptured by Victor to notice our absence. I could only stumble after my husband, who jerked me so relentlessly that my arm felt wrenched from its socket. "William," I said. "William, please."

But he did not slow as he took me from the room and down the hall out to the porch. He bit off an instruction to the servant to fetch the carriage.

"I don't understand." I grabbed William's arm to stop him. "What happened? I don't understand."

He shook off my arm as if he couldn't stand my touch. "Is that how he does it?" William spat. "Does he control you so easily? My God, they were like puppets. Puppets! And you're the worst of them."

I wanted to cry. What was happening now, it was not real, it couldn't be real. "Don't be absurd, William. He—"

"He's like a god in there, *creating* people. I was right. Damn it, look what he's done to you." William nearly shoved me into the carriage. He put his fist to the ceiling, and we were off. I huddled in the corner until we were at Seaward. When we went into the house, William took my arm and yanked me up the stairs, and I was so miserable and confused that I let him. I said nothing when he propelled me through the door of our bedroom and slammed it shut behind us. Even when I realized how he planned to punish me, I did not fight him.

"Did he spend the night with you in our bed?" he asked me, pushing me back upon the mattress, tugging off his coat, jerking upon his collar.

I turned my face away from him.

"How long has it been going on, my sweet angel? How long have you been his whore?"

He was on me. He shoved up my skirts, and I lay there, numb and still, and let him. He was naked—I had felt him that way only once before, on our wedding night.

He muttered more, other obscenities, so wretched and horrible that I stopped hearing him. I could not even feel him. When he was finished, he lay there for a moment longer, covering me, and then he left. I did not hear him or know where he had gone. I moved my head and felt a warm wetness on the pillow beside me. His tears, I realized in a slow burn of regret. My own eyes were dry.

Notes from the Journal of
Victor Leonard Seth

It is over. My experiment with Eve is over. Her husband has removed her from my care, and I find that I have no choice but to relinquish her. Dear God, to lose her this way . . .

I tell myself it is for the best: I have done the research required for my paper; I have no doubt that when I present it to the Neurology Association this fall, it will receive the accolades it deserves. And it is best to withdraw from her now, before I begin to question my motives in keeping her. I must ask myself why I continued to work with her when I had succeeded in doing what I set out to do. I have felt desperate at the thought of losing her, and my rational mind says this should not be so. She is a patient, nothing more. My worries these last days, when I have felt her questioning, beginning to withdraw; when I have seen suspicion in her eyes, suspicion planted by her friends, by the man who calls himself her husband—suspicion of me, who has saved her!—I have not been myself. She remains my creature. And yet perhaps I did not completely see. Experiments flourish best in a controlled environment, and Eve's environment is not within my hands.

I find it best to focus on writing my paper. I cannot fight for her without her husband creating a scandal, and I cannot allow such a thing to besmirch my findings. I lost myself for a time; I had been so enthralled with Eve's development that I had forgotten it all must end. The experiment is over. The results are gathered. I cannot think of her. I must not think of her. I <u>must not want her.</u>

Chapter 24

The door was locked from the outside. William had made me a prisoner. There was no connecting room, no way to escape unless I chose to jump the two stories from the balcony. My chest began to tighten in that familiar way, the way I hadn't felt for months. I went to the bed and sank onto it, forcing myself to breathe, to calm, and the things I had refused to think of came into my head: Victor's and my kiss at Bailey's Beach, William's anger, his threats. I heard Millie's words again—*It's unhealthy the way he controls you . . . as if he has you under his spell,* and I was afraid because I knew it was true and I knew that of all of us, I had lost the most. Because he had changed me, and I could not go back to who I'd been. I had felt, in those last moments, Victor's surrender to William, his release of me, and I knew he would do what he could to save himself.

I went to the balcony and stepped out into the cool air, staring at the sea that was only a stain of darkness beyond. The moon had fallen, and there was a heaviness in the air that spoke of heat tomorrow. I felt a dread that made me unsteady, so I sat on the wicker chair near the doors. Tomorrow. I saw the faint edges of dawn lighting the horizon. Tomorrow was here; it would be daylight soon.

But it was not until dawn was lighting the sky, making the sea look darker than ever, bringing breezes that were already warm enough to break perspiration on my skin, that I saw a man walking along the seawall. I rose and went to the railing, clad only in my dressing gown, my hair loose and blowing into my face. I watched the familiar walk, the way a borrowed morning coat flapped against the back of his thighs, and it was then that I hurt, that the pressure of it seemed too much to contain. I leaned out over the railing to call to him. Before I could, he stopped and looked up at me, and then he turned a little, and I saw William step from the porch to stand on the lawn, waiting as I waited on the balcony above him.

Victor came up the lawn toward the house. I was afraid to say anything; William's hands were clenching at his sides, and I saw in him the mindless fury that had driven him to punish me. My own hands were so tight on the railing that I ceased to feel my fingers. It seemed to take Victor an eternity to make his way to the house.

When he came close enough, I saw the dissolution of the night on him, rumpled evening clothes, boots covered with wet sand, beard shadow. But his presence was still so compelling to me that when he stopped before William, my husband seemed shrunken and wan, like a ghost before a live and vibrant man.

"I want you to leave my house," William said, barely controlled, and Victor nodded.

"No. . . ." I had not meant to say anything. The sound was a breath. But they both heard it. Victor looked up at me, and William looked over his shoulder.

"Get into the house," he said. "This is between me and Victor."

Victor looked weary. "Go inside," he said softly. Strangely, I found myself doing so. I went into my bedroom and sat on the bed, and then I heard the two of them come into the house, the closing of the back parlor door, the rise and fall of voices. My worry weighted me as the voices went quieter and quieter. My dread grew so that I went to the door and tried the knob again, though I knew it wouldn't give.

Then I heard the parlor door open and footsteps on the stairs—Victor's steps. I rattled the knob. "Victor," I called. "Victor, he's locked me in." There was no answer, only the brief pause of footsteps, then their resumption as he went to the back bedroom.

It was an hour before I heard them again, along with the brush of something heavy against the walls. His bag. I pounded on the door. "Let me out," I called. As the footsteps kept going, I called more loudly. "William, you must let me out. Victor!"

I rushed to the balcony, throwing myself on it so abruptly that my dressing gown flew open. I stood there with my nakedness exposed as Victor stepped off the porch, William beside him.

"Victor, no!" I cried. He did not look up; I saw nothing to show he had even heard me, and then they were gone, around the corner of the house where I could no longer see them. He could not be leaving me, not like this, not without a word.

In the distance I heard the wagon, David's voice, the crack of reins, the starting creak of wheels. The road was on the other side of the house; I could not see him go. I could only listen until the sound of the wagon retreated.

He had left me.

William came around to the porch. When he caught sight of me still standing there, he frowned.

"Go inside, Lucy," he said. "You've forgotten yourself. You're indecent."

"Where did he go?"

"I won't talk to you about this here," he said.

"Where did he go?" I had raised my voice; I heard it echo out over the beach.

William said, "Calm down."

I did just the opposite. I went into the bedroom and pounded at the door with all my strength, until he hurried up the stairs and pushed open the door. He stepped inside, closing it tightly behind him, saying, "Calm down, Lucy. For God's sake, what if the neighbors should hear?"

"I don't care."

William's expression was tight and mean. "He used you, Lucy. I should think you'd be glad that he's gone."

"Where has he gone?"

"It doesn't matter."

"It does to me."

"Why? You're my wife. He's gone from your life for good."

I went to the armoire, threw open the doors, and took a traveling bag from the cluttered depths.

"What are you doing?" he asked.

I said, "I'm leaving you." I began tossing things into the bag, gowns and underclothes, a pair of shoes.

"Lucy. Lucy, you don't know what you're saying."

"I know exactly what I'm saying. I'm leaving you."

"Think of who you are, Lucy. God damn it, I won't let you go. You're a Carelton. You're my wife. And that's what you'll be until you're in the grave."

I was stopped by his words. His face was as cold as I had ever seen it, the rawness of his emotion bared. I saw once again the inflexibility of his will, and a vision came to me: a grave marker, my name chiseled in marble, CARELTON at the very top, with *Lucille Marie Schyler Van Berckel* beneath. The truth of William's words struck me, its very permanence, so I had to shake myself a little to forget it.

"Let me go, William," I said. "It would be best to let me go."

"I won't do that."

"I don't want this life any longer." The bag could hold no more. I fastened the buckles and put it on the floor, and then I pulled out the traveling gown I'd arrived in and threw off my dressing gown so I was standing completely nude before my husband. I saw him flush and step back; he had never seen me so carelessly naked. It made me feel curiously powerful, dispassionately sensual in a vengeful way, and I let him watch as I pulled on my drawers and stockings, my chemise. I threw back my hair to pull on my corset.

His face was white. "You aren't going anywhere. You're my wife, damn it. You'll do as I say."

I tried to shove past him. "Not anymore."

He threw me back in the room as easily as he had the night before. His strength made me angry, so I tried to push past him again. "Let me go," I said. "I don't love you. I don't want to stay."

"I don't give a damn what you want," he said, and this time he shoved me so hard I went sprawling to the floor. "You're my wife. You're a Carelton."

He left me, shutting the door firmly. I heard the turn of the key in the lock, the thin echo of his voice as he said, "I'm sorry, Lucy, but you aren't yourself just now. It's best if you go to bed. I'll call the doctor right away."

William didn't return. As the morning crept into a dully hot afternoon and I began to sweat and grow light-headed, I took off the corset and put on my dressing gown again. I sat on the balcony watching the sea until the afternoon turned to evening. I began to hear music floating on the breeze, and I realized that things were moving on exactly as they always had. Somewhere there was a supper I had been invited to, a supper where they were gathering and drinking and gossiping, and for some reason, I found my vision blurring with tears. I went back into my room and lay upon the bed, falling into a restless sleep where dreams plagued me, until I heard someone knocking on the door.

It was dark. William came into the room bearing only a candle. He stood in the doorway and looked at me steadily, his eyes seeming to glow in the darkness. He held a glass of lemonade.

"I thought you might be thirsty," he said. "It was a hot day."

I was captured still by the dreams; this seemed only another restless image. I sat up and nodded. I *was* thirsty; I'd had nothing to drink all day. He put the glass in my hand and said, "Drink it all, Lucy," and I obeyed him. The drink was strange, a little warm, with a familiar taste, but my throat was dry and I drained the glass.

He took it from me and backed away. "Go to sleep now," he said, and then he was gone.

The next morning I woke groggy and dull, my mouth bitter with laudanum. I could barely move. William had drugged me, I knew that, but the morphia made me helpless. I could not care. I could only stare blankly as he came into the room with a hearty-looking man wearing bushy muttonchop whiskers and dressed soberly in black. He held papers in his hand, which he looked at often.

"You see?" William said. "She cannot even rouse herself to modesty." The man nodded, and his gaze raked over me where I lay exposed on the bed. I could barely bring myself to show any interest in him until he came over and took my wrist, his fingers curling around it. Then I wrenched away from him violently, remembering Victor's fingers just that way. I backed up against the headboard, twisting my hands together and wrapping myself around them so he could not get them.

The man looked at me sorrowfully. "Mrs. Carelton, can you hear me? Can you understand me?"

I began—inexplicably—to cry.

He did not try to touch me again. "I understand your situation," I heard him say to William, and my husband came over to the bed.

"I'm sorry," he whispered. "Lucy, my dear, I am sorry. But you must realize what a danger you are to yourself."

I turned away from him and heard him sigh. Then he went to the door and said something, and two men came in—David, who averted his eyes hastily when he saw me, and someone else, some man-boy I'd seen in town. His stare locked upon me greedily, but I didn't care. I could barely bring myself to wonder why they were there, what they wanted.

Sadie came in behind them. She looked sad and anxious. Quickly she went to the armoire. She pulled out drawers and petticoats, a chemise, a corset, my traveling gown, and brought them over to where I lay on the bed. "You two go on out," she ordered David and the other. William said, "Wait in the hall," and as they left, Sadie urged me to sit up.

"Come on, now, Mrs. Carelton," she whispered. "Let's get dressed, shall we? That's a good girl."

I was too limp to care or to help her. "Where are we going?" My voice sounded slurred even to my own ears.

"Why, out," she said, glancing at William. "It's a good sunny day. Wouldn't you like to go for a ride?"

"William won't let me," I said. "I'm his prisoner."

"Don't be absurd, Lucy," he said impatiently, coming to the bed to help Sadie. "Let's get you dressed."

They pulled me up and I stood on unsteady feet. I held on to the back of a chair as my dressing gown was pulled off. My eyelids were heavy, my limbs slack. It was as if they dressed another body or a doll. The layers were put upon me one after another: chemise and corset, petticoats and skirt. The corset made me woozy, so when they ordered me to sit down, I did so, watching as they shoved my feet into boots, the flash of the buttonhook in the light.

"Her hair?" Sadie asked.

William shook his head. "We've no time. They're waiting for us. Believe me, they won't be surprised."

Sadie gave me a pitying look.

William said, "Come now. Let's go."

The bag I'd packed was still there, buckled and ready. He picked it up and called for the boys and handed it to David. Then he took my arm and we went down the stairs.

I felt a niggling worry: This was odd, even for a dream. Real but unreal—where was I going? Who was waiting? But I couldn't muster the strength to ask those questions. I forgot them nearly the moment I thought of them.

We went from the house. The carriage was there, and William bundled me inside and put my bag on the seat. He muttered something to Sadie, then climbed in beside me. I felt the shudder as David climbed onto the box, another jolt—it must have been the other boy—and then we started off.

The rocking motion of the carriage immediately lulled me to sleep. I was awakened by the sound of voices. I blinked and tried to sit up. The carriage had come to a stop. I looked out the window to see two men approaching, both in dark suits, both sweating beneath their hats. William stepped from the carriage and spoke to them. I heard him say *laudanum*, and the taller man nodded and came to me.

"Mrs. Carelton," he said in a quiet voice. "How nice to see you. How are you feeling?" He seemed familiar, but I couldn't place him, and I was too sleepy to try.

He held out his hand for me, and there seemed to be nothing to do but take it. He helped me from the carriage and handed the other man my bag. William came up to me and said, "They're going to take care of you, Lucy," in a mild voice that made me afraid.

"Take care of me?" I managed.

"Go with them, darling," he said.

I began to feel panicked. "Where are they taking me? Where am I going?"

"You'll go on the steamer into the city," he said. "Back to the Row. Your father is waiting there for you."

"Papa?"

"Newport has been draining for you, I know," he said. He squeezed my arm, kissed my cheek. "I'll meet you there in a few days. I've some . . . things to finish up here."

I looked past him to where David and the other boy stood looking hesitant. The two men stood waiting for me, one of them holding my bag. I was too tired to resist, and I wanted to be away from my husband. When each of the men took one of my arms, I went with them down the dock and onto the steamer. They took me into some little cabin, a room I'd never seen before, appointed with comfortable settees and lamps, with windows that clouded as the ship began to move from the dock into the sea.

When the door closed behind us, one of the men stood beside me, too close. He put his hand on my arm, and I started to chastise him when I saw what he held: a syringe. He was rolling up my sleeve.

When I opened my eyes, I was in a carriage. The leather shades at the windows had been drawn, but now the door was open, and I saw past the darkness to dim lights that illuminated a stone wall, an entranceway.

"What's happening?" I murmured. "Where am I?"

I heard the creak of leather. I felt the press of warmth against my leg. It was then I recognized the tall man who sat across from me. Dr. Little. I looked at him, and he gave me a thin smile. "Welcome to Beechwood Grove, Mrs. Carelton. I expect you'll be very happy here."

PART III

Beechwood Grove Asylum

July 1885

Chapter 25

My God," I said. I grabbed on to the strap hard. "No. No. Take me back. Take me back this moment."

Dr. Little smiled. "Come, come, Mrs. Carelton. Everything's taken care of."

"No." I shook my head. "No. I don't belong here."

"I'm afraid everything is quite in order. Your husband secured the opinions of two doctors, and a judge has agreed with them. Please, Mrs. Carelton. We'll take good care of you here. You need a rest."

"I don't want a rest." I backed into the corner, disbelieving. "I don't belong here."

The doctor sighed. "Please, Mrs. Carelton. It would be best if you didn't make this difficult."

"Take me back. I want to go back."

"I would rather not do this, but I'm afraid you leave me no choice." Dr. Little opened the carriage door and motioned to two women who stood outside. They came forward. They were stronger than they looked, twin monoliths. One grabbed my wrist, twisting it from the strap so I cried out. The other seized my other arm and yanked me forward. I fought them, but they pulled me stiff and struggling from the carriage, wrenching me down the step so hard that I stumbled and slid on the wet grass and mud.

"You see, Mrs. Carelton, we can be quite persuasive," the doctor said. "Do you think you can walk now, or do you still need assistance?"

"I'm not going anywhere," I said.

Dr. Little turned to the second man who had brought me here. "I do think we can take care of things from this point on," he said.

As the man turned to leave, I called out in sheer panic, "No! No! Don't leave me here!"

He didn't pause but climbed into the carriage and shut the doors. I struggled against the women, who held me fast. One of them said, "Now, now, dearie, it's best if you don't fight."

The driver slapped the reins, and the carriage was off. I tried to think what to do, but my mind was still so fuzzy. It was dark; the road the carriage had disappeared down was deserted. It ended here, at a tall iron gate that was being closed by two men. There was darkness all around: trees, bushes . . . the only lights were the lamps at the entrance, whose light we stood within.

"Your husband is quite concerned about you, Mrs. Carelton," Dr. Little said in a soothing voice that only fed my fear. "It seems you have lately caused your family much worry."

"No," I whispered.

He said, "Please believe me when I tell you that it would be best if you let Charlotte and Greta show you to your room. I believe you will be quite comfortable."

There seemed no other option. I was drained, and all of this was impossible, like some terrible nightmare. I wanted sleep. I wanted to wake up and find this was all an illusion.

He led the way from the gate onto a cobbled path that

opened to the vast stone entryway. Lamps gabled from the door, which he opened to usher us in. The nurses did not release their hold, and I was grateful for it. My legs were weak with my acquiescence, with my growing horror.

They took me upstairs to another great door, which the doctor opened with a key from the chatelaine hanging inside his suitcoat.

"This way," he said, and we were past the door and into a hallway that was softly lit by gas lamps and lined with doors, all closed. For a moment I relaxed. I felt oddly as if I were a guest in some well-appointed house in the country, being led to my room for a fortnight's stay; there would be chocolate brought in the morning with freshly baked buns and nothing but a day of riding and socializing to look forward to.

Then I heard the scream. One of the nurses tightened her grip on my arm. The doctor looked up but kept walking.

"Mrs. Meyers again?" he asked.

"She wouldn't take her medicine tonight, Doctor," said the other nurse.

"Send Maddy to take care of it," he said. Then he smiled at me. "These interruptions are quite infrequent, I assure you. They shouldn't intrude upon your sleep."

Before I could answer, we stopped at a door. Dr. Little swung it open easily. "Your room, Mrs. Carelton."

I had a vague image of dimity curtains closed against the darkness, hangings of chintz, carpets, a bed.

"It's quite late," Dr. Little said. "Will you need anything else this evening?"

I shook my head, feeling numb and strange. "Nothing."

"Then we'll wish you good night."

He backed from the doorway. The nurses released my arms. I didn't move as they left me there. The door closed; I heard the clinking of his chatelaine, the key in the lock, and then their footsteps.

I stumbled to the bed, hitting my shin at the corner, which was oddly sharp. I lifted the bedcover and saw that the wooden posts were heavy, with iron bands fastened by screws. The whole of it was bolted to the floor, as were the bureau and the chair in the corner.

I sank onto the mattress, burying my face in a pillow that smelled vaguely of dirty hair and sweat beneath the scent of harsh soap. I turned my face away. Then I saw what had been carefully hidden by the closed curtains: the pattern cast on the window by a light from outside. Narrow bars.

I woke to a loud, insistent knocking on my door. I slitted my eyes—it was still dark outside—and turned over, ignoring it. I heard the click of the lock, the door opening, and then someone was shaking me.

"Get up, Mrs. Carelton."

"It's too early, Sadie."

"I ain't Sadie, Mrs. Carelton. Wake up now, dearie. We've a schedule here."

The shake was rougher, the voice coarse. I started truly awake, uncertain where I was, and then I remembered.

"Leave me be," I said. "Let me sleep."

"Get up, Mrs. Carelton." The woman's hands were on my arms, pulling me up. "Come on, now. I guess you're dressed already—that won't happen again, will it? You can get yourself washed. Or you want me to do that too?"

I was bleary-eyed. Her face, round and plain as a potato with severely pinned brown hair, wavered before me. I blinked to bring her into focus. Her expression was unpleasant, her dark eyes narrowed.

"This ain't your house in the city, and I ain't your servant. You'll do what I say or you'll regret it. Do you understand me?"

I was taken aback. "Who are you? Where is Dr. Little?"

"My name's Maddy. I'm your nurse," she explained. "If you just follow my orders, we'll get along fine."

"I demand to see Dr. Little."

Maddy smiled smugly. "You'll see him, all right." She grabbed my arm hard, so I had no choice but to get to my feet, and then she shoved me over to the tin washbasin painted in crude flowers. "Let's just start off on a good foot, hmm? I'll ask you again. Are you going to wash yourself? Or do you want me to do it for you?"

"I'll do it," I said.

She smiled again. "I thought you might."

I waited for her to leave, but she only crossed her arms over her breasts and stood back to watch. I poured tepid water into the basin, splashing my face. I could not bear to do more than that while she watched me. It seemed to satisfy her, in any case. When I was finished, she said, "We'll go on down to breakfast now."

"I'd prefer to have it in my room."

"Oh, you would, would you?" She shook her head, muttering something about the spoiled rich, and then she went to the door and opened it. "Come on. They'll throw it out if you don't get there."

I hesitated, and her eyes narrowed again.

"I'll put a jacket on you if I have to, dearie, and take you down in chains. I promise you won't like that one bit."

I didn't know what a jacket was, but the thought of chains was too much, so I did as she commanded. I would not be here for long. I held to that conviction desperately. I could bear anything for a day, even two. I would tell Dr. Little everything the moment I saw him. I would explain it all: how William had sent me here against my will, not because I was insane, but because he was humiliated by my affair with Victor. I would tell the doctor how much better I'd become, how the fits that had once

plagued me were gone, how I should not be here. I would demand that he call my father.

Other doors were open now, other women being led to the
stairs. They were dressed soberly, for the most part, with their
hair simply done. They were quiet and subdued, pasty-faced and
sad-looking. I saw curiosity in some of their expressions. Others
were so blank-faced they disturbed me. They all walked with
their hands folded before them. I realized that some of them
walked that way because their hands were encased in leather mittens bound by chains.

I tamped down my panic violently, forcing myself to remember that this would end soon, that it was a mistake.

They led us down the stairs and through the foyer. Beechwood Grove had apparently been a great estate once. The foyer
was large, marble-floored, with a great wooden stairway rising
from the center with carved polished banisters and stained-glass
windows cut in patterns above. Paintings on the walls depicted
calm, gold-lit landscapes and bucolic rolling farmlands dotted
with sheep and horses. It was beautiful, much like our summer
home on the Hudson, though much larger, and I felt it wrap
around me with familiarity and comfort, as if to belie my words
that I didn't belong here. That frightened me more than anything else.

We were taken into a large room that had been an elegant
dining room. A gasolier hung overhead, and deep brown drapes
were pulled back to reveal barred windows through which the
faint light of dawn cast the sky slate blue, with dark trees shadowed against it. The room was nearly filled with two long tables, upon which were set bowls and spoons. The nurses
ushered each of us to a stiff, high-backed chair. A far door
opened, and out came two women pushing carts of heavy,
steaming pots laden with the scent of cornmeal. Together, as if
they'd done this many times, they went down the length of the

table ladling mush into each bowl with quick, efficient movements. They spilled scarcely a drop.

But for the wet slap of mush into tin bowls and the squeak of
the cart wheels, there was not a sound. The nurses stood against
the wall watching us, and as if on cue, each woman dipped into
her bowl, eating silently. There was no sugar, no cream, and
only black coffee to drink.

I did as the rest of them did, only because Maddy stared
evilly at me from the wall. The women on either side of me kept
their elbows close to their sides, as if concerned they might
bump me, and neither even glanced at me as we ate. The mush
was foul and tasteless, with lumps the size of peas, but I was
hungry. It settled like a stone in my stomach.

When we were finished, the nurses came again. Maddy took
me aside as the others were led out a side door. "They're going
for exercise," she explained. "You'll get your turn tomorrow. For
now the doctor wants to see you."

Dr. Little. I went with her gratefully as she led me from the
dining room into the foyer and back down another hallway. We
passed more closed doors and one or two that were open to
show nicely appointed sitting rooms, empty but for upholstered
chairs and bookcases and small tables. At the end of the hallway,
Maddy stopped and opened the door.

"Mrs. Carelton, Doctor," she announced.

"Yes," came an unfamiliar voice. "Bring her in."

I frowned. "Dr. Little?"

"You'll see him later this afternoon," Maddy said. "This is Dr.
Rush. He's going to do your examination."

I felt hot. "My examination?"

"Come along, now, Mrs. Carelton," she said. Her hand curled
around my arm, and she pulled me through the door into a small
room that held a desk and two tightly jammed bookcases. A
graying, jocular-looking man waited by a small window.

"Welcome to Beechwood Grove, Mrs. Carelton," he said,

squinting at me with rheumy blue eyes. "You came in so late last night that we didn't have time to get acquainted." He seemed to expect some kind of response.

"Yes," I said.

"Every new patient receives a full examination. We'll be seeing each other regularly."

Maddy closed the door. The room felt too small, too close. The doctor went to a door in the far wall and opened it, and I saw an examination table, instruments, things too familiar to mistake.

"I've had enough examinations," I said.

"I'm sure you have." He smiled, revealing stained teeth. "I assure you, this is quite necessary. Dr. Little and I have taken over your care. Therefore I will need to examine you." He jerked his head to Maddy, and she pulled me ungently to the other room.

"Let's get undressed, Mrs. Carelton," she said to me.

There was no dressing screen, and when I glanced at her in question, she gestured to me roughly, and I understood that I was expected to undress in the open. When I did nothing, she came over and stripped off my gown and petticoats with practiced movements. Her broad, flat fingers tugged at the fastenings of my corset until it came loose. When I was clad in only my chemise, she bade me sit on the examination table, and Dr. Rush came in, wiping his hands on a towel.

I hugged myself, feeling exposed and miserable and powerless in a way that I had never felt before. I had had examinations like this so many times, but always because I wanted to be well, always because I hoped the doctor would find the answer.

"Now, Mrs. Carelton," the doctor said. "You've been diagnosed with uterine monomania. Your husband indicates that you've been unable to conceive during the length of your marriage."

I could almost see the goose pimples on my thighs beneath the thin lawn of my chemise.

"I'm sure this is familiar to you, Mrs. Carelton. Maddy?"

The nurse forced me onto my hands and knees. I closed my eyes against her rough hands pulling my chemise up over my hips, baring me to the doctor. I felt his hands, the cold speculum, and I could not stand it. "I don't belong here."

The doctor sighed. The sound was tired and irritated; there was no attempt at pity. "Yes, my dear, I know. No one does."

Chapter 26

Through all of this, I refused to think of Victor, though he was always hovering in the back of my mind. I told myself that I would think of him and his abandonment after I convinced Dr. Little of William's treachery. When I was free again, I would decide what to feel about Victor. Beyond that I would not contemplate. For now all that mattered was freedom.

When Maddy led me to Dr. Little, I was resolved. His office, through a maze of close hallways and many rooms, seemed to take forever to reach. When she closed the door behind me, I heard the squeak of a chair in the hallway—she was waiting—and that filled me with an odd sense of importance, as if they expected me to turn into a raving lunatic at any moment. Dr. Little sat at a large desk in the corner of the room, against a window where the sun came streaming in. The room was quite warm, and I had a moment of confusion—the office was so like the one I'd visited him in before, with its plaques and books. But here the wallpaper was plain brown with no design. Only the chairs, with their rich silk upholstery of deep maroon, and the highly polished desk gave any nod to decoration.

I stood in the middle of the room, my hands folded before

me, feeling nauseated. There was so much at stake; I had to convince him, and yet I could not think of the words.

He studied me through round spectacles—like Victor's, I thought briefly, though they perched on top of a fleshy nose. "Mrs. Carelton," he said, rising. "Please, sit down."

I settled myself on the very edge of a chair.

He took up a paper from his desk and scanned it, then his brow furrowed as if he sought some answer in my face. "You've had your examination with Dr. Rush this morning?"

"Yes."

He tapped his finger on the desk. "His examination seems to bolster my previous diagnosis of uterine monomania. According to your husband, you've only grown worse in the time since I saw you last."

"No," I said. "I haven't. I've been much better."

The doctor sat on the corner of his desk, crossing his arms over his chest, dangling the paper from his fingers. He looked thoughtful. "Your husband says that you were engaging in delusions and hysterical fits, Mrs. Carelton. That you were immodest and uncontrollable. He lists several examples of your unacceptable behavior: that there were several instances of"— here he reddened—"reckless and disturbing sexual conduct, that you began drawing obsessively, and that you frequently embarrassed neighbors and friends with your talk and actions."

When his words registered, I was so disbelieving that all I could think to say was "But that's not true."

"Which part?"

I felt a rising panic. "William knows . . . he *knows* I've been getting better. That's why he sent me here, you see, because he was threatened by it, because I humiliated him."

"How did you humiliate him?"

"I—I had an affair," I said desperately. "With my doctor."

"Your doctor?"

"Yes. Yes. William found out and he sent me here. He drugged me first, so I wouldn't protest."

"You had an affair with your doctor, so your husband sent you here," Dr. Little repeated.

"Yes. He says I'm insane, but he's lying."

"Lying?" Dr. Little gave me a sad smile. "My dear Mrs. Carelton, why would he do that?"

"To keep me here. To imprison me."

"Do you really believe that?"

"Yes, I do. I do." I could no longer contain my anxiety. I rose jerkily from the chair and began to pace. "I embarrassed him, and this is all simply to remind me of who I am."

"I see." Dr. Little exhaled. "You did not begin drawing obsessively?"

I jerked to a stop. "What?"

"It's a simple question, Mrs. Carelton. Were you drawing obsessively? I have here several reports—not just from your husband but from others, your father as well—that you were."

"My father?" I sank again into the chair. "My father knows I'm here?"

"Yes." Dr. Little's look was pitying.

Papa had helped William imprison me. The realization silenced me.

"Mrs. Carelton, it says here you were drawing in your every spare moment. Your maid says it. There is also an account of how you left a party to draw in the courtyard. Is this true?"

"Yes," I said, unable to think. "I suppose it is."

"Did you embarrass your friends?"

"I suppose so. I don't know."

"Did you display uncharacteristic sexual behavior?"

I could not believe this was happening. Not this interrogation, not Papa's involvement, not anything. I began numbly to see that I would not escape this place, that the reprieve I'd hoped for was not coming. Papa would not help me. William had put me here. And Victor . . . oh, Victor. I squeezed my eyes shut. "I only wanted William to kiss me. But he was afraid I would sap his energies."

"In other words, Mrs. Carelton, you have done every one of the things I've mentioned."

I felt the chains binding me ever more tightly.

"Mrs. Carelton, I understand how this must all seem quite overwhelming, but the fact remains that your husband loves you and wants the best for you. He informed me of your mother's unfortunate history, and I know that he and your father fear you will repeat it. They both believe that Beechwood Grove is where you should be just now. I must admit that, confronted with your behavior these last months, I have no choice but to agree. Rest is what you need. Rest and medication." He came before me, squatting until his face was even with mine. "Mrs. Carelton, is your husband lying?"

I thought of how I had changed beneath Victor's care, how I had become someone I didn't know, how it must have seemed to William. He was my jailer, true, but I knew also that William believed he loved me. We had been bound together in hope and hopelessness for years.

I shook my head and whispered, "No."

Dr. Little smiled. "As I thought." He stood and went to the door, muttering something to Maddy before he turned back to me and said, "Maddy will take you back to your room, Mrs. Carelton. We will meet again tomorrow."

I barely registered the walk back to my room; I knew only that we were there, and that someone had unpacked the bag I'd forgotten about, had hung my clothes on the wall hooks and filled the bureau drawers. I saw what I had thrown into the bag in my haste to leave William: a silk dress embellished with lace, a ball gown, a gown of muslin, things so inappropriate for this place.

Maddy took my nightgown off the bed and handed it to me

with the curt direction to change. From the window I saw that it was merely early evening, but time no longer mattered. I did as the nurse bade me, and when I was done, there was a knock on the door. It cracked open to show another nurse, one from last night. Greta, with her great thick arms and dirty-blond hair covered by a cap. She held a bottle and a cup.

"I've come with your medicine, ma'am," she said.

Maddy motioned for her to come in. "Now, I see it this way, dearie," Maddy said. "You either take your medicine like a good girl, or I use the wedge on you. Might even break a few of your pretty teeth, which I don't think you'd take to kindly." She reached into the pocket of her apron, bringing out a piece of wood angled into a wedge. I could see the teeth marks cut deep into the grain.

I had not planned to argue.

Greta measured medicine into a cup and went to the pitcher to add a bit of water. She put the cup into my hand, and the pungent green smell of chloral reached my nostrils. I downed it in one gulp.

"Now, then, that's a good girl," Maddy said, taking the cup from me, leading me to the bed. "You just lay down now, dearie. You'll feel better in the morning."

I woke before dawn, confused and frightened. I did not know where I was; the shadows were strange; I couldn't hear the ocean. It was hot . . . hadn't the windows been left open? I thought I remembered Victor padding naked to them, flipping the catches, throwing them open.

But then I saw the faint play of light on the ceiling from lamps outside, and it came to me. Victor was not here.

I crawled out of bed. I felt drowsy, my limbs were heavy, there was a nasty taste in my mouth—the chloral. I stumbled against the bed stand and sat on the edge of the mattress, and the sadness and pain of Victor's abandonment rose to drown me.

I wanted to hope it was all a lie, a terrible delusion. I lurched to my feet, fumbling with the buttons on my nightgown, impatient to have it off, to see my own body, to find a mark—a bruise from his kisses, perhaps, something to show me he had been there, that he had loved me. I stood there naked and desperate. I touched my breasts, searching for the memory of his hands there; I ran my fingers over my waist and hips, across my thighs. I remembered every encounter, every time he'd touched me with his long fingers, every movement studied and elegant, every touch arousing. Had he ever loved me? Or had it been as I feared, that he had used me and controlled me? Had I only seen what I wanted so much to believe?

There was the key in the door. Startled, I reached for the nightgown I'd dropped on the floor, but before I could, the door opened. Maddy went still when she saw me, her hand frozen on the doorknob, and then her dark brows came together in a thunderous frown.

I hastily grabbed up my nightgown, holding it before me to shield my nakedness.

She yanked it away, so I was forced to cover myself with my hands. "They warned us about this," she muttered. "Dr. Little will want to know about this."

"Please," I said. "I was just getting dressed."

She went to the door, which she had not bothered to close. Anyone walking down the hallway could see. "Greta!" she called. There was a flurry of footsteps. The burly maid came to the door.

"What is it?"

"Mrs. Carelton here has been gratifying herself." Maddy spat the words as if the very thought was repulsive.

"No," I said, growing frightened. "No, I was merely getting dressed." I tried to go to her, but the chloral had left me drunk and unbalanced. I fell to my knees.

"Tell Hilary I'm bringing her down."

Greta smiled. "Will you need the muff?"

Maddy turned to me. "Will I need the muff, Mrs. Carelton? Or will you get dressed and come with me like a good girl?"

"Go where?" I asked, huddling, trying desperately to cover my nakedness from those who peered inside the door as they made their way to breakfast.

Greta reached into her pocket and took out a pair of leather mittens fastened with a chain.

"Not those," I said. "Please, not those."

Maddy gave her fellow nurse a grin. "I think we'll do just fine without them, Greta. Go tell Hilary."

Greta went off, and Maddy shut the door at last. I was grateful until I saw the way she looked at me. "Now, then, dearie, think you can get dressed? Or do you need my help for that?"

I scrambled to my feet. She handed me my nightgown. "That's good enough," she said, and I didn't question her. I put it on as quickly as I could, ashamed of my nakedness, of the way she never took her eyes from me, of the shameful, humiliating thought that she was looking too closely—indecently—at my breasts. When I had it on, she opened the door and grabbed my arm—I was beginning to learn that Maddy never did anything gently—and took me down the hall, away from the dining room. Again I was lost in a maze of stairs and narrow hallways until we came to a room. It was cold and austere, with stone floors and no windows. There were full-length tin bathtubs everywhere, and coiled hoses leaking water, and iron bedsteads covered with thin gray mattresses. There were drains on the floor.

I remembered Elmira, the water cure. This did not seem as benign. I stopped at the doorway. "No," I whispered.

Maddy pulled me forward. "This is the punishment for women like you who can't keep their hands off themselves." She smiled. "Hilary!"

A woman came through the far door. She was wearing a gray

apron that looked to be made of rubber and heavy boots. "That her?" At Maddy's nod, she jerked her thumb toward a bed in the corner. I dug my heels in, but Maddy dragged me easily. Hilary spread a rubber sheet, and before I knew what was happening, she had grabbed the collar of my nightgown. I heard the pop of buttons; the gown slithered to the floor.

I tried to wrench from Maddy's hold, but she slapped me hard. My ears rang, and my vision blurred. They forced me to the bed, and I convulsed at the touch of the freezing-wet sheet they laid over me.

They bound my arms to my sides, wrapping me so tightly I could not move, and then they covered me with more sheets. They strapped a cap filled with ice to the top of my head, and within moments my teeth were chattering; I could not feel my limbs. Whenever the sheets began to warm, they wet them again, pouring ladles of cold water from a nearby tub.

I had no idea how long they kept me there. As that cold gradually seeped into my bones, a languor came over me. My thoughts were scattered and strange: Dr. Little, Victor, and William pulsed and moved like bright colors in my mind. I could not keep them straight. There was Victor, standing beside me, but the words that came from his mouth were not his words, not his voice. *How long have you been his whore, my sweet angel?* I shook my head mutely, unable to move my lips, they were so stiff and cold.

Maddy was at my side, feeling at my throat, taking my pulse. She leaned close; her face filled my vision. "You going to be a good girl now, Mrs. Carelton? You going to mind your manners?" and I saw my father and William. *You are a lady. You are not yourself.* Then there was Papa telling me to be a wife, to make William's home a castle. A hundred directions, a single road.

What if I can make you into the woman you were meant to be?

When they took the ice cap from my head and unwrapped the sheets, I lay there, unmoving. Maddy's hand burned where she touched my cold skin. They dressed me in my torn nightgown and paraded me down the hallway, back to my room, with nothing to hold the gown together. Maddy went to close the door, and I heard myself whisper through inflexible lips, "Laudanum." She smiled meanly and said, "Well, now, that'd make it easy for both of us."

She left briefly. I lay on my bed, burrowing beneath the blankets, shivering, and then she was back with a bottle and a cup.

What if I could make you into the woman you were meant to be?

I sipped the medicine gratefully. This was where I wanted to be, this calm, motionless place, where I could not think—not about the husband whose love was slowly killing me, not about the man who had used and abandoned me so that his ambitions could fly. For once I had what I wanted: a medicated world where my dreams were formless and fleeting and mine alone. I lost the desire to leave them.

August 3, 1885

Dear Mr. Carelton,

I believe it remains wisest for your wife to have no contact with you. Therefore I must ask that you cancel your planned visit to Beechwood Grove and keep to our original plan of waiting some weeks before a visit. I usually recommend—in fact, in most cases I require—that three to six months pass before allowing family to visit, but I do understand your need for haste. Still, I cannot help but think that seeing you at this time would further disturb a woman who is already extremely troubled.

I also wish to beg you to reconsider the time in which you wish us to effect Mrs. Carelton's cure. I understand that you wish for her to be if not well then at least capable for the ball celebrating the opening of your new home. I wish to emphasize that at this time I find it extremely unlikely that Mrs. Carelton will be in any condition to re-

sume her wifely duties and obligations, much less host a ball. She is very fragile. The move to the new house, along with the crush of friends and neighbors, will undoubtedly be too much for her.

I would like to be optimistic that this will not be the case, but I have no reason for optimism. Mrs. Carelton was quite distressed when she came to us, and we have had to take some steps in calming her. I regret also to say that her erotomania has worsened. At Beechwood Grove we are possessed of the most current methods for treating someone of Mrs. Carelton's sensibilities, and we have taken appropriate steps to curb your wife's unfortunate tendency for self-abuse. It seems to have had the desired effect, though she now refuses to speak and has regressed into a type of catatonia. You would, I think, not recognize her. I must ask that you not contact her until such time that I advise you it is safe to do so. I continue to hope for the best, but I regret to say that I have changed my original prognosis. I believe she is worsening by the day.

I urge you once again to reconsider the dilemma you have put upon us. You must begin to come to terms with the fact that your wife may indeed need to remain here for some time to come. Unfortunately, it is impossible at this time to come to any other conclusion.

Yours sincerely,

Dr. Robert Little

August 19, 1885

Dear Mr. Carelton,

I understand your need for a quick resolution to your wife's case, though I am distressed at your insistence that she be capable by the end of September. I am afraid that is quite impossible. Her prognosis is worse than ever and may be quite hopeless. I have ceased daily meetings with her because she is incapable of communicating. She has begun to have extremely violent nightmares, wherein she has attempted to harm her nurse. We have had no choice but to increase her medication, which calms her, but she continues to thwart our every attempt to force her to speak.

I have asked my associate, Dr. Rush, for his esteemed opinion regarding her catatonia, and he believes we should consider an ovariotomy. Of course, we will perform no surgery without consulting you.

I dislike having to send such a negative report, but I believe you must face the truth about your wife. Please do not continue to insist upon having her well in time for your planned soiree. It is impossible.

Sincerely,

Dr. Robert Little

August 28, 1885

Dear Mr. Carelton,

I understand completely. We will do all in our power to have Mrs. Carelton ready to face her responsibilities by the end of September. Your instructions—as well as your <u>assurances</u>—have been duly noted.

I will be leaving Beechwood Grove for several days this week to attend a meeting in Albany. My associate, Dr. Rush, will be attending in the meantime, in the unlikely event that you should need to contact us.

Sincerely,

Dr. Robert Little

Chapter 27

The morphia invaded my dreams so that I could not tell what was true and what was delusion. A part of me knew I must escape from this place; it murmured seductively in my ear: *You have only yourself to rely on, Lucy. Your life is in your own hands now.* In that world I lived, thinking, plotting, praying. I dreamed of escape, of fleeing to Rome, to anywhere, and one night my dream was so real that I actually felt Maddy's hands all over me, her weight on my body, as I tried to get out of bed. The hallucination pinched and mauled my skin, and I fought it. I tried to strangle the dream with my bedclothes, and then I rose from the bed and ran down the hallway, thinking only of escape, of finding my own life, my real one.

But then I woke again, and though Maddy was gone, I was heavy with the effects of the drug. To speak was too difficult. Moving was such an effort I remained still. The world seemed to spin by me in unfocused color—people moved too quickly for me, their words were too fast, hard for me to concentrate on, so it was easier to close my eyes and retreat into the world I'd made for myself, to delusions of escape that dulled the reality of my surrender.

When Dr. Little came into my room one morning, I stared at him, unable to place him.

"Good morning, Mrs. Carelton," he said, coming to a stop a few feet from my bedside. I had no answer to give, and he sighed and went on. "Your husband is very worried about you."

My husband. It took me a moment to remember. William.

Dr. Little put a finger to his lips thoughtfully. "I was just in Albany. At a meeting of alienists and neurologists. I met a man there—a quite brilliant man, actually, who delivered a quite brilliant paper. He had a patient who reminded me very much of you, whom he managed to cure through hypnosis. I spoke to him of you, and he believes that he might be able to help you."

I had no idea what he was talking about, and I didn't care.

He ignored me. "He's waiting in the hall to see you, Mrs. Carelton. His name is Victor Seth."

The name cut through my confusion. It was another hallucination. A wretched dream. Little stepped back, looking startled, and then my nurse came in. Not Maddy, but . . . Jenny. Her name was Jenny. She carried a bottle and a cup.

She hurried to me, murmuring, "Here now, ma'am. You calm yourself now." Her face filled my vision. Round and freckled. Pale eyes. She pulled the cork from the bottle.

"No," I murmured, and then, more strongly, "No."

"Don't give it to her." The voice came through the fog.
Victor.

Jenny stepped away, and he came into view. The same. Not the same. It was Victor, but he had shaved; there was no hint of a beard, no mustache. His hair had been cut short, and he wore a fawn-colored flannel suit. But it was his eyes that startled me. There was no recognition in them, only polite interest. There was no indication that he knew me, that we had ever been anything to each other.

This was the cruelest hallucination of all.

"You see?" Dr. Little said. "She is quite beyond communicating."

"You mustn't give her any more laudanum," Victor said. He frowned and took the bottle from the nurse. "It will kill her."

"Oh, come now, Dr. Seth," Dr. Little said. "Most of our patients use morphia of some sort. It's quite safe if administered correctly."

"I cannot work with her if she's drugged," Victor said tersely.

"But—"

"See that she doesn't have any more. She'll suffer for a few days, but then she'll be fine."

"She's had terrible nightmares."

"I'm sure I can manage her." Victor crossed his arms. His fingers went to stroke a beard that was not there and stopped mid-motion.

"She tried to strangle her nurse," Dr. Little said. "The woman had to be removed. Though she was a huge creature, Mrs. Carelton did considerable harm. Dr. Rush has been considering an ovariotomy, and I find myself inclined to agree with him."

Victor frowned. "An ovariotomy? That's hardly an enlightened treatment."

"It is a last resort. We've tried everything else."

"Why have you brought me here?"

"I had thought you might be able to help her. Your paper indicated remarkable success with a similar patient, and I must admit we're desperate. Her husband—"

"Yes, yes," Victor said impatiently. "Very well."

"Excellent. Excellent. We can arrange for tomorrow—"

"Tomorrow I will be on my way back to the city," Victor said. "Unless I find that she responds positively to my methods. Leave me alone with her."

Dr. Little sighed. "You mean to begin now?"

"Yes. As soon as the drug wears off. But first I must examine her. Leave us."

"Yes, of course." Dr. Little started to the door. "I'll leave Jenny."

"She can wait outside the door."

Dr. Little looked stunned. "Mrs. Carelton can be quite violent. Especially when the medication wears off."

Victor scrutinized me dispassionately. "I assure you, I'll be in no danger."

Dr. Little cleared his throat. "Very well, then. I'll leave you. Jenny will be in the hallway should you need her."

"I expect not," said Victor.

Jenny followed Dr. Little from the room. The door closed behind them with a thick, satisfying thud. Victor and I were alone.

He put aside the laudanum bottle and came to my bedside quickly, kneeling beside me, and the disinterest fell from his eyes; I saw what looked like despair. "Lucy," he whispered. "Lucy, what have they done to you?"

He didn't touch me, and he said nothing more. He simply sat on the chair, staring out the window, there when I fell asleep, still there when I woke. As the hours passed and the fog of morphia began to fade into feeling, I began to believe in the truth of him.

"You're not . . . an—" I swallowed hard; my throat was dry. I struggled for the word. "Illusion."

"No," he said. "I'm quite real."

"You would . . . say that even if you were an illusion," I pointed out hoarsely. "I . . . want for you to be . . . real, you see. I want to believe it was all . . . real."

I saw pain cross his face, and it made me glad. He closed his eyes. When he opened them again, he stared at me as if for the first time. He rose and came to me. He touched my hair; his fingers tangled in the unbrushed, unpinned mass of it, tugging slightly, a little pain that cut through what was left of my tor-por—too sharp. My skin felt raw.

"What are you doing, Victor?" I whispered, anguished. "What game are you playing?"

"No game."

"Then why are you here?"

"Why shouldn't I be here?" He sounded as if he despised him-self. "You're my prize patient. You've won me the acclaim I hoped for."

I felt a growing dread, a sense I'd had before, in Newport, that he was not who I wanted him to be, that he was a fallible god after all. With that feeling, my dream fell away. My mind cleared, and I realized with a sudden jolt that it *had* been an il-lusion, that my love for him had not been real, that I had been away from him too long. My mind was my own again. I did not love him any longer, but I was hungry for him still; the desire I'd felt for him was there, still real, still mine. But as for the rest, I felt strangely free.

"You left me," I accused. "You had to know what William would do."

He shook his head. "No. No. I didn't know. I never thought he would go so far. William said you'd gone on an extended trip to the continent, and I believed him."

"Yes, of course you did," I said. "It had nothing to do with your wanting to believe him."

"That was part of it," he said quietly. "But then you were gone, and I . . . I couldn't bear the loss of you, Lucy. You must believe that if nothing else. I came the moment I found where you were."

"I don't understand why. Why not just leave me?"

He sat on the bed. "Dr. Little came to me at the Neurology Association meeting. He'd heard my presentation, and he told me about you. Apparently William has given him until the end of September to cure you. He was quite desperate."

"The end of September? Why?"

"Your house will be finished. Your ball is scheduled for October sixth."

I felt ill. "He can't mean . . . He can't want me there. Not after—"

"Perhaps it's a measure of his love for you," Victor said carefully. "He wants you well. He wants to redeem you."

"I don't want to be redeemed," I said.

"How can you not?" he asked me. "It's the only life you've known."

"It was destroying me."

"But you said you wanted it. You begged me to give it to you. *Make me like them,* you said."

"You sound as if you're agreeing with William."

"I only want you to be certain."

"Certain of what?"

He took a strand of my hair between his fingers and rubbed it. It seemed I felt the pain of that touch in my skull.

"You haunt me, Lucy," he whispered, "so I can't sleep for thinking of you."

Bitterly, I said, "What other fame can I provide for you?"

He leaned closer. I felt his warmth at my side, his breath against my jaw, and it roused my desire. "I love you, Lucy. Isn't that what you want from me? If I told you that I could take you from this place, that we could be free forever—"

I did not want to trust him, but such a habit was hard to unlearn. My heart said no, but the memory of the feel of him stole over me. I wanted him, yes, my body yearned for the satisfaction of him, but I was frightened of him too, of the control he'd once had over me.

He kissed my collarbone. "We haven't finished, you and I."

"What do you mean?" My voice did not sound like my own. I struggled to keep hold of it.

"The culmination of everything," he whispered, and there

was desperation in his voice, such raw emotion—something I had never seen in him before, a lack of control, and my fear disappeared. I understood for the first time the power I had over him. My mind was my own again, and I realized that we were equally matched, that he had not lied to me. I *did* haunt him. I was his obsession, as he had once been mine.

It was exhilarating. It inflamed me, because I understood how to take what I wanted; I knew how to be free.

"Very well," I said to him, and he smiled in satisfaction. He leaned to kiss me again, and when he was near my lips, I whispered, "But this time, Victor, I get what *I* want."

To those at Beechwood Grove, it was a miracle.

When Dr. Little came back into my room, he found me awake and speaking again. "This is quite remarkable," he said.

Victor nodded. "She's a curious case, Dr. Little, but I find myself intrigued. And as you can see, my methods seem to have been very effective."

"My God, yes. I must admit I'm surprised. I had not thought—"

"Yes, I know. You were ready to attempt surgery."

"Will the effect last?"

"For a time. I would like to pursue this further, if you don't mind."

"Yes, yes, of course."

"I would require that I be her only doctor. And that my instructions be followed to the letter."

"Her husband—"

"Ah yes, that's the other problem. It's important that he not be told I'm treating his wife."

There was a pause. "This is quite irregular."

"I think if you examine it from his point of view, you won't find it so unusual. You said yourself that most people are wary of hypnosis. It's still very experimental. There's no need to cause him undue worry. Nor hope. I cannot say with any exactitude how effective I can be."

Dr. Little winced. "Yes, I see."

"Good. Then we're agreed. I'll stay on here for a time and hope we can make some progress with Mrs. Carelton. I will need rooms of my own."

"Of course."

"I will need to return to my own practice, you realize, but I've found that hypnosis can achieve fairly quick results. I don't expect my treatment to take long."

"How soon?"

"My first goal will be to break her of the laudanum habit. That could take some time. After that it's hard to know. My best estimate is that it will take a few weeks."

"Thank God," Little murmured. "I'm most appreciative. Mr. Carelton has been very distraught. If his wife can be cured . . ."

"I can't promise a cure."

"No, no, of course not."

"But I do think she'll be much improved."

"We must hope so, Dr. Seth. For her sake, and her husband's, we must hope so."

"Yes," Victor said slowly. "It's her husband I'm thinking of."

Chapter 28

Nearly three weeks had passed since Victor's arrival when Dr. Little came to see me in my room, nearly trembling with satisfaction.

It was the start of October; I had been at Beechwood Grove over two months, and my behavior had so improved that everyone spoke of it as a miracle.

"I have already spoken to Dr. Seth of this," Dr. Little began without preamble, "and he suggested I come to you with the news. I had written to your husband to tell him how improved you are, and I've had a letter from him today."

"No doubt he's delighted," I said.

"Yes, he is. Quite delighted. As are we. In short, Mrs. Carelton, I've told your husband that you are ready to return to your former life. Dr. Seth is most agreeable to this. He did say he'd spoken to you. I imagine his own practice suffers from neglect, and it is time for him to return to it. I trust he has already informed you of this decision?"

I nodded, and he went on quickly, as if afraid I might collapse before he could get the words out and cause him misery again. "Good. Good. Your husband is sending a man to collect you and bring you home. Unfortunately, he himself is unable to come, but he hopes you will understand."

I smiled. "And when will this be?"

"In two days. You have made a startling recovery, Mrs. Carelton. You should be quite proud of yourself."

"Yes, I am. I'm looking forward to resuming my life."

"As you should be," he said.

Soon after he left, Victor knocked on my door. He came behind me at the window, hidden from view in the event that anyone walked by.

"Dr. Little's been here?" he asked.

"Oh yes. William's delighted, the doctor's delighted, you're delighted."

He laughed softly in my ear. "Indeed. We're all quite pleased with ourselves."

"I'm leaving in two days," I said.

He touched my shoulder. My skin was still so sensitive from all the morphia that I flinched and felt him draw slightly back. "Yes. Everything's ready," he said.

"When will I see you again?"

"I'll come to you tonight," he said. "After that, I'm not certain. It would be best, I think, if we waited a little while. There's no point in arousing suspicion all over again. If you need me—"

"I won't," I said.

He laughed a little uncertainly. "How confident you are, Lucy. You must be careful."

"Yes," I told him. "I will be. Have no doubt of that."

That night he came to me near midnight. The moon shone blue and bare, sending the silhouettes of my barred windows onto the walls, so it seemed we were animals in a dark and shadowed zoo. As he covered my body with his own and murmured in my ear, I heard the sound of waves crashing against the hull of a ship on a faraway shore, and I dreamed of the Rome of my girlhood, the Rome I did not know.

*   *   *

Two days later, I was brought into the great reception room, where Jimson waited uncomfortably.

Dr. Little made a speech about how gratified he was at this happy circumstance, and I was bundled into the carriage with my only bag. The horses were given a short slap with the reins, and Beechwood Grove was behind me.

It was late when we arrived in the city. I had lapsed into a fitful sleep, and when I woke, I saw the streetlights of Central Park. For a moment I expected to go past it and move on to the Row. It was disconcerting when the carriage stopped, when Jimson opened the door.

"Welcome home, Mrs. Carelton," he said.

We were before a huge home built in the style of a row house, yet much larger, with double staircases curving around to a front door and electric lights glittering from the narrow windows. The grounds looked barren and ghostly, but as Jimson helped me from the carriage, I saw the shadows of shrubs and hedges, the rounded spine of a trellis.

Jimson followed me up the walk. The front door was opened for us immediately by Harris, who smiled and nodded at me and said, "How good it is to have you back, ma'am," and took my bag from Jimson.

The floor was checkered in white and pink marble. The dome William had promised arched over the foyer, over the alabaster nudes Millie had chosen, over Jean-Claude's bronze Pompeiian sculptures, over the elaborately carved stairway. Plaster cherubs decorated the border of the rose-colored glass, their plump little arms extended as if they held it aloft. The dome itself was dark. I had to admit it was beautiful.

Harris took my cloak. "How was the continent, ma'am? I trust your journey was comfortable."

"Yes," I said. "Where is my husband?"

Harris cleared his throat. "Mr. Carelton sent a message,

ma'am. He's been unavoidably detained. He'll be home quite late. He was most distressed that he could not be here to welcome you home."

"I see."

Harris pushed a button hidden in the wall behind the door, and in moments a woman with hay-colored hair and pale skin came in.

"Bridget," Harris said, "please show Mrs. Carelton to her room."

"Bridget?" I asked in surprise. "Where is Moira?"

"I believe Mr. Carelton felt it best to dismiss her," Harris said.

So almost nothing was to be the same. Wordlessly, I followed Bridget up the stairs to the third floor. The maid opened one of a row of doors that flanked a broad hallway. "Here, ma'am," she said.

Inside, the lights were bright. I was assailed by gold—chairs upholstered in gold toile, fragile tables, gold draperies. It was a large room, with two sets of windows—the ones I had begged William for—but I didn't go to them. I had no interest in seeing the view. It was not Washington Square; that was all that mattered. An archway, with folding doors pressed open, separated the sitting room from my bed, which was a monstrosity of white and gold, with angels decorating each of its posts, swarming on the headboard and footboard. The bed was laid with a heavy gold-fringed bedspread.

Bridget, no doubt well trained by Harris, was already going to the gilt-laid armoire, pulling out a nightgown I'd never seen before. Apparently William had decided new clothes were in order as well. I stood silently and allowed her to undress me, then dress me again in pale lawn and lace. I let her lead me to the vanity and comb out my hair. When she was done, I bade her good night.

I was finally alone, but I felt William's presence everywhere I turned, in every detail, every golden latch, every bar. I forced myself to crawl into the bed that William had chosen for me, to wait for my husband.

It was late when I heard the faint knock on the door. It opened slowly and carefully to show William. I had not been asleep. I'd turned off the electric lights and lit a candle, and it was by that dim light that I saw him for the first time in almost three months. He looked tired and worried, but when he saw me awake, he came to sit on the edge of my bed.

"Lucy, darling," he said, with outstretched hands. "Forgive me for not being here. How I've missed you. . . . Have you seen the house? What do you think of it?"

I let him take me into his arms. I pressed my face briefly against his chest, but my skin rebelled against him; I could not stand to touch him. It was all I could do to keep my expression impassive. "It's lovely, William," I said. "But you knew that."

"Do you like your room?" He gestured about. "It was quite easy, actually, to find the look of it. Everything in it reminds me of you. It's so delicate. So fragile." He gave me an anxious look as if trying to find something in my face to reassure him. "Dr. Little says you're quite recovered. Is it true?"

"Oh yes," I said. "I feel much better."

"His letters over the last months were distressing."

"Thank goodness you had the house to comfort you," I said.

He frowned. "You can't think it meant more to me than you. I was desperate, Lucy. You must believe me. I had no idea what to do. After what Seth—"

"I don't want to talk about him," I said quickly.

William looked surprised, then comforted. He said carefully, "Should I take this to mean that you are . . . that you are quite . . . finished with him?"

"My mind is clear, William," I said quietly. "I am certain of my course in a way I have never been."

"Then your stay there was successful." He let out his breath in a rush. "You cannot know how anxious I was. To think I hadn't done the right thing . . ."

"You should not have worried."

Apprehension flashed in his eyes. He ran a hand through his hair, which was growing sparser, I noticed. He looked haggard, in fact, as if he had not been sleeping, and I felt a moment of pity. That I had worried him I didn't doubt. But William's love was something I couldn't think about. It had almost killed me.

"What did you tell everyone?" I asked.

"That you had gone to the continent," he said.

"I imagine they were relieved."

He seemed relieved himself that I had mentioned it. "Yes. They weren't sure what to make of the summer. I assured them that there had been nothing between you and Victor. I told them his only role as a doctor had been to prescribe a sleeping draft for you."

"They believed that?"

"They said they did." His expression hardened. "Especially when I told them that he had made advances toward you. I said you'd repulsed them but that I could not in good conscience continue to call him a friend."

"You ruined him socially," I said.

"He ruined himself, Lucy, when he seduced you," he said angrily.

"Let's talk of something else," I said smoothly. "What did I miss while I was away?"

He turned eagerly to the topic. He told me of what had happened in the last months: how the new horse show had progressed, what dinners he had attended. Julia Breckenwood had taken an unexpected trip to her parents' home in Boston after catching Steven with his latest mistress, and Steven had followed to beg her forgiveness. Caroline Astor had cut Daisy Hadden at the opera because Daisy had slighted her in some ridiculous way William could barely remember. Antoinette

Baldwin was engaged to marry an earl she'd met during the early summer—much to her dismay, it seemed.

"I should leave you to sleep," he said reluctantly. "Tomorrow will be a big day." He went to the door, then paused, his hand on the knob. His face softened. "How are you really, Lucy? Are you truly well? Should I believe it?"

I made myself smile. "I am not as fragile as the furniture, William," I told him, and he smiled back, but tentatively.

"Good. That's good. I should hate to think that you aren't ready. It distressed me so to send you there, Lucy. I'm not sure I could bear having to send you back."

My smile felt frozen. I heard the threat in his voice, his tacit *behave*. "You won't have to do that," I promised him, and he nodded and left. All I could think was how I could not bear to be in his company a moment longer. How much I yearned to be away.

After breakfast in the huge dining room with me seated at one end of a table meant to seat at least twenty while William watched me anxiously from the other, he begged me not to lift a finger. Every detail had been already attended to. I should rest in my room and prepare for two hundred of our closest friends to descend upon us this evening. He hoped I would wear the burgundy silk with roses. And the diamonds.

I spent the afternoon watching the servants scurry around, polishing, dusting, arranging. The dining room table was extended to its full length, which seated sixty-four, and other tables were brought to make up the rest. Candles were set everywhere. There were roses bunched in vases on every table, in every corner, in colors ranging from pink to yellow to red. The house was full of their scent, along with that of turtle soup and roasting beef, and I felt a growing agitation that made me glad to do as William had suggested and retire to my room. I took a short nap. When I woke, it was time to prepare.

"I'll wear the jet tonight, Bridget," I said as I stood before the mirror, clad in the burgundy silk appliquéd with roses and trimmed in black lace.

The girl frowned. "The jet, ma'am? Not the diamonds?"

"I prefer the black," I said. She looked at me strangely but reached obediently into the case I'd opened. She took out the jet, a web of beads and stones, and put it around my neck, where it fell against my skin like shadows. I fastened on the matching earrings, jet drops that dangled against my jaw. It was a look that matched my mood this evening.

I said to Bridget, who hovered behind me, "You may leave me now."

She nodded and curtsied. When she opened the door, the sound of music drifted in—the orchestra, which had arrived an hour or so ago. I heard William's voice shouting orders: There were only moments before the first guests arrived, why were the candles not lit?

The door closed again, leaving me with the muffled sounds, the constant rush of footsteps. I adjusted the lace of my sleeve, the décolletage. I patted my hair. I was perspiring, though my hands were like ice.

From below I heard the opening of a door. Voices. I went to the window, pushing aside the drapes to see the view. My room looked out over Fifth Avenue. It was a wet night, and foggy. The rain had stripped leaves from the trees to gather on the street, where they had been crushed into mulch by carriage wheels. Central Park was gloomy, its trees shrouded in fog, ghostly in the arc lights. The edges of carriages were blurred. Drivers hurried from their damp perches to open doors, people huddled into their coats and capes, a man paused to adjust his beaver hat before he rushed his partner beneath the canopy William had erected over a burgundy-colored carpet leading up the steps.

I should go down, I thought. *I should greet our guests.* But I knew how they would look at me, the things they would wonder.

They would remember William's words. *He'd made advances . . . she repulsed them . . . I can no longer call him a friend.* They would wonder what of that was true, and they would secretly believe that I had had an affair with Victor. They would talk about it: *Wasn't it scandalous, how she kept him? As a guest in her own house? We suspected it, of course, who wouldn't? I heard she'd gone to the continent.* Ultimately I would be forgiven; I was a Van Berckel, after all, but it would always be a stain.

I let the curtains fall and backed away from the window. I imagined myself moving down those stairs—an interminable length, a promenade. Everything in me was measuring, measuring. Every beat, every moment. I heard them arrive, more and more. Twenty and then thirty. There was a knock on the door.

"Mrs. Carelton?" Bridget called timidly. "Mr. Carelton's asking for you, ma'am."

"Tell him I'll be down shortly," I said.

The music was louder, no longer tuning up. I heard the rise of talk, appreciation, footsteps. My throat was dry. I imagined them gathering, the rustle of rich silks, jewels glinting in the electric light, the smoke of candles, the salty, fishy scent of oysters borne by a dozen servants.

"Mrs. Carelton?"

"In a moment."

"Do you need help, ma'am?"

"No."

The clatter of hooves on the cobbled drive, the squeak of leather hinges, doors opening, the slip of heels on wet rock, laughter. My hands were cold and clammy within my gloves. It was growing late. They would expect me to be there. They would all be wondering. William would be wondering.

It was time.

It was as if a clock had chimed the precise hour within me. I straightened. I was ready to go down. But there was one last thing to do. I went to the armoire, plunging my hands through

silks and satins and lawns to find the bag I'd brought from
Beechwood Grove. My fingers stumbled across it. Soft, well-
oiled leather, a hard buckle. I pulled it out, ignoring the clothes
I pulled with it, scattering them on the floor. My fingers trembled on the buckle, but I pulled it open, stretching its jaws wide,
thrusting my hands past a grayed chemise, stockings, an inappropriate ball gown, a dressing gown, brushes that had never
seen the light of day at the asylum. Searching, searching . . .

My fingers came upon it. Smooth, cold metal. I sighed in relief and took it into my hands, pulling it loose so it gleamed in
the too bright light.

I grabbed my evening bag from the chair and slipped the gun
inside.

It was not hard, then, to do the rest.

I went out of my room and down the stairs. The lights glittered upon gold and wax, melted upon roses. The smell of the
flowers was overpowering, along with a hundred different perfumes. My hand slid along the soft, polished wood of the banister; my friends were below. They smiled at me as I came down,
their eyes measuring as I smiled back, as I went down and down
and down, into their midst, past servants holding silver trays,
past candles, through silks and satins. *Hello, Lucy, how are you,
Lucy? How well you look! How was the continent?* I moved easily past
them into the dining room. I saw Millie down the hall and
waved to her with a bright little smile, and her own smile died;
she lifted her hand as if to stop me.

She came toward me at the same moment I saw William,
holding a glass of bourbon. I willed her to stay away and finally
had to focus on my husband, who caught sight of me and
smiled. For a moment, I went numb. I thought, *I can't do this . . .
after all this time . . . how ridiculous.*

And then suddenly I could.

I opened my bag. I saw Millie coming, and I shook my head
at her. William was moving toward me quickly now, looking

worried. The bourbon was spilling over his hands, spotting his cuffs. I reached into the bag, almost expecting that the gun would not be there, but there it was, sliding into my palm. My fingers grasped the handle, cradled the trigger.

I pulled it loose and dropped my bag, and from the corner of my eye I saw people turn to me; I felt their hesitation. I paid them no heed. I waited until I heard the startled scream, until William came to a shocked stop. Our eyes met, and I saw astonishment there, then concern. I waited for the fear, and when I saw it, I felt a surge of satisfaction. Then I lifted the gun and pulled the trigger.

The blast nearly sent me rocking back; the crack echoed in the arched ceilings, too loud. The glass in William's hand went flying, shattering on the floor, spilling bourbon. I heard the screams, and I saw the stunned horror in the eyes of those around me. I saw the blood spreading across the marble floor, the women stepping back as if concerned it might soil their hems and their pretty shoes. It was as if I watched from afar while the shock faded and men set upon me, their shouts like echoes against my ears, their hands hard upon my arms, reaching for the gun, prying it from my fingers. They were shouting questions, I think, though I could not be sure because I couldn't take my eyes from the red of the blood creeping across the floor. How dark it was, darker than I'd expected. I wondered whether it would still be warm if I touched it.

That is all I remember about that night, except for one other thing. When the president of the Board of Police arrived, and my father gave the order for the men to take me to my room and lock me inside, I did not feel regret.

All I felt was free.

PART IV

The Tombs
October 1885

Chapter 29

I heard the noises downstairs, the chattering of the guests as they were sent away, the splashing of the rain against carriage wheels, and then the clatter of a police wagon arriving. I listened with some far-removed part of myself. I was too busy remembering the look of surprise and alarm on William's face, the way his glass went flying, the way he jerked back and fell, arms wheeling as if to keep himself afloat.

I had no idea how long I stood in my room. I was freezing, I was aware only of that. I had some vague thought that William must have installed central heating; why wasn't the furnace stoked?

Then there was a knock on my door, the sound of the key, and I turned to see the president of the Board of Police enter my room. He was flanked by two officers who would not look directly at me. But Stephen French was an old friend of my father's, and he did not flinch. I thought of all the times I had seen him across my father's table, laughing at some joke, his large white mustache twitching.

"Lucy," he said, hesitating before he stepped across the threshold. "Lucy, my dear, do you realize what has happened?"

"Yes. That is . . . didn't I shoot my husband?"

"Don't you know for certain?"

I began to shiver; it was uncontrollable. "This house," I murmured. "This terrible house . . ."

One of the officers ventured to Stephen, "She don't seem quite well, sir."

Stephen nodded. His expression seemed so sad. Gently, he said, "You understand, my dear, that I've no choice but to arrest you for murder. It's out of my hands. There were witnesses, you understand. But one thing I can do for you—we won't take you to the station house. I'll vouch for you myself. You won't be able to leave here, at least for now. I've posted officers at every entrance. Do you understand me, Lucy? You're a prisoner here."

"It's no different than it's ever been, then," I said.

He cleared his throat. "Your father wants to speak to you," he said.

"Yes, of course," I murmured, and the door shut behind them. I heard their voices in the hall, and then it was still again, and I was alone. The scene in the dining room reeled through my head like a drunken vision, each time bringing another detail into focus, something I'd missed. A scream, the calling of my name, the way someone had put an arm around me to hold me close. I heard a voice—my own—asking over and over again, "Is he dead?" and then, at a curt *yes*, the sound of harsh, jagged breathing—again my own.

The key turned once more, and my father came inside, followed by another officer. There must be police all through the house.

Papa looked haggard. He sighed heavily. "My God, Lucy. My God, do you know what you've done?"

There was something about his expression—the dismay, the unspoken fury—that made an impossible laugh bubble from my chest into my throat. I couldn't keep it down. I started to giggle—a high, tight sound that made my father recoil. Then I began to laugh in earnest, cackling like a witch, like a lunatic. I'd heard that laugh at Beechwood Grove upon occasion, lingering in the walls.

"She's mad," Papa said. "Look at her—she's mad!"

"No sir," the police officer said. He came over to me and put his arm gingerly around my shoulders, leading me to a chair while I laughed so that my ribs hurt. "There, now, Mrs. Carelton, you'll be all right. You'll be all right, you'll see." He clucked his tongue as if I were a child. My laugh turned rough. It hurt my throat, but I couldn't stop it, and before I knew, it had turned to coarse, raucous sobbing that robbed me of voice and breath.

The officer handed me a handkerchief. I held it to my face, blocking the sight of my father standing there, and perhaps it was that, or perhaps it was the smell of the policeman's sweat on the handkerchief, but my sobs settled into my chest, deep first, then shallower and shallower, and I could breathe again. I had hold of myself.

The man took his arm from around me and got to his feet. "You all right now, Mrs. Carelton?"

"Yes." I nodded. "Yes, thank you. I—I'm fine."

"Good. Now, here's your da to see you. I think it's best if you listen to him."

"Yes, of course. I will."

The policeman nodded, then said, "I'll wait outside." He went out into the hallway, but I still felt his presence. I wiped at my eyes and crumpled the handkerchief in my hand.

"Good God, girl, what's wrong with you?" my father murmured.

I looked down at the gold and white carpet. "Nothing."

"It seems that . . . that *place* did you no good at all. What were you thinking, Lucy? Why?"

I didn't answer him.

"I'm going to call Sullivan," he said. "He's a good lawyer."

"I don't want him," I said.

Papa frowned. "What?"

"I don't want Robert Sullivan," I said again. "I don't want a society lawyer."

"They're accusing you of murder, girl. You'd better have the best lawyer my money can buy."

"I want William Howe," I said.

"What?"

"I want William Howe."

My father looked stunned. "William Howe? His reputation—"

"—is for winning," I finished. "He's the one I want."

Papa's face was thunderous. "Absolutely not. By God, I'll call Sullivan and—"

"I will refuse him," I said. "I don't want him. Papa, you go to William Howe. If you don't, I'll find someone who will. It would be best, don't you think, if you were the one who hired him? You could control him that way. After all, who knows what he might say or what he might discover?"

My father stiffened. I saw a dawning surprise in his eyes.

"It's quite late now, I think. Perhaps you should try to rouse him from his bed. I'm sure a visit from the esteemed DeLancey Van Berckel will be enough to do so."

He was studying me. His voice was quiet when he said, "What has happened to you, Lucy?"

"It's growing late, Papa. Unless you want to see the Van Berckel name further marred by the scandal of a daughter in Sing Sing, I suggest you contact Mr. Howe."

He said, "I don't think you completely understand. He's a showman. He'll drag your name through the mud."

"As if it hasn't been there already."

"This will be worse, Lucy."

"How many reporters are in Hummel and Howe's pockets, Papa?"

He looked startled. "My God, how do you know of this?"

"It doesn't matter." I lowered my voice. "What matters is that he understands this city as no one else does. That's what I need, Papa, you know this as well as I."

He was quiet. Then he said, "How did you get to be so clever, girl?" He didn't wait for an answer. "Very well. I'll see if Mr. Howe's services can be engaged."

"Thank you."

"Just tell me, Lucy, when you shot William—"

"I didn't know what I was doing," I lied to him. "I can hardly remember doing it."

"Yes," he whispered. "Yes indeed. I understand."

I let him believe he did.

The rest of the night passed restlessly. I was aware of the constant motion downstairs. The police wagon did not move from the drive, but in the early morning another carriage came. When I saw it was the morgue wagon, I drew my curtains. In place of my numbness was anxiety. I wondered if my father had engaged William Howe. I wondered when they would take me to court. I wondered even what they would do with William's body, whether his parents might come to his funeral, whether I would meet them at last.

There was only one person of whom I dared not think. I would not allow myself even to think his name.

William Howe did not make an appearance. As the hours dragged on, I began to believe my father had failed, and desperation and fear joined my nervousness. I began to imagine terrible things, my future behind bars, crowded with other women, listening to their snores, breathing their breath, and I grew panicked—was I destined to spend the whole of my life in a cage?

"No," I whispered, calming myself, and then "No." I thought of William Howe and prayed Papa had hired him.

As if I had conjured him, I heard a knock on the door and an officer say, "Mrs. Carelton, you've a visitor." He opened the bedroom door—it was the same officer who had held me last night.

Now he was formal, almost stern. "You've a visitor in the parlor, ma'am." When I stood there, unmoving, he frowned. "Ma'am?"

"I don't know where the parlor is," I whispered.

If he found it surprising, he showed no sign. He only nodded curtly and motioned for me to follow. I had no awareness of this house, of *my* house, as he took me down some stairs to a closed door. I found myself glancing down the hallway, involuntarily, wondering if they had cleaned the dining room, if I would ever have to see it again. Then the officer opened the parlor door, and I was face-to-face with William Howe.

Howe was unmistakable; no one who had lived in New York for long could fail to know him. In the papers they called him "Big Bill," and it was not just his size—he was a man who obviously enjoyed a good meal—that dictated his nickname. He was larger than life, flamboyant, a man who'd bought life from nearly certain death sentences with his rhetoric and his crocodile tears. Today he wore a bright green vest with sparkling buttons that vied for attention with the diamond stickpin in his lapel and a large, clustered diamond ring. Behind him was a small, thin man with sparse brown hair, wearing an ordinary brown suit, carrying a leather-bound journal and a pocketful of pencils.

Howe said, "Mrs. Carelton, I am William Howe, and this is my assistant, Mr. Blake. He is the soul of discretion, I assure you."

The little man nodded, murmuring a hello in a reedy voice. Howe gave the police officer an impatient glance, and the man drew back, stopping only when I said, "When we're finished, I'll call you. Will you escort me back?"

"Of course, Mrs. Carelton," he said. He left, closing the door behind him. Mr. Blake opened the journal and took a pencil from his pocket.

I took a deep breath to steady myself. So much depended on

this visit. "Please, Mr. Howe, do sit down," I said, as if this were a social call. "Shall I ring for tea?"

"No, thank you," Howe said. He perched on the very edge of the nearest chair like a fat robin upon a fence rail. Mr. Blake leaned against the wall as if accustomed to never sitting. He didn't stop writing as Howe said, "There will be a bail hearing soon, within the next few days. I expect you'll be free then to go about the city as you please. For now you should know that there are reporters clamoring to talk to you, to hear 'your side' of the story."

"I don't want to talk to anyone," I said hastily.

"Oh, but you will," he said. "And soon. I've handpicked one of them, a woman by the name of Elizabeth Adler. She writes for the *World*."

"The *World?*" I asked, horrified.

"My dear Mrs. Carelton, the readers of the *World* will be ready to vilify you simply because you're a member of the mon-eyed class, unless we have someone there to raise their sympa-thy. Believe me, in a case such as this, we need all the public support we can rally. I think you'll find Elizabeth to be quite sympathetic to your plight—you will have paid her a fortune to be so. When she visits, you will be contrite and regretful. You will say you remember nothing of what happened. You will tell her that your husband was a monster."

"But William was—"

"I don't care what he was," Howe said. "For the purposes of the *World*, he was intolerable. Do you understand, Mrs. Carel-ton? You've hired me to make sure you don't spend the rest of your life at Sing Sing. I will require that you follow my direc-tions to the letter."

I nodded. "I understand."

"Excellent." He glanced at Blake, who nodded and turned a page. "Now, then, let me tell you what the district attorney has said. At your arraignment, which I expect to take place in about a week's time, they will charge you with murder in the shooting death of your husband, which is a very serious crime. Unfortunately, there can be no doubt that you did it, as there were several witnesses. There is much that can be done with the testimony of witnesses—I assure you, no one sees exactly the same thing—but there were several, and though I can shake their credibility in the eyes of the jurors, I can't make the entire scene disappear. I must tell you, Mrs. Carelton, that if you were going to shoot your husband, I wish you'd chosen a more private place." His voice softened. "Why don't you tell me what happened last night?"

"I don't remember much. It comes to me in bits and pieces." The lie was easy to say. "I remember being nervous. It was our first party in this house—it's just been finished, you know, and I am not accustomed— Then I was in the dining room, and he looked up. He had . . . bourbon. And when I shot him, it went everywhere."

"Bourbon," said Howe thoughtfully. "Yes."

"He was anxious that I do well. I'd only just got back—"

"Yes, I'd heard. From the continent."

"No. From Beechwood Grove."

Howe frowned. "Beechwood Grove?"

"A private asylum. On the Hudson River. William had me committed there in July."

"Good God." Howe's whole body seemed to become sharp and angular. Blake paused in his writing. "He had you committed to an asylum?"

"I was there for nearly three months."

"Who knows of your confinement there?"

"My father," I said. "My doctors."

"No one else?"

"Only the men William hired to take me there. I don't know their names."

"Your husband told your friends that you were visiting the continent. An extended visit, no doubt."

"Of course."

"And did none of them suspect anything different?"

"I don't know. I couldn't say."

"Just when did you return, Mrs. Carelton?"

"The night before the party," I told him. "The fifth of October."

"I assume we're talking of a lunatic asylum. Beechwood Grove *is* a lunatic asylum?"

I nodded.

Howe was avid. "Did he commit you there with your full consent?"

"Hardly," I said bitterly. "He drugged me with laudanum. I had no idea. I would have fought him."

"Why would he do such a thing?"

"I had grown . . . inconvenient," I said. "I'm sure you'll discover that I've been treated by many doctors over the last three years."

"For?"

"Hysteria. What they call uterine monomania."

"We'll need the names of those doctors," Howe said. He said to Blake, "Did you get all that?"

"Yes sir."

"What did these treatments consist of?"

I took a deep breath. "I took the water cure at Elmira. I was given morphia of all kinds. There were various other tortures."

"Did none work?"

"Only one," I said. I crumpled the silk of my gown between my fingers. "This is why I became inconvenient."

"How so?"

"My last doctor was somewhat of a visionary. He began treating me with hypnosis and electrotherapy. There were . . . surprising results. I began to feel much better. I was so much improved, in fact, that I think William began to believe I wasn't the wife he'd married. He had wanted me well, but once I became well, it had consequences he didn't like."

Howe appeared fascinated. "Such as?"

"I began drawing. He didn't care for that. Nor for the fact that I began to do things on my own, that I no longer cared so much for social niceties. I stopped holding a calling day. I much preferred to be outside."

"Inconvenient," Howe murmured.

"Yes. And there was more. At the beginning of my treatment, William insisted that my doctor accompany us everywhere—under the guise of a friend, you understand. It was when we removed to Newport for the summer . . . Well, William was so busy, and I required my doctor, and William began to believe . . ." I shrugged. "You see?"

"Yes," he said thoughtfully. "I think I do begin to see."

"There was . . . an incident," I went on. "William took badly to it. He banished the doctor from the house and imprisoned me in my room. He gave me laudanum. It was truly as if I had gone insane. I no longer knew what was real, Mr. Howe, nor what was illusion. Without the doctor I'd grown to rely on—at William's insistence—I was quite undone."

"That's a remarkable story."

"A true one, I fear."

"Did anyone but your husband witness this . . . incident?"

I shook my head. "No."

"And this doctor of yours, will he corroborate this?"

"I believe so."

"What is his name? Do you know where I can locate him?"

"Oh yes," I said. "His office is on Lower Broadway. On the corner of White Street. There's a little shop below. I believe it's called Jenson's."

"I've got it, sir," Blake said.

"And his name? Is it Jenson as well?"

"No," I said. I met William Howe's gaze. "His name is Victor Seth."

Howe rose, smiling, his eyes sparkling. "Well, well. I will contact him immediately. I must tell you, Mrs. Carelton, that until today I had little hope for this case."

"And now?" I asked him.

"Now? Now I think our chances are considerably improved." He chuckled, shaking his head. "An asylum. Can you believe it, Blake? An asylum?" He and his associate went to the door. He turned back to me. "I'll be visiting you again soon. In the meantime, there's that reporter—"

"Elizabeth Adler," I said.

"You are the sympathetic victim in all this, Mrs. Carelton," he said. "Don't forget that."

"I'm not likely to, Mr. Howe," I said.

His expression went blank. "No," he said. "I don't expect you will."

THE WORLD

New York, Tuesday, October 13, 1885

EXCLUSIVE Interview
Society Murderess Begs for Understanding
Carelton Marriage Made in Hell

All of New York society was shocked by the murder last Tuesday evening of prominent New York stockbroker William Carelton, who was shot by his Knickerbocker wife as guests danced the night away in the elegantly appointed ballroom of the Careltons' new Fifth Avenue mansion. Mrs. William Carelton (née Lucille Van Berckel) was promptly arrested for her husband's murder.

This reporter was given an exclusive interview with Mrs. Carelton in her home, where she stays confined to her room, haunting the murder site like some weeping specter. She was

*enervated and pensive, a Rossetti painting come to life. She
was dressed somberly in a gown of gray wool, with her dark
hair severely pinned back, a study in quiet rectitude.*

A Terrible Nightmare

"*Every morning I am horrified to find I have done this
terrible thing,*" *she said, tears falling copiously from her
large brown eyes.* "*And every night I go to sleep praying
that I will wake from this nightmare.*"

*It is indeed a nightmare of which Mrs. Carelton speaks:
a nightmare encompassing four years of marriage to a man
who drove her to illness with his incessant demands.
"William was a stockbroker," she tells us, "and he was quite
ambitious. I'll never know what drove him, but he could be
unmerciful. He was determined to belong; he insisted that I
play the part of a society wife even when my constitution required that I rest."*

*Her friends confirm that Mrs. Carelton was often ill and
that the strain of her marriage kept her nearly bedridden.*

"*I'll never know what made her marry him,*" *says one
anonymous friend.* "*She was so quiet and frail, and he was
so completely overpowering. There was something not right
about him. And, of course, he was not one of us.*"

A Prayer for Clemency

"*He wanted me out of the way,*" *Mrs. Carelton tearfully
explained as she told how her husband had committed her
to Beechwood Grove, a private lunatic asylum.* "*It was
much easier to control my money when I was not there to
question him.*"

*The night Mrs. Carelton returned home from Beechwood
Grove, her husband threatened to send her back if she did
not behave.*

"*I was so afraid. It was as if a black cloud came over me.
I hardly remember what I was doing or what I thought.*"

Mrs. Carelton shed tears throughout. "*I have no hope of
God's forgiveness for the terrible thing I did. All I can hope
is that I am not judged too harshly. I know only that I had to
escape that hell.*"

*The accused was unable to control her sorrow and re-
gret, and it is clear that to judge her solely as a society wife
is to do her a grave disservice. Mrs. Carelton's humanity
shines from a face wet with remorseful tears. Her devotion
to her husband, despite his cruelty, is amply documented. To
hear her cry for clemency is to answer the call of all people
in their fight against oppression. We can only hope the judge
and jury in this case treat her with compassion and mercy
despite—or because of—her unremarkable life.*

Chapter 30

The rush to William's funeral was unseemly, held as it was only three days after his death. Papa said William's body was deteriorating badly, though I knew the truth was that he was afraid I would insist upon attending if I were free, which Howe assured me I would be after my bail hearing, scheduled for the next day. So I was absent from seeing my husband laid to rest—appropriate, I suppose, as I was the one who had sent him there.

From my room I could hear the ringing of the church bells as he was eulogized, but it was left for Papa to tell me about. The service had been short and attended by many of William's colleagues, stockbrokers and Long Room traders and message boys. But those whom he would have wanted at his funeral—our friends, the people he made money for—had, for the most part, stayed away.

It was hardly surprising. My friends had never truly accepted him, even when his genius in the stock market made them money. The parvenu stink had never left him. Between the two of us—me, with my Knickerbocker heritage, and William, whose origins were unknown but always thought to be inferior—I was the one to whom they would lend their support, even with the taint of an asylum hanging above my head. The article in the *World* was only one in which William was portrayed as greedy and controlling. The irony was that had our friends known of my commitment to Beechwood Grove before William's death, I would have been the pariah. For now, confined as I was, with the judgment of a trial still awaiting, I could be their horribly persecuted daughter.

I was more than ready when the day came for my bail hearing. Papa had made arrangements to take me there himself, and he and the carriage were at the house early that morning. I went downstairs quickly, smiling weakly at the police officer guarding the door, wanting only to be free of this house, of William's presence, of the cursed dining room. The day was damply chill, with pregnant gray clouds overhead. I breathed deeply of the manure-scented air and longed to be free.

In no time we were there, and my father took me inside the District Court, where officers were waiting to escort me into a small open room lined with benches upon which sat all manner of men. At the front of the room was a desk, slightly raised, behind a barred railing.

As I entered, there was a gasp. Some of the men on the back benches swiveled, and I saw that many of them were scribbling away—reporters. I did not wonder what they saw: a woman dressed somberly in gray, no doubt exhausted-looking. I thought grimly of how they would portray me in the papers, how New York City would choke down my description with their breakfast and coffee. My stomach fell; my nerves rattled. A man in the front turned, and I saw with relief that it was William Howe. He smiled reassuringly and nodded slowly, and my nervousness faded.

"Is this Mrs. William Carelton?" asked the judge.

The officer on my right nodded. "Yes sir."

"Bring her down."

They led me down the aisle. The judge stared at me as if evaluating my every step, my every expression. As we reached the front, Howe stood.

"Your Honor," he said, "I'm serving as Mrs. Carelton's attorney."

The judge looked surprised and irritated. He shot a glance at me. "Is Mr. Howe your attorney, Mrs. Carelton?"

"Yes," I said.

"Dear God." The judge heaved a great sigh. "Very well, then. I see there is probable cause to hold Mrs. Carelton pending a charge in the murder of William Stephen Carelton, lately of New York, originally of Newport, Rhode Island."

Newport, Rhode Island. I hadn't known that. He had told me— What had he told me?

"Mr. Scott is the district attorney in this matter, I see. Mr. Scott, we're here to address the issue of bail. Have you—"

"Your Honor," Howe interrupted. "We are asking that bail be set for Mrs. Carelton. She is an esteemed member of New York society. Her movements are carefully watched at all times." Howe reached into his pocket and pulled out a scrap of paper. "If I could just read what the new society page, *Town Topics*, has to say of her . . ."

"That won't be necessary, Mr. Howe."

"I believe it shows how strong Mrs. Carelton's ties are to the city."

"I'm sure it does." The judge looked at the district attorney. "What are your feelings on the matter, Mr. Scott?"

Mr. Scott stood. He was tall and thin, with dark blond hair that fell boyishly into his face. His voice wasn't boyish at all. It was deep and resonant and completely serious. "We're requesting that Mrs. Carelton be held without bail, Your Honor," he said. "Regardless of Mr. Howe's statements, we have some evidence indicating a fragile mental state, and she has ample means to flee should she desire to do so."

Howe protested, "Your Honor, Mrs. Carelton has responsibilities. She employs several servants who rely on her, and she has many friends. Her father resides here. Mrs. Carelton's lineage stretches back to the Knickerbockers, sir; her ancestor was a Dutch ambassador. Mrs. Carelton has lived her entire life in New York City—"

"She's committed murder," Mr. Scott interrupted. "We believe she's a danger to society."

Howe harrumphed so loudly that Scott flushed. "She's accused of killing *her husband*, Your Honor. She hardly poses a threat to society. And as you can see, her father is here, ready to put up his considerable estate."

"Yes, yes, I see," the judge said. He glanced behind me to Papa. "Hello, DeLancey."

"How are you, George?"

"Do you think you can keep a leash on your daughter until her trial?"

Papa's voice was strong. "I guarantee she will be here."

"Your Honor," Mr. Scott protested, "this is highly irregular."

"This whole thing is irregular," the judge said. "I find that I agree with Mr. Howe. Bail is set at one hundred thousand dollars. Mrs. Carelton, you are free to go once the bond is posted. You cannot leave the city, and you must return for your arraignment after formal charges are filed. Mr. Howe, you will acquaint Mrs. Carelton with her obligations?"

"Yes, Your Honor."

"See the bailiff. Mrs. Carelton, I assume you will stay out of trouble. Your father has guaranteed it."

"Yes sir," I said.

I heard the rapid scratch of pencils on paper, a murmur that seemed to hover at the back of the room.

"Next, please."

It was over.

*   *   *

As the carriage started off, Papa closed his eyes and took a deep breath. "Well, thank God. I've made arrangements to take you back to the Row, Lucy. I thought you'd be more comfortable there, given the circumstances. I've removed Harris from . . . the other house and told the other servants they were dismissed as of this morning. And I've moved my things from the club, so I can be with you."

"You needn't have," I said.

"It's quite obvious you need someone to watch over you," he said. "And I gave my word, as well as my money." He grunted and glanced out the window. "What an incredible circumstance. I never could have imagined it. Not even when . . ."

He left the words for my imagination to fill in, which it did, neatly: . . . *your mother was alive*. I supposed my father would always thank God that my mother had the grace to kill herself before she could embarrass him as fatally as I had.

It was drizzling now, gray and foggy. I was cold inside the carriage, even huddled as I was against my father's bulk, with the traveling blanket over my lap. I wondered if I would ever be warm again.

We arrived home to a smiling welcome from Harris and another new lady's maid, one Papa had hired for my return. Her name was Gillian, and she was a quiet, biddable girl who had dark hair and apple cheeks. Her wide blue eyes regarded me with wariness.

"It was hard enough to find someone," Papa said gruffly. "Once they heard who they were serving. I hope she's efficient enough, but I doubt it. Had to pay her an exorbitant wage just so she wouldn't run off in fear the moment she saw you."

"If you don't mind, Papa, I'm quite tired."

He nodded, and I hurried to my room, to quiet safety. But when I walked through the door and lit the gas, everything was different. This room was no longer quiet or safe, no longer mine. I had been gone too long; I had tried to make too many other places my own. I realized suddenly, with a strangeness that I could hardly reconcile, that although William had understood nothing else about me, he had perceived this: that the room kept me the girl I'd always been. I was no longer comfortable here but cocooned. I remembered standing before the mirror, feeling like a stranger to myself. I wanted to laugh at how fine and ephemeral those feelings seemed to me now, how weak they'd been compared to this strangeness. How much older I felt, how unreconciled to these things of mine, to that bed, that chair. I did not belong here any longer.

But where I did belong—I dared not think of that now. Not now. There would be time enough later.

On Thursday morning I prepared myself for the calls that Papa had been certain would come. *They won't dare snub you*, he'd said before he left that morning, but I was not so certain. I sat in nervous anticipation, wondering what I would say, wishing I could avoid it all. When there was a knock on the door shortly after one o'clock, I rose from my chair and smoothed my skirt, taking a deep breath for strength. I was relieved when I saw it was only Millicent.

She entered the parlor fluttering, nervously smiling, patting at the pink-throated thrush on her hat. She carried a beribboned box, which she set before me as I embraced her and urged her to sit.

"What is this?" I asked.

"Nothing, really," she told me. "Some of those pastries you like so much. I thought . . . Well, I didn't know you couldn't go out before, or that you wouldn't."

"How lovely," I said. "How thoughtful of you."

She smiled weakly. "You've decided to come back here, then?"

"For the time being," I said. "Until the trial is over."

She winced at the word *trial*, and I realized what this visit was to be like when she said, "Did you hear that Consuelo Martin's daughter is engaged to some duke?"

I poured tea and watched her drink it. I watched her fumble with the cakes Papa's new cook had created—delicious little cream-filled things that neither of us had the appetite for. We talked pleasantly, as if nothing had happened, as if she had not watched me pull a gun from a beaded purse and shoot my husband. After fifteen minutes had passed—the allotted time for an afternoon call—she said, "Mr. Howe has asked me to serve as a witness on your account, Lucy. I'm not to have any contact with you until then. I haven't told anyone I was coming here today, but I felt I should come first and let you know."

I stared at her in surprise—we had been talking of a dinner party I'd missed, and I had thought the conversation would continue in that vein. "Oh."

She loosened her bag from where it had tangled at her feet. "I—I would do whatever I could for you, Lucy, you must know that."

"How good of you," I said sincerely.

She looked at me, and I had the sense that she was trying to see through me, to my soul, perhaps, to find the answers she wanted. "I'm your friend," she said simply, and perhaps that was all it was. The words were so quiet and sure that I felt tears come to my eyes.

"Yes," I said, "I believe you are."

She made a quick, definitive nod as if she had discharged a duty and now meant to go purposefully on. "I'll take my leave, then," she said. "You must take care of yourself, Lucy. Promise me you will?"

"Yes, of course," I said.

She paused, and then she said, "You mustn't be too hard on them, you know." I needed no explanation to understand of whom she spoke. Our friends, who I realized would not be coming to say hello or show their support. "They don't know what to think. No one does."

"I understand," I whispered.

"I hope you do," she said, and she rose and smiled and said her good-byes, and I was alone again, in a parlor filled to over-flowing with bronze statues and marble sculptures, silent and unmoving. The clock ticked on.

She was the only visitor I had that day. Or any other.

I did receive a few invitations. I was surprised until I saw who they were from—the faster crowd, Alma Fister and the like. With an unpleasant start, I saw that I was notorious, a fine en-tertainment, as Victor had been this summer, or as a European actress might be—with all the rumor and innuendo attached to an immoral life.

"You should go, my dear," Papa told me. "Show your face. Show them you're a Van Berckel. I'll accompany you if you like."

Two nights later, my father and I arrived at Alma Fister's door and were shown to a parlor already filled with guests where an effusive and beaming Leonard Ames held court.

"Why, DeLancey, why, Lucy, how good to see you. Lucy, how fine you look; if I didn't know the truth, I would have thought you'd been to the continent."

Papa flinched; I attempted to keep my smile. In the corner was the notorious Italian opera singer Alma had ostensibly held the party to celebrate. He was superbly dressed and handsome in a darkly Mediterranean way. He was rumored to have several mistresses, and I had no doubt that was true. Alma was talking urgently to him. She caught my gaze and whispered something in his ear. An appraising look came into his dark eyes—eyes that reminded me of someone else's.

I reached for the nearest glass of champagne. I had not been out since my return home. Millie had been the only person I'd seen, except for Papa and the servants. I had known it would be this way; I had known there would be whispers. Naively, I had not known they would be so uncomfortable.

Alma came over in a rustling of deep violet silk shot with silver. "My dear Lucy," she said, purring. "How good of you to come. And to bring your father too. Dear DeLancey, you haven't been about for the longest time."

"No, of course not," he said sharply.

Alma nodded commiseratingly before she turned to me. "Lucy, how wonderful you look. Especially after such a terrible ordeal." She shuddered dramatically. "Well, you will tell us all about it, won't you? Sergio is quite curious. When I told him who you were—he's read the papers, you know, though I was surprised to find he could read English. Apparently he's quite educated."

If I'd had any doubt that I'd been brought to serve as the evening's amusement, it fled with her words. When she brought the opera singer to us, my father squeezed my arm as if to give me strength, though the truth was I didn't need it. I understood my role now.

The crowd was faster even than I'd expected. Leonard, of course, and Alma, but there were others too, men from the Belmont clique who never missed an opportunity for notoriety, women I barely recognized who stared at me with unsuppressed glee.

"We should leave, my dear," Papa whispered into my ear. His hand on my arm was shyly insistent. "It won't do to be seen here after all."

He was right. This crowd was too scandalous. But I shook my head and took another glass of champagne and wondered why this didn't distress me. I'd been abandoned by my own crowd, though they pretended to favor me for the newspapers. Here I was not quite accepted, but curiosity would not be gainsaid. It became clear as the night went on that they expected some show from me, some little trick of insanity, something to amuse them. We sat in Alma's darkly wallpapered dining room and ate from Minton china embellished with deep blue borders and exotic birds. The room was small; we were so close together we bumped elbows, and still I was watched. I was, if possible, better behaved than I had been in years, but they were not quite sure what to do with me—how could they be? How does one look at a murderess over roast fowl in claret sauce? They didn't need a trial to tell them what I was. They had all heard every detail. Some had even been there. But I saw doubt in their eyes. Their memories were already growing faint. Had I really done what they thought I had? Here I was, well behaved, with my well-connected father beside me, and no outward sign of hysteria or insanity—could it really be true? And there were the newspaper reports as well, the article from that Adler woman. Poor persecuted Lucy. And William—they had never liked William, never really trusted him. . . .

They wondered, and I let them wonder. I drank champagne and ate and listened to Sergio's lovely baritone as he sang for our pleasure, and I only smiled when they asked their questions, because I knew that they had invited me not just to be an entertainment but because I had come down in the world, because I was not so untouchable, and that reinforced their own sense of superiority, their need to make their lives secure. *I will never be like her*, they told themselves, and I did not disabuse them of the notion. I didn't tell them what I knew: that it was easy to be like me. All it took was a slip, a step from the path we'd all been trained to tread. We were none of us different from the others; that was the lesson I had learned. We were all capable of anything.

They charged me with first-degree murder on a Tuesday and set my trial for early December. That afternoon William Howe lounged in my father's parlor, drinking brandy from fine leaded crystal. He looked out of place there, decorated as he was with jewels, too flashy for the pale blue walls that had entertained the best of Knickerbocker society for decades. But I was out of place here too—not because of what I wore, which was black, as befitted my status as a recent widow, but because the black was so heavy with irony it was hard to walk within.

Howe exhaled deeply and held his glass up to the light from the open window, swirling the brandy. "Well," he said, looking around him, "I must admit this is unusual for me. Most of my clients aren't so high-toned."

I had to restrain myself from going to the window. "It's all happening so fast," I said. "I'd thought the trial wouldn't be until spring, at least."

"They're torn between wanting to show the world that the rich aren't different and wanting to have it all behind them. Those newspaper articles have won you support. It's worked to our advantage. There's no need to stretch things out."

"I suppose not," I said.

"Mrs. Carelton, I know this is difficult for you. Trust me, I don't believe the end of this will find you behind bars. Wouldn't it be better to have the uncertainty done with more quickly?"

"Yes, it would."

"Your father tells me that your friends have been too busy to visit you."

"Let's not hide behind niceties, shall we?" I said. "I've become a curiosity. Curiosities are not the kinds of people Caroline Astor wants at her suppers."

"As long as they continue to join ranks behind you publicly, it doesn't matter if they cut you at every opportunity."

"How easy for you to say."

His expression became quizzical. "Come now, Mrs. Carelton. You should have expected this would happen when you decided to shoot your husband."

"I told you—"

"Yes, yes, I know." He waved my comment away. "I've heard

more excuses in my career than you could possibly imagine. It doesn't matter. In the end this case comes down to one thing."

I frowned. "What's that?"

He fingered his watch chain, stroking a jeweled cross that hung from it. "What we're presenting is not a regular insanity defense. I'm going to argue that you were laboring under a momentary 'irresistible urge.' You were sane before you pulled the trigger, you were sane after you pulled the trigger. But when you pulled the trigger . . . let's just call it 'temporary insanity.'"

I laughed incredulously. "Who will believe that?"

"The jury, when I'm finished with them," he said confidently.

"But I was in an insane asylum."

He smiled. "The burden of proof is not on us, Mrs. Carelton, you should remember that. It would be the state's responsibility to prove beyond a reasonable doubt that you were insane, which they won't do. Remember, punishment is what they're seeking. They don't want an insanity dodge. Mr. Scott will try to prove that the murder of your husband was cold-blooded and premeditated. They will certainly call the superintendent of Beechwood Grove, and he will no doubt say that you were quite sane when he released you. After all, it would be highly irresponsible of him to release a madwoman into the public. None of this worries me."

"Why is that?"

"Because we have two things that will convince the jury. First, it will be clear to them that you were not yourself when you pulled the trigger." His smile became smug. "I've spoken to Dr. Seth, and I think we have cause to plant ample doubt in the jury's mind about what happened that night."

I kept my voice as neutral as I could. "You said there were two things."

"Ah yes." He played with his watch chain again. "What did your father tell you about your husband's funeral?"

"That it was a short service."

"Did he tell you who attended?"

"Not many of our friends, I take it. Mostly the men who worked with William."

"Yes, well, there were others. One woman in particular who interested me very much."

He was happy about this news, I knew, yet I could not help feeling a twinge of dread. "Who was that?"

"William's mother."

I went numb and still. William's mother. I remembered telling Victor that I'd never met William's parents, that I wasn't interested in them. I could not imagine how his mother's coming could help me, why it shouldn't hurt me unbearably. How could I look her in the face after I'd killed her son?

"His mother?" I asked carefully. "Not . . . his father?"

"Apparently the man died two years ago," Howe went on. "His mother said she'd never met you. Now, I found that curious. She'd never met her own son's wife, and it's not due to distance. Why, she only lives in Newport. Where you and William spent every summer."

I remembered the bail hearing. *William Stephen Carelton, lately of New York, originally of Newport, Rhode Island.*

"Newport," I repeated.

"You didn't know?" Howe asked.

I shook my head.

"Why is that, Mrs. Carelton? How could you not know your husband's own parents?"

"I don't know," I said. I sank onto the edge of the settee. "He never spoke of them. I assumed, I don't know, that he was estranged from them. Or that they were dead. I had no idea they lived so close. I would have insisted on meeting them."

Howe leaned forward. "Do you know anything about them? Or about William's relationship with them?"

I shook my head, and he leaned back again. The many-colored floral pattern clashed with his garish vest—also floral, in greens and oranges and an odd shade of red. I had to turn my gaze away.

"Mrs. Carelton, listen to me closely. I must ask you to tell me whatever it is you know about your husband's parents. Anything at all."

"I don't know anything," I said. "I already told you, William never spoke of them. Why? Is something wrong?"

Howe shook his head. "Wrong? I should say not."

I watched him carefully. "Then why all the questions? Is there something I should know?"

"Mrs. Carelton, I would prefer it very much if you didn't know," he said, wheezing as he rose. "And that is why I won't tell you. You must trust me about this."

"But if there's something that could have a negative effect on my trial—"

He laughed, a short burst of sound that silenced me. "Don't worry about your trial, Mrs. Carelton," he said.

But that was exactly what I did. As the weeks passed and the date came closer and closer, Howe's words became even less reassuring. That there was something I didn't know, some plan I wasn't privy to—I began to worry as I hadn't before. The idea of a future in a prison cell was no longer so unreal.

Howe's visits came less and less often. Little Mr. Blake told me he was busy preparing. I was not to worry. But I had nothing else to do. I'd lost the desire to go out. Invitations became less and less frequent; too much time had passed, and I was no longer the topic of conversation. It was easy to forget me in the bleak snows of winter, when the wind was so bitterly cold.

But the day of the trial came too soon.

William Howe sent Blake to my door nearly with first light. I was awake; I'd been unable to sleep. Howe's assistant gave me terse instructions.

"He insists you wear black, Mrs. Carelton. You are in mourning for your husband. Dress as somberly as you can but not se-

verely. He wants the jury to notice how"—he swallowed uncomfortably—"how attractive you are." He reached into the
pocket of his coat and pulled out something wrapped in cloth.
He handed it to me. "You're to wear this."

I unwrapped it to find a mourning brooch—a wreath made of
braided dark hair. I looked up at him in surprise. "William's hair?"

He shook his head. "No, but the jury'll never know the difference."

I smiled. "Of course not."

"Are you ready for this, ma'am?" he asked.

"Yes," I said. I took a deep breath. "I'm quite ready."

He left, and I did as he bade. Gillian helped me into the black
wool gown I'd ordered for just this event. It was beautifully cut,
appliquéd with satin, jet-buttoned. The fabric fell over the bustle in sedate ruffles and folds. It made my skin look very pale and
enhanced my slenderness. I looked as if I might not have the
strength to carry the bustle. I added a hat—very simple, very
tasteful, decorated with black feathers and tulle that did not
cover my eyes. I carefully fastened the brooch Blake had given
me over my breast. I wondered whose it had been, whose hair
had been woven for this adornment.

I was ready when the carriage was brought, and Papa and I
made our way to the Halls of Justice—the Tombs, as it was
called, quite appropriately, grim as it looked with its Grecian ar-
chitecture. William Howe was waiting for me in the courtroom,
along with Mr. Blake, who murmured a greeting.

Howe smiled when he saw me. "You look perfect," he said,
and then he held out a chair for me between himself and his assistant. Papa sat in the row behind. Howe leaned down to whisper in my ear, "We're before Judge Wilfred Hammond. He's a
decent judge—we could have done far worse. He'll make sure
Scott doesn't try any tricks, but he's not disposed to like you.
The man doesn't trust women."

I shrank at his words. I hazarded a glance at Judge Hammond, who was busy with his papers and didn't look at me. He was an older man, in his midsixties, I guessed, with thinning silver hair and a rather bulbous nose. He grumbled and muttered to himself as he worked, and when the district attorney came into the room, he glanced up with a smile and small wave. Obviously the two knew each other. I gave Howe a worried glance.

"Don't worry," he assured me. "Randolph Scott is the nephew of the captain of the Harbor Police. Hammond knows him, but I don't think they're particular friends." Howe smiled wickedly and whispered, "Scott has a penchant for tenderloin brothels, and Hammond knows it. They once pulled him from a raid. Kept it all very quiet, and Scott's cleaned his nose a bit since then, but there's no love lost there. Hammond's not a fool."

I wasn't reassured.

Judge Hammond cleared his throat. "We're here to seat a jury in *People v. Carelton*. Are you gentlemen ready?"

Howe straightened and nodded. The lights caught on the silver threads in his brightly checkered vest and glinted on the ornate buttons. "The defense is ready, Your Honor."

"As is the state," Mr. Scott said.

The judge turned to the bailiff. "Bring them in."

The door opened, and in filed men of all ages, dressed in all manners. As they took their seats, they stared at me so intently I felt myself go hot. Howe had told me to look at them as they came in, but I could not.

Beside me, Blake put a reassuring hand on my arm. "They're curious, Mrs. Carelton," he said. "They'll look for a while, and then they'll lose interest." But even after Howe stood and introduced me, their scrutiny was so hard that I didn't have to feign the tears filling my eyes.

"Is she the one?" one of the men asked, and the hatred in his gaze alarmed me. "Is that the she-devil who killed her husband?"

After that everything passed in a blur. I heard Howe's questions of the men, and Scott's questions, the virulence of some who were summarily dismissed. Howe had not warned me about this. Who I was and what I'd done were a threat to these men. I sat in shocked silence, letting their abhorrence whittle away at my calm until, at the end of the day, I was a trembling mass of nerves.

We had twelve jurors, most of them businessmen and merchants.

Howe turned to me with a wry look. "Well, we've got it, Mrs. Carelton. A jury of your peers."

I looked up at Howe uncertainly, and it was as if he sensed my distress. He sat beside me. "This is not as bad as it seems," he said. "You must trust me."

The echo of other words, another time. As then, I had no other choice. I nodded my assent. "And tomorrow?" I asked.

He sighed. "Tomorrow we begin the trial. I should warn you, there will be reporters everywhere—but that's not my worry. We own enough of them. The seats will be full, some with your friends, many who are simply curious. You must ignore them all. Today you were quite effective. If you can manage to look as distraught tomorrow—"

"It shouldn't be too difficult," I said quietly.

He gave me an admiring look. "Yes, that's just the expression we want. And Mrs. Carelton"—he hesitated—"I must warn you that there will be things said tomorrow. . . ."

"There could not be anything worse than today," I told him.

I was wrong.

The next morning, after a breakfast that I couldn't eat, I went again to the courtroom. Papa was not allowed inside. He was to testify in my defense, so he left me in the hall. As I turned to go in, he touched my arm. "I'm here for you, my girl. Don't you think I'm not." Though I had never before thought that we looked alike, now I saw myself in the slope of his jaw, the set of his eyes, and I had the not entirely unwelcome idea that I was truly my father's daughter.

"Thank you, Papa," I said, and then I went into the courtroom.

Howe had said the seats would be full, but I had not imagined the crush. Every space was taken, even against the walls. There were not just men but women too, many of whom had brought huge picnic baskets for the lunch break, no doubt so they would not lose their place. Some I recognized. Daisy Hadden was there, as were Alma Fister and Leonard Ames. Millie wasn't; she was also a witness. Nor, of course, was Victor, though there was a moment when I searched for him, when the noise and motion seemed suspended.

I sat down at the defense table beside Blake. William Howe came into the courtroom then, like a triumphant gladiator. He was all smiles, flashy and diamond-laid, with his stickpins and rings. Today he wore a fawn suit with a vest of scarlet poppies on a black ground. It seemed he knew nearly everyone in the courtroom. He shook hands, he grinned, he laughed, he won the crowd with his flamboyance and his ease. I only hoped the jury would be as easily influenced.

The district attorney entered as long-faced and boyishly earnest as ever. It was hard for me to imagine that he had a penchant for the tenderloin brothels, as Howe had said, though I had spent my life in a world where facades were all-important. I knew vices lay beneath.

Mr. Scott was followed by his secretary. They sat at the prosecution table. Then the judge nodded to the bailiff, and the jury was led in. The crowd silenced, watching as, one by one, the men took their seats.

"Gentlemen," Judge Hammond said, looking at Howe and Scott, and then, "Gentlemen of the jury. We're here today to decide the fate of Mrs. William Carelton, who sits before you

charged with the murder of her husband. We'll start with opening statements. Mr. Scott, are you ready?"

"I am, Your Honor," Scott said.

Howe laid his hand on my arm and leaned close to whisper,
"Prepare yourself, Mrs. Carelton."

I took a deep breath, and it felt as if I did not release it during the whole of Scott's statement.

It was horrible. Randolph Scott laid the scene well: October
sixth, ten P.M., just before dinner was to be served. He was as
much a storyteller as anyone I'd ever heard. I saw myself come
down the stairs smiling, talking with my friends. I saw my eyes
lit with chilling fury as I pulled the trigger. The pictures he
painted were extraordinary. Had I not been there, I would have
thought his detail incredible. As it was, I felt myself pulled into
the scene he imagined.

At the end he went to the jury box and leaned on the rail, his
voice vibrant and deep. "Gentlemen, the defense will attempt to
prove that Mrs. Carelton is insane, but we will show that she is
not, and that the shooting of her husband was a cold-blooded,
premeditated act. She meant to free herself of his loving control
and take command of the fortune he administered so admirably
for her benefit. And why is this? Why would she do such a
thing? Because Mrs. Carelton knew that as long as her husband
was alive, she would not be free to carry on with her lover."

There was a gasp—it was my own. Howe tightened his grip
on my arm in warning.

"Insanity has nothing to do with this case, gentlemen. In the
end you will have no choice but to find Mrs. Carelton *guilty* of
first-degree murder."

Scott turned. His gaze lit on me for an instant, then flickered
to Howe in triumph before he took his seat. The courtroom was
quiet. I felt eyes on me, and I did as Howe had instructed me. I
lowered my gaze, I bit my lip. I felt frail, undone.

Howe rose. Under his bulk, his footsteps had resonance. He

walked to the jury box, his hands in his pockets, and then he sighed.

"This is a sad case," he said, shaking his head. There were actually unshed tears in his eyes. "A very sad case. Mrs. William Carelton is a fine, upstanding citizen of this community. Her family is descended from our first settlers, from the original Dutch ambassador to New York. She grew up coddled by her parents, admired by her friends. In short, there was no reason to think that Mrs. Carelton might not have the kind of life most of us envy. But for one thing.

"She married badly. On the outside William Carelton seemed a fine man. He was certainly intelligent. He was a successful stockbroker who made a great deal of money for many people. On the surface their marriage seemed to be a love match. It was anything but.

"In the four years of their marriage, William Carelton abused his wife to the point of illness. Mr. Scott is correct when he says that William Carelton controlled his wife and his wife's money, but it was not a loving arrangement. Over the years she saw countless doctors for the relief of hysteria and neurasthenia. And when she finally found one who could help her, Mr. Carelton panicked. He forced his wife into a lunatic asylum, lied to their friends, and found himself in full control of her estate—without her interference.

"Gentlemen, we shall prove that Mrs. Carelton was not in her right mind when she shot her husband, but was in thrall to an irresistible urge, an undeniable, desperate attempt to free herself from his manipulations and torture. Our expert witnesses will testify that Mrs. Carelton was not in control of her emotions or her mind. We will also show that Mr. Carelton was not the man he seemed to be, and that even his wife had no knowledge of the truth of him.

"Mrs. Carelton's shooting of her husband is the saddest story of all, gentlemen, because it shows what can happen when a man abuses the sacred contract that God Himself put down between men and women. This case is not about seeking the control of money or about the freedom to be with a lover. This case is about what can happen when a man does not temper his superiority and strength, does not offer kindness to the fragile woman in his care. When Mr. Carelton denied the charge put to him by God and society, Mrs. Carelton was forced by desperation and fear to take the only avenue she could. Gentlemen, this fine woman had no other choice. In the moment that she pulled the trigger, she was driven to a desperation that knew no rationality or logic. She could no longer live in the world of his making."

Here Howe paused. He lowered his eyes in abject sorrow.

"Yes, gentlemen," he said. "This is a sad, sad case. But it is not Mrs. Carelton we should blame but her husband. I trust you will find in your hearts the ability to understand this poor woman. I trust you will right the wrongs that have been committed against her." He pulled them in with his gaze. His voice was huge, dramatic. "I trust that you will prove to be wise men."

THE WORLD

New York, Monday, December 7, 1885

SOCIETY MURDER TRIAL

Police Testify
"She Knew She Done Wrong"
SOCIETY ATTENDS TRIAL

Today began the murder trial of Mrs. William Carelton. Mrs. Gerald Fister and Mrs. Moreton Hadden were in attendance, as were Mr. Leonard Ames and several lesser luminaries of the city. As Mrs. Hadden said, "Of course we will stand by Lucy Carelton. She's one of our own."

Mrs. Carelton wore a black wool gown with satin and jet

decorations, and a hat decorated with black feathers. She constantly fingered a mourning brooch—a brooch, Mr. Howe told us, that was made from her husband's hair. Mrs. Carelton was tearful throughout and obviously deeply disturbed by the proceedings.

The first witness called by the prosecution was Officer Edward Boyd, one of the men called to the Carelton residence on the night of the murder. Officer Boyd described the scene in grisly detail. "The house was lit like the Fourth of July," he claimed, with electric lights. There was an orchestra in the room, but they were silent. "I never heard such a sound," Officer Boyd told the district attorney. "Or, I should say, such a nonsound. There was all these people there, all huddled around whispering, and it was like being at a funeral." The officers rushed directly to the dining room, where they found the fallen body of William Carelton lying in a pool of his own blood, the mortal wound one that had struck his chest. "It was from close range," the officer said. "He was splayed open like a butchered hog." Several of the ladies in the courtroom swooned at his description. Mrs. Carelton bent her head and cried silently while Mr. Howe put a hand on her shoulder to comfort her.

"She Wanted to Be Punished"

Officer Boyd said that he had gone with the president of the Board of Police, Mr. Stephen French, to Mrs. Carelton's sitting room, where she had been led from the slaughtered body of her husband. Officer Boyd said that she "was perfectly calm. Dry-eyed, if you want to know the truth. Nothing like I expected her to be."

Mr. Scott asked, "And how was that?"

"Well, most females who've done in a man like that, they're pretty shook up."

"And Mrs. Carelton was not?"

The officer shrugged. "Not to my eyes." He then told the jury that Mrs. Carelton did not seem to him to be in any way insane. "She agreed with Mr. French's terms as calm as you please," he said. "It was like she wanted to be punished. Like she knew she done wrong."

The defense attorney, Big Bill Howe, asked the officer if he was qualified to judge a woman's insanity. Officer Boyd answered that he'd seen enough crazy women to know the look of one.

"Could it be that Mrs. Carelton was in shock over the sight of her husband?" Mr. Howe asked. "That she was not calm, as you suggest, but deeply horrified by what she'd just done?"

Officer Boyd answered that it might be so.

"And isn't it true, Officer Boyd, that you have never spent time in a lunatic asylum, and that you have no way of judging the different ways in which insanity might claim a victim?"

Officer Boyd was clearly uncomfortable when he admitted that Mr. Howe's statement was correct. Mr. Howe dismissed him after asking if he had known Mrs. Carelton prior to her arrest, and if he had any reason to know what her demeanor normally was when she was in shock or upset. Officer Boyd said he did not.

This reporter would have to say that although the officer's description of the crime scene was vivid and disturbing, Big Bill Howe clearly was the victor in the determination over Mrs. Carelton's state of mind upon her arrest.

The court reconvenes tomorrow morning at nine A.M.

Chapter 31

I could not forget the words the officer had said, how William had looked to him like a butchered hog, and it was this description above all else—a description I knew but could not remember—that kept me tossing and turning restlessly through the night. That and my dreams of Victor, of how I'd last seen him, limned by moonlight in my room at Beechwood Grove. I was pale and tired as I went to the courtroom the next morning.

Mr. Scott had been thorough. He first called Julia Brecken-wood, and though Howe had told me her name was on the list, I was startled by her appearance. She was dressed in dark green, elegant and self-possessed as they swore her in, and yet I remembered her in Millie's dining room at Newport, confused as she woke from a trance, straining to hear the music on the beach. I remembered her quiet humiliation when I told her it wasn't so, and then I remembered William's insinuations about the weekend she and Victor had spent at Daisy Hadden's country house, and I realized uncomfortably that I had no idea what she would say.

Mr. Scott came over to her and smiled. He rested his hand on the witness box and said, "You were invited to the party Mr. and

Mrs. Carelton gave on October sixth to open their new house, were you not?"

"Yes," she said.

"And did you go?"

"Oh yes. Everyone went."

"It was quite an occasion, then?"

She nodded. "William had been talking about the house for nearly a year. He was very excited."

"What about Mrs. Carelton? Was she excited as well?"

Julia glanced down at her hands, and I tensed with apprehension. "Well, it was odd, you see. I don't know. She never spoke of it. I would have spent every moment decorating, but Lucy seemed . . . she seemed not to care."

"Did she ever tell you why that might be?"

"No." She shook her head. A tiny curl came loose to bounce at her cheek, and she pushed it aside with a nervous movement. "She never confided in me. We were friends, but not . . . good ones."

"I see. But you had known Mrs. Carelton for many years, hadn't you?"

"Oh yes." She smiled thinly. "We shared the same friends. We even shared the same doctor."

I went still.

"The same doctor," Mr. Scott repeated. "And who was that?"

"Victor Seth."

"What kind of doctor is Victor Seth?"

"A new—a neurologist." She smiled in embarrassment. "It's a hard word to say."

"Do you know what the word means, Mrs. Breckenwood?"

"I believe he's some kind of brain doctor."

"And who recommended Dr. Seth to you?"

"Why, it was William," she said. "William Carelton. He said that Lucy had seen Dr. Seth for some little irritability and that she was doing remarkably well."

"Objection," Howe said. "Hearsay."

"Sustained," Judge Hammond ruled.

Scott nodded. "Did that seem to bother him, that his wife was doing remarkably well?"

"Objection!" Howe said.

But before the judge could rule, Julia answered. "Oh, goodness no. He was quite pleased. Exultant, I would say."

"He was exultant." Scott nodded. He stepped away from the box and looked meaningfully at the jury. "And this Dr. Seth, did you have occasion to see him socially?"

Here Julia bit her lip. "Yes."

"How so?"

"He was quite often at social occasions in the city, and when we removed to Newport, he was a guest at Seaward."

"Seaward? What is that?"

"The Careltons' summer home. Actually, I believe it belongs to DeLancey Van Berckel, but he is never there."

"Who was at Seaward this summer, Mrs. Breckenwood?"

Julia kept her gaze steadfastly turned from me. I pressed my hands to my stomach to still the fluttering there.

"Lucy Carelton," she said. "And Victor Seth."

"Not Mr. Carelton?"

Slowly she said, "He came on weekends at first, and then there was a month or so when he didn't come at all."

"So Mrs. Carelton was alone with Dr. Seth?"

"Yes."

"Did you find that strange, Mrs. Breckenwood? That Mrs. Carelton should be alone all summer with a male guest?"

"Usually I would not have thought so," she said reluctantly. She was pulling at her gloves. "But Dr. Seth was quite attentive to Lucy, and . . . people wondered."

"I see. Did Mr. Carelton seem satisfied with this arrangement?"

"I thought not," she said. "And then I was sure of it when he came to Newport in July."

"What made you so sure?"

Julia pulled again at her gloves. "Well, there had been an unusual entertainment that summer. Dr. Seth could make people . . . do things, you see. He called it hypnosis. He could put them in a trance and give them direction. It was all in fun. It was very entertaining. He could make them hop like a frog or bark. It had become a favorite diversion. This night that William came to Newport, Dr. Seth put someone into a trance and . . ." She hesitated.

"What happened, Mrs. Breckenwood?"

Julia swallowed. "William became quite upset."

"Upset? How do you mean?"

"It was odd. He took Lucy from the party without even an excuse. He seemed angry. Everyone noticed it—it became the talk of the night. Later, he told us that he'd discovered Dr. Seth had made improper advances toward her. I wasn't at all surprised. I'd suspected it all along. All of us had. It was obvious they had a relationship beyond that of a doctor and patient."

Howe raised an objection, but the judge merely silenced him and let Mr. Scott go on.

"What happened after that night?"

"I don't know," Julia said. "Lucy was gone the next day. William said she'd gone to the continent."

"I see." Mr. Scott clasped his hands behind his back and paced to the jury. "When was it that you next saw Mrs. Carelton?"

"At the ball. The opening of their house."

"How did she seem to you?"

"When I came in, she was coming down the stairs. I waited for her to greet me, but she walked on by. It was as if she didn't see me."

"She seemed distracted, then?"

"Oh yes. Terribly. But driven too. As if she was on her way someplace and didn't wish to be interrupted."

"Did you see where she went?"

Julia nodded. She looked ready to cry. "Oh yes. Everyone did."

"Where did she go?"

"To the dining room."

"Did you follow her?"

"Yes. I was right behind her. I'd only thought to greet her, to ask her how her tour was."

"But you never got a chance to do that."

"No."

"Why was that, Mrs. Breckenwood?"

"Because she went into the dining room, and I saw her reach for something, and then there was this terrible sound—like an explosion—and smoke. Someone screamed, and then there was Lucy, holding a gun, and William was on the floor. He was dead." Julia was crying. Mr. Scott reached into his pocket for a handkerchief and handed it to her, and Julia dabbed delicately at her eyes.

"Now, tell me, Mrs. Breckenwood—yes, I know this is very distressing, but if you could please tell the jury if you're certain it was Mrs. Carelton who held the gun."

She sniffed and nodded. "Yes, it was."

"Was it she who pulled the trigger?"

"Yes. No one else was near her."

"Did this act of Mrs. Carelton's surprise you?"

"Surprise me?" Julia paused. The handkerchief was suspended in air. "Why, yes. It surprised me greatly."

"You would not have thought Mrs. Carelton capable of such a thing?"

"Lucy? Goodness no. Not at all."

"Did you see any sign of distress or anger on Mrs. Carelton's face?"

"None. Only that distraction, as I told you."

"Did she seem in possession of her faculties?"

"Certainly. Yes. Yes, she did."

"She did not seem to you to be a wild beast?"

Julia shook her head. "A wild beast? Oh, goodness no."

Mr. Scott once again propped his arm on the witness box. "Have you ever observed Mrs. Carelton to act in such a way as to make you think she was not in her right mind?"

Julia frowned. "No, not at all."

"Did Mrs. Carelton appear to be in good health?"

"Well, she was frail, and often ill. And she *was* seeing Dr. Seth. She had fits sometimes, where she fainted, and she was often absent with the headache."

"But nothing evidencing insanity?"

"No. Nothing like that."

Mr. Scott looked puffed up, self-satisfied. I sat there in a dull fog. I wondered how I had been so unaware of how much Julia disliked me.

"I'm done with this witness," Mr. Scott said, and Judge Hammond nodded to Howe, who rose without preamble and went to Julia, leaning close enough that she sat back in her chair.

"Mrs. Breckenwood, you said that you and Mrs. Carelton were not good friends, isn't that true?"

"That's true," she said quietly.

"Mrs. Carelton did not confide in you?"

"No."

"Would you say you knew her well enough to know the circumstances in which she lived?"

"Well . . . yes."

"I see. You stated that she was often ill, that she had headaches. Did she ever confide in you as to why that might be?"

"No."

"Did she ever confide in you as to her relationship with Dr. Seth?"

"No." Julia squirmed.

"So when you said that it was obvious Dr. Seth and Mrs. Carelton had an intimate relationship, this was complete speculation on your part?"

"Not just mine," she protested. "Others said the same thing."

"But it wasn't unusual, was it, for Mrs. Carelton to have male guests at Seaward?"

Julia paused. Her voice was nearly a whisper. "No."

"Was it unusual for a man like William Carelton to be away from Newport for long periods of time?"

"I suppose not."

"Most husbands attend to their wives there only during the weekends, isn't that true?"

Reluctantly, she said, "Yes."

"Was Mr. Carelton different from the others in that way?"

"No," she admitted.

"Now let me ask you: Would you think it unusual for a woman such as Mrs. Carelton, a woman you say suffered headaches and 'fits,' and who seemed to be improving under a doctor's care, to have that same doctor attend to her day and night?"

Julia straightened. "I wouldn't know about that."

"Wouldn't you?" Howe stepped back, exaggerated surprise on his face. "*You* wouldn't know? Didn't you just say that you and Mrs. Carelton shared a doctor?"

"Yes."

"And that doctor was Victor Seth?"

"Yes."

"Why were you seeing Dr. Seth, Mrs. Breckenwood?"

"I don't care to say," she said.

"Isn't it true that he attended to you during a weekend stay at Mrs. Moreton Hadden's country home in early June?"

She said nothing.

"Isn't it true, Mrs. Breckenwood?"

"Yes," she whispered.

"Were you having an affair with Dr. Seth?"

"No." She blushed furiously. "No, of course not."

"What was the purpose for him to accompany you there?"

"He was my *doctor*," she said. "He was treating me."

"For what, Mrs. Breckenwood?"

Julia's full lips thinned. "I don't understand why that should be important. It's nothing to do with this business."

"Please answer the question, Mrs. Breckenwood," the judge said.

She flushed again. "For my nerves. He was treating me for my nerves."

Howe nodded. "So, Dr. Seth also attended to you day and night, and you were *not* having intimate relations. The same could be true of Dr. Seth and Mrs. Carelton, couldn't it?"

Julia frowned. "I . . . I suppose so. But—"

"What exactly did Mr. Carelton tell you about Dr. Seth's relationship with his wife?"

"Objection," Scott called out. "Hearsay."

"You opened the door yourself, Mr. Scott," said the judge. "I'll allow it. Please continue, Mrs. Breckenwood."

Julia bowed her head. Her voice was so soft I had to strain to hear it. "He said that Dr. Seth had made advances toward Lucy."

"Did he say how Mrs. Carelton reacted to those advances?"

Julia would not look at him. "He said she had rejected him."

"Do you have reason to believe those words aren't true?"

"No," she whispered. "I suppose not."

"So you have no real knowledge that Mrs. Carelton and Victor Seth were having an affair?"

"No."

"Now, Mrs. Breckenwood, I have only a few more questions. How long have you known Mrs. Carelton?"

"All my life."

"And yet you did not know her well."

"We were never good friends, as I said."

"But you claim to know her well enough to understand her state of mind as she walked down those stairs to the dining room the night of October sixth?"

"Well, I—"

"In fact, you don't know what Mrs. Carelton was thinking, do you, Mrs. Breckenwood?"

"I can assume—"

"But by your own admission you didn't know Mrs. Carelton well enough to assume. Isn't that true?"

There was a pause. Julia glanced at me, and her gaze was so hostile it felt like a slap. "Yes," she said.

"Are you acquainted with the symptoms of insanity, Mrs. Breckenwood?"

She said, "Why, it's easy enough to tell."

"Have you spent time in a lunatic asylum?"

"Of course not!"

"Are you a doctor?"

"No, but—"

"You don't know what a doctor might call insanity, do you, Mrs. Breckenwood?"

She was silent. Howe went on as if she'd spoken. His voice raised dramatically. "In fact, Mrs. Breckenwood, not only do you have no knowledge of Mrs. Carelton's illness, you have no knowledge of her life beyond what you've seen at the opera and at parties, do you?"

"No."

"So you are hardly qualified to judge if Mrs. Carelton was indeed insane the night she shot her husband, isn't that right?"

Julia sighed. "Yes."

"And what about Mr. Carelton? When did you meet him?"

"When we all did. About a year before Lucy married him."

"Do you know where he came from?"

"No."

"Did you know anything of his history?"

"No."

"What did you think of Mr. Carelton?"

"What did I think of him?" She looked puzzled.

"Yes."

"He was . . . We were all surprised when Lucy married him."

"Why is that?"

"Well, he wasn't of our class."

"I see." Howe smiled indulgently, as he might toward a naughty child who had decided to behave. "Thank you, Mrs. Breckenwood. You've been most enlightening."

Howe was exultant, but the rest of the day was torture for me. Mr. Scott next called Hiram Grace, a man who certainly had no love for me. I was not a good wife or a woman who knew her place, he said. He found these things as disquieting as murder. But as for insanity . . . I'd made foolish decisions. I was perhaps drinking. That was what he thought, and no wonder—any female who had married so far beneath herself must be unhappy. But I'd brought it on myself.

And what did Hiram Grace think of William? Howe asked. Hiram answered that William was a good stockbroker, that he'd made Grace some money over the years, but even DeLancey Van Berckel, William's own father-in-law, had not been able to get William into the Knickerbocker Club.

"DeLancey sponsored him, but there was something about him. Not quite of our class, you know," Hiram Grace said. "No one knew where he came from. Newport, you say, hmmm? No, I didn't know. No one did."

Chapter 32

The next day the district attorney questioned Dr. Moore, who had been so ready to prescribe my laudanum, and who stated with assurance that my only illness lay in the fact that I coddled my moods like any other woman. After that, Mr. Scott called Dr. Little to the stand.

The asylum superintendent was dressed in a dark brown suit buttoned so high that his dark satin necktie puffed just beneath his chin. His thinning hair was shiny with oil, and his glasses were gone, revealing the dull mud of his eyes. He did not look at me as Mr. Scott called him to the stand, and he sat with an air of noble superciliousness that had reporters muttering.

Howe squeezed my arm and leaned close to whisper, "He'll play right into our hands."

I nodded and pulled away, twisting my fingers in my lap. I was almost sick with apprehension, more so than I'd been with any of the other witnesses.

Dr. Little told the jury of his credentials. Mr. Scott started the testimony by asking, "What is insanity, Dr. Little?"

"That's a complex question, Mr. Scott," Dr. Little said. He laid one hand over the other, resting them on his dark-clad knee.

"But I suppose, in layman's terms, that a person is insane if he cannot control his impulses—and, more importantly, if he cannot tell right from wrong."

Mr. Scott smiled. "That's a precise statement indeed, Doctor. Can you tell us how you know the defendant?"

The doctor paused. Now he looked at me, with a sad, pitying expression. "She was a patient of mine."

"When did you first see her?"

"She and her husband consulted with me a little over a year ago. She was having hysterical episodes. I made a diagnosis of uterine monomania."

"What exactly is uterine monomania?"

"Abnormalities in Mrs. Carelton's uterus cause a reflex action in the nervous system, subjecting her to extreme mood changes, which may range from mild depression to intense hysteria."

"Did you suggest a treatment?"

"I did. I suggested she be placed in an asylum."

Mr. Scott nodded gravely. "Did Mrs. Carelton follow your advice?"

Dr. Little looked affronted. "She did not."

"In your opinion, was that a good idea?"

"Absolutely not. I warned her and her husband that she would grow worse."

"What did Mr. Carelton say to that?"

"That they planned to have a child, and he felt that would solve Mrs. Carelton's problems. I warned him that a child might make her problems worse."

"I see. Did you see Mrs. Carelton again after that visit?"

"Not until a year later. July twentieth, to be exact."

"Under what circumstance?"

Dr. Little glanced at me again. I bowed my head to study my hands. "Mrs. Carelton was being committed to my care at Beechwood Grove."

"What is Beechwood Grove?"

"A private asylum."

I heard a murmur from the back of the courtroom, the scratching of pencils, loud whispers. I did not dare look at the jury, but I felt them watching me with pitying curiosity.

"How long was Mrs. Carelton at Beechwood Grove?"

Dr. Little's voice became clipped. "She was there until October fifth. About two and a half months."

"Do you know, Dr. Little, what took place the next day, October sixth?"

Dr. Little's face looked cast from stone. "I understand that she killed her husband."

"Is this something you could have anticipated, Doctor?"

Little shook his head. "It was most emphatically not. Mrs. Carelton made excellent progress. At Beechwood Grove we pride ourselves on our exacting care, and Mrs. Carelton received the very best treatments available. Had there been any doubt of her sanity, she would be there still. I assure you, Mr. Scott, that when Mrs. Carelton left us, she was quite sane, as I told her husband she would be."

"Did she have control of her impulses?" Mr. Scott asked.

"Yes. Very much so."

"Could she tell right from wrong?"

"Oh yes. Certainly."

"Would you say that she would have understood the consequences of her actions?"

"Mr. Scott, she was as sane as you or I."

"Could she have been clever enough to fool you?" Mr. Scott asked.

Dr. Little reddened. "I am a highly qualified physician, Mr. Scott, and she is only a woman."

"Yes, of course. You're saying there is no possibility at all that she could have been insane when she left Beechwood Grove?"

"None at all. I told you, we made excellent progress. When

she left, she was in perfect health. I would stake my reputation on it."

"So, in your considered opinion as a doctor who has treated Mrs. Carelton: Would you say she was in her right mind when she shot her husband?"

Dr. Little stared at me. I felt all the eyes in the jury box following his gaze. "Absolutely. Yes. I believe she knew exactly what she was doing when she killed her husband."

I waited for Howe to protest. When he did not, I whispered in his ear, "How can you let him say such a thing?"

Howe gave me a quiet smile. Mr. Scott finished his questioning, and Howe's expression was reassuring as he stood and went to the witness box.

"Dr. Little," he said. "When Mrs. Carelton first came to see you, what results was she hoping for?"

"What results?"

"Yes. What did she want your treatment to provide?"

"She wanted her health to improve."

"Would you say she was disturbed by her bouts of hysteria?"

"Oh yes. Very disturbed."

"And she wanted profoundly to live a normal life as wife to her husband?"

"Yes."

"Did you see any signs at all that she disliked her husband or was angry with him?"

"Not when I examined her."

Howe nodded. He turned to the jury, and in a deeply dramatic voice, he said, "I see. So would you characterize Mrs. Carelton as a woman who wished to be rid of her 'uterine monomania,' and who wanted to find peace and contentment with her husband?"

"Yes," Dr. Little said carefully. "That is how I would characterize her."

"How was it that she came to be at Beechwood Grove, Doctor?"

"By carriage."

Howe rolled his eyes and smiled. There was a snicker from the jury. "I meant under what circumstances."

"She was committed for treatment."

"Committed? Do you mean involuntarily so?"

"Well, yes," Dr. Little said. "Her husband was very concerned."

"In your opinion, was Mrs. Carelton happy about being taken to Beechwood Grove?"

"No." Dr. Little took a deep breath. "But that is not unusual either. Many of our patients are so ill they don't realize that Beechwood Grove is the best place for them."

"Do most patients argue with you, Dr. Little?"

Little nodded. "Oh yes."

"What was Mrs. Carelton's argument?"

"She tried to tell me that her husband had made a terrible mistake, that she was, in fact, much better."

"You didn't believe that?"

"No. Given my previous diagnosis, that would have been very difficult to believe. Such stories are a common tactic among the insane. She also told me that Mr. Carelton had her committed because she embarrassed him."

"How so?"

"She said he discovered that she was having an affair with her doctor."

Another loud murmur. I squeezed my eyes shut.

"You didn't believe her?"

"No sir, I did not. It is not at all uncommon for those suffering from monomania to experience delusions. Mr. Carelton had said she was behaving inappropriately, that there were several instances of reckless sexual behavior. He was very disturbed by it, but I know for a fact that he did not believe Mrs. Carelton was having an affair with her doctor. He told me so himself."

"Tell me something, Dr. Little: Isn't it true that Mrs. Carelton did not begin to make progress at your asylum until you brought in another doctor—a specialist who'd had some experience with women's nervous disorders?"

Dr. Little frowned. "Why, yes."

"How did Mrs. Carelton respond to his care?"

"Very well. Very quickly. We were all quite amazed."

"Amazed enough to begin utilizing some of his techniques yourself?"

Dr. Little nodded. "Yes. We've had good results."

"Could you describe this treatment?"

"Hypnosis," Dr. Little said. He leaned forward as if sensing the need to defend himself. "I know it seems odd, but it's been remarkable, how well it can be used for cases of Mrs. Carelton's type."

Howe nodded. "You told us earlier that Mrs. Carelton was quite sane when she left Beechwood Grove, isn't that so?"

"Yes, yes."

"And you would attribute that sanity to this doctor?"

"Why, yes," Dr. Little said, but warily, as if he had begun to smell something unpleasant.

Again Howe turned to the jury, raising his voice so it echoed against the smoke-stained ceiling. "What was the name of that doctor?"

"Victor Seth."

There was more than a murmur. There were hushed whispers, nudging, shuffling feet. I kept my gaze on William Howe, on Dr. Little. I didn't dare turn around for fear of what the reporters might see on my face.

"Were you aware, Dr. Little, that Victor Seth was the same doctor Mrs. Carelton had been seeing previously? The one who was with her in Newport, the one who treated her in New York City, the one she claimed to have had an affair with?"

"Objection!" Scott was on his feet. The judge waved him quiet.

Dr. Little looked genuinely shocked. "No," he said. "He never said anything. She never said—"

"He had good results, you say?"

"Yes, yes." Dr. Little was pale.

"She was not insane when she left Beechwood Grove?"

"No." It was a whisper.

Howe smiled as he turned from the witness box. He made a dismissive gesture. "That is all."

"Tomorrow it's our turn," Howe said, settling into a chair in my parlor. He smiled, and I smiled nervously back.

"Who will you call first?" I asked him.

"Your father," he said, and then he slanted me an assessing glance. "Are you worried?"

I shook my head. "There's nothing he could say that I haven't already heard."

"After that I'll call your friend Millicent Wallace."

I was almost afraid to say the words. "And then . . . Victor?"

"Ah yes, Victor Seth." Howe sighed. "You must tell me something, Mrs. Carelton, and I want the truth."

"Of course." I waved my hand at him. "Whatever you want."

"Were the things you told Dr. Little true? Were you having an affair with your doctor?"

I couldn't look at him.

"Forgive my bluntness: Were you intimate with him?"

I nodded.

Howe went still. I felt him watching me. Then he said, "Did your husband know this?"

I took a deep breath. "You remember the 'incident' I told you about?"

"Yes."

"William discovered us . . . together."

Howe looked so somber—which was hard enough to do, given the bright orange-and-green-checked vest he wore—that I found myself embellishing my story. "I believe now that it wasn't what William believed. It wasn't even what I believed."

"How so?"

"When we first . . . when Victor and I . . . I think he believed that our . . . intimacy was a kind of treatment, that it would help me be healthy again." I looked at the wall, at the painting that had hung there as long as I could remember, Saint Beatrix with her face turned to the light, to truth, to God. "I may have . . . mistaken things."

"Is that why you shot your husband, Mrs. Carelton? To be with Dr. Seth?"

I stared at him. "I don't know why I shot my husband, Mr. Howe, I've already told you that."

He shook his head chidingly. "The truth, Mrs. Carelton."

"That is the truth," I lied. "It is the only truth I know."

My father took the stand with the dignity that had sustained him throughout this entire ordeal. I could spot strands of gray in his hair that had not been there before, and new lines in his face. He was wearing stark black, as if he were in mourning, and I suppose he was. The only question was for whom: me or William.

I tried not to think such ungracious thoughts. He had done everything for me since I'd been arrested. He had hired William Howe; he had defended me staunchly to every paper in the city and to all our friends. But I could not rid myself of the feeling that I would pay for this later, that he would extract his pound of flesh for standing by me.

He spoke slowly, as if his words were weighted, as if his sorrows were too great to be borne. "Lucy was a sensitive child.

From the time she was very young, her mother and I worried over her. She formed such quick attachments. It wasn't normal."

"Quick attachments, Mr. Van Berckel?" Howe asked. "What exactly do you mean?"

"First there was religion. Now, we went to church, you understand—we're good Episcopalians, we've a pew at Saint Thomas now, and Grace Church before that—but Lucy took it too far. She fancied she would join a nunnery when she was old enough. She wasted away to nothing, praying all the time, fasting. It was distressing."

"What came of that?"

"Eventually she outgrew it. Then she took on poetry. It was the same thing all over again. And then it was painting. She was delirious with it. I feared for her health, which was always fragile."

"I see. Your daughter was often ill?"

"Yes. She suffered headaches and aches and pains from the time she was a girl."

"Even into her marriage?"

Papa's face was grief-stricken. "It seemed to grow worse then."

"Why do you think that was?"

"I don't know." Papa took a deep breath. "I talked to her often. I urged her to find happiness in her marriage, in her duties as a wife."

Howe frowned. "She was unhappy being a wife?"

Papa waved his hand dismissively. "No, not as you'd think. It was simply that she was not good at keeping a house. She often had trouble with servants."

"Why do you think that was?"

"It was due to her health."

Howe nodded sympathetically. He looked more like a compassionate friend than a lawyer. His voice was somber and quiet when he said, "Were you worried for her, Mr. Van Berckel?"

"Worried? Well, yes, I was."

"Why was that?"

Papa seemed confused. "She was my daughter."

"But there was another reason you were worried, wasn't there, Mr. Van Berckel?"

Papa hesitated, then said reluctantly, "Yes. Lucy was—Lucy is—very like her mother."

"Is Mrs. Van Berckel still alive?"

"No. No. She died twenty years ago."

"How was Mrs. Carelton like her mother?" Howe went on.

"Irene was fragile herself," Papa said slowly. "She was often melancholy. I blame myself for her death."

"You blame yourself for her death? How can that be?"

Papa lowered his head. "I was not as gentle with her as I should have been. She was unhappy."

"How did Mrs. Van Berckel die?"

"She drowned," Papa said.

"How so?"

Papa said nothing. The jury murmured among themselves. The crowd grew restless. Judge Hammond looked up sternly. Howe waited one horrible second before he said, "Isn't it true that Mrs. Van Berckel—your wife, Mrs. Carelton's mother—took her own life?"

Someone—Daisy Hadden, I thought—gasped. My father squeezed his eyes shut. For a moment I thought he would deny it; it was too damning, too irredeemable. But he sighed and said, "Yes."

"When your daughter married William Carelton, did you warn him of this unfortunate defect in her heritage?"

"Yes. I told him he must treat her with the utmost care. As if she were a child."

"And did he?"

"William was possessed of great energy. I thought he would be good for Lucy. I see now that he couldn't possibly know how to handle her." Papa didn't look at me as he spoke. He knew, as

I did, that William had done exactly what Papa had said, that he had treated me just that way: like a child. Papa had finally taken my side against William. I should have been glad, but the truth was, it was too late. I no longer needed Papa, and I felt a bitter sorrow that William should be maligned like this by the one man who had supported him unconditionally. "I was . . . sorry . . . that I had allowed her to marry him."

"Why was that?"

Papa said, "He didn't have the right background."

"You mean he was not of your class."

"Yes."

"Hmmm. I'm curious, Mr. Van Berckel. Why *did* you allow your daughter to marry so clearly beneath her?"

"I made a deal with the devil," Papa whispered. He clasped his hands together, fat fingers squeezing tight. "I'm not happy about it, but William made me a great deal of money when I needed it. I was . . . grateful."

"Grateful enough to give him your daughter?"

Papa's cheeks flushed in anger. "If she had not loved him, I wouldn't have. But she did."

"I see." Howe stroked his chin thoughtfully. "She loved him to her detriment, wouldn't you say?"

"I'm not sure what you mean."

"Yes, I'm sure you don't, Mr. Van Berckel," Howe said. Before Papa could protest, he went on. "Do you know the circumstances that sent Mrs. Carelton to Beechwood Grove?"

"William told me that she had made a scene in Newport, then had taken an overdose of laudanum. She had done that before, and I was worried. When he said he wanted to commit her to the asylum, I agreed that it would be best."

"An asylum seems a drastic solution. Wasn't it?"

"As I said, I was worried. Lucy had been acting strangely. She wasn't herself."

"What do you mean by that?"

"She had always been so biddable, and now she was not."

"Did you discuss this with her husband?"

"Yes."

"What did he say?"

"That Lucy was under the care of a doctor. That she was improving. The doctor had said she might go through a phase of this kind, and we were not to be concerned."

"But you were concerned."

"Yes."

"Because your daughter was not so frail, or so ill, or so biddable?"

Papa squirmed. I looked down to hide a smile I couldn't control.

"You haven't answered the question, Mr. Van Berckel."

"She was not herself," he said. "I agreed with William that she should have a rest."

"In an asylum?"

"Yes."

"Did William tell you that he feared she was having an affair with the very doctor who said she was going through a phase?"

"No," Papa said. He looked stonily at me. "He said nothing of the kind."

When Millie came to the stand, she supported Papa's contentions. I had been a frail child with an intense imagination; I carried things too far; I made myself ill with my yearnings.

"She fairly threw herself into things," she said. The peacock feathers in her bright blue hat bobbed against her cheekbone. "For example, when she began decorating for their new house, she had the clerks at Goupil's in a frenzy."

"Their new house? The same new house she didn't care for?" Howe's expression was exaggeratedly puzzled.

"Yes, at first that was true," Millie said. "We were all surprised she didn't seem to be excited about it. But then that changed. She was intent on finding the right things for it."

"Why do you suppose that is?"

"Because William asked her to," she said. "And she was determined to please him."

"Was this usual for Mrs. Carelton? Did she often attend to her husband's desires so wholeheartedly?"

Millie hesitated. "In most cases. She did long for William's approval."

"Were you at Newport this summer, the same time Mrs. Carelton was there?"

"Yes," Millie said.

"Did you observe her with Dr. Seth?"

Millie was holding a blue beaded bag. She fidgeted with the clasp. "Yes. I did."

"Did it seem innocent to you?"

"No."

"What did you believe was their relationship?"

"In the beginning I assumed they were having an affair." Millie reddened. "But then I talked to Lucy about it, and she confessed that he was her doctor and had come to attend her during the summer."

"Did you believe that?"

"I wanted to."

"Did you have any evidence otherwise?"

"No," she said.

"Did you think that Mrs. Carelton was better under Dr. Seth's care?"

"Yes," she said. "She seemed much better."

"Mrs. Wallace, did you think that Mrs. Carelton was happy?"

Millie frowned at him. "Happy?"

"Yes, happy. Was she happy with her husband? With her life?"

Millie looked at me, her eyes expressionless. "I think Lucy

tried to be happy," she said slowly. "But I don't think she was. I don't think she ever was."

I breathed a sigh of relief when Millie was done, when it seemed that there would be no real surprises after all. The courtroom was quite warm; I was reaching for a handkerchief to wipe my brow when Howe went to the front of the courtroom. With a flourish of pure showmanship, he said, "Your Honor, I call Mrs. Wilhelm Brock to the stand."

I abandoned the handkerchief in sudden wariness. Mrs. Wilhelm Brock? I'd never heard the name before; I had no idea who it could be.

I turned when the audience did, as the doors at the back of the courtroom opened. A woman clothed in black came inside. She wore a small hat with a dark veil that hid her face. She was compact—an older woman, I thought, though she walked with steady purpose. I watched curiously as Howe helped her into the witness chair. I sent him a questioning glance, but he only smiled. He leaned down, whispering something to the witness, and she reached up and lifted her veil.

I gasped.

I was looking at a woman with William's face.

Chapter 33

She stared at me as if trying to memorize me. I felt the jury's gazes riveted to us.

Howe was still smiling. "Mrs. Brock, do you recognize the defendant?"

Mrs. Brock shook her head. "I don't."

"Do you know who she is?"

"I've heard of her," she said. Her voice was light and melodious. "She's Mrs. William Carelton."

"How do you know this?"

"You told me who she was," she said. "And I've read the papers."

"What relationship do you have with Mrs. Carelton, Mrs. Brock?"

She hesitated. I did not know what she would say, or who she was, and I was angry at Howe for surprising me this way.

She looked right at me when she said, "I'm her mother-in-law."

I felt the blood leave my face. The audience broke into surprised whispers; there was a whoop from a reporter; even the jury began talking among themselves. Mr. Scott rose from the prosecution table, calling, "Your Honor, please."

Judge Hammond slammed his gavel. "I will have silence in this courtroom. Mr. Scott, sit down. Mr. Howe, proceed."

The murmurings died down, though they didn't completely disappear. Howe was smiling so broadly it seemed his skin stretched to his ears. I saw him try to rein it in. He bent back to Mrs. Brock, who was still watching me with eyes that were as blue as William's.

Howe said, "William Carelton was your son?"

"Yes," she said quietly. "He was my son."

"You have a different surname, ma'am. Did you remarry?"

"No sir. My son changed his name." Her eyes watered as she spoke, as if it was still painful for her. "When he was born, we named him William Guilden Brock. The only thing he kept was the William."

Howe's voice became soft, cajoling. "When did he do this, Mrs. Brock?"

"When he was fifteen. Just before he left town."

"Which town is that, ma'am?"

"Newport, Rhode Island," she said.

Again I heard the echo of the bail hearing, the oddity of the thing I had not known. *William Stephen Carelton . . . originally of Newport, Rhode Island.*

"Why did your son change his name, Mrs. Brock?"

Her tone was resigned. "Because he was ashamed of us. Ashamed of his own father and mother. He was afraid someone might find out where he came from."

"Why do you think that was?"

"Because he never wanted anything but to belong to *them*." She emphasized the audience, me, with a jerk of her chin. "His own father was a lawyer, but that wasn't good enough."

"When did you last see your son, Mrs. Brock?"

"I saw him just the other day. In his grave." Her voice broke again, in sorrow or anger, though I was unsure where it was directed.

"Before that?"

"About five years ago," she said. "Before he got married."

"To Mrs. Carelton?"

"Yes."

"It was a big society wedding, I understand?"

"Four hundred people," she said, looking up. "At Saint Thomas. There were tea roses and lilies. The bride wore a Worth gown in white satin, with appliqués of lilies and a bodice beaded with seed pearls." She recited it with a sad pride. "I read it in the paper."

"You didn't attend?"

"We weren't invited. William said he would tell them about us eventually, but he was afraid the great DeLancey Van Berckel might cancel the wedding if he found out who William really was. He said that these people trusted him, that he had made his way into high society. He was marrying a society girl, you see—the same girl he'd wanted for years and years. Oh, he used to watch the Van Berckels, you know, when they came to Seaward. He used to talk about her. Lucy Van Berckel, how she was the prettiest thing. How one day he was going to marry her."

I began to feel ill.

"And you accepted that?"

"We had to." She began to cry. When Howe handed her a handkerchief, she dabbed gracefully at her eyes. "We loved our son, and William loved his wife. He was afraid he would lose her. I wanted him to be happy."

"You were his parents," Howe said gently. "Surely Mrs. Carelton would have accepted you if she truly loved her husband."

"William wouldn't allow it." She closed her eyes. When she opened them again, they were full of pain. "I loved my son, Mr. Howe, and I am sorry he's dead, but I knew what he was. The truth is, as much as William might have loved her, he was ambitious too. Maybe what William really loved was the thought of her and the things she could bring him. He wanted to be rich and respected. When I think about it now, I wish we'd left Newport. It would have been easier for William to understand his place. But with all those cottagers there every summer, having parties, driving their carriages around like they were lords of the town . . . it changed him. Nothing was ever enough for him."

"Does it surprise you, ma'am, how your son ended up?"

She shook her head sorrowfully. "I wish I could say it does. But he was too ambitious. He was never going to be happy with his place. More, more, more, that's all I heard from him."

She came up to me later, as I was climbing into the carriage to go home. It was Papa who saw her first, and his hand tightened on my elbow, stopping my ascent. I turned to see her standing there, looking like an angel in the light snowfall, her small form haloed by a streetlamp. She was looking at me with hungry eyes. "My, aren't you pretty," she said. "Prettier even than he said you were."

I straightened and pulled away from my father, who stood back, suddenly perceptive when I wanted him not to be. I was afraid of her. I spoke quickly, hoping she would understand. "I didn't know about you. I hope you know that. He wouldn't talk about his parents. I thought . . . I thought you were dead."

She nodded. "I won't bother you after today. I just wanted to see you one time. To talk to you one time. It always seemed strange to have a daughter-in-law I didn't know."

I said again, because I could think of nothing else, "I never knew."

"I just want you to tell me," she said, "why you killed my son."

"Because I wanted to be free," I whispered, because she was

his mother and she deserved to know, and to despise me for it. It was the only thing I could give her.

She sighed, and then she smiled weakly and took my hand. "It was nice to meet you," she said, then released me, turning away as if I were a stranger she never expected to see again. But of course, that was what I was.

Chapter 34

I woke long before the sun rose and lay nervous and still. There had been a sound from somewhere, a crash, the dismay of a servant, but that was not what had awakened me. It was the knowledge of what would happen today that had me tossing and turning and staring blankly into the darkness. Today was the day Howe would call Victor to the stand.

The courtroom was as full as any other day, and the whispers when I came in and sat down were the same, the scribbling of the reporters no different. Howe was smiling when he saw me and leaned down to whisper, "Word is we're winning." Before I could ask him how he knew, the judge was sitting, and Howe went to the front of the courtroom and called out in a large, expansive voice: "Please bring Dr. Victor Seth to the stand."

I froze in my seat, afraid to look when I heard the doors open, the sudden rush of talk, and his step. I had never been aware of hearing it before, I had always thought he moved too quietly to hear, but I realized now that I knew it. His stride was self-assured, almost too confident. I heard the talk die to whispers as he came down the hall, and I knew they were struck—as I had been, as William had been—by his bearing.

It was not until they swore him in and he took his seat that I looked up.

He had changed little since the last time I'd seen him. He was still beardless, but his hair was longer, just brushing his collar, which was stiff and white, and he wore a suit I'd never seen, of a fine dark wool with a matching vest. His watch chain was gold, but those charms still hung from it, and I had the panicked thought that I had never found out what those charms were. It seemed absurd that I had not. Perhaps I didn't know him as well as I'd thought.

He glanced at me, and I calmed, and then Howe was speaking.

"Dr. Seth, could you state your qualifications, please."

Victor said, "I'm a neurologist. I studied at the University of Leipzig, and then with Jean-Martin Charcot at the Salpêtrière until I went to Nancy. There I studied with Hippolyte Bernheim."

"A neurologist," Howe said. "I'm not familiar with that term, sir."

"Neurologists study the brain and the nervous system," Victor said easily. "We specialize in organic disorders, especially as they apply to illnesses that most people think of as nervous conditions."

"Such as insanity?"

Victor nodded. "Among other things. Neurologists tend to treat those who are still functioning outside of institutions."

"I see. So you are a physician?"

Contemptuously, Victor said, "I am a physician, but I hardly assume ancient medical knowledge has validity. I'm a scientist first and foremost. Medical knowledge is increasing day by day. The brain and nervous system have been unknown continents before now. In time science will solve every puzzle of human behavior. We will be able to cure anything."

Howe raised a brow. "Even madness?"

"Especially madness," Victor said.

"How truly extraordinary," Howe said. "How then, sir, would you characterize insanity?"

"Insanity can be measured only by comparison with a person's normal behavior."

"So if one day someone's behavior changed dramatically, that could be seen as insanity?"

Victor nodded. His eyes were so dark it was hard to read his expression. "Possibly."

"Would you say that, oh, a carpenter, for example, who one day was calmly making cabinets, and who had always been of an even temperament, and then the next day violently decapitated his wife with an ax might be insane?"

Victor allowed a small smile. "That could be one possibility. I would need to know more about the circumstances of the particular case."

"But you do believe that someone might be so overtaken by some emotion, some irresistible impulse, that he might temporarily lose control of his actions?"

"Certainly. I've seen it for myself."

"What generally triggers such a thing?"

"Great distress," Victor said. "Physical or emotional."

"I see. Where is your practice, Dr. Seth?"

"Here in the city."

"And what is your specialty?"

"I specialize in nervous disorders—hysteria, neurasthenia, morbid fears, and the like—especially in women."

"Is that how you came to know Mrs. Carelton?"

Victor glanced at me. He steepled his fingers beneath his chin. "Yes. She came to me in January of this year. She desired treatment for hysteria. At the time her husband said they were quite desperate. Apparently she'd seen many doctors throughout the years. None had been able to help her. Mr. Carelton intimated that I was their last hope."

"Other doctors diagnosed her with uterine monomania."

"They were wrong," Victor said flatly. "There was no irregularity with her uterus, nothing to indicate monomania at all."

"How did you ascertain this?"

"With a simple examination," Victor said. He exhaled in disgust. "This is the problem with most physicians today. They're too quick to find fault with the reproductive system. Mrs. Carelton was quite normal, although she had been unable to conceive."

"Wouldn't one assume that this was because she was not normal?"

Victor's smile grew faintly patronizing. "One could assume this, but one would be wrong. Mrs. Carelton had no abnormality in her uterus or her ovaries. She did indeed suffer from hysteria and sexual neurasthenia, but I attributed those things not to her womb but to her husband."

"Her husband?"

"Yes. Mr. Carelton declined to do his part to relieve his wife's systems. He said he was afraid of defiling her. What he meant was that he didn't want to be of the class of man who might have a passionate woman as a wife. In her desire to please him, she followed his instruction in everything. Because of that, her own desires were thwarted, and she took refuge in hysteria."

Howe nodded. "Did you believe you could cure her of this hysteria and—what else did you call it?"

"Sexual neurasthenia," Victor said. "Yes. I did believe I could cure her."

"How long did your treatment of Mrs. Carelton last?"

Victor looked pained. "Until her husband committed her to an asylum."

"Because she was insane?"

"No, Mr. Howe. Because she was well."

There was a stirring in the audience. Judge Hammond looked up sternly.

Howe's thick brows rose in surprise. "She was *well*, and he had her committed? Why was that?"

"In my conversations with him, I discovered that Mr. Carelton preferred his wife to be helpless and dependent upon him. He preferred her ill. When she began to deny him, he was angry."

"What did she deny him, Dr. Seth?"

"The opportunity to dictate her every action."

"But isn't that what husbands are supposed to do? To lead their wives gently in the proper direction?"

Victor said firmly, "It is certainly a husband's prerogative to direct his wife in proper behavior, but I believe Mr. Carelton's ambition made him unduly harsh. I ask you, Mr. Howe, who would have been the most cognizant of proper behavior: Mrs. Carelton, who is descended from the Knickerbockers, or Mr. Carelton, who was not?"

"A good question, Dr. Seth," Howe said, looking pointedly at the jury. "A very good question indeed. Now, Doctor, you are of the opinion that Mrs. Carelton was well when her husband had her committed to Beechwood Grove. Why do you say that?"

"I was directing her treatment. She was making great strides."

"Would you say your relationship with Mrs. Carelton was intimate, Doctor?"

"I would say any doctor-patient relationship is."

"Yes, of course. However, Mrs. Breckenwood claimed earlier that Mrs. Carelton was having an affair with you. Is this true?"

Victor didn't look at me. "No. It is not true." His lie was so smooth and confident even I nearly believed it.

"You were not having a personal relationship with Mrs. Carelton?"

Again Victor sighed with exasperation. "Part of Mrs. Carelton's treatment required some exploration of her physical symptoms, yes. This is a usual medical procedure. Mr. Carelton knew this. We discussed it. He did not seem to find it unreasonable."

"What else did her treatment consist of?"

"Electrotherapy, to treat the sexual neurasthenia. Hypnosis for the hysteria."

"Hypnosis?" Howe turned his gaze to the jury as if he might find understanding there. "What exactly is hypnosis? A kind of mesmerism?"

"No. Mesmerism is a parlor trick. Hypnosis is a medical procedure that uses suggestion to change behavior."

"Suggestion? How does that work?"

"A person is put into a trance state," Victor explained patiently. "During the trance, the conscious mind is inactive—asleep, if you will—and the unconscious mind is then receptive to suggestion."

"Objection," Scott called. "What relevance does any of this have?"

"We have a right to raise a defense," Howe said. "And the state has already mentioned Dr. Seth's unique ability—"

"Yes, yes," said the judge. "Continue, please, Doctor."

Howe smiled and turned back to Victor. "Now, Mrs. Breckenwood testified earlier that you performed this 'hypnotism' at parties."

"Yes."

"She said that you could make anyone do anything. Is this true?"

Victor shook his head and smiled slightly. "Hardly. Not everyone can be put in a trance state, nor does everyone respond to suggestion to the same degree."

"So there are some for whom hypnotism doesn't work?"

"Yes."

"And what about Mrs. Carelton? How did she respond to hypnotism?"

"I found during my first examination of Mrs. Carelton that she was extraordinarily suggestible."

"What exactly do you mean by that?"

"She responded quite well to suggestion," Victor said. "To a degree I'd never seen. For example, if I told her she would be numb, she became so."

"I see." Howe turned from Victor and faced the jury. He seemed about to deliver a cautionary tale. I found myself leaning forward, waiting to hear.

"You said earlier that you could not *make* anyone do anything, as Mrs. Breckenwood testified. But in fact you did have the skill to put everyone into a trance when you were entertaining at Newport, didn't you?"

"Yes," Victor said. "But that was only because I chose my subjects well. Experience has taught me who will go into a trance and who will not. There is a certain indolence about the eye, a willingness to be led." He shrugged. "It was not so difficult to choose those who could be hypnotized."

"And you say that Mrs. Carelton was especially susceptible to hypnotism?"

Victor's voice deepened as he said, "Yes. Yes."

"How often did she follow the suggestions you planted during a trance state?"

"Every time," Victor said, and his vanity over it was obvious. "She followed every suggestion I made. As I said, it was extraordinary."

"Is it possible to make a suggestion that the subject acts upon at some later point in time?"

"Yes. Posthypnotically."

"So you could, for example, make a man bark at the moon after the party is over and everyone has gone to bed?"

"Yes."

"Would he still be in a trance state?"

"No. The suggestion has been planted in his unconscious. It lingers there until it receives a signal. Perhaps I've made the suggestion that he bark at the moon at midnight. At midnight he will wake and do so."

"Remarkable," Howe said. "That's hard to believe, Doctor."

Again that confidence, that shining vanity. "Ask anyone who was at Newport last summer. They saw it quite clearly."

"Did Mrs. Carelton also respond to— What did you call it? Posthypnosis?"

"Posthypnotic suggestion," Victor said. He leaned back in the witness chair, self-possessed. "Yes. That is exactly what reduced her distress and her hysteria."

"You said that Mrs. Carelton followed every suggestion you made to her. Could you make her do something that she wouldn't normally do?"

"Yes."

"Even if it was morally abhorrent to her?"

I gasped softly. The jury glanced at me. Victor glanced at me.

"What are you suggesting?" he asked quietly.

"Answer the question, Dr. Seth," Judge Hammond said.

I saw Victor struggle. I saw when his vanity seemingly won the battle. "Yes," he said. "Even that. I can make Lucy do any-thing."

This time Judge Hammond did not attempt to quiet the courtroom. It was Howe, my own lawyer, who held up his hand for silence and turned to Victor.

"You were aware, weren't you, of the position Mrs. Carelton occupied in New York City society?"

"Of course," Victor said.

"And you were aware, Doctor, of Mrs. Carelton's consider-able fortune? A fortune of her own that was controlled by her husband, as well as the fortune that would come to her upon her father's death—and also be controlled by her husband, if he were still alive?"

Victor's expression became stony. "I understood she was wealthy, yes," he said. "I was unaware of the details."

"Were you?" Howe asked, and then he turned away and smiled at the jury. "Were you indeed?"

THE WORLD

New York, Tuesday, December 15, 1885

DOCTOR CONTROLS SOCIETY MURDERESS!

Trial of the Decade
JURY TO DECIDE HER FATE

Victor Seth: Conspirator or Master?

Yesterday testimony was heard from Mrs. Carelton's physician Victor Seth, who defined his controversial new specialization—the science of neurology—and described his personal expertise in hypnosis, a scientific procedure much like mesmerism, wherein Dr. Seth put Mrs. Carelton into a trance and controlled her "unconscious" mind. Dr. Seth admitted under oath that he could dictate Mrs. Carelton's behavior even when she was no longer in a trance, and that he could make her perform acts that might normally be reprehensible to her.

During this testimony, Mrs. Carelton sat mute, obviously still under the influence of her doctor, who had a spellbound control not just of her but of the courtroom. Her mind was clearly not her own while Dr. Seth spun his tale of control and foreknowledge of Mrs. Carelton's vast wealth. Only when he was gone from the stand did she become herself again. Her spine seemed to droop, and she was quite beside herself, so that Mr. Howe, her attorney, had to remove her from the courtroom during the lunch break.

"An Urge I Could Not Control"

When court resumed, Mrs. Carelton herself testified. When Mr. Howe asked her if she had been under the doctor's control, she said, "I don't know. I was aware I relied on him. I felt I needed him, and I didn't know why. Later, I began to understand that he had done things to ensure I would not leave his treatment. I don't know what he may have had in mind, but I do know that when I killed my husband, I was in the grip of something irresistible. It confused me, but it was an urge I could not control."

Mrs. Carelton told the jury that she loved her husband and wanted to please him, and that she had done everything in her power to be well. She had been innocent of her husband's past, had never met his parents, and believed, in the trusting manner of all gently bred women, that he loved her and desired to protect her. She said the news that her husband had used her to gain social position was "a terrible shock."

Schemer or Victim?

In closing arguments, the district attorney, Mr. Scott, argued feebly that Mrs. Carelton was a scheming woman who desired control of her fortune and conspired with her lover, the doctor, to kill her husband. This despite the fact that several witnesses, including Mr. DeLancey Van Berckel, Mrs. Carelton's father, declared she was faithful to her husband.

Mr. Howe argued the extremely compelling evidence that Mrs. Carelton was a woman in the grip of forces she could not control. Given the dishonesty of her husband in both character and mien, her forced commitment to an asylum, and the oft-repeated testimony that William Carelton was a social climber who married his wife to gain access to society circles and denied his own parents in order to achieve his ambitions, Mrs. Carelton easily could have been the victim of an "irresistible urge," or emotional insanity. Howe also told the jury that it seemed likely Mrs. Carelton was also the unwitting victim of a doctor who was willing to use her "extraordinary suggestibility" to achieve his own ends. "Mrs. Carelton has said repeatedly that she does not know why she killed her husband. Perhaps she didn't, but her 'unconscious' did. Her unconscious knew just what to do, because Dr. Seth told it what to do."

In either case, said Mr. Howe, with tears in his own eyes, Mrs. Carelton was not responsible for her actions and was in fact a terrible victim of injustice who should be acquitted.

Chapter 35

I don't know how long they'll deliberate," Howe said.

It was late the next morning. The window of my father's dining room afforded me a view of clouds and thickly falling snow. My uneaten breakfast of oatmeal and cream was abandoned on the table, and my coffee cup was still full; I had taken only a single sip. Howe poured a cup for himself and sat without invitation at the table.

"You seem so certain," I said.

He smiled in the affable way that had kept most of the courtroom on his side. "Mrs. Carelton, I have to admit that it's seldom I have a case so predisposed to succeed. A husband who hid his past and committed his wife to an asylum? A doctor who admits he can control his patient? Good God"—he laughed out loud— "if they don't come back with an acquittal, I'll shoot them all myself; they'd be too stupid to live anyway."

I could not make myself smile. It was true, everything he'd said. I had known it myself, sitting in that courtroom, listening to the testimony. I had seen sympathy on the faces of the jurors as I told my story complete with tears and unbearable anguish.

But I had spent too long in a world made by other people; I was afraid to hope for freedom now.

"I don't know if I can bear to wait another moment," I said.

Harris came to the door. "Madam," he said. He held out a note. His hand shook slightly, though his expression was as impassive as ever. "I believe it's quite important."

Before I could take it, Howe reached for it. "From the court," he said, with an *I told you so* look. He tore open the message. "The jury's back," he said after scanning it. "We'd best go."

My hands trembled. I pressed them hard into my stomach and tried to take a deep breath. It wouldn't come; it felt as if my lungs had frozen. A shallow sigh was all I could manage. Papa came down at that moment. He took one look at me and his face went ashen.

"They're back," Howe told him.

"Then we must go," Papa said. "We must go now."

It seemed to take forever to reach the courtroom. The stairs of the Tombs were covered with ice; my thin boots slipped; my feet were numb with cold. Howe took a firm hold on my elbow and led me into the building while Papa followed behind. Then we were once again in the overheated room, with its smells of wet wool and sweat and steaming bodies. Now I smelled the deeper odors, the ones that lingered in the hard wooden seats, in the scarred floor. The scent of must, of fear, of lingering sorrow. I would not have thought those things had a smell, but they did. I puzzled why I had not breathed them before today.

The courtroom was full again. I wondered how all these people had known to come. Had they been waiting outside in the snow and ice for word? Who had told Daisy Hadden? It was not yet noon; how had she managed to pull herself from bed? How had Millie known? There she was. Her mouth trembled when I looked at her. The little stuffed bird on her hat dipped and moved as if it were singing a bright song or an elegy, I could not tell. There were newspaper reporters, Miss Adler among them.

She smiled at me as I passed. In the front, at the prosecutors' table, sat a dour Mr. Scott.

"You see?" Howe whispered into my ear, nudging me slightly. "Even Randolph knows when he's beaten."

I didn't see Victor anywhere. I had not expected to.

Howe led me to the table. Mr. Blake was already there. I had never seen him smile, but he did now. Howe eased his corpulence into the chair beside me and watched as the jury was marched in. I felt him studying each one of them. I could not make myself look, afraid I would see the result on their faces, not wanting to know, not yet.

Howe took my hand and squeezed it. He bent to say something to me, but just then the judge came in, and we were bade to stand. When we were seated again, the judge addressed himself to the jury: "Have you reached a verdict?"

The foreman—a graying, spindly man who was impeccably dressed, a warehouse owner, I remembered—nodded. He rose and handed a paper to the bailiff, and we all watched that paper as it made its way across the room into the hands of the judge, who read it and passed it back. The pressure built in my skull; the sounds in the courtroom were a meaningless buzz.

"Will the defendant please rise," the judge directed, and I had a fleeting thought that he meant me, but I was paralyzed. Howe rose and took my arm, lifting me gently to my feet. I swayed into him as the judge commanded the foreman to read the verdict.

"We . . . jury . . . find the defendant . . ." The words were like music, lifting and falling through the buzz in my ears. I caught one and then another, like a conversation barely heard amid the traffic of Broadway. ". . . not guilty by reason of temporary insanity."

My knees gave. I fell into my seat. There was whooping all around me. My father leaned over the bar to rest his hands on my shoulders. Howe was beaming, shaking Mr. Blake's hand so hard I wondered if it might not come off.

I was free.

I let my attorney and his assistant and my father surround me. I didn't smile at Daisy Hadden, I did not even nod in Millie's direction. Reporters crowded around, shouting, begging for a word. Howe puffed out his chest dramatically and said, "Justice has been done. Mrs. Carelton's days of suffering are over!"

The walk out of the Tombs into the icy, snowy streets to my father's waiting carriage was the longest one I had ever made.

Jimson smiled at me and helped me inside. When I was seated, he tucked a thick wool blanket around my legs, and I was bundled and warm again, like a child. When he backed out, my father came inside. The smell of his cologne was overpowering in the small space, more overpowering than he was. How shriveled he looked, I thought. How weak.

Howe leaned in. "Mrs. Carelton, should you ever find yourself in trouble again—"

"I trust that Lucy's troubled days are over," Papa said firmly. "We appreciate all you've done, Mr. Howe, but I doubt we'll be seeing you again."

The door was closed in Howe's face. I felt the shudder of the carriage as Jimson climbed onto the box, the lurch as the horses pulled into streets so rutted and icy and jarring that we rocked back and forth against the walls.

Papa sighed. "Well, thank God that's over." He shook his head. "Time to get on with things, I suppose. We'll want to decide what to do about that house of yours. I've thought about selling it. God knows it'll just sit there empty and useless unless we do. But I suppose that can wait a few days. Once everything is back on course—"

"Back on course?" I laughed.

"What is it?" he asked, frowning. "During the trial, it was best to be about—couldn't have everyone thinking you were guilty—but now I think we should keep to ourselves for a bit. Give people time to forget. A trip to the country. I've made arrangements for us to leave the day after tomorrow—had them made just in case, you know. It'll be good for you to be coddled, I think. Yes, I do think so. I've been corresponding with a doctor—Weir Mitchell, in Philadelphia. He believes it would be best if you rest. Plenty of bed rest and good, rich food. Cream and butter and the like. No thinking at all, no more drawing or reading or any of that nonsense—you'll be yourself in no time." He patted my knee through the thick blanket and my heavy skirts. "I'll take care of you now, my dear. You've nothing to worry about."

I regarded him clearly. "This is what we shall do," I said. "There is a ship leaving tomorrow for London. The *Lysander*. You will send Harris to procure me a ticket. A first-class cabin. I will be on it in the morning, and I will stay away for some time."

I saw shock in his expression. His mouth moved as if he might speak, and then he swallowed before he said, "A ship? Certainly not! We will do as Dr. Mitchell suggested."

"I will not be seeing another doctor," I said calmly, adjusting the blanket. "I am a married woman, Papa. A widow. I have control of my own fortune, and I will do as I please."

"You will not—"

"Papa, I ask you to remember what happened to the last man who told me no." I gave him a pleasant smile and was rewarded by my father's dawning comprehension. I rested my head against the seat. "I'll require the ticket by this evening. But I think I won't have dinner with you tonight, Papa. This has all been quite draining. And I've so much packing to do if I'm to make the ship."

At last his words were gone. I reveled in the silence.

* * *

Early the next morning I stood waiting at the front door. My trunk was already packed and tied onto the carriage in the street. The ticket had been purchased; I held it tight in my hand. On the table in the hall was a vase full of roses, sent by Mr. Howe, along with a telegram of congratulations. It was the only one I received. From my friends there was only quiet, and that would continue, I knew. In spite of my acquittal, I was too scandalous to receive in New York City.

I tapped the ticket against my gloved hand. Harris came into the hallway. "Your father begs your understanding," he said, "but he cannot leave his breakfast just now. He sends his best wishes. He expects that you will write."

I smiled and opened the door onto a world swirling with white. It was a week until Christmas, and the maid had festooned the front gate with greenery, which was sagging beneath the weight of snow. A carriage was emerging in Washington Square from the fog of snow like a ghostly vision. Before me, Jimson waited.

I got into the carriage and settled myself and watched the passing scenery as we made our way to the transatlantic docks on the Hudson. I did not expect to see these places again soon.

When we arrived, the docks were alive with people arriving and departing, men shouldering trunks. I said good-bye to Jimson and paid a porter to carry my trunk to my cabin, then I made my way there myself, up the gangplank, past the staff, who waited at the top with friendly smiles, who did not know who I was or where I'd been, only that I held a first-class ticket.

Someone showed me to my cabin. It was like all the others I'd occupied since I'd been old enough to travel. A bedroom, a sitting room with a settee and a polished dining table and lovely plush chairs. I threw off my cloak and sank into one. This was where I would stay until the ship was well under way. There would be no one waiting to bid me good-bye from the docks, no one who cared if I was gone. No one to see the flexing of my wings.

There was a knock on the door. I felt a rush of excitement, a pull of desire like gravity. I went to the door and opened it, and there he stood.

Victor.

"You took your time," I said.

"My appointments calendar is full," he said. "I had to tell them all I'd been called away. They will have to wait until I return."

"If you return," I said, and I stood back to let him in.

He smiled. "Oh, I'll return," he said. "And you will too. Someday." He reached for me, and I went into his arms, feeling that pull tighten and hold when he put his hand in my hair and kissed me and whispered, "I told you it would work, Lucy, didn't I? What a remarkable creature you are."

"Yes," I murmured back. "We are so clever."

"I love you, Lucy," he said. "Just think of how we will be together," and I smiled. He was so confident. He still thought he could control me, and I wanted him enough to let him believe it. For now. Yes, we would be together for now.

Until the day I cut the thread that bound us.